LOVE
AT FIRST BITE

LOVE
AT FIRST BITE

SHERRILYN KENYON

L.A. BANKS

SUSAN SQUIRES

RONDA THOMPSON

St. Martin's Paperbacks

This is a work of fiction. All of the characters, organizations and events portrayed in this book are either products of the author's imagination or are used fictitiously.

LOVE AT FIRST BITE

"Until Death We Do Part" copyright © 2006 by Sherrilyn Kenyon.
"Ride the Night Wind" copyright © 2006 by Leslie Esdaile Banks.
"The Gift" copyright © 2006 by Susan Squires.
"The Forgotten One" copyright © 2006 by Ronda Thompson.

ISBN: 0-312-34929-7
EAN: 9780312-34929-5

Printed in the United States of America

St. Martin's Paperbacks edition / October 2006

St. Martin's Paperbacks are published by St. Martin's Press, 175 Fifth Avenue, New York, NY 10010.

10 9 8 7 6 5 4 3 2 1

CONTENTS

UNTIL DEATH WE DO PART

by

Sherrilyn Kenyon

PROLOGUE

Romania, 1476

He was coming for her. She knew it. Esperetta of the house of Dracul could hear him out in the cold darkness. Unseen. Fearsome. Threatening.

And he was getting closer.

Closer.

So close, she could feel his breath on her skin. See his evil eyes as he relentlessly stalked her through the night while she ran from him, hoping to find some way to escape.

He wanted her dead.

"Esperetta . . ."

There was magic in that deep, sultry voice. It'd always had a way of making her weak. Of lulling her into a stupor. But she couldn't afford that now. Not after she knew him for the monster he really was.

She stumbled through the darkness as the fog seemed to wrap itself around her, slowing her down, pulling her back toward where he waited to devour her. The cry of wolves echoed on the wind that sliced through her dirt-stained gown and cloak as if she were naked in the woods.

Her breathing labored and painful, she tripped and fell against a wall of solid black steel. No, not steel.

It was *him*.

Her hand was splayed over the frightening gold emblem on his armor of a coiled serpent that mocked her with its venom. Terrified, she looked up with a gasp into those deep, dark eyes that seemed to penetrate her. But that wasn't what scared her. It was the fact that she was in her white burial gown. The fact that she'd clawed her way out of her own grave under the weight of the full moon to find herself alone in the church cemetery. She'd stared down at the tombstone that had held her name and death date for almost an hour before she'd found the courage to leave that place.

No longer in Moldavia as she'd been when she went to sleep, she was in a small village outside of Bucharest. In the churchyard by her father's castle, where she'd been born. Needing to understand what had happened to her, she'd made her way toward her father's home, only to find an even worse horror than waking in her own grave.

She'd seen her husband kill her father before her very eyes. Seen him gleefully hand her father's head off to his Turkish enemies. Screaming, she'd run from them, out into the night.

And had run without stopping until now. Now she was in the arms of a man whose black armor was covered in her father's blood. A man she'd sworn to love for all eternity.

But it wasn't this man she'd loved. This was a coldhearted monster. A liar. He might bear the same imposing height. The same long black wavy hair and sharp, aristocratic features, but it wasn't Velkan Danesti who held her now.

It was the devil incarnate.

"Let me go!" she snarled, wrenching herself away from him.

"Esperetta, listen to me!"

"No!" she shouted, moving away as he tried to touch her again. "You killed me. You killed my father!"

He scowled at her and if she hadn't seen his darker side for herself, she might even believe the sincerity he feigned. "It's not what you think."

"I. Saw. You. Kill. Him."

"Because he killed *you*."

She shook her head. "You lie! You're the one who gave me the poison. You! Not my father. He loved me. He would never have hurt me."

"Your father stabbed you through the heart when he saw you dead to make sure you weren't feigning."

Still, she didn't believe him. He was lying and she knew it. Her father would never have done such a thing. When Velkan had given her the sleeping balm he'd told her that it would make her sleep so soundly that no one would know she was alive. He'd promised that no one would bury her, since that had always been her fear. Side by side, they were supposed to awaken from their sleep so that they would be free to stay together forever.

But she hadn't awakened in her bed. She'd awakened in her grave.

Now, she knew what he'd planned all along. To kill her and her father so that he could avenge his own father and take their lands for his family. Velkan didn't love her. He'd used her and like a fool, she'd played into his hands and cost her father his life.

She ran for the woods again only to have Velkan overtake her.

She tried to pull away, but he held her arm in a fierce grip.

"Listen to me, Esperetta. You and I are *both* dead."

She frowned at him. "Are you insane? I'm not dead. I only slept as you said I would. What madness are you trying to convince me of?"

"No madness," he said, his eyes burning into her. "When we wed, I bound our souls together with my mother's sorcery. I told you that night that I didn't want to exist without you and

I meant it. When your father killed you, I swore vengeance against him, and after he killed me, a goddess came and offered me a bargain. I sold my soul to her so that I could avenge you by killing him. *For you.* I didn't understand when I made the bargain with Artemis that it would involve you, too. Because I live, you live. We are joined together. Forever." Then he did the most unbelievable thing of all. He opened his mouth to show her a set of long, sharp fangs.

He was an upyri!

Her heart pounded in terror. It couldn't be! This wasn't her beloved husband, he was an unholy demon. "You're in league with Lucifer. My father was right. All of the Danestis are an evil who must be purged from this earth."

"Not evil, Esperetta. My love for you is pure and good. I swear it."

She curled her lip at him as she pried his grip from her arm. "And my love for you is as dead as my father," she spat before she ran through the fog once more.

Velkan forced himself to stand still and not follow her again. His bride was young and she'd been through a shock tonight.

She would return to him. He was certain of it. In all the violence and horror of his life, she'd been the only thing he'd ever had that was good and gentle. She alone had touched his long dead heart and caused it to live again. Surely, she wouldn't stay angry at him. Not when all he'd done was protect her.

She would see the truth and she would return to him.

"Come back to me soon, my Esperetta." And then he uttered the one word that had never left his lips before. "Please."

1

Chicago, 2006

"Just out of curiosity, can an immortal choke to death on a bagel?"

Retta Danesti cut a vicious glare to her best friend as she tried to swallow the bite that was lodged painfully in her throat. As a shape-shifter who'd befriended her almost four hundred years ago, Francesca was well aware of the fact that Retta's husband had sold their souls to the goddess Artemis and by default made Retta immortal.

And Francesca's latest news had stunned her so badly, she'd sucked a piece of bagel down her windpipe, where it burned like fire.

Francesca pounded her gently between the shoulder blades. "C'mon, babe, I knew it would piss you off, but I didn't mean for it to kill you."

Retta reached for her bottled water and finally cleared her throat even though her eyes were tearing up unmercifully. "Now what did you just tell me?"

Francesca put her hands in her lap and gave her a level stare. "Your husband is opening the Dracula theme park in Transylvania next summer and the key attraction is the mummified remains of Vlad Tepes—Dracula himself. Apparently Velkan's going to release the body to scientists so that they can verify the remains through tests and prove that it really is the impaler of medieval legend."

Every part of Retta seethed. "That rank bastard!" She cringed as she realized several heads in the deli turned toward her.

Francesca lowered her voice and spoke behind her hand. "He doesn't really have your father's remains, does he?"

Retta recapped her water as she wished a thousand vile things on Velkan's head. Including pestilence and plagues that would cause a certain part of his anatomy to shrivel up and rot off. "It's possible. After all, Velkan killed him and was probably the one who buried him. Although I doubt he has the head since he gave *that* to my father's enemies."

She clenched her bottle even tighter. "Damn him! First he gives Stoker that ridiculous book, then he starts the tours, then the Dracula restaurant and hotel, and now this. I swear, God as my witness, I'm going to get an ax and kill him once and for all."

Francesca's light blue eyes were warm with concern. Even though she was a wolf in animal form, those eyes were very catlike when she was human. The only thing the human Francesca shared with her wolf counterpart was her thick, dark chestnut hair. And speedy reflexes. "Calm down, Retta. You know he's only doing this to get under your skin."

"And it's working."

"C'mon, he wouldn't really do this."

"To get back at me? Yes, he would." She ground her teeth in frustration as she continued to call down the wrath of hell on his head. For centuries Velkan had done nothing but strike at her and her family. "I hate that man with every fiber of my being."

"Why did you marry him then?"

That was something she didn't want to think about. Even

five hundred years later, she could still see the night they'd met clearly in her mind. She'd been on her way home from the convent, for a visit with her father when her party had been attacked by Turks. They'd killed everyone but her and were well on their way to raping her when all of a sudden her assailants had been beheaded.

Too scared to scream, she'd lain on the ground, covered in their blood, waiting for her own death as she looked up at the men in armor who were routing the few attackers who'd managed to run.

Dressed in his dull black armor that held a gold serpent emblem, the knight who'd killed her would-be rapists had quickly wrapped her in his fur-lined cloak and picked her up from the ground. Without a word to her, Velkan had carried her on the back of his destrier to his home, where he'd made sure she was well tended and fed.

She could still remember the sight of his fierceness, the raw power that had bled from every part of him. He'd worn a black basinet helm that'd been fashioned to look like a bird of prey so that it inspired fear in his enemies. And it had definitely scared her to the core of her soul.

She'd had no idea of his features until later that night when he'd come to check on her. But it wasn't his handsomeness or his strength that had captivated her, it'd been his uncertainty around her. The fact that this man who'd been so intrepid and strong before the Turks had actually trembled when he reached out to touch her.

It'd been love at first sight.

Or so she thought.

Her heart aching from the memory, Retta curled her lip as she banished that memory and reminded herself that in the end Velkan had betrayed her and murdered her father. "I was young and stupid, and had no idea what I was letting myself in for. I thought he was a noble prince. I had no idea he was barely one step up from a monkey." She grabbed the printed-out page that Francesca had brought to lunch from Yahoo! News. "I take that back and I deeply apologize to all the primates of the earth for insulting them. He's not worthy of monkeydom. He's a slimy slug trail."

Francesca dipped her french fry into ketchup. "I don't know, I think it's kind of sweet that he keeps doing these stunts to get you to come see him."

Yeah, right. "That's not why he's doing this. He's trying to torture me and get back at my father. This isn't about tender feelings. It's about a man who's ruthless. A man who, even after five hundred years, can't let my family rest in peace. He's an animal." Sighing, Retta tossed the paper back to the table and reached into her purse for her Treo phone.

"What are you doing?"

"I'm booking a flight to Transylvania so that I can kill him in person. Then I'm going to stop these antics once and for all."

Francesca snorted. "No, you're not."

"Yes, I am."

"Then make it two."

Retta would have questioned that, since shape-shifting Were-Hunters could teleport from one location to another, but for some reason Francesca had always liked to travel with her. Of course, if Retta were smart, she'd make Francesca teleport her, too, but she hated to travel that way, even though it was virtually instantaneous. She might be immortal, but Retta liked to pretend she was as normal as possible. Besides, if Were-Hunters didn't know the area and shifted to it, they could hit a tree or manifest right in front of someone. Both experiences had nasty repercussions.

She paused in her dialing to watch Francesca pour more ketchup. "Why are you coming?"

"After all these years of listening to you rant about Prince Dickhead, I want to meet him for myself."

"Fine, but remember to avert your gaze from his. He'll

suck the goodness right out of the marrow of your bones and leave you as morally bankrupt as he is."

Francesca let out a low whistle. "Dang, remind me not to make you mad. I mean, really. How bad can he be?"

"Trust me. They don't come any worse than him. And you're about to see just how right I am."

2.

Retta had forgotten the beauty of her homeland. But as they made their way up the narrow mountain pass toward the hotel where she and Francesca would stay, old memories slammed into her. Even with her eyes wide open, Retta could still see this land as it had been when there were no power lines or modern buildings to mar it. No roads except for dirt paths worn by horses as they traversed the Wallachian landscape on their way to villages and Bucharest.

God, how she missed the mountains of her childhood. As a young woman, she'd spent countless hours staring out at them from the windows of her convent. No matter the season, they'd always been breathtaking—like a piece of heaven that had fallen to earth. It had never failed to capture her imagination and make her wonder what it would be like to fly over the mountains and explore distant countries.

Of course in her human lifetime that had been an impossible dream. Since her death, she'd traversed the entire globe trying to escape Velkan's cruelty.

As they rode in the taxi, they passed many thatched cottages that seemed lost in time. Some she could have sworn were here five hundred years ago when she'd fled this land to escape her husband.

She'd vowed that night to never return.

Yet here she was. And she was every bit as uncertain now as she'd been then. Her future every bit as unclear. The only thing that had kept her going back then had been Francesca's friendship. Francesca had joined her in Germany as Retta had been making her way from Wallachia to Paris. They'd met in a small inn where Retta had stopped for food.

There had been an awful rainstorm that had come up suddenly while she dined. It was so bad that her driver had refused to go onward until it stopped. Because of that, there weren't any rooms left for rent. Francesca had been kind enough to share her room with Retta.

Since that fateful night, they'd been virtually inseparable. There was nothing she'd treasured more over the centuries than Francesca's loyalty and wit.

"You okay?" Francesca asked.

"Just thinking."

Francesca nodded as she looked out the window. "Is it the way you remembered it?"

She didn't comment as she realized the driver was looking at them in the rearview mirror.

"Goat!" Retta shouted in Romanian as the animal darted into the road in front of them.

The driver slammed on the brakes, causing her and Francesca to tumble forward in their seats. They both let out "umphs" as they hit the back of the front seat and had the breath knocked out of them. Exchanging looks of aggravation, they resettled themselves back into place.

Francesca fastened her seat belt.

The driver smiled at them from the rearview mirror. "You are one of us, eh?" he said in Romanian. "I thought you looked like a natural daughter."

Retta didn't respond. How could she? He'd die to know

just how natural a daughter she was. After all, it was her infamous father who had made this little corner of the world such a tourist spot.

That thought made her ache as she remembered the turbulent time of her mortal years. This land had been covered in blood as battle after battle was fought between the Romanian people and the Turks. Between her family and her husband's as they vied for political power. She'd foolishly thought that by marrying Velkan she could ease the war and hostility between their families so that they could focus on the land's invaders.

That mistake and the well-known tragedy of their lives during the fifteenth century was what would lead a man called William Shakespeare to write *Romeo and Juliet* roughly a hundred years later. And just like his couple, their secret marriage had led to both their deaths.

But it'd been her husband's black sorcery that had led to their resurrections and immortality. Damn him! Even after all these centuries she couldn't forgive him. Besides, what few times she'd weakened, he'd always done something to renew her anger.

She pushed that thought aside as they reached the hotel. She got out first while the driver went to pull their suitcases from the trunk. Retta looked up at the quaint hotel with its highly arched roof and stylized black trim. Dusk was setting as she took her suitcase from the older man and paid him his fee.

"Thank you," he said.

Retta inclined her head as she and Francesca made their way toward the hotel's blackwood stairs.

Francesca frowned at a flyer that was on a bulletin board at the base of them. It was identical to several others except for the fact that it was written in English. "Did you see this? Dracula tour begins in an hour at the old church."

Retta seethed. "A pox on both his testicles."

Francesca laughed at that. "That's harsh."

"Yes, it is. But he deserves a lot worse. Bastard."

"May I help you with your bags?"

Retta jumped at the deep, thickly accented voice that appeared suddenly. Where the hell had he come from? Turning around, she met the gaze of a handsome man in his late twenties who stood just in front of her. A man who looked enough like Francesca to be her brother—right down to the dark chestnut hair and strikingly blue eyes. "Are you with the hotel?"

"Yes, my lady. My name is Andrei and I will be here to serve you in any manner you wish."

Francesca laughed, but Retta had a sneaking suspicion that his double entendre wasn't from trying to speak a different language. He knew what he was offering. "Thank you, Andrei," she said coldly as she handed him her bag. "We just need to check in."

"As you wish . . . madame?"

"She's a madame, I'm a miss," Francesca said, handing him her suitcase as well.

"I knew I should have left you in Chicago," Retta mumbled as Francesca winked at the handsome Romanian. Yet she wasn't flirting with him, which for Francesca was a first.

"I am sure you will both enjoy your stays here at Hotel . . ."—he paused for effect before he rolled the next word with true Romanian flare—"Dracula. We are having a special tonight. Staked steak with a tart raspberry sauce and minced-garlic mashed potatoes for keeping away those evil vampires." There was a devilish gleam in his eyes that Retta didn't find charming or amusing.

Rather, it just pissed her off.

"I imagine the garlic will keep away much more than vampires, eh, Andrei?" she said sarcastically.

He didn't speak as he led them up the stairs to the hotel's doors. There was a stereotypical winged vampire head on each door that opened into the blood-red lobby. There were pictures of different Hollywood depictions of Dracula everywhere, along with sketchings and paintings of Retta's father.

And her "favorite" was the golden cup in a case with the plaque that declared it to be the cup her father had set out in the central square of Tîrgovişte. He'd proclaimed his lands so free of crime that he'd put it there to tempt thieves. Terrified of him, none had ever dared to touch it. It'd stayed in the square all throughout his reign.

Right next to that was what appeared to be a stake with dried blood on it and a plaque that said it was the one her father had used to skewer a monk for lying to him. Bile rose in her throat.

"Ever feel like you've walked into a nightmare?" Retta asked Francesca.

"Oh, c'mon. Enjoy it."

Yeah, right. The only thing she would enjoy was kicking Velkan's balls so hard that they came out of his nostrils. Hmmm . . . maybe she was her father's daughter after all. For once she understood her father's deep need to torture his enemies.

Andrei led them across the lobby. "Would you like tickets for tonight's tour?"

Retta spoke without thinking. "Like another hole in my head."

He frowned at her.

"That's American slang for 'no thank you,' " Francesca said quickly.

"Strange. When I was in New York it was slang for 'no fucking way.' "

"You were in New York? When?" Francesca asked in a stunned tone.

"A year ago. It was . . . interesting."

Something strange passed between them.

Retta shook her head. "It must have been quite the culture shock for you."

"It took a little getting used to, but I enjoyed it there."

"What made you come back?" Retta asked.

His gaze bored into hers as if he knew who and what she was. "Once Transylvania is in your blood, it never leaves you."

Retta disregarded that. "Tell me, Andrei. Do you know a Viktor Petcu?"

He arched one handsome brow. "And why would you wish to speak to him?"

"I'm an old friend."

"I somehow doubt that, since I know all of his old friends and I would have remembered a woman so beautiful in his past."

Someone tsked.

Retta turned toward the counter to find a woman moving to stand before the old-fashioned ledger that was there. Appearing around the age of forty, she was dressed in the traditional Romanian peasant blouse and loose skirt. Tall and quite striking, she was someone Retta hadn't seen in over five hundred years.

Surely it couldn't be . . .

"It is not Viktor she wants, Andrei," the woman said, indicating Retta with a tilt of her chin. "She is here for Prince Velkan."

"Raluca?" Retta breathed as she stared in shock at the woman.

She bowed to her. "It is good to have you home again, Princess. Welcome."

Her jaw slack, Retta approached the woman slowly so that she could study her features. She looked only slightly older than she'd been when Retta had last seen her. Only then Raluca had been a servant in Retta's father's castle.

"How is this possible?"

The woman glanced to Andrei before she answered. "I am a Were-Hunter, Princess."

Were-Hunter. They were akin to the vampires or Daimons her husband had been created to kill. The Daimons had once been mortals who'd run afoul of the Greek god Apollo. A group of them had assassinated the god's mistress and child. As a result, Apollo had cursed them all to having to drink blood to live and for all of them to die at the tender age of twenty-seven. The only way for them to live longer was to steal human souls. Dark-Hunters had been created by Apollo's sister Artemis to kill the Daimons and free the human souls before they died.

Several thousand years after that, an ancient king had unknowingly married one of their cursed race. When his wife had decayed on her twenty-seventh birthday, he'd realized that his beloved sons would meet their mother's fate. To save them, he'd magically merged the souls of animals with their race until he'd found a way to save them. Thus, the Were-Hunters had been created. Able to bend the laws of physics and with highly developed psychic sense, the shape-shifters lived for centuries.

But it was rare for a Were-Hunter to be near a Dark-Hunter, never mind serve one. Since Dark-Hunters were created to kill their Daimon cousins, most Were-Hunters avoided them at all costs.

Most.

Retta looked over her shoulder to Francesca, who was now squirming uncomfortably. A bad feeling went through Retta as she realized that Francesca had befriended her just weeks after she'd fled Romania. They'd known each other almost fifteen years before Francesca had confided the truth of her existence to Retta.

Now she had a suspicion that sickened her.

"Lykos?" Retta asked Raluca. That was the Were-Hunter term for their wolf branch.

"Raluca is my mother," Francesca said quietly. "Andrei and Viktor are my brothers—it's why I never used a surname. I didn't want you to realize I was one of the family."

Retta couldn't breathe as she stood there with her emotions in turmoil. Anger, hurt, betrayal. They were all there and they each wanted a turn at Raluca and Francesca, but most of all, they wanted Retta to beat her husband. "I see."

"Please, Princess," Raluca said, her bright blue eyes burning with intensity. "We're only here to help you."

"Then call me another cab and get me back to the airport ASAP."

Francesca shook her head. "We can't do that."

Retta glared at her. "Fine then. I'll do it myself." As she moved toward the phone on the desk, Raluca pulled it away.

Retta saw the sympathy in Raluca's eyes as she cradled the phone to her chest. "I'm truly sorry, but you can't leave here, Princess."

"Oh yes, hell I can and I am." Retta started for the door, only to have Andrei block her path.

"You are in danger, Princess."

She narrowed her eyes on him. "Not me, buddy. But you are if you don't move out of my way."

Francesca took a step toward her. "Listen to him, Retta, please."

She turned on Francesca with a hiss. "Don't you dare start on me. I thought you were my friend."

"I *am* your friend."

"Bullshit! You lied to me. Deceived me. You knew how I felt about Velkan and yet you never once told me that you serve him."

Francesca glared at her. "Yes, Retta. Prince Velkan sent me to watch over you because he was afraid for you to be alone. As you've said repeatedly over the centuries, you were young and naive. You spent the whole of your life behind a convent wall. The last thing he wanted was for you to be hurt again, so I was charged with your care. Is that really a crime after all we've been through together?"

"I didn't need a babysitter. How could you play both sides of the fence when you knew how much I hated him?"

Those blue eyes singed her with sincerity. "I never played you. Okay, so I didn't mention that he'd sent me to stay with you originally. So what? We *are* friends."

"Uh-huh. Friends don't lie to each other."

"What lie?"

"You said you never *met* him."

"She has never met him," Raluca said quietly. "I am the one who sent my daughter after you at the prince's request. She was the one closest to your area when you left here. But Francesca has never met His Highness. Not once."

That made Retta feel better than she wanted to admit, but still it didn't rectify any of this. They'd all deceived her and she was too tired to play this game anymore. "It doesn't matter. I'm going home."

Andrei blocked her way again. "You *are* home, Princess."

"Like hell." She feinted to the right, then rushed left, past him.

He caught her in his arms before she could make it to the door.

"I don't want to hurt you, Andrei, but so help me, I will."

Before he complied, Francesca went to the door and locked it with a key. "You're not leaving."

"Damn you!"

"Look, spew at me all you want, but you need to be aware of why I brought you here."

Retta crossed her arms over her chest. "Let me guess. Velkan wants to see me?"

"No," Raluca said, joining them. "The only thing His Highness would like to see in regards to you, Princess, is your disembowelment."

Now that surprised her. "Since when?"

It was Andrei who answered. "Since about halfway through the sixteenth century when it became obvious that you had no intention of returning. He's been cursing your name ever since. Loudly, too, I might add."

Raluca nodded eagerly.

For some reason Retta didn't want to think about, that actually hurt her feelings. She'd assumed that all of his attempts to besmirch her father's name and reputation had been his way of getting her to contact him. Of course, she'd had no intention of ever doing that since she still wasn't convinced he hadn't intended to kill her the night he'd given her his sleeping potion.

"Then why am I here?"

Andrei took a deep breath before he answered. "Because of Stephen Corwin."

She was baffled by the name. How in the world could *he* fit into this madness? "The investment broker?"

"Among other things," Francesca said. "Remember when I told you I had a weird feeling about him?"

"You have weird feelings all the time. Nine times out of ten, they're attributable to either pizza or spoiled beer."

Francesca gave her an unamused stare. "Yeah, right. Remember when I told you that his scent bothered me? That I couldn't place it? Well, I did some checking and it turns out he's a member of the Order of the Dragon. Sound familiar?"

Retta rolled her eyes. Both her father and grandfather had been members. Their epitaphs of Dracul and Dracula had stemmed from their membership. "That order ceased to exist not long after Velkan killed my father."

Raluca shook her head. "No, Princess, it didn't. They merely went underground and wanted the rest of the world to think that. It was a cousin to Mathhias Corvinus who lost his wife to a Daimon. Horrified by the demon who claimed her life and soul, he reestablished the order to purge the world of the undead. They went on a killing spree of Daimons, and he called for his brethren to help him. But they didn't stop there. They killed our people and countless Dark-Hunters as well.

They don't distinguish between us. To them, one preternatural being is the same as the other and all of us should be exterminated. Even now, centuries later, they hunt us without discrimination, brutally slaughtering all they find."

Retta felt terrible about that, but it still didn't explain why they wanted her to stay here. "What has this to do with me?"

Francesca took a deep breath before she answered. "I think Stephen was sent to *kill* you."

Retta scowled at her friend. "Are you insane? There's no way."

"Remember the tattoo on his arm you told me about? The one of a dragon coiled around the cross? It's their emblem. He's one of them, Ret, trust me."

"Trust you? After all these centuries when you were lying to me? Think again. Stephen wouldn't hurt me. He's had ample time to try."

Francesca gave her a deep, meaningful stare. "Are you sure?"

Retta hesitated, then hated herself for it. Stephen had never once given her an indication that he was anything more than an acquaintance who wanted to be more significant in her life. But since she was still technically married and an immortal, she'd kept him at bay. "Of course I'm sure."

"Then why has he been sniffing around you?" Francesca asked coldly.

"Because maybe he likes me?"

"Or he was trying to use you to get to Prince Velkan," Raluca said. "That has been my theory. It is why the prince made sure that all mentions of you and your mother were purged from historical records. He didn't want anyone to learn that Vlad Dracula had a daughter, and most especially he didn't want them to know that you had married him. He knew that the order would pursue you to the ends of the earth if they ever learned of your existence."

"It makes sense," Andrei added. "The Corvinuses and the Danestis have a long history of bad blood between them."

Still Retta discounted their argument. "This is not the Middle Ages, people. In case you haven't noticed, the wars are over."

"No," Andrei said, glancing past her, toward the door. "I think the war is only beginning."

Frowning at his dire tone, she turned her head to see what had his attention.

Her heart stopped beating as she saw the tall figure dressed in black armor, complete with helm and heraldry.

It was Velkan's.

And he was heading straight for her.

3

Retta couldn't so much as draw a breath as Raluca opened the door and Velkan swaggered in. At six foot four, he'd seemed like a giant to her when she'd been human. And again, she remembered the first time she'd seen him. Blood had coated that black armor. The blood of those out to rape and kill her. She could still recall the sound of steel scraping steel as he moved. The sight of his dexterity even though every inch of his body had been covered by armor.

More than that, she remembered the beauty of his face . . . the tenderness of his callused hands as they caressed her bare skin. The way he'd held her as if she were unspeakably precious, as if he feared she would shatter in his arms and leave him alone again.

Those memories surged and buried all the anger and hatred she'd nursed against him. There for a moment, she wanted to go back to the beginning of their marriage. Back to the days when she had lived and died for this man. When she had trusted him without question.

He had been her entire world.

She'd known this moment would come, and in her mind she'd practiced a thousand things to say to him.

A thousand and then some.

But every one of them fled her memory as he approached her and some foreign part wanted to embrace him after all these centuries. She wanted to rush into his arms and just feel him hold her again.

She'd expected him to curse her or kiss her. To stare at her as if he couldn't believe she was here. To try to strangle her. Something. Anything. But in all her imagined scenarios nothing had come close to what he did next.

He walked right past her as if he didn't know her and seized Francesca in a fierce hug before he danced around the room with her.

Baffled, Retta put her hands on her hips as a wave of rage whipped through her body. How dare he grab another woman and not even acknowledge her! She opened her mouth to speak only to be hushed as the knight started laughing in a tone that was nothing like Velkan's. It was light and almost boyish.

"Oh, my little sister! It's been far too long since I last saw you. How have you been?"

"Viktor," Raluca said with a laugh. "Put Francesca down before you bruise her."

Francesca pulled the bird-shaped helm from his head, exposing his laughing features, as opposed to Velkan's serious countenance. With brown hair and teasing blue eyes, Viktor quickly complied with his mother's orders and set Francesca back on her feet. Laughing, she hugged him close while Retta let out a long breath.

That had been close. Too close in fact and it made her realize that she didn't want to meet Velkan on *his* terms. She needed to make sure that she had control of their first meeting. That her emotions and body didn't betray her again.

"It's so good to see you," Francesca laughed at her brother. "I've missed you so much."

And those words tugged at Retta's heart as she saw the affection her best friend shared with her family. Retta's own brothers had died hundreds of years ago, as had their entire lineage. There was no joyous homecoming for her. No parents.

No husband.

Nothing.

That hurt most of all.

Viktor paused as he realized that they weren't alone. "Princess Esperetta?"

"Yes," Raluca answered for her.

Panic flickered in his blue eyes. "We must get her out of here before the prince sees her."

Finally someone who actually saw reason.

Raluca waved his words away. "He won't come here this early."

Viktor shook his head in denial. "She can stay the night, but come the morrow, she needs to leave before he learns that she is here."

Francesca argued with him, "I brought her here for protection. She must stay."

"No," Retta said, growing tired of the way they spoke about her like she was a lost puppy who was out in the garage. "I came here because Velkan is planning on putting my father's remains on display."

They exchanged a puzzled frown as Francesca turned a bit sheepish.

Absolute rage tore through Retta's entire being. "Don't tell me you lied."

Francesca cringed. "Only a little. I knew if I told you that, that it was the one thing that would get you to leave Chicago."

In all her life, Retta had never been more livid. "Unbelievable! Un-friggin'-believable. How could you do such a thing?"

Francesca was completely unrepentant. "I did it to protect you."

Retta held her hand up as pure disgust filled her. "Thanks, Frankie. It's not like I have a life as well as clients who need me."

"You can't have clients if you're dead. Besides, Trish is handling them. They won't even miss you."

"Save me the bullshit." She looked at Viktor. "Get me a cab and I'm out of here. Right now."

He started for the counter.

"Viktor," Raluca said in a thick, drawn-out accent. "Touch that phone and you will regret it for the rest of your existence."

He arched both brows as he froze in place. "But Mother . . . the prince will—"

"I will deal with the prince. You need to prepare yourself for the tour. Now go."

Retta could tell he wanted to argue but didn't dare. Instead, he cast a sullen look her way before he complied with his mother's orders.

"Where is Velkan?" Retta asked Raluca.

"Not to be flippant, Princess, but he is wherever it is he wishes to be."

"You won't tell me?"

Raluca hesitated before she answered. "I will not allow you to blindside him in his home after all he has suffered for you, Princess. I know of your feelings toward him from my daughter."

"And still you side with him?"

Raluca's gaze went toward the blunted spike tip on the wall. "I will protect His Highness with every breath I hold in my body. But for him, I would have been impaled, too." And with those words spoken, she turned around and left Retta alone with Francesca and Andrei.

Retta gave Andrei an expectant look.

"He will be in the Bloody Dungeon later."

"The what?"

"It's a club," Francesca explained. "One where Daimons tend to pick off tourists who want to meet real vampires."

Well, didn't that make perfect sense? "What time does he go there?"

Andrei shrugged. "Any time between now and dawn."

"You are just so helpful, Andrei."

"I try to be, Princess."

"And you fail with such panache."

He ignored her sarcasm.

Sighing, Retta looked at Francesca. "I don't suppose I could talk you into just poofing me home again, could I?"

"You don't like to teleport. It makes you queasy. Besides, I thought you didn't like me anymore."

"I'm bordering on it. But you are the only family I have. Good or bad, and right now it's definitely bad. Let me go home and I will forgive you."

"I can't do that, Retta. Sorry. But trust me, this is for your own good."

Fine then. Come morning, she'd slip away from them one way or another. She looked back at Andrei. "We are one hundred percent sure Velkan won't come to this hotel, right?"

"Oh, I can absolutely guarantee it. He wants nothing to do with your family. He only ventures here once in a blue moon."

That just made her all warm and toasty inside. "Then why do you run this place?"

He grinned at her. "The money. We make a killing on it."

Great, just great. "Whatever. I'm going to bed now. Give me a key and let me put this whole nightmare behind me."

Francesca frowned. "Aren't you hungry?"

"No. I just need to sleep and forget this whole day has happened."

Andrei went behind the counter to sign her in. "Would you like Dracula's Suite?"

Retta narrowed her eyes at him. "Keep pushing, Andrei, and you and I are going to play a game."

"And what game is that, Princess?"

"Find the Ball in My Hand."

He frowned. "I don't see a ball, Princess."

"Oh, you will, just as soon as I snap it off your body."

He flinched.

Francesca laughed. "She's teasing, Andrei. Her bark is always worse than her bite."

Wishing she'd left her friend at home, Retta took the key card from his hand. "Where's the room?"

"Top floor."

Without a word, Retta grabbed her suitcase and headed for the elevator. She got in and turned around to see Francesca and Andrei teasing each other as the doors closed. Pain sliced her heart. How she wished she could have her family back again. She'd adored her two little brothers. They had been one of the greatest joys of her human life. And a twinge of guilt went through her that she'd deprived Francesca of hers. She hated they'd been apart all these centuries.

But that had been Francesca's decision, not hers.

Sighing, she rode the elevator up to the room, and as soon as she pushed open the door she felt the need to go downstairs and hurt Andrei and Raluca. To say the place was tacky would be an insult to tackiness. The suite was large and airy, with blood-red walls that were decorated with every kind of wood-cutting imaginable that depicted impalements.

She rolled her eyes as she headed for the bedroom, then stopped dead in her tracks. Unlike the sitting room, this one was done in black, white, and gray and was identical to the bedroom from Bela Lugosi's *Dracula*, where he'd bitten his fair maiden.

"You people are sick," Retta said, grateful that at least in here there were no reminders of her father.

Setting her suitcase down, she peeled her coat away from

her body as she toed off her shoes, then headed for the bed. She'd take a little nap to get the edge off her exhaustion and then she'd see about finding a rental car to get back to the airport. One way or another, she was going to get out of this place and go home.

She pulled the covers back and tucked herself into the large bed that cushioned her like a cloud, and before she knew it, she was sound asleep.

But her sleep was far from peaceful. In her dreams, she could hear her father's voice calling out to her. She could see Velkan delivering the death blow that had ended her father's life as his serpent emblem drifted through her mind, over all the images.

You are the daughter of the dragon.... Death to the Danestis.

She came awake with a start. Retta lay silent as she listened to a fierce wind whipping against her windows. But that wasn't what had disturbed her.

She sensed a foreign presence in the room. It was powerful and frightening.

Reacting on pure instinct, she quickly rolled to her feet and struck out at where she sensed the presence. There was nothing there but air.

Now the presence was behind her.

She whirled about to confront the intruder only to find herself face-to-face with the last person she expected.

Velkan.

He stared at her with eyes so black she couldn't even tell where the iris stopped and the pupil began. Dressed in a pair of jeans and a tight black shirt, he wore his long, wavy black hair pulled back into a ponytail. He still had the same sharply chiseled features. The same feral look that announced to the world this was a man who not only could take your life but one who would relish the killing.

God, he was unbelievably sexy. Tall and commanding, he

made every part of her warm and breathless. And as she stood toe-to-toe with him, she was tormented by images of being held between those muscular arms while he made love to her. Of being kissed by that perfect mouth. Of fingering the long scar that ran from the outer corner of his left eye to his chin. A scar that in no way detracted from the beauty of that masculine face. If anything it added to it.

She couldn't even think as a wave of pent-up emotions seared her to the spot.

Velkan couldn't breathe as he stared into eyes so blue they reminded him of the summer sky he'd not seen in over five hundred years. The scent of her hung heavy in his nostrils, reminding him of a time when that scent had clung to his body. Her skin was still as pale as a snowy field. Her hair the deep auburn red of a fox.

Not once in all these centuries had he forgotten her beauty. Her scent. The sound of her voice calling out to him.

The sound of her voice cursing him to death.

It was a mistake to be here. He knew it.

Still he was here, staring at a woman he wanted desperately to kiss.

A woman he wanted to kill. He'd given her everything he had and more, and in return she'd spat at him. He hated her for that even as a buried part of him loved her still. He'd lived and died for her. Had died a death no human being should ever have to suffer. And for what? So that she could run from him and deny they'd ever loved each other.

His father had been right. Women were useless outside of the bedroom and only a fool would ever give his heart to one.

"What are you doing in my room?" she breathed, finally breaking the taut silence that was rife with their bitter emotions.

His gut tightened at the sound of her cadent voice that was so similar to what he remembered and at the same time alien. She no longer bore her native accent. Now she sounded like the women in the American TV shows that Viktor watched.

Velkan ached to reach out and touch her, but honestly he didn't trust himself not to choke her if he tried. Anger, lust, and tenderness were at war inside him and he had no idea which of them would ultimately win. But none of it boded well for the woman in front of him.

"I wanted to verify your presence with my own eyes."

She held her arms up in a sarcastic gesture. "Obviously, I'm here."

"Obviously."

She stepped back, her eyes guarded. "Well then, you can leave." She gestured toward the door.

It was hard to stand here when all he wanted to do was pull her into his arms and taste those mocking lips. The air between them was filled with their mutual hatred. Their mutual desire. He still didn't know how it had come to this. How a man could love a woman so desperately and still want to kill her.

It didn't make sense.

A million thoughts clashed inside his head. He wanted to tell her that he'd missed her. He wanted to tell her that he wished she were dead. That he'd never laid eyes on her.

Most of all, he just wanted to stay here and soak in the beauty of her features until he was drunk on them. *You are one sick bastard.* This was a woman who'd abandoned him five hundred years ago.

He might not have much in his life, but he did have his dignity. Be damned again if he'd allow her to take that from him. With a curt nod to her, he stepped back and turned toward the window to leave.

"I want a divorce."

Those words stopped him cold. "What?"

"You heard me. I want a divorce."

He laughed bitterly as he looked at her over his shoulder. "As you wish, Princess. But make certain that you take a camcorder to the courthouse, as I would like to see the look on their faces when you present them with our marriage scroll and they note the date of it."

"That's not what I mean," she said coldly. "I want to be free of you. Forever."

Those words tore through him like a hot lance and did twice the damage. Grinding his teeth, he looked out the window, into the black night that had been his only solace all these centuries past. "Then take your freedom and leave. I never want to see your face again."

Retta didn't know why his words shredded her heart, but they did. They even succeeded in bringing tears to her eyes as she watched him turn himself into a bat before he flew through her open windows.

In spite of everything, she wanted to call him back, but her pride wouldn't let her. It was best this way. They would both be free now. . . .

Free for what?

She was still immortal. And no matter how much she hated it, she was still in love with her husband. Tears flowed down her cheeks as she realized the truth. She should never have come back here. Never.

But now it was too late. After all this time, she knew the truth. She loved Velkan. Even with all the lies and the betrayal. He still held her heart captive.

How could she be so stupid?

Closing her eyes, she saw him as he'd been on the day they'd married. It'd been a small monastery in the mountains. For the first time since childhood and in order to honor her, Velkan had laid aside his armor and wore a simple doublet of black velvet. Still unrefined even though he was a prince, he'd left his long hair loose to trail over his shoulders. She'd been dressed in a gown of dark green samite and velvet, trimmed in sable that matched her fur mantle.

It'd been the only time she'd seen him clean-shaven. His dark eyes had scorched her as he stared at her and uttered the words that would bind them together before God.

What she hadn't known then was that Velkan's mother had been a sorceress who'd taught her son well. And while he and Retta had taken holy vows, he'd bound her to him with the darkest of arts.

Without telling her.

What he'd done was unforgivable. So why then did a part of her ache to forgive him?

Retta tilted her head as she heard a light scratching at her door.

"Velkan?" she whispered. Her heart leaped at the prospect of it being him again.

Before she could stop herself, she rushed to the door and opened it. Her jaw dropped at the sight of the last person she'd expected to be there.

Tall and blond, he was a far cry from her darkly sinister husband. And for the first time, she realized he was pale in comparison to the man she'd left behind.

"Stephen? What are you doing here?"

His light blue eyes were filled with sympathy. "My name is not Stephen, Retta. It's Stefan."

Before she could ask him what he meant by that, he blew something into her face.

Retta staggered back as her senses dulled. Everything shifted around her. Reacting on instinct, she kicked her foot out, catching him right between the legs. He doubled over immediately. But as she tried to close her door, her sight went black and she fell to the floor.

4

Velkan landed on the balcony of his mansion that overlooked the quiet valley, and shifted back into human form. Five hundred years ago, this place had been accessible by a dirt road that led up the mountainside to his courtyard. It was a road he'd closed and let be overgrown two hundred years ago when he realized how often he watched it, waiting for Esperetta to return.

Now that road was completely covered by brambles and vines as the forest had reclaimed it. The only way to venture here was by flight or teleportation. Two things that helped to keep away anyone who had no business here.

Velkan paused on the carved-stone balcony to look back toward town. He'd already cleared out the Daimons who'd come to town to prey on the tourists and he still had hours before dawn. His house was completely dark and silent in the night. Viktor had chosen to stay at the hotel with his family—no doubt in fear of Velkan's mood.

And the man had every right to be afraid. Velkan didn't like surprises and Esperetta's arrival had definitely qualified as that. The Weres should have told him to expect her. What they'd done was unforgivable to him.

The gilded French doors to his room opened silently at his approach, then slammed shut behind him. Long ago, his wife had been terrified of his supernatural powers. What he had now made a mockery of the ones he'd borne as a mortal man. Back then, he'd been limited to simple premonitions, curses, potions, and spells that had to be worked with blood and ritual.

Now his powers were truly fierce. Telekinesis, shape-shifting, and pyrokinetics. Over the centuries, he'd become the monster Esperetta had feared. He held his hand out and the bottle of bourbon flew to him. Uncorking it, he drank the bourbon straight from the bottle as he walked past a mirror that didn't cast his reflection.

He laughed at that. Until he neared the fireplace where Esperetta's painting hung. The look on her face froze him to the spot. And as always, it took his breath.

He'd commissioned it right before their wedding. He'd hired Gentile Bellini and had practically been forced to abduct the man out of Venice for the work. But Velkan had known that no one other than that artist would have ever been able to capture her youth and innocence.

Bellini hadn't disappointed. If anything, he'd excelled past all of Velkan's expectations.

Esperetta had been so nervous that day. With bright summer flowers in her dark auburn hair and dressed in a light gold gown, she'd been an absolute vision. Bellini had placed her in the garden outside of Velkan's residence—a garden that was now a gnarled, unsightly mess from lack of care. She'd been fidgeting unmercifully until she'd spied Velkan sitting on the wall, watching her.

Their eyes had met and had held, and the shyest, most beautiful smile that ever graced a woman's face had been captured by the artist. It was a look that could still bring Velkan to his knees.

Snarling at the picture, he forced himself to walk onward,

away from it. He should have burned it centuries ago. He still wasn't sure why he hadn't.

In fact, he could send a blast to it even now and burst it into flames. . . .

His hand heated up in expectation. But he balled it into a fist as he left his room, then descended the stairs to the first floor, where Bram and Stoker waited for his return. Calling out to his Tibetan mastiffs, he made his way to his study, where his fire had all but gone out.

He shot a blast of fire into it, making it roar to life. It bathed the room in a dull orange light and caused the shadows to dance eerily along the cold stone walls. He petted his dogs as they welcomed him home with joyful barks and licks. Then they bounded off to retake their seats beside his padded chair. Sighing, Velkan took his seat so that he could stare into the fire that did nothing to warm him. The light was painful for his eyes, but honestly he didn't care.

He glanced over at the dogs on each side of him. "Be glad that you're both neutered. Would that I had been so fortunate." Because right then, his body was hard and aching for the one woman who would never again submit to his touch.

His anger mounting, he took another swig only to curse over the fact that the alcohol couldn't do anything to him. As a Dark-Hunter he could never get drunk. There was no escape from this pain.

Growling, he threw the bottle into the hearth, where it shattered into a thousand pieces. The flames sparked in greedy consumption of the alcohol. The dogs lifted their heads in curiosity while Velkan raked his hand through his hair.

As bad as it had been before, it was so much worse now knowing that she was only a short distance away. Her scent still hung in his nostrils, making him even more feral than he'd been before.

You should go to her and force her to take you back.

That was what the Moldavian warlord Velkan Danesti

would have done. He'd have never allowed a slip of a woman to lead him about.

But that man had died the night an innocent young woman had looked up at him with eyes so blue, so trusting, they had instantly stolen his heart. Perhaps this was his punishment for having lived such a brutal human life. To want the one thing he couldn't have. Esperetta's peaceful, soft touch.

Restless with his thoughts, he rose to his feet. Bram rose as well until he realized that Velkan was only going to pace the room. The dog settled back down while Velkan did his best to banish his memories.

But unfortunately, there was no way to cleave his heart from his chest and until he did that he knew he would never escape the prison his wife had condemned him to.

Retta came awake to a stinging headache and found herself tied to an iron chair. The room, which was industrial, like an old warehouse or something, was dark and damp, with an awful stench that was similar to that of a pair of old gym socks mixed with the smell of rotten eggs. It was all she could do to breathe past the stench as she tried to wrest her wrists free of the ropes that held her down.

She could hear faint voices from an adjoining room. . . .

She strained to hear them, but all she caught was a faint whisper until a loud roar rang out.

"Death to the Danestis!"

Great chant, especially since she was technically one of them. Granted, she didn't want to claim kinship, but on paper . . .

"She's awake."

Retta turned her head to see a tall, gaunt man in the doorway. Dressed in black slacks and a turtleneck, he reminded her of a slick city drug dealer, complete with a gold-capped tooth. And he eyed her as if she were the lowest life-form on the planet.

"Thank you, George," an older man dressed in black slacks and a blue button-down shirt and sweater said as he moved past him. There was something innately evil about the older man. He was definitely the kind of guy who'd like to pull the wings off butterflies as a kid. Just for fun.

And pulling up the rear was her "good" friend Stephen, tall and blond. She'd originally liked him because he was the complete antithesis of her husband. Whereas Velkan's features were sullen and intense, Stephen's were wholesome and sweet. He'd reminded her of a very young Robert Redford.

If only she'd known that Stephen wasn't the boy next door. At least not unless you happened to live next door to the Munsters.

She glared at him with every ounce of hatred she felt. "Where am I and what am I doing here?"

It was the older man who answered. "You are our hostage and you are in our . . . place."

Gee, he was ever so helpful. "Hostage for what?"

It was Stephen who answered. "To get your husband to come to us."

She burst out laughing at the absurdity of that statement. "Is this a joke?"

"No joke," the older man said. "For centuries my family has been hunting him, trying to kill the unholy, unnatural creature he has become."

"And we've been hunting you," "Slim" said as he stepped forward from the doorway.

The old man nodded. "But always you and he escaped us."

"Wow, that doesn't say much about your skills, since I didn't even know I was being chased."

He rushed forward as if to strike her, but Stephen caught him. "Don't, Dieter. She's only trying to provoke you."

"She's doing a good job."

Retta cleared her throat to draw their attention back to her. "Just out of curiosity, why have you been hunting me?"

Stephen stepped closer to her and offered her a cocky smile. "Because you are the one thing we know that will draw Velkan out into the open. He's never responded to any lure we've cast at him . . . yet."

"Yeah, well, bad news for you, pal. He won't come for me, either."

Dieter scoffed at her. "Of course he will."

She shook her head. "Hardly. News flash, guys. All of you have committed a felony for no good reason. I saw Hubby earlier tonight and he made it plain that he never wants to see me again."

The men exchanged puzzled stares.

"Is she lying?" the old man asked Stephen in German.

Retta had to force herself not to roll her eyes. Surely they weren't so stupid as to think she couldn't speak German?

"She has to be," Stephen answered abruptly. "Good God, the man was impaled for her. In all the centuries while our kind have watched him, he's never been with another woman or we would have used her to get to him. There's not even a record of a one-night stand, and he keeps tabs on Esperetta constantly. Face it, the werewolves would never have sacrificed a daughter to stay with her if he wasn't absolutely adamant that she be protected. Those aren't the actions of a man who hates her."

Slim concurred. "The werewolf I tortured and killed said that he keeps her room just as she left it five hundred years ago. It even has the gown she wore when they married. There's a painting of her when she was human in his bedroom and photographs that have been sent to him to prove that she lives and is happy. He stares at the photographs every night. There's no chance that he doesn't hold her sacred. If he hated her, he would have destroyed all traces of her centuries ago."

"Likewise," Stephen said with a hint of rancor in his voice, "she lives as a nun. I couldn't even get a kiss from her the whole time I've known her. She's only trying to protect him. I'm sure of it."

Retta couldn't breathe as she heard those words. It was true. She'd never touched another man. Had never even been interested in one. Of course, she'd told herself that once burned, a thousand times shy. And she couldn't very well date, let alone marry, a human man who would begin to wonder why she didn't age. After all, there were only so many ways to lie about plastic surgery before it became obvious she was immortal.

And in all this time, she'd convinced herself that Velkan hadn't been as faithful to her. During their lifetime, no woman would have ever expected fidelity from her husband. It was absurd. Even her father, who was adamant about his Christianity and who demanded absolute faithfulness from his subjects, had been known to have mistresses.

So she'd convinced herself that Velkan had never really missed her. That he'd taken what he wanted and used her to kill her father.

Could it be that Velkan really did love her? That he missed her?

If it were true, then she deserved to die at their hands. Because if it were true, then she'd been punishing a man for centuries for no other crime than loving her.

No one should be hurt because of that.

Surely she hadn't been that stupid. Had she?

I am such a rabid bitch. No wonder Velkan had told her to get lost. She was lucky he hadn't choked her. Clenching her teeth to staunch the pain that ached inside her, she tried her best to remember what he'd said the night she'd left Romania. She could see the moonlight on his face, the blood on his armor.

They'd argued, but now she couldn't remember anything other than her confusion and fear of him. She'd been absolutely convinced that he'd tried to kill her by burying her in the ground. That he'd lied about the tonic he'd given her.

But had he?

Please don't let me be wrong. Please. "He won't come for

me," Retta said from between clenched teeth. "I know he won't."

Dieter narrowed those rodent eyes on her. "We shall see. Not that it matters. Either way, we kill *you*."

It was almost five in the morning when Velkan found himself alone in his bedroom. Then again, he was always alone in his bedroom. God, he was such a fool. Any man worth his salt would just find a willing female and sate the ache in his loins for a woman's body.

But Velkan refused to forsake the oath he'd taken to Esperetta. He'd vowed before his father's God to honor her and to keep himself for her only, and he'd stood by that oath.

Even though he hated himself for it.

There was only one woman who held his attention and it was why he despised her so much. She'd left him with nothing. Not even his manhood.

Damn her.

Suddenly there was a knock on his door. "I told you to leave me alone, Viktor," he snarled, thinking it was his Squire.

"It's not Viktor," Raluca said from the other side of the doorway.

How unlike her to venture here so close to the dawn. Not that the dawn held any sway for her, but normally Velkan would be preparing for bed.

Frowning, he opened the door with his thoughts to find her there, wringing her hands. Her sons and Francesca were behind her and all of them echoed their mother's worry. His stomach shrank. "What has happened?"

Raluca swallowed. "They have taken her."

He knew instantly that Esperetta was the her. "Who has?"

"The Order of the Dragon," Andrei said, his voice tinged by anger. "Once they notified us that they held her, we tried to get her free, but . . ."

"But?" Velkan prompted.

Francesca stepped forward. "They have her tied inside a cage. An electric one. There's no way for us to get to her without it immobilizing us."

Velkan gave them a droll stare. "Fine, let her stew there, thinking about how much she's betrayed me. When the sun sets, I'll go get her."

The Weres exchanged a nervous glance before Raluca spoke. "It's not that simple, my prince. They've put her on a small stool with no rungs. And that stool is on an electrified floor. If she puts her legs down at all or slips from the stool, it'll kill her instantly."

Francesca nodded. "They have enough juice on that floor to light up New York City."

He wanted to tell her that he didn't care, but the fear in his heart told him exactly how much of a lie that was.

But before he could move, Raluca was by his side, with her hand on his arm. "You know you can't go, either."

He narrowed his eyes on her. "I'm not afraid of them."

"It's too close to dawn," Raluca insisted. "You'll end up like Illie if you go. They know our weaknesses."

Velkan took her hand in his and squeezed it gently. Illie had been her mate who'd died at the hands of the Order. Five years ago, he'd been captured when one of their Order had used a Taser on him. The electricity had shot through his cells, turning him from man to wolf and back again. It was one of the few things that could completely incapacitate a Were-Hunter. Enough electricity would ultimately kill them.

And if the Order had Esperetta, then they already knew Velkan's weakness.

"Would you have her die?" he asked Raluca.

He saw the pity in Raluca's face. She'd been Esperetta's nurse before his wife had been oblated to the convent.

"Not by choice. But better her than you."

"Mom!" Francesca snapped. "No offense, but I choose Retta in this. She's an innocent victim."

Her mother turned on her with a snarl. "And the prince has guarded us for centuries. But for him, I would be dead now and so would your brothers."

"We're wasting time," Velkan said, cutting them off. "I need you to take me to her so that I can free her before the sun rises." He saw the reservation in Raluca's eyes. "It's why you came, is it not?"

She shook her head. "I came only because I knew you would be angry if I failed to tell you what had happened."

She was right about that. He would never stand by and see Esperetta harmed—even if he did hate her. "Don't fear. You can teleport me there and I can turn off the electricity, then you can teleport both of us out, long before the sun rises."

Francesca screwed up her face. "It's not that easy. The switch is inside the cage. You'll be electrocuted trying to switch it off."

He sighed at the prospect, but it changed nothing. He just wished he could use his telekinesis on it. But electricity was the one thing he couldn't move with his mind. Its living nature made it highly unpredictable, and he could accidentally hurt or kill someone by trying to manipulate it mentally. He would have to manually shut it off. "Fine. It won't kill me." It would just hurt like hell.

"There's more," Viktor said quietly.

This he couldn't wait to hear. "That is?"

"They have a generator rigged and another switch that is also inside another electric cage. If you turn it off, it won't give us enough time to reach her before they fry us, and unlike you, we're not immune."

Raluca nodded. "And they have her out in a courtyard. The wall of which is surrounded by mirrors to reflect the rising sun directly onto you should you go to her. Their intent is for none of us to survive this."

And they'd done a good job setting this trap.

Velkan let out a tired breath as he considered what was about to happen. But it didn't matter.

"My wife is in danger. Take me to her."

Retta ground her teeth as every muscle in her legs ached from the strain of keeping them off the floor. The effort showed itself in small tears in her eyes. This had to be the most excruciating pain she'd ever experienced. Honestly, she didn't know how much longer she could stand it and not rest her legs.

The dry hum of electricity was a cold reminder of what would happen to her if she didn't keep them lifted. . . .

"You can do it," she whispered.

But what good would it do? They were determined to kill her regardless. Why was she even fighting the inevitable? She should just put her feet down and get it over with. Put herself out of her misery.

Velkan wouldn't come for her. Francesca couldn't. It was over. There was no need to delay the inevitable, and yet Retta couldn't make herself give up. It just wasn't in her.

"What is it about you and this country that you are ever finding yourself in peril whenever you're here?"

She jerked her head up as she heard that deep, resonant voice that went down her spine like a gentle caress. "Velkan?"

He stepped out of the shadows and neared the edge of the electrified floor that separated the two of them. His face was awash with shadows and yet he'd never looked more handsome to her. "Is there anyone else stupid enough to be here?"

She glanced up at the sky that was growing lighter by the second. "You can't stay. You have to go."

He didn't say anything as he turned into a bat and flew toward her. Her heart pounding, she watched as he neared the cage, but the wire was too tight for him to fly into the cage with her.

She could swear she heard him curse before he turned back into a man. And as soon as he did, the force of the electrical current threw him back ten feet, onto the grass. This time there was no mistaking his fierce curse.

"Forget it!" she said, looking up at the sky again. It was too close to the dawn. "There's no need in both of us dying."

Shaking his head, he ran at the cage and grabbed the wire. Retta cringed at the sound of his skin frying as he seized it. His entire body shook from the force of the electricity. It had to be unbearable. And still he held on, pulling at the wire until he'd torn through it. Amazed by his strength and courage, she was crying by the time he threw the switch and turned the electricity off.

"There's another—" Before she could say more the electricity returned. She jerked her feet up as a thousand curses came to her mind for the people who'd rigged this damned place.

Velkan grabbed ahold of the cage and snarled an instant before he punched straight through the metal floor. Two seconds later, he pulled a thick wire up from underneath and tore it in half.

The humming ceased as the electricity vanished again.

Too scared to put her faith in that, she waited for it to return. And as each second ticked by while she watched Velkan's frayed appearance, relief coursed through her.

He'd done it. Her tears coursed down her cheeks as gratitude swelled in her heart. In spite of the fact that she wasn't worth it, he'd come for her. And in that moment, she remembered exactly why she loved this man. She remembered all the reasons that she'd wanted to spend her life by his side.

Velkan reached for her.

Until sunlight cut across his body. Hissing, he jerked back, instinctively covering his face. Then he took another step toward her only to have more mirrors turned to him.

Even so, he crawled toward her, while Stephen and the

others kept the mirrors on him, so that he could loosen her hands. She quickly freed herself.

Her rage mounting, Retta tried to wrap herself around her husband, but she wasn't large enough to cover him from the deadly rays that made his skin blister and boil. His entire body was smoldering as he tried to make it toward the wall where there were still shadows.

He staggered at the same time Stephen and the others left the house. They were coming to finish Velkan off, but she'd be damned if they'd get to him without fighting her.

Retta stood her ground, ready to battle until she felt someone grab her from behind. She turned to strike but caught herself as she saw a friendly face.

"It's me," Francesca said as she flashed them from the garden.

One second Retta was a hair from death, and in the next she was in a room she hadn't seen in centuries . . .

Velkan's bedroom.

Retta's heart pounded in fear. "We can't leave him."

"We didn't."

She looked around her as Viktor flashed into the room with Velkan in tow before he sank to the floor between Andrei and Viktor. Horror filled her as she stared at what remained of him. He was bloodied and scorched. The scent of burnt hair and flesh invaded her senses, making her queasy.

But she didn't care. Terrified that he was dying, she rushed to Velkan's side and rolled him over. Tears gathered to choke her as she saw the damage done to him. "Velkan?"

He didn't speak. He merely stared at her and blinked.

Pushing her aside, Viktor and Andrei picked Velkan up from the floor and moved him to the bed.

Retta followed, wanting to help.

"You should go," Viktor said coldly as Andrei struggled to peel Velkan's shirt from the flesh that seemed to be melted to it. "You've done enough damage."

"He's my husband."

Viktor narrowed his cold blue eyes at her. "And you walked out on him five hundred years ago. Remember? Do him a favor and let history repeat itself."

"Viktor!" Francesca snarled. "How dare you."

"It's all right," Retta said, calming down her friend. "He's only doing his job."

Then Retta moved to stand beside Viktor. This time when she spoke, she lowered her voice and let her raw emotions show in every syllable. "Get in my way again, boy, and you're going to learn that Velkan isn't the only one in this family who has fangs." That said, she pushed her way past him to reach the bed where Velkan lay.

She wasn't sure if he was still conscious until she paused by his side. Her stomach shrank at the sight of his blistered and charred skin.

But it was the pain in his eyes that took her breath. In spite of the part of her that wanted to run from the horrible sight of him, she reached out and placed her hand to an undamaged part of his cheek.

He closed his eyes as if he savored her touch.

"Thank you, Velkan," she breathed.

He took a breath as if he would respond, but before he could, he passed out on the bed.

Viktor moved to stand next to her. "Are you going to just stare at him or are you going to actually help us tend him?"

She looked to Viktor, whose face bore all the rancor of his voice. "You're such an asshole, Viktor."

He opened his mouth to respond, but Francesca covered his mouth with her hand. "Lay off, little brother. They've both been through a lot today."

Curling his lip, he moved to the other side of the bed, where Andrei was still trying to get the shirt off. Retta helped him undress Velkan, but as she saw a fierce scar in the center of Velkan's chest, just over his heart, she paused. That hadn't been there when he'd been mortal. It literally looked as if someone had staked him through the heart.

"What on earth?" she said, fingering it. It was at least six inches wide and four deep. "How did this happen?"

Viktor gave her a droll stare. "Can't you handle the sight of your father's handiwork?"

She frowned at Viktor. "What are you talking about?"

"The scar," Andrei said quietly. "It's where the lance left his body after your father ordered him impaled."

Retta jerked her hand back, not wanting to believe it. "I don't find your humor funny."

"I'm not joking."

Nausea filled her as she looked back to Velkan's blistered face. Then she looked to Raluca, who nodded grimly.

"I don't understand," Retta whispered.

Raluca's eyes were kind as she explained. "After your father killed you, Princess, he viciously turned on Velkan. He tortured him for weeks until he finally had him impaled in the square at Tîrgovişte. That's how he died and was able to become a Dark-Hunter."

Still, she had a hard time believing it. Her father had loved her so much. Would he really, even in anger, have killed her? He may have hated the world, but to him, his children had always been sacred. "Why didn't Velkan tell me?"

Viktor snorted. "Oh, I don't know. Maybe because you ran from him when he tried and didn't stop running."

"Viktor!" Raluca snapped.

"Everyone stop 'Viktoring' me. I speak the truth that all of you are too scared to say. She ought to understand what he's gone through to keep her safe. What he suffered as a human. For. Her." Viktor turned back toward Retta. "He didn't mind his own death—he'd planned on that. It was yours that destroyed him. He'd surrendered himself to your father, knowing the bastard was going to impale him. He thought that by having you drink the sleeping potion your father would see you dressed for burial and leave you be. His plan was for my mother to take you to Germany, where Francesca was living, and to keep you safe while your father tortured him. He never dreamed your father was going to stab you in the heart while you lay dead."

That hadn't been the plan Velkan had given her. They were to lie side by side as if dead and then awaken once her father was safely gone and convinced of their deaths. Velkan was then supposed to take her to Paris, where they could be together without fear of her father's reprisal against Velkan. Free of the war that was waged between their families.

She looked to Francesca for the truth, but for once her friend was speechless. "Velkan surrendered to my father?"

"What did you think he was going to do?" Viktor asked angrily.

"He told me we would both drink the potion and that my father would see us dead, then leave us in peace."

Viktor nodded. "And you drank it first."

"Of course, and then I saw him drink it right after me."

Viktor shook his head. "He never swallowed it. Once you were unconscious, he spat it out and placed you in state for viewing. He was afraid that if you were both unconscious your father would behead both of you. So he remained conscious and told your father that you'd died of disease. Your father promised him that once he saw you, he would be content to take Velkan and leave. Velkan submitted to him and had to watch him kill you."

And she had run out on him. . . .

Again, her gaze went to Francesca for verification. "Why didn't you tell me?"

Her gaze sad, Francesca sighed. "You didn't want to hear it. If I ever tried to take his side, you yelled at me, so I learned to drop the subject."

It was true and Retta knew it. She had no one to blame but herself.

Retta's heart ached as she thought about how many

years . . . no, centuries she'd deprived herself and Velkan of because she'd been stupid and unforgiving. No wonder Viktor hated her. She deserved it.

Clenching her teeth, she looked up at the picture over the fireplace—the one that had been her wedding portrait. Tears gathered in her eyes as she recalled the day it'd been sketched. The sight of Velkan on the wall, watching her with nothing but adoration on his face. He'd looked like a woodland sprite come to life to stand guard over her.

She blinked away her tears before glancing back at the bed where her husband lay. "We have to get him healed."

"Why?" Viktor asked.

"So that I can apologize."

But getting Velkan healed proved to be easier said than done. The sun damage was hard for even an immortal to overcome. Not to mention they still had the threat of the Order out there wanting them dead. At least here in Velkan's home the Order couldn't get to them.

"You should go rest."

Retta looked up at Raluca's voice. The older woman stood in the doorway with a chiding look on her face.

Retta stretched in her chair to ease her sore and cramped muscles. She'd been by Velkan's side for the last four days while he slept. At first his continued sleep had seriously concerned her, but Raluca and Viktor had assured her that it was natural for a Dark-Hunter to sleep like that whenever he was injured. It was what enabled his body to heal.

True to their words, every day Velkan's skin did seem better than the day before. Now he merely looked as if he had a serious sunburn and the bruises were all but gone.

"I don't feel like resting," Retta said quietly.

"You have barely eaten or slept."

"It's not like I can get sick or die."

Raluca tsked at her as she turned around muttering. "Fine.

I'll bring your food here, but trust me. If the prince awakens he will be grateful *he* doesn't have a heightened sense of smell."

Highly offended, Retta daintily sniffed at herself to make sure she didn't stink.

"Relax. She was only teasing."

Her heart stopped beating as she heard that deep voice. "Velkan?" She shot from her chair to the bed to see his eyes open.

"I thought you'd be gone by now."

She swallowed against the tight knot in her throat. "Hardly. I have much to do."

"Such as?"

Retta swallowed against the lump in her throat before she answered. "Apologize to you."

"Why would you do that?"

"Because I'm stupid and pigheaded. Judgmental. Unforgiving. Mistrustful—you can stop me at any time, you know?"

One corner of his mouth lifted to taunt her. "Why should I? You're on quite a roll. Besides, you missed the worst flaw."

"And that is?"

"Hotheaded."

"I learned that one from you."

"How so?"

"Remember that time when you threw your boots into the fire because you had trouble getting them off?"

Velkan frowned at her words. "I never did that."

"Yes, you did. You also gave your favorite saddle to the stable master because it scratched your leg as you dismounted and told him he could have it but, personally, you'd burn it, too."

That one he remembered well. He still bore the scar from it. But what surprised him was the fact that she remembered the incidents. "I thought you banished all traces of me from your memory."

She looked away sheepishly. "God knows I tried, but you're a hard man to forget." When she looked back at him, their gazes met and locked. "I've been so stupid, Velkan. I really am sorry."

He lay there completely stunned by the heartfelt emotion in her voice. There had a been a time when he prayed to hear those words from her lips. A time when he'd pictured this moment.

"Can you ever forgive me?" she asked.

"I could forgive you anything, Esperetta, but I could never trust you again."

Retta scowled at his words. "What do you mean?"

"When you left and didn't return, you proved to me that you had no faith in me as a man or a husband. You were so suspicious of me that you honestly thought I could kill you. Obviously, we had a lot of problems in our marriage that I didn't know about."

"That's not true."

"Then why didn't you come home?"

Because she thought he'd kill her. She really had. "I was young. We lived in turbulent times. Our families had spent generations killing each other—"

"And you thought that the only reason I married you was to kill you." He shook his head. "You know as well as I do that I was disowned by my family when they learned we'd wed."

It was true. His family had turned them out. His father had sent an army to seal this house and make sure that Velkan would never enter it again.

But the worst had been his father burning everything that had held Velkan's symbol or name. Even the family crest book that bore the Danesti lineage had been burned and a new one created that left no trace of Velkan's birth.

"I thought that you'd had enough of running from our families. And we both know that had you returned home after killing me and my father, your father would have welcomed you back."

Those black eyes burned her. "I made my decision as to who held my loyalty on the day I bound myself to you, Esperetta. I knew the cost and the pain our union would cause my family and still I thought you were worth it. You spat on me and you spat on the love I wanted to give you."

"I know I hurt you."

"No," he whispered. "You didn't hurt me. You destroyed me."

Tears welled in her eyes. "I'm so sorry."

" 'Sorry' doesn't even begin to fix five hundred years."

He was right and she knew it. "Why did you tie our souls together without telling me?"

His eyes burned her with sadness. "I didn't want to live without you . . . in either this life or the next. I had intended to tell you what I'd done, but your father ran us to ground before I had the chance. Little did I know that when I sold my soul to Artemis for vengeance your soul would go with mine."

What he didn't say was that she'd caused him to suffer the very thing he'd wanted most to avoid . . . a lifetime spent without her.

In that moment, she hated herself for what she'd done. And she didn't blame him for not forgiving her.

He'd given her the world and she'd spurned him. Unable to stand the mistake she'd made, she got up. "Are you hungry?"

"Yes."

"I'll get you something to eat. Hang tight." Retta paused at the door to look back to where he lay on the large bed. It was the bed she'd lost her virginity in. She could still see that night so clearly. She'd been terrified and excited. Velkan for all his ruthlessness had left her untouched and in a room down the hallway.

He'd promised to take her the next day to her father's agents and release her. It'd been the last thing she'd wanted. Her father would have sent her back to the convent to live out a life of prayer and hard work—not that anything had been wrong with either of those. But she'd already fallen in love with her dark warlord and she didn't want to go back without a small token.

Her intent had been nothing more than an innocent kiss. But the moment their lips had touched, Velkan had swept her up in his arms and she had submitted to him willingly—even more eager to taste him than he was to have her.

Closing her eyes, she could still remember the feel of him inside her as he clutched her leg to his hip and thrust against her. "I will never let you go, Esperetta," he'd whispered fiercely in her ear.

And then he'd given her a kiss so hot that her lips still tingled from it.

How had she ever turned her back on that? A tear slid down her cheek before she brushed it away and headed downstairs to the kitchen. She scratched Bram on the head as she passed the giant animal that reminded her more of a cow than a dog.

"Good to see you out of that room," Raluca said as she set her tray down that was filled with food.

"I'm only here because Velkan is awake and hungry."

Francesca snorted as she entered the kitchen behind her. "And you're here getting food? What kind of stupid are you? I'd be in bed with him."

"Frankie!" Raluca snapped. "Please. I am your mother."

"Sorry," she said, but her tone was less than apologetic.

Retta sighed as she straightened up the flower in the vase Raluca had put on the tray. "It doesn't matter what I want. I blew it with him a long time ago."

Francesca shook her head. "You can't blow it with someone who loves you that much."

"I daresay you're wrong. I just wish you guys would let me go home."

"The Order would be all over you now that they know for a fact you're real. You can never go home again."

And she couldn't stay here. How perfect was this?

Raluca gave her a sympathetic smile. "He loves you, Princess. He's hurt, but underneath that is the man who went through a fate far worse than death trying to save you. He won't let something as cold as pride keep you from him."

"It's not pride, Raluca. It's broken trust. How do you repair that?"

"That's up to you, Princess. You have to show him that you want to stay with him."

"And how do I do that?"

"You close your office and have Andrei and Viktor bring all of your belongings here."

"What if he won't let me?"

"How can he stop you? You're the Lady Danesti. This home is half yours."

Retta smiled as she considered that. But in order to stay here, she'd have to give up everything.

No, not give up. So she couldn't be a divorce lawyer in Romania. She wouldn't be able to keep up her practice too much longer anyway. Some people were already getting a bit suspicious because she hadn't aged.

She looked around the stone walls that somehow managed to be warm and inviting. Stay with Velkan . . .

Somehow that was nearly as frightening as it had been. But in order to stay, she'd have to reclaim the heart her husband had closed to her. *C'mon, Ret, you're made of sterner stuff than this.* And she was, too. She wasn't going to walk out on him again.

But as Raluca said, she'd have to find some way to show her husband just how serious she was.

5

Velkan ached with a pain that was second only to impalement. His Dark-Hunter powers should have healed him by now . . . it told him just how severe his injuries had been that he was still hurting from them.

He turned as he heard the door open.

It was Esperetta, and there for a second he was back five hundred years ago when they'd shared this room together, when she had willingly joined him here every night.

Once he'd reclaimed this house after his death, he'd taken great pains in making her room down the hall look just as it had when she'd lived here. But though her personal items were there, she'd never really used it for anything other than dressing. In contradiction to the customs of their time, she'd shared this room with him for sleeping . . . and for other things the memory of which warmed him completely.

Wincing, he could still imagine the way her scent had clung to his sheets and pillows . . .

The way it had clung to his skin.

Be strong, Velkan. He had to be. The last thing he wanted was to let her hurt him any more than she already had.

She came forward a bit hesitantly before she set the tray down on the table by his bed. Her long hair was pulled back into a ponytail and she looked extremely tired. And yet she managed to be the most beautiful woman he'd ever seen. "Do you still prefer your steak served with onions and stewed apples?"

Her question surprised him. He couldn't believe that she'd remembered that. Nodding, he watched as she pulled the silver top off the platter and then uncovered the onions.

"Are you not eating?" he asked as she handed him the plate.

"I'll just take some of the bread. I'm not really hungry."

He shook his head at her. "Bring the bread plate and split this with me."

"You need it."

"I will live and I can send for more. Now bring me the plate."

She arched a brow at his sharp tone.

"Please," he added, softening his voice.

Retta paused at that. This was a man who was used to issuing commands. To her knowledge, he'd never even uttered "please" before. Her heart softening, she picked up the plate and did as he asked.

"Thank you," she said as he halved his food with her. "By the way, I have a bone to pick with you."

"Only one?"

She smiled in spite of herself. "At the moment."

"Then I can't wait to hear it," he said before tasting his steak.

" 'Bram' and 'Stoker'?"

He laughed, a deep, resonant sound. "It was fitting, I thought."

Retta growled at him. But she didn't mention her room, which she'd seen the night of her arrival. It had been an eerie reminder of their past, and it had brought home to her just how much Velkan loved her. Even if he denied it, she knew the truth. Everything had been laid out as if he'd expected her to return at any moment.

When she'd seen it, she'd actually sat down on the floor and wept over her own stupidity.

Forcing that thought away, she cleared her throat. "Did you have to give that man that awful book about my father?"

He shrugged those broad shoulders before he wiped his mouth. "I was stationed in London at the time and bored. He'd been working on the book and had been calling the lead character Radu—which, no offense to your uncle, isn't nearly as compelling as Vlad Dracula. Besides, it's not my fault the book took off. It would have been forgotten completely if not for the movie decades later."

She narrowed her eyes on him suspiciously. "I heard you had a hand in that, too."

"That is a rumor of which I'm quite innocent."

"Uh-huh." Even so, she wasn't really angry at him. At least not now. A century ago, she'd wanted to cleave his head from his shoulders, but strangely, now that she was here, she felt an odd kind of peace. It was so bizarre.

He set his plate aside.

"You're not through, are you?"

"I'm not really hungry."

The only problem was that she was starving . . . and it wasn't for food. What she really wanted a taste of was that delectable mouth of his. He was sinful and decadent. He'd always been that way, and it had been so long since she'd last had a kiss.

Velkan could barely focus as his body burned for a taste from his wife. How cruel to be this close to her and to not be allowed to sate the need that burned so furiously inside him.

She finished her food, then moved to retrieve his plate. As she did so, she turned to look at him. It was a mistake.

Unable to stand it, he buried his hand in her soft auburn

hair and pulled her closer to him. He expected her to push him away.

She didn't.

Instead, she met his lips with remarkable passion. It was as if she wanted to devour him.

Velkan growled at her enthusiasm. It'd been the last thing he'd expected from her. But God, how good she tasted. It was the most incredible moment of his life and all he could think of was pulling her naked body flush to his.

Retta couldn't get enough of him as she folded herself into his arms. At least not until she eagerly brushed her hands against his ribs and felt him cringe from the pain of his injuries. "I'm sorry," she breathed, pulling back.

But he didn't let her go far. He pulled her back to him and gave her a kiss so sizzling that it melted her completely. With a teasing laugh, she nibbled his lips. "You're still hurt."

"You're worth a little pain," he whispered before he buried his lips against her throat.

Retta groaned as chills spread over her, and her body heated up immediately. It'd been way too long since they'd been together. She'd all but forgotten how good this felt. How good Velkan felt. Leaning back, she pulled him with her until his weight was pressing her into the bed. Still his lips didn't leave her neck as he unbuttoned her shirt. His eyes were dark with hunger as he cupped her breast while his thumb slipped beneath the lace to touch her skin. She shivered at his hot touch as she pulled his shirt from over his head.

His skin was still burnt and angry looking, but even so, she'd never seen anything more exquisite. He was so lean and ripped that she could see the outline of every muscle on his chest. And she remembered the first time she'd seen him naked. He'd been hesitant, afraid of hurting her. And she'd been stunned by the size of him. By the contrast of his masculine body to hers. Where she was soft, he was hard. Where her skin was smooth, his was chafed by battle scars and calluses. And his scent . . .

It was warm and masculine, all-consuming.

Shivering, she reached around and undid her bra, then let it fall to the floor.

Velkan could barely breathe. He still couldn't believe she was allowing him to touch her. Not after all the anger she'd spewed. All the insults that had gotten back to him over the centuries. If he were smart, he'd send her packing. But how could he? No matter the anger, he knew the truth.

He still loved her. He still wanted her.

She was everything to him.

And she might change her mind. . . .

That would be too cruel for words. Cruel even for the daughter of Vlad Tepes.

Her eyes dark with longing and passion, she moved from the bed to divest herself of her pants. Velkan thought he was going to die as she reached for her panties. His breath came in short, sharp bursts as she licked her lips, teasing him, exciting him. The tips of her fingers went beneath the black satin fabric.

"Do you want me to leave?" she asked as she hesitated while he waited for her to lower that damned skimpy piece of fabric.

What, was she insane? Or just plain cold?

"Hell, no," he growled.

Smiling, she slowly pulled the panties down her legs until she could step out of them. In that moment, it was a struggle not to come from the sheer pleasure of seeing her naked alone. Damn, but she had the hottest body the gods had ever gifted to a woman. Granted her breasts weren't very large and her hips were a bit wide, it didn't matter to him. There was no woman more perfect.

Retta loved the power she felt as he watched her with hooded eyes. Even so, she could tell how eager he was. But that was nothing compared to how badly she wanted a taste of him.

She pulled the covers away from Velkan's body, then crawled back onto the bed between his legs while never breaking eye contact with him. Her mouth dry, she finally dropped her gaze down the bulge in his pajama bottoms. She could have sworn she heard him whimper.

But still he didn't move while she moved her hand so that she could cup him through the flannel. He hissed as if it were sheer torture, and yet she knew by the look of relief on his face that he was enjoying it immensely. It still wasn't enough. Her heart hammering as her entire body burned for him, she dipped her hand into the slit of his pants to seek him out. His skin was so hot and smooth as she touched his cock. He was already wet and leaking. She brushed against the tip of him, making him arch his back as if he were being tortured on the rack.

Laughing in delight at his response, she pulled her hand away so that she could taste the salty sweetness of him.

Velkan was absolutely on fire as he watched her lick the tip of her finger. But that was nothing compared to how he felt as she reached for his waistband to pull his pants off. He lifted his hips to accommodate her even though her slowness was starting to piss him off. He wanted to savor this, and at the same time he wanted inside her so badly that he could barely contain himself. It was all he could do not to seize her and whip her under him.

But his patience paid off as she tossed his pants over her shoulder, then dipped her head down to take him into her mouth.

The sight of her hair fanning out over his lap while she tasted him was almost more than he could suffer. She looked up at him and met his eyes with nothing but raw hunger in her gaze. . . . He had to grind his teeth to keep himself from his orgasm. But it was hard and he didn't want this over so quickly.

He had to lean back and stare at the ceiling just to control himself, and even so he still felt the moist heat of her mouth as she tongued him from hilt to tip.

Retta groaned deep in her throat as she saw Velkan clutching the sheet in his fists. He lifted his leg between hers, and when his thigh touched her core she almost came from the sheer pleasure of it.

But that wasn't what she wanted. She wanted to make amends to him for all the centuries she'd allowed her unfounded fears and stupidity to keep them apart. She owed him so much and she wasn't going to leave him until he knew just how sorry she was for what she'd done to both of them.

Her body throbbing, she slowly kissed her way from his cock to his navel. Then she moved to his nipple so that she could lave it while he sank his fingers deep inside her. Closing her eyes, she savored his touch as she moved herself so that she straddled his hips.

He moved his hand and cupped her face before he kissed her, and in that moment every bad thought she'd ever carried for him melted and she couldn't remember what about him had ever made her flee. Closing her eyes, she savored his tongue and mouth. Savored the feeling of his hands on her face before she lowered herself onto him.

Velkan shivered as she took him in all the way to his hilt. He'd dreamed of this moment for the last five hundred years. And all those dreams paled in comparison to this one moment in time. He inhaled the sweet fragrance of her skin as she rode him slow and easy.

This was all he'd ever wanted in his entire life. Esperetta in his bed. His body inside hers. He growled deep in his throat as she continued to ride him, driving both their pleasure onward. She nipped and licked the pad of his finger as he gently traced the curve of her lips.

Needing to touch her, he dropped his hand down so that he could cup her breast in his hand and let her hardened nipple tease his palm. He lifted his hips to drive himself even deeper into her.

Retta smiled and took Velkan's hand into hers while she gave them both what they needed. The look of pleasure on his face only added to her own. It felt so good to be back with him. So natural. For the first time in centuries, she honestly felt like she was home.

And she was never going to leave it again.

That thought swept through her an instant before her body shuddered and spasmed. In a glorious flood of ecstasy, her body splintered. Crying out, she leaned forward over Velkan as he quickened his strokes, heightening her pleasure even more.

And when he came, he whispered her name like a breathless prayer. That gave her more hope than anything else that he'd forgive her.

Her heart pounding, she laid herself on his chest while he held her close in the firelight. There was no sound in the room except their breathing and the sound of his heart thumping under her cheek. Closing her eyes, she inhaled the scent of them and caressed the muscles of his arm.

Velkan lay quietly as he felt every inch of her body pressed against his. He loved the sensation of her flesh on his. Of her hand gliding over his arm. But he knew this couldn't last.

He knew he couldn't trust her.

No matter what he felt right now, the past stood strong in his mind. And it was a past he didn't want to relive. Learning to get through each day while that pathetic part of him had kept watching the road, thinking, no, praying, she would come back to him.

She might be with him now, but she didn't trust him. She never would. And that burned through him like a stringent poison.

"What are you thinking?" she whispered.

"I'm wondering when you'll be on the next flight out of here."

"I'm not leaving, Velkan."

"I don't believe you. You have a business to run. A life to get back to."

Retta grew quiet at that. He was right . . . and he was wrong. "I've had other businesses in the past that I had to walk away from. I can leave this one as well. I belong here, with you."

He didn't say anything, but the doubt in his eyes tore through her.

"Will you at least give me another chance?"

"At what?"

"Being your wife."

"Do you think that could make you happy? I'm stationed here in Romania. In the backwoods of the world that you've embraced. You wouldn't be happy without all the conveniences you're used to. Besides, Dark-Hunters aren't married. They're not supposed to have any kind of emotional ties whatsoever."

"Then we'll get our souls back and be free."

"And if I don't want that?"

She was taken aback by his question. "You'd rather stay in Artemis's service?"

"I'm immortal, and I'm an animal, remember? I live for war."

"You would choose that over me?"

His black eyes burned her. "You chose much less than that over me."

Retta looked away, ashamed. He was absolutely right. Her heart heavy, she slid herself off him. Her gaze fell to the areas of his body where his skin was still blistered from his rescue of her. "Then I guess there's no future for us."

He let out a tired sigh. "We were never meant to be, Esperetta."

She ground her teeth in frustration. "Then do we divorce?"

"Why bother? Death has already separated us."

Not true. Stupidity had separated them, not death.

Retta scooted from the bed and gathered her clothes before she dressed without another word to him. She didn't know what to say. "So that's it then?"

"That's it."

She nodded as she opened the door to the hallway. She hesitated. "I have to say I'm surprised."

"By what?"

"Your cowardice. I always thought you had more guts than this."

He turned in the bed to give her his back. "Then we're even."

"How so?"

"I misjudged you, too. I once thought you were worth dying for."

The door slammed shut in her face.

Retta stood there staring at the wood, her mouth agape, his words ringing in her ears. She glared at the door, half-tempted to kick it in and beat him. But she wouldn't give him the satisfaction of it.

Fine. If he wanted to play it that way, so be it. Far be it from her to argue. As he'd pointed out, she had a life in America. Lifting her chin, she turned and walked toward her room down at the end of the hallway.

And with every step she took, more tears gathered in her eyes as pain filled her. Her heart broken, she opened the door to find Raluca in her room, shaking her head at her.

Retta cleared her throat. "Don't give me that look. You don't understand."

"I do understand." Raluca crossed the small distance between them and held her hand out to her.

Needing to feel comfort, Retta took Raluca's hand and then gasped as a spike of hotness tore through her. It ripped her from this room out into a lightless void that was searing and frightening. She heard winds howling in her ears as something whipped against her body. She held her hand up to protect her eyes as a sudden light pierced the darkness.

No longer in the manor, she found herself in the small cottage where she'd taken refuge with Velkan after their families had learned of their marriage. His family had disowned him and her father had vowed to see Velkan dead. And it'd been her father who'd found them first.

Completely disembodied, she stood in the corner where she could watch Velkan, who was kneeling beside her comatose body. Because they were in hiding, he didn't wear the armor of a warrior. He was dressed in a simple tunic and hose. To her utter shock, there were tears in his eyes as he held her hand in his and kissed her fingertips. She'd never seen him look so vulnerable.

"I won't let anyone hurt you," he whispered, lowering her hand from his face. "Raluca will see you safe for me. Please don't be angry that I'm leaving you. It's the only way I know to free you to live the life you deserve." He rose up so that his lips were only an inch above her own. "I love you, Esperetta. Always." And then he pressed his lips to hers before he tore away with a growl.

Still, she saw the lone tear that slid from the corner of his eye, down his whiskered cheek. He brushed it away before he turned and opened the door to their cottage.

There before him was her father with his army. Dressed in armor, her father wore no helm to cover his stern, chiseled features. His long black hair brushed his shoulders as he narrowed his black eyes on her husband. She winced at the rage that contorted her father's face. Never once had she seen this side of him. To her, her father had only been loving and indulgent. Kind. Velkan drew his sword and stood there as if to take all of them on.

"You're outnumbered, boy," her father snarled. "Is this how you would die?"

"In battle, aye. It's what I prefer." Velkan glanced back

over his shoulder. "But you promised me that you'd allow my servants to take Esperetta home for a proper burial. Do you still swear it?"

Her father's lip curled before he nodded.

Velkan planted the blade of his sword into the ground beside his foot. "Then I surrender to your . . ." he paused before he said, "mercy," from between gritted teeth.

Two of her father's men dismounted before they came to take Velkan. As soon as they held him, her father slid from his horse. He came forward with an angry swagger.

"She's dead," Velkan spat, trying to free himself. "Leave her in peace."

Her father scoffed as he entered the cottage and moved to stand beside her. Retta held her breath as she saw the pain that darkened his brow. His lips quivered ever so slightly as he looked down on her body. He lifted his hand to press it against her mouth and nose so that he could hold them closed.

"I told you," Velkan said, his voice rife with anger. "She's dead."

Her father jerked the dagger from his waist as he turned on Velkan with a fierce curse. "She's nothing but a Danesti whore." And then her father plunged the dagger straight into her heart.

Velkan let loose a cry so anguished that it made every hair on her body stand up as he shook off the men who held him and grabbed his sword. Before he could pull it free, two arrows were shot into his back—one striking his shoulder, the other to the left of his spine. Velkan stumbled to the side, and when he failed to go down, another arrow was shot into his leg. He cried out, reaching for the fallen sword. Until another arrow was embedded into his forearm.

"Don't kill him!" her father roared. "Not yet!" He kicked Velkan's sword out of reach before he shoved the arrow at the small of Velkan's back deeper into his body. Velkan growled, trying to move, but there was nothing he could do.

Instead, he looked to where she lay inside. "Esperetta," he breathed in a tone that was filled with tragedy and loss.

Her father seized Velkan by the hair and pulled him back. "She's the least of your concerns, you bastard."

Velkan tried to fight, but he was too wounded to have much effect on the knights who were better armed.

Unable to bear it, Retta turned away. "Take me out of here, Raluca. Now."

She did, but still she didn't take Retta back to the manor. Instead, Raluca took her to where her father was torturing her husband. Retta's breath caught in her throat as she saw him bleeding and bruised as they laid hot pokers over his skin.

"Stop!" she screamed, closing her eyes and covering her ears. "Take me home. Now!"

To her instant relief, Raluca obeyed her.

Retta glared at her in anger. "What was the point of that?"

"Understanding."

"I got it, okay? I was willing to—"

"No, not for you. I know you were ready to start over. But now you know why Prince Velkan isn't. You couldn't even look at what your father did to him and you didn't even see the worst of it." Raluca's eyes blazed in anger as she glared at her. "What do you think he'd have given if he could have simply closed his eyes and told me to take him home?"

Retta swallowed against the knot in her throat. Raluca was right. He'd endured hell for her.

"I can't undo what I did and he won't forgive me. If you have some magic trick in your bag that will give us common ground, then by all means pull it out. But at this point, I'm not the one being stubborn here. And I'm not the one who has to forgive. I've apologized. There's nothing more I can do."

Raluca let go her hand before she gave a curt nod. "You are absolutely correct, Princess. Forgive me."

And before she could even blink, Raluca vanished from the room.

◆ ◆ ◆

Velkan tensed as he felt a presence behind him. He turned quickly in bed to find Raluca staring at him with a gimlet look that was unsettling.

"Is something wrong?"

"Yes." She reached out and touched his arm.

Velkan sucked his breath in sharply between his teeth as his vision dimmed. Suddenly he wasn't in his room. He was in complete darkness with an awful weight pushing down on his chest. It was hot and stifling. Oppressive. Something smelled like rotten earth. Damp and cold. It choked him. He couldn't breathe as a putrid terror coursed through his body. Desperate, he pushed against the darkness.

It wouldn't budge.

More desperate than before, he shoved even harder. Only this time, it caused something to rush in on him. He coughed and choked as his entire face was covered with heavy black dirt. The weight of it was excruciating. The thick, grainy taste filled his mouth and nostrils as he kept pushing and digging, trying to free himself of it.

He'd never felt anything like this. Every movement only made it worse. Every second ticked by with an excruciating slowness as he fought against his prison. Eternity seemed to have passed before he finally broke free of it. Wheezing and vomiting earth, he found himself climbing out of a grave that bore a single name and date.

ESPERETTA D. 1476

Confused, he looked down at his hands, only they weren't his. They were feminine and they were torn and ravaged from the digging. They were Esperetta's.

Still coughing, he tried to move free of the grave, but the weight of his dress pulled him back toward the coffin. Afraid of falling, he kicked his feet, tearing the hem, and used his trembling arms to get his weight out of the grave.

And as he lay on the ground, trying to remove the taste of dirt from his mouth, his thoughts whirled.

What had happened?

We'll be together, Esperetta. Trust me. When you awaken, I'll be there by your side. We shall go to Paris, just the two of us, and start our lives over. No one will ever know who we are.

Only they weren't together. There was no sign of Velkan now. Panic set in as Esperetta looked about the cold, desolate cemetery. Where could he be?

A wave of terror went through her as she feared for him. Surely he wasn't dead. Not her Velkan. He'd always been so strong. So fierce.

"Please," she begged as tears gathered in her eyes. She had to find him. The last thing she wanted was to live without him. He meant everything to her.

Unsure of where to go, she headed through the cold darkness toward the town lights, desperate for him. It wasn't until she'd reached the street that she realized she wasn't far from her father's home.

Why was she here? She'd taken her serum far away from this place.

With Velkan.

With nowhere else to go, she headed for her father's palace. But she never reached the doors. Before she could do more than slip inside the gate, she'd heard the sound of swords clashing.

And then she'd heard her father cry out.

Without a clear thought, she'd run toward the sound only to skid to a stop as she saw her father lying dead at Velkan's feet. Her mouth worked a soundless scream as she watched her husband kick at her father's body and curse him. But that wasn't the worst of it. The worst came from the single sword stroke that separated her father's head from his body.

The cold satisfaction on Velkan's face burned her eyes as he gripped her father's head by the hair and pulled it up from the ground. "Death to the house of Dracul. May you all burn in hell." Those words rang in her head.

Velkan was a monster!

This time her scream came from deep within her soul.

Velkan jerked as that scream resonated through his memory. He tried to free himself of Raluca's tight grip, but she refused to let him go.

"Enough!" he roared. "I don't want to see any more."

She finally released him.

Velkan's breathing was ragged as he stared at the Were-Hunter. "How can you do that?"

She folded her arms over her chest. "My father was a Dream-Hunter. I inherited a few of his abilities, such as manipulating reality so that you could experience that night as Esperetta."

"Why would you do this?"

"Because I lost my mate to the hatred of an Order that should have never existed. There's nothing I can do about that, but you two have lost each other because you're both too prideful and stubborn to admit you're wrong."

"How could I ever tru—"

"Velkan!" Raluca snapped in a tone he'd never heard before as she called him by his name. "You have seen that night through her eyes. It wasn't her fault. You kept the truth of her father from her. You never once let her know as a mortal how demented Vlad was. No one did. To her, he was a decent and caring father. She never saw his brutality. But you . . . you she saw. On the night you met, you beheaded a man on top of her. She was just a young woman who'd been sequestered in a convent. Can you imagine the horror of that?"

He looked away as he remembered just how scared Esperetta had been. Her entire body had quaked in his arms the whole way home and she'd been racked with nightmares for months on end. He'd held her in the darkness and sworn to her that he'd never allow anyone else to ever hurt her again.

Until her father had killed her.

But that changed nothing. Esperetta didn't love him and he would never expose himself to that kind of pain again. "You ask more than I can give."

"Very well, but know this. The princess hasn't left your side since you were brought here. She could have tried to escape us, but she hasn't. She's stood watch over you like a lioness guarding her pride. And for five hundred years I have sacrificed my daughter and her happiness to watch over Esperetta for you. I've had enough of that. If the princess leaves, she leaves alone."

"I forbid it."

"I am your servant, my lord. My daughter isn't. If you want the princess guarded, then I suggest you do it yourself."

Velkan gaped at her words. She'd never spoken to him like this. Never once. "You're not serious."

"Oh, but I am. Francesca isn't getting any younger and I want grandchildren. It's time she was free to find her mate. You threw yours away by choice. Francesca should at least have the chance to be so stupid, no?"

He honestly had no response to that. What could he say? He was a fool. But how could he put aside the centuries?

How could you not?

"You lie there, Prince, in your bed alone. I'm going to book a flight out for the princess. She's a big girl. We'll let her find her own way in the world." And with that Raluca left him alone.

"Good riddance," he said sullenly under his breath, but even as the words left him, he knew better. He couldn't allow Esperetta to leave here. Not while the Order was out there. She wasn't strong enough to protect herself from them.

They were a cunning bunch.

He would simply go to her and . . .

Beg her to stay.

He flinched at the voice in his head. He'd never begged for anything—not even mercy while her father had tortured him. He would order her to stay. And she would . . . laugh in his face most likely.

You'll have to beg.

"Then she can leave." But he knew better than that. In fact, he was already stepping out of his bed. His emotions torn, he quickly dressed in a pair of pants and a loose-fitting button-down shirt.

As he started for the door, it swung open and almost hit him. Aghast, he watched as Andrei and Viktor entered with a large trunk between them. Esperetta followed them into the room.

He was baffled as they placed the trunk at the foot of his bed. "What is this?"

The men didn't answer. In fact, they refused to meet his gaze as they hastened from his room.

"There's another trunk that needs to be moved, too," Esperetta told them.

Viktor cringed as he looked at Velkan, then nodded. "Yes, Princess."

"What trunk?" Velkan asked, stepping closer to his wife.

"My trunk. I'm moving in."

"In where?"

"My room. Here."

Completely stunned and flabbergasted, he opened and closed his mouth, unable to speak.

Esperetta walked over to him and placed her finger on his chin before she closed his mouth. "I know you don't trust me, but tough shit."

He would have gaped again at her profanity had her hand not prevented it.

"This is my home and you're my husband. I made a mistake and for that I'm sorry, but I'm through being an idiot."

He pulled back from her. "Dark-Hunters can't be married."

"Well then, someone should have told Artemis before she made her bargain with you and brought me back to life, huh? You were created as a married Dark-Hunter. I hardly think they can complain now."

She did have a point about that.

"But—"

She ended his words with a kiss.

Velkan growled as she explored every inch of his mouth and buried one hand in his hair. "Esperetta—"

"No," she said, tightening her grip in his hair. "I won't hear any protests from you."

He laughed at that. "I wasn't protesting. I only wanted to say welcome home."

Retta drew her breath in sharply at his words. "Really?"

He nodded, but even so she could tell that he didn't truly believe her. But at least he was allowing her to stay. It was a start, and it was one that gave her hope.

The door opened again as Viktor and Andrei brought in the next trunk. They paused in the doorway.

"Should we come back later?" Andrei asked.

"Yes," Velkan said, his voice thick. "And take your time about it."

The men reversed course.

Retta laughed until Velkan kissed her again. Yeah, this was what she needed, at least until he pulled back and glanced at the trunk. "You didn't arrive here with trunks."

She bit her lip sheepishly. "It's symbolic," she confessed. "They're actually empty." Then she frowned as she realized he was dressed. "Where were you going?"

"No place."

She arched a brow at that as a sneaking suspicion went through her. "No?"

She saw him hesitate before he spoke in a deep, emotionally

charged voice. "I was going to find you and ask you to stay."

"Really?"

He nodded. "I don't want you to leave, Esperetta."

"You're willing to trust me then?"

He hedged. "Well . . ."

"Velkan!"

He kissed her lips, melting her anger. "I will trust you, but only if you swear to never leave here again."

She wrapped her arms around his shoulders and met that dark gaze levelly. "I will only leave if you're with me. Promise." Then she rubbed the tip of her nose against his before she met his lips and sealed that promise with a scorching kiss.

EPILOGUE

In all the centuries, Velkan had never bothered with the Order. He'd left them alone to run amok without his interference. But all that was about to end.

They'd threatened Esperetta and had almost killed her. Now that he had his wife back, he wasn't about to let anyone take her from him again.

Without preamble, he used his powers to open the door to Dieter's home. Velkan strode through the doorway as if he owned it. Dieter and Stephen looked up with a gasp, as did five other men.

And before Velkan could move, an arrow was shot at his chest. He caught it in his fist and tossed it to the floor. "Don't even try that again," he snarled.

"W-what are you doing here?" Dieter said as a fine sheet of sweat appeared on his forehead.

Velkan pinned each member there with a hostile glare that should adequately cow them. "I'm here to bury the proverbial ax. Where exactly I bury it is entirely up to you. Either we can bury it in the ground and let bygones be bygones or I can bury it in the heart and head of every one of you here. Either way, the persecution of my wife and her friend stops now."

Dieter stiffened. "You don't come in here and order us about."

Velkan shot a blast that knocked him off his feet. "Be smart. Take the out I'm offering you. I promised Esperetta that I wouldn't be a barbarian anymore. So I'm trying to be civilized about this and let you live even though the warlord inside me would rather I bathe in all your entrails."

"We are sworn—"

"Save it," Velkan snapped, cutting Dieter off. "I was one of the members of this Order five hundred years ago and I know the oath you've all taken. And I've taken a new one. The next man or beast who threatens my wife or my servants will not live to regret that stupidity. Is that understood?"

He waited until each man had nodded.

Velkan took a deep breath. "Good. Now that we have an accord, I'll leave you in peace."

Turning toward the door, Velkan caught sight of something from the corner of his eye. Before he could react, a single gunshot rang out.

He snapped his head toward a corner of the room where Esperetta stood with Raluca, Francesca, Viktor, and Andrei.

Esperetta was holding the gun in her hands. Her eyes were narrowed on the men in the room. "Anyone else want to try and go for my husband's back?"

Velkan looked to see Dieter lying on the floor with a single gunshot in his chest. Stunned, Velkan met Esperetta's gaze.

She didn't speak as she moved forward to take his hand while the wolves stood their ground. "Gentlemen," she said quietly. "I think most of you have met Illie's family and I believe they'd like a word with you. Alone."

Stephen came to his feet. "Retta . . ."

"Save it, Stephen. You already told me what I needed to know."

Velkan wasn't sure what he should do, but as Esperetta pulled him from the house, he followed. And as soon as the door was closed behind him, he heard the screams of the men.

He stared in stunned awe of his wife. "I thought you wanted them spared."

"I'm not the girl you married, Velkan. I'm a woman who now understands the way the world works. They wouldn't have stopped coming for us. Ever. Frankie and her family owed a blood debt for what the Order did to her father. I say *bon appétit.*" She stepped into his arms and placed a chaste kiss to his cheek. "Thank you."

"For what?"

"For trying to be a gentleman when I know it had to go against every part of your nature."

He took the gun from her hand and threw it into the woods before he cupped her face in his hands. "For you, Esperetta, anything."

She gave him a speculative look. "Anything?"

"Yes."

"Then come and get naked with me. Right now."

Velkan laughed before he kissed her lightly on the lips. And for the first time in his life, he gladly submitted to someone else's orders. "As you wish, Princess."

RIDE THE NIGHT WIND

by

L. A. Banks

This story belongs to my Street Team . . . those folks who have embraced the Vampire Huntress Legends series and who ride it like the night wind. THANK YOU! The whole concept of doing backstories for each of the series Guardians within anthology shorts came from your fantastic, avid support. Feel the love coming right back atcha . . .

BIG PHILLY HUG,
Leslie!

1

The Legend of Neteru Guardians

After the fall of the dark angel, after man and woman were deceived and ousted from Paradise, the legions of evil beset humanity with all manner of strife and hardship to sway their choice. Earth became the Gray Zone of choice, where free will could manifest for good or evil, and a soul could be compromised in this fragile environment that cast shadows of darkness amid the light.

The angels on High wept as they watched the fate of humankind in their struggle against demonic forces, mere flesh and bones and the hope of earthbound spirits crushed by plagues, pestilence, famines, disasters, violence . . . no mercy. The cry for help that went up to heaven from the peoples of the earth was heard.

From the twelve scattered tribes, twelve Guardian Councils were mission-anointed and made up of honorable, courageous men and women of all positive faiths and all races, working as a united front, quietly moving behind the scenes, each battling evil in their own corner of the globe. The balance could not be easily tipped; their fight was vigilant. But just as the forces of evil had human helpers to reinforce the negative spheres of soul-killing influence, the forces of good had the Guardians . . . those who held the line no matter what challenges befell them. They would not allow the Light to be extinguished.

And from those twelve armies came the Covenant—one from each Guardian Council, twelve members in all, the bravest of the brave, the wisest of the wise, the keepers of the faith and the knowledge between worlds.

Only the Covenant could foretell the coming of the Neteru, although they would never know whether this mortal superbeing would come as male or female. All they could do was prepare a special Neteru Guardian Team as they searched for the prophesied being.

Anointed with the Divine mission to protect the Neteru, this elite category of spiritual warriors was chosen to surround their charge with heightened extrasensory awareness, superior physical and inner strength, unmatched courage, keen battle strategy, and unparalleled skill. These strengths not only protect but also reinforce the Neteru's learning curve and developmental life preparation for his/her own perilous mission.

Each Guardian's mastery was a lone, hard-won trial by fire and a baptism of struggles until their faith was made impervious to doubt. They come from the ranks of the unwashed, huddled masses, the tired, the poor, the downtrodden, the nameless, the faceless, the obscure—but they are mighty . . . for in the last days ". . . the first shall be last and the last shall be first."

EAST LOS ANGELES, 1990

He was having the same dream again. Could smell the sulfur, see the swirling, billowing, horrible clouds of smoke. The angry mass almost seemed like it was alive as it wrapped around him and the finest woman he'd ever been with in his life. The thick smoke covered her face, but there was always the strange sense that he knew her. She reached out, calling to him for protection.

As frightening as the dream was, that was always the best

part . . . the part where they'd escape from the cloud, riding on the back of his bike to safety—then get naked. Oddly, her face was always obscured then, too. Shadows, half moonlight—he couldn't see her face, but her body was undeniably awesome. He tried to will the dream to skip to that part.

Por dios, she was *fine.* He'd only copped some tail a few times in high school, since he wasn't one of the serious ballers who got all the females. If you weren't an athlete or dealer, forget about it. Now that he was out of school, broke, and didn't have a fly ride—just a motorcycle—female company found at the clubs was a costly habit that he couldn't afford . . . so he snuggled down deeper into the pillows, not even afraid of the hellish scene playing out in his dreams.

His body was ready to fast-forward to the soft skin . . . the breathless panting, gorgeous, firm breasts with toffee-colored nipples. Jesus . . . wonderful, tight ass and long legs wrapped around his waist out in the middle of the desert. His name a cry on the wind. Silky dark brown hair in his hands. Screw the demons in his dreams; he'd ride through smoke and hellfire to get to all of that. He shifted uncomfortably in his sleep, the pulsing erection a killer. C'mon, where was the girl, this time?

"Jose!"

Wrong voice. Reality jerked him awake like a splash of cold water. Jose could smell the hotel cleaning products wafting off his mother's skin from the doorway of his bedroom before he even opened his eyes. Oh, shit. . . . Maybe if he pretended he was still asleep, she would just go away, *por favor.*

The fight would be the same. It always was. He finally opened his eyes and simply stared at the woman. The dream had flitted away, just like his arousal. If he could have died from embarrassment he would have. His mother glared at him, her angry gaze raking his body with a disgusted click of her tongue. *How did time manage to make a once beautiful thirty-seven-year-old woman seem like an old crone so fast?* he wondered, bracing for the inevitable.

"Jose, this has got to stop!" his mother said, folding her arms over her chest, crushing her maid's uniform. "It is nearly six o'clock at night! What have you been doing all day, huh? Are you taking those drugs, or smoking those funny cigarettes? You're almost twenty-two years old and still living here like a bum. Well, not under my roof! I can't support a grown son who won't get a job. It was bad enough that your father left me, then died. Now, you sleep all day and then go out with those gangs at night—and when I come home, not a dish is washed, nothing around the house is done. I'm tired of this!"

Jose sat up slowly, scratching his head, searching for words. "Momma, listen—"

"No, you listen, Jose! You listen to me for once! You've been out of high school now for three years already, and what do you have to show for your life? Where's your ambition?"

He let out a weary breath. "I bring home money every week to help the household and—"

"I don't want drug money!" she shrieked, coming into the room to stand over him.

He was on his feet. "It's not drug money!" he shouted, wishing he could just make her understand. "I draw for them, paint their jackets, and detail their cars! They pay me to do my art, Momma."

"Art," she snapped, disbelieving, "is for the rich. Like all that foolishness about one day playing in some stupid band. Instruments, motorcycles from drug money, no doubt, are all over this place. Besides, you don't need to be doing gang emblems. It's all such a ridiculous waste of time."

He stood facing her, not knowing where to begin. Her eyes traveled over him as though she wanted to spit in his face for merely existing. There was no arguing at this point; her mind had already been made up and was closed. He watched his mother fold her arms tighter against her chest and scan his room with her nose turned up.

"I'm not a bum, Momma," he whispered. "One day, I'm gonna move us both—"

"Oh, stop dreaming," she said with a wave of her hand. "How, with no job, Jose?"

"I have a job. Drawing."

"Don't speak to me," she snapped. "You must be high." She began fussing around his room, inspecting, each step a brittle, agitated, jerky motion.

He could only look at her as she walked through his room snatching up clothes from the floor and flinging them onto the chair, violating his haven. High? Him? The smell of weed, or anything else for that matter, made him sick as a dog . . . his boyz always teased him about that. How could she have given birth to him and still not know him at all?

If she would have listened, he would have told her that drawing for the *hombres* was better than having to run drugs, go to prison, or die. Being the local artist was like being their mascot. It was a way to live between worlds in a place where few options existed. He swallowed thickly, holding back the pain her angry eyes caused. She didn't understand. All through high school, nobody picked on him, nobody tried him, and nobody forced him to prove his manhood or gang loyalty by dropping a body—all because he could design the baddest logos . . . could turn a leather jacket or beat-up car into a prize with his custom work.

It had put food in the house when her small checks couldn't stretch. His so-called foolishness had even helped pay rent from time to time. Didn't she know how many storefronts had his signature on them? Bodegas and other small shops went graffiti-free because his one-of-a-kind designs marked them as off-limits. Auto-body joints called for him *by name*. He was *not* a bum! He was not a bad son.

But as he looked as his mother's exhausted expression, he couldn't remind her of all of that, because to do so would be a slap in her face. Tears of frustration glittered in her eyes, and he knew in his soul they came from much more than his messy room.

Who stole her laughter, her beauty, her soft side, her hugs? Her hair was pulled back in a severe bun and wrapped in a black fishnet. Her brown eyes were dull and lifeless, just like her skin. Her figure was gathering rolls from disuse in the middle, and she was still so young. No one came to take her anywhere nice. No one had come to her since his father. No, as her son, he was both the man of the house as well as the enemy species. By now, he was used to the tirades.

So a reminder of what he'd done to support himself for as long as he could remember would be a stab in her heart. As the only man who still loved her, he couldn't say those vicious things to her, no matter what. He was her son. She was his mother. Madonna in a dirty housekeeper's uniform. The brutal truth would be just like saying she was a bad mother—a young girl who had had him too soon, had to endure a shotgun wedding, a woman-child who had made bad choices, and *that's* why her life had turned out the way it did, from her own decisions. Then she would have the right to beat him and cry and tell him that if he'd been aborted, her life would have been different and so much better. Maybe it would have. That was the part that tortured him the most.

"I'm trying to get my money together to go to art school, Momma," he finally said in a quiet voice while beginning to gather up the mess in his room so she could calm down. "Maybe once I graduate and get a good job, you can retire from cleaning rooms, and I'll be able to support us both so you can rest. I—"

Her attention jerked up from the floor as she slowly straightened her spine and balled up a dirty towel in her fists. "Art school? Art school! You need to get a *real* job, take up a trade, a vocational-tech program that makes sense, and stop dreaming . . . just like your father. I cannot deal with this."

"I got a mural job, Momma. I was waiting till you came home to tell you." Pure defeat claimed him. How could he ever get her to understand that he'd go nuts in a factory, where his soul would shrivel up and die? He didn't want to work the hotels or landscape the lawns of the wealthy. Something so much greater was calling him, but at the moment, he couldn't name it for her approval.

"Two choices," she said, her tone a low warning. "You enroll in a vo-tech program tomorrow, or you pack your bags and go live on the reservation in Arizona with your grandfather. Maybe your father's family will have you, and allow you to be *an artist* there."

They both stared at each other, mother and son locked in a quiet, urgent struggle. There was no way in hell he was going out to Arizona to live with some old, superstitious Creek Indian shaman and his Navajo wife. Been there, done that, when he was a little kid. His mother had left him there once, when she and his *papi* were breaking up. Now she was threatening to send him back there again? To the crazy people? The only one he'd really connected with was the wild biker who had passed through . . . a guitar player. If Jack Rider was there, cool. Jose remembered it like it was yesterday. Each summer when his momma was insistent about getting him off the streets while school was out, he and Rider had some really wild times out there together. But who knew where Jack Rider was now? The guy was like the wind . . . something he wanted to be. Free.

"So, what is it going to be, Jose?" His mother's gaze had narrowed, the ultimatum a thick wall between them.

"I'm gonna go paint the mural, get enough money to enroll in the first semester of art classes at Santa Monica College, and—"

"Walk out of my door tonight, young man, and your bags will be packed at the door when you get back."

He passed his mother without saying a word and headed toward the bathroom in their tiny apartment. If he had to sleep on the streets to follow his dream, so be it! He was *not* a bad son.

◆ ◆ ◆

Jose stared up at the vacant apartment building by the 405 Expressway. It was the most beautiful canvas he'd ever seen in his life. A city program had pulled him off the most-wanted-graffiti-artist list and had given him a jewel, instead of a record. God bless America!

He quickly parked his gleaming silver and black Harley chopper and yanked off his helmet so he could see the building better. Breathing in deeply, he allowed the night air to enter his lungs and fill his spirit. Adrenaline rushed through his system as he braced the helmet under his arm and stared up. The scaffolding was already erected in his honor. They'd given him brushes and said they'd make paint available, but he preferred spray cans. It was all about sensing the pressure of the color release, the texture of the building that would be anointed.

A can of white, to begin the outlines, whispered to him from his motorcycle saddlebags. The city program wanted an anti-drug message . . . or something positive and community-reinforcing to be splashed on the walls. *Hombres* from the neighborhood who had heard about his good fortune wanted him to make sure their gang territorial markers and names of their dead soldiers were emblazoned on the side of the building that faced the highway—while he was up there. But he had this image in his mind that he couldn't shake. It was a part of the recurring dream.

She was gorgeous . . . all curves . . . wide brown eyes haunted with fear . . . if he could only get the rest of her face to come forward through the smoke. Monsters and demons were all around her. A Thunderbird totem loomed in the background as she ran toward it. Native American shamans war-danced while ghostly Chicano ancestors drew dead Conquistador blades and rode horrifying phantom horses toward the flying demons.

Jose closed his eyes, seeing the mural come to life in his mind. A young man stood with a gleaming revolver pointed at the monsters, splattering gook with the ancestor spirits. Yeah. That was the ticket. He could tell the city program it was his artistic interpretation of how youths were being lost and hunted by the demonic forces of drugs and violence in the streets and how the spiritual past of the people was their hope. He smiled. Total bull, but it might work.

Then he could tell the gang brothers that the guy with the gun was one of them—all he had to do was tie the right color bandana around the *hombre*'s head in the mural to play it off. He'd then kick some game about how all the demons and whatnot were *the man* and how the girl was running toward the hype brother with the stoopid gun because she was fine, like the women they all had. Yeah . . . he'd make that gun real big to keep down the static. Jose chuckled quietly to himself. Being an artist with skills had certain privileges, the greatest being that everyone expected you to be crazy and didn't challenge your artistic interpretations.

Inspired, he slung his helmet onto his motorcycle seat and quickly pulled two cans of white spray paint out of the bike gear carrier. Tucking them into the pockets of his gray hoodie, he rushed over to the scaffolding and began to climb.

The night was his. He loved it as though it were a woman. It was daring and free and passionate and dark . . . the sounds it contained were so different, just like the scents changed as the sun went down. As chaotic as the neighborhood was, the darkness provided a certain peace that stilled his soul.

Jose hoisted himself up to the top platform three stories higher and stood before his beloved blank canvas, suddenly king of the world. The scent of bricks and mortar made him reach his palms out flat and lightly touch the surface of the building with a caress, studying where to begin.

Shadowy motion passed by a darkened, broken window and gave him a start. But given how long this building had sat abandoned, cats, rats, crack addicts, the homeless, anyone or anything, probably inhabited the joint. Jose had to focus and was not about to allow some stray cat to chase him away. He blew out a nervous breath and ran his fingers through his hair, determined.

Once he laid the foundation of the drawing, then cool. People could stop and stare; the *hombres* could smoke reefer below and holler up at him with music blaring from cars. That was the only thing he didn't like about doing outside, mural work. It wasn't private. An artist needed a studio, a place to intimately commune with his work without commentary from a street peanut gallery. So, a piece of the night stolen while the brothers were drag racing, clubbing, or getting booty was the time to think out the wall until he had the image perfected.

A spray can tumbled into his hand as he dug into his pocket, his sole focus on the wall, his eyes unseeing, only envisioning the image that would grace it. Then, he began to work. Before long, his back and chest and armpits were damp. The cool night stung his scalp through his wet hair. Glorious images careened through his mind, sparked impassioned motions through his outstretched arm, his body bending and swaying in a choreographed union with his art. Soon blue and red lights dappled the walls. The familiar whoop of a police siren stopped the dance, broke the divine meditation, and made him stand up straight, hands in the air.

"Get off the scaffolding!" an angry voice yelled through a loudspeaker.

Jose turned slowly. "I'm an artist that's been—"

"Down. Now, buddy!"

Two officers exited their patrol car.

"We are sick of you little bastards destroying property!" one officer shouted. "An artist my ass!"

Jose closed his eyes, keeping his arms outstretched. "Man, I've got a letter from the city in my pocket that says—"

He heard gun holsters unsnap. He opened his eyes quickly and remained as still as possible. "I need my hands to climb down, man!"

◆ ◆ ◆

"Where are you going?" Juanita's mother blocked the door and looked at her hard.

"Only out with my brother, Momma. He has a friend he wanted me to meet, and there's a party—"

Her mother made the sign of the crucifix over her chest. "Your older brother breaks my heart with his friends. They're all dope dealers and—"

"You don't know what you're talking about, Momma," Juanita pleaded. "I stayed home after I went to work and watched—"

"That's right, you should stay home and watch your little brother after work! What else more important do you have to do? I work sixteen hours a day to keep you all fed. Now I should feel guilty for wanting my daughter to be here, to stay away from the streets that have taken my eldest son?"

"I'm almost twenty, Momma. You act like—"

"I act like what? Who is this friend?"

Juanita measured her words. What could she tell her mother when she was in a state like this? The woman wasn't rational. There were young girls in the neighborhood who were sixteen and had more freedom than her. After her father died she'd done her best to stand by her mother's side, to help her out as much as she could. But it seemed as if her life was not her own!

"Juan's friend is a cousin of the Riveras and just a little older, plus he's—"

"*Madre d'Dios*! Men from that family have been spawned by the devil himself. Lucifer! How many young women have fallen to their lusts?" Her mother's gaze roved over her. "Look at you, dressed like a tramp! Red halter. Jeans. Fancy little sandals and hair all over your head, with makeup like a whore. And you want me to believe this *Rivera* person or whoever, cousin of Satan, is some sort of saint—"

"He's Juan's *friend*!" Juanita shrieked. "Because of you,

Momma, and Juan threatening to shoot anyone who would come near me, nobody has ever asked me to a dance! No one has ever dared set foot in this house to come see me! No one! This is the first real chance any of his friends took notice! I don't want to be like you!" She turned away from her mother, tears brimming to fall and smear mascara. Her mother spun her around with a hard yank and slapped her hard enough for her to see stars.

"Never do you speak to your momma with such disrespect! Who fed you? Who clothed you? Who kept a roof over your head! Who kept you clean, kept you from being pregnant and thrown away like all your girlfriends? Me! Your mother who loved you and deserves respect!" She smoothed her hands down her floral-print housecoat. "So, now, because I'm fat, and old, and my hair isn't pretty . . . because my face has wrinkles from worry over my children, I know nothing of the world? I don't deserve your ear to hear me?"

Guilt and shame collided with hurt until Juanita couldn't breathe. She just wanted to be normal, have fun, and not waste being young cooped up in a house with her praying momma and aging grandmother to become some old maid.

Looking at her mother through teary eyes, Juanita held the side of her face. "You said 'loved,' not 'loves,'" Juanita whispered.

Her mother's angry gaze narrowed. "Who could love a daughter who is so ungrateful? I swore that if my own treated me that way, she would be dead to me." Her mother turned away, sniffed hard, wiped her eyes, and strode into the kitchen. "Take off that harlot's outfit and go wash your face!" she yelled over her shoulder.

Juanita remained rooted to the floor where she stood. Her own mother had said such things and meant it? Her own momma? Covering her mouth, Juanita stifled a sob. How could she? Hadn't she graduated from high school, gotten a job, and gone to work at the corner pharmacy, never once complaining that the dream to go to college to study business was a dream deferred, because no provisions had been made for her education? She was a good daughter, who understood why no one had thought about the future when she was conceived. Until now, she'd accepted that no one cared that she had been the babysitter, the maid, the cook, the one to run a household while her mother worked herself to death night and day.

Her brother Juan was supposed to be the man of the house but was destroying the house. Yet, even for all her vicious words about Juan, her Momma still doted on him, even knowing where his money came from. He never had to lift a finger around the house because he was a so-called man. Didn't Momma know *she* was the stable one, the one who could be counted on? Of course she didn't have babies early; she'd seen what taking care of an infant was from constantly watching her younger brother—*work*. She knew what running a full household was—*work*. She was the maid! Her middle name was Work, her last name was Duty hyphenated with Commitment . . . and for the offense of wanting to go out with a handsome friend of her brother's, she'd been struck?

That was it. The battles were over. No matter how much she tried to get her mother to see, the woman was still blind. A whore? A harlot? She had never even been with a man yet, at her age, and her mother had called her those terrible things?

Pure heartbreak made Juanita's legs move her toward the door. Alienation and defeat helped her quietly slip out of the house. She wouldn't wait for Juan to come home to pick her up. She didn't want to meet this fine friend of his who had a street hustle. She didn't want to be called a whore while still a virgin. She no longer wanted to carry the weight of her mother's fury or frustration or bitterness. She couldn't take all the superstition and omens about demons in her mother's shrieking dreams. No more. She couldn't stand by and watch another year go by, hoping, wanting, her nose pressed to the glass of approval for change.

The double standard propelled her quickly down to the end of the block. Her brother could be a male whore, drink, sell drugs, and do whatever, but she had been struck for thinking about a party . . . for hoping that this friend of Juan's might dance with her, flirt with her . . . might even kiss her one day. Bitter tears fell as she began to run blindly into the night, avoiding neighbors' waves, cars, and pedestrians she didn't know.

Following the bus route, she hurried down blocks, unafraid. She'd never go back home, would never cross that threshold again. She was grown! She was a good daughter! She had a job and would get her own place, somehow.

A bus rolled by and slowed at the corner. Juanita got on and fumbled for change and bills, dropping coins in her distress. Numb, blank stares greeted her as she pushed her way to the back of the lumbering vehicle, and she clasped a pole for support with her eyes closed.

God, just take me away from here. Anywhere but her mother's house. Take her away from the hurts and insults, the verbal lashings, the constant suspicion and accusations. There had to be a place out there somewhere where beauty replaced the ugliness within human souls . . . where the air was clear and clean, where the stink of city garbage didn't exist. A place where there were flowers and trees and quiet beauty . . . a place where someone loved her for who she was, not who he thought she was. She missed Papi, his warm bear hugs and the way he called her princess and made her feel like she was just that—his baby doll.

Her father was the only one who didn't think her dreams were foolish and who calmed the night terrors when she dreamed of monsters . . . her mother thought she was possessed when she saw those things. Her momma said her visions were coming from the evil resident within her.

Blessed Mary, Mother of God, have mercy on her and send her into arms that would protect her from the cold, dead night.

2

Spread-eagled on the hood of the police cruiser, Jose gritted his teeth as his legs were kicked open and his body frisked for a weapon. His letter from the city might as well have been toilet paper, for all the good it did him. Anger fused with spray paint, engine fumes, gasoline, and the cops' dank sweat plus a hint of sulfur made him want to hurl. But he knew better than to argue with LA cops down in the barrios. Going to lockup was the least of his worries; getting shot and beat down was a high probability.

But the scent of something was raising the hair on the back of his neck in the darkened street. A shadow flitted past his peripheral vision, and in reflex he jerked his head up, only to have it slammed down again.

"You resisting arrest, punk?" one burly officer said.

"Naw, man," Jose said between clenched teeth. "I saw something outta the corner of my eye."

The two officers glanced at each other.

"Better check it out," the tall, lean one said. "Might be more of 'em out here with this one. They always work in packs."

"Call for backup," the thick officer with a barrel chest warned.

"Gimme a minute. You stay here with this punk. I'll just do a quick recognizance; then we can haul his ass in."

Jose was yanked back by his shirt.

"Get in the car."

The officer who was still with him had opened the door, taken the safety off his revolver, and begun to shove him into the vehicle when they all saw it. The building came alive, blackness pouring over the edges of the windows, sliding out from under the bolted doors. The two officers backed up, and the three men stood paralyzed for a second by terror.

It seemed like the ooze had created a yawning blackness that was darker than the night, and then within the fragile seconds it took for natural human reaction, the surreal darkness separated, took flight, and hundreds of bats fanned out in the air.

"Oh, shit!" the burly officer yelled as tiny beasts swarmed him in a billowing funnel cloud.

Gunfire ripped from his revolver as his bellows turned to screams. Fearing what he was seeing more than a shot in the back, Jose made a break for his motorcycle. He immediately smashed on his helmet to keep the vicious flying creatures from attacking his head.

Jose turned to glance over his shoulder only once to see a swarm gather around the other cop and then become a large singular entity masquerading as a bald, jaundiced-hued, black-suited man with hooked claws, red gleaming eyes, and fangs. He was out.

Stomping down on the motor, he careened away from the highway underpass near the scaffold-clad building, heading for open, wide streets that were populated by something that made sense—people. In a blur, a wisp of red fabric stabbed into his vision from the sidewalk. The high-pitched scream of a woman became a Doppler effect in his mind, welding it to the piercing decibel of screeches from the things that flew.

Billowing sulfur-tainted smoke obscured all but the woman's terror-stricken brown eyes as he drove, turning to look over his shoulder, hunkered down to keep control of the bike. The sound of guttural moans, then the stench of blood made him hock and spit in the wind as his bike raced down the center of the lonely street. He wasn't stopping for shit!

"Oh, my God! Help me!"

The female voice rang in his ears behind him. The familiar scent dragged his bike to a pivoting spin. Two beasts had her cornered against a vacant building in a huddled mass. He reached, one-handed, into his saddlebags and found paint. His bike became a weapon, hitting the curb and barreling down the sidewalk playing chicken with the unknown. Something landed on his seat behind him with a heavy thud, but his Harley was a part of his body, and Jose instantly whirled around to blacken gleaming eyes with paint, sending the invader shrieking to the ground clutching its hideous face.

Kicking and screaming, the woman covered her head as a predator bent. But the thing looked up too late to avoid Harley wheels burning at 80 miles an hour. Jose braced for the tumble, expecting the collision to throw him from the bike. Instead the entity parted in a foul splatter of sulfuric green gook that wet his helmet, chest, and the sidewalk.

"Jump on!" Jose yelled. "Up now, or I'm leaving you!"

The woman scrambled to her feet and immediately mounted his bike. Gone in seconds, he zigzagged them into traffic, popping a wheelie as they entered a busy intersection to make cars stop and give way.

His heart thudded, sweat blinding him along with demon gook on his helmet shield, forcing him to snatch it off and let it bounce away in the street. Frightened hands clung to his chest, and a feminine face pressed to his shoulder blades. He rode like the night wind itself, still smelling approaching sulfur.

Lead the mass of shrieking demons to his mother's home?

Impossible. Stop riding? Not likely. Talk to this chick on the back of his bike and figure out how to ditch the unexpected passenger along the way? Not. Oh yeah, hang around and try to explain that he hadn't butchered two cops? Suicide. Stop? Oh, *hell* no. Not until he ran out of gas. Not until he was somewhere safe. Not until his heart stopped slamming into his chest. Not until he reached the only place in the world where he knew people who believed in such things and had something to deal with it—Grandpop's.

They came to a stop on an old dusty road on reservation lands. An old man sat on the porch chewing the stem of a worn corncob pipe with a smile.

Jose's grandfather stood with effort, his tattered red and gray plaid shirt loosely blowing in the just-before-dawn breeze. He came to the edge of the porch rail and waited and shoved his hands in his brown corduroy pants. The old man simply nodded as the coyotes howled. Waning moonlight washed across his silver hair which hung in two long braids over his chest.

"The Thunderbirds sent you," Jose's grandfather murmured, and then looked up at the moon. "You smelled them?"

Jose leaned his head against the bike handlebar, too spent to immediately respond. "I'm freaked out, Pops. No riddles right now."

"I was on the bus," the girl clinging to him sobbed. "I was; I was . . . Then the bus stopped at the end of the line. I got off!" she said, her voice rising in hysteria. "It was deserted and I was afraid, so I headed toward police lights in the distance, and then . . . and then . . . oh, dear Mother of God . . ." She pressed her face to Jose's back and wept.

"We know," the old man said calmly. "The council of elders had a vision. It is the season for these things."

Jose felt the woman behind him cringe but lift her head. He

looked at his grandfather with a harsh glare. "This wasn't gypsy moths, Pops! The season? The freakin' season! Do you know what they did to two cops? Have you any idea what—"

"Yes," his grandfather said in a calm tone. "Your training to guard the innocent begins with a harsh lesson, because you bear the totem of the Thunderbird. You are a sensor. Your gift is like that of the wolf, a tracker, but you fly like the night wind, and portend the rains of change." He sighed a calm, satisfied sigh. "Come into the house, wash, and eat. The women have clothes for her. I have clothes for you. We've been waiting for you both for a very long time."

Jose watched his grandfather go into the house with quiet dignity. His serene acceptance of their story was both comforting and unnerving. Trying to piece together the fragments of reality that still existed within his mind, Jose finally turned to the woman on the back of his bike.

"Listen, sis . . . this ain't no place to be. I'm sorry I didn't drop you off in LA, but shit. . . ."

He rubbed his hands down his face and kicked the bike stand down so he could dismount. She still had her palms covering her face, breathing into them slowly as though holding back a scream. He knew exactly where she was at—freaked out.

Rather than dismount, he turned to her and touched her tousled hair. "What's your name?"

She didn't answer, just dragged her breaths in and out of her lungs as though about to have an asthma attack. "I saw it all in my dream," she whispered. "The same one I have almost every night. I never saw his face . . . the man on the bike. But the demons, the street . . . the dead cops—I saw it all!"

"Whoa, whoa, whoa." Jose grabbed her by both arms. "Come again? Tell me the dream!" he nearly shouted.

As she lifted her head slowly from her hands, the same eyes he'd seen night after haunting night stared back at him until her gorgeous heart-shaped face was revealed. Tears and terror had made circles under her eyes from bled mascara. But it was her. He let his gaze trail down her torso. Oh yeah . . . it was *her*. Violet-laden perfume, Dove soap, and adrenaline-spiked pheromone got separated out from her skin in layers to attack his senses with dream-memory. The scent bottomed out in his stomach and made it clench.

"I never saw his face," she murmured, "because he wore a black helmet." She allowed her gaze to slide down Jose's torso. "But he was wet with sweat. And I know the bike. . . ." Her words trailed off as she glanced at his hands. "I know those hands," she added quietly. "Same grip."

Jose let his hands slowly loosen and then fall away from her arms. "Your people . . . you need to call home, and let them know you're all right."

"Okay . . . but my mother doesn't care. She said I was dead to her."

He watched new tears rise in her eyes, and something he couldn't understand drew his fingertips to wipe them away from her pretty, flushed cheeks as they fell. "Call her anyway," he said in a gentle voice. "I have to call my mom, too."

She nodded, adjusting the strap on her halter top, suddenly feeling exposed. It had to be the insane terror that had released butterflies in her stomach. She lifted her chin; no matter what her mother had said, she was no tramp. But those intense gentle, quiet brown eyes and strong grip made it hard to breathe. She studied the line of his solid jaw and then let her gaze travel over broad shoulders, and lean, sinewy arms that had held the bike steady to save her.

"You came back for me. Bless you with all the gifts of heaven."

"I couldn't leave you out there like that without trying . . . not after I saw what they could do."

She stared up at him and swallowed hard. "You could have been killed."

He gave her a half smile. "But I wasn't and neither were you."

She touched a finger to his lips. "Thank you. Say no more. Let me just work this out in my head for a minute."

He didn't move or blink while he watched her process it all. She was a still life, something his hands ached to immortalize in wet paint, charcoal, pencil, any medium that would hold her. There was a level of serene acceptance beneath her stricken state. In the moonlight, even with smeared makeup and wild hair, she was the most beautiful woman he'd ever been this close to. It was reflex that sent his hand to stroke her hair and pull her into a hug. Why he was feeling like this at a time like this was way past crazy.

But the sensation of her silky hair under his palm and the way her breaths entered and exited her mouth to pour warm heat over his chest was beyond comprehension. The urge to take her mouth defied all logic, just as what they'd experienced was surreal. Rather than make her more nervous than she already had to be, he simply hugged her and nuzzled the crown of her hair.

"You'll be safe here tonight. You can call home, get a shower and some hot tea, something to help you chill out . . . and some rest. My grandfather has some strange ways, but he's a decent old man. Real cool like that."

She nodded and pulled away from the embrace to stare up at him. "You'll stay in the house with me, though . . . I mean . . . you won't be too far away?"

"Yeah," he said, trying to keep his voice from cracking. She wanted him near? Thought of him like he was some kinda protection or something—a hero? Whoa.

Needing to move or else kiss her, he got off the bike and helped her down. For some reason, she snuggled in close to him, and for some reason, his arm threaded around her waist. They entered the house practically in tandem. His grandfather's

Navajo wife looked up, smiled, and brought a pile of towels and clothing forward. She petted the young woman's face and turned to Jose for an introduction. It was only then that he realized he didn't even know her name.

"Uh, we just met, and—"

"I'm Juanita," the young woman beside him said shyly.

"Oh yeah, I'm Jose," he said to the woman he'd saved, and then offered his grandfather's wife an apology with his eyes.

The older woman said nothing, just simply handed off the pile of towels and clothing to Juanita, then kissed them both, held their faces for a moment, and left the house to go wait on the porch.

Jose's grandfather nodded toward him. "My wife will gather with the women to make strong medicine to give to you both, but especially her, the one with the eyes of the night."

Jose stood very, very still. He knew a little something, as memory served him, about old shaman ways—none of which made him feel comfortable in the least. If an all-female tribal *night* conclave was being convened to make serious medicine before dawn, then the men would be in a heavy spiritual ritual within a sweat lodge. He and his grandfather shared a knowing glance.

"Do not worry," his grandfather said, setting his jaw hard as he fetched his gray felt hat with the eagle feather down from the wall. "You passed the first test—she is not dead; you also live unmarked by the beasts. This house cannot be entered by the shadows. Strong medicine keeps the path clear and this home untouched." He strode toward the door, unfazed. "Besides, the man with a good heart who played the guitar taught you how to shoot a rifle. He is a good teacher. There is a rifle with special shells on the mantel."

Jose nodded. Jack Rider had definitely taught him how to shoot, how to ride, and how to play a little guitar. The reference to his old mentor's presence at the house brought back good memories. But, still, Jose wished his grandfather had decided to stick close to home. He wasn't no punk, but damn. They were gonna leave him and Juanita there all by themselves? What if something else wack jumped off? Learning how to shoot a rifle years ago, with a wild-man guitar player while drinking Jack Daniel's and hanging out on bikes, was not exactly commando training!

Jose glimpsed the mantel, and then Juanita. She stood stock-still, like a paralyzed deer caught in the gun-barrel sight of a hunter. Her knuckles were losing color as she clutched the pile of fabrics to her chest. Girlfriend looked like she was about to pass out, and he couldn't blame her.

"Uh, listen . . . why don't you call your mom, tell her you're okay? I'll call mine. Then you can get a shower and I'll root around in the fridge to see what's to eat."

"You know how to shoot that gun?" Her gaze ricocheted from him to the mantel and back.

"Yeah, I'm okay at it."

She shook her head in a slow, frightened daze. "I can't go into the bathroom alone . . . it has a window, right?"

"Yeah, but—"

"Uh-uh! No," she whispered, panic strangling her voice. "Please don't leave me alone in any room at any time."

"But what if you have to pee?" he said, trying not to smile.

"So!" She began walking in a tight circle. "You can bring the gun in there, stand by the window, keep your back to me, and then when I tell you I'm decent, you can turn around."

"The bathroom ain't but so big, 'Nita." He chuckled and raked his fingers through his hair.

She looked up at him, a plea in her eyes. "What did you call me?"

"'Nita. Why?"

She glanced away, her face flushed. "That's an old nickname. Only people who know me real well ever call me that."

He shrugged, new tension threading through him as he stared at her beautiful, stricken face. "Well, sorta makes sense that we get real cool real fast, if we're gonna listen to each other pee, don't you think?"

She just stared at him for a second and then burst out laughing. The sound of her voice ran through him and tightened the tense muscles in his spine.

"Good to see you finally relaxing." He looked down at his grimy, gook-splattered clothes. "I'll ransack the fridge after I wash up, on second thought."

"You're still gonna go in the bathroom with me, with the gun, right?" Her eyes searched his face for a commitment.

"Yeah. No problem," he said, feeling an odd mixture of nervousness and excitement. This woman didn't know him from Adam, yet trusted him not to be some weirdo. She was gonna allow him to guard her, naked in a shower, and not try to violate her. Deep. Jose went to the mantel and turned to face her. He watched her shoulders drop an inch in visible relief.

3

The responsibility weighed on him heavily in several ways as he ushered Juanita to the bathroom. Part of him stood taller, felt a sense of quiet, resounding pride that a woman as beautiful as her actually thought of him as some sort of neighborhood knight. Him? A kid from the barrios without any real money beyond chump change to his name? But every glance she offered was filled with awe and respect like he'd never been given by any female eyes. Yet another part of him was extremely worried. What if his grandfather had been wrong and those things that attacked them came back . . . what if he wasn't able to fend them off this time? What if they hurt her in some way? That outcome was totally unacceptable now, especially when she'd scooted into the bathroom behind him and shut the door, seeking a lock.

"My grandparents don't believe in locks in the house," Jose said, turning his back to Juanita.

Her eyes darted between him, the window, the door, and the shower. The man hadn't lied; the bathroom was so small that both of them could barely turn around within it, but every horror movie she'd ever seen converged in her rapid pulse.

"Check the shower," she said, whispering. "Please."

Jose flung the curtain back with bravado, brandishing the weapon, using the rifle barrel to hold back the white plastic. "It's cool."

She sighed and closed her eyes. "Good."

Perhaps it was the expression of relief on her face or the way the statement had come out on a breathy rush, but it made him need to turn around to pull himself together.

"I'll, uh, just stay like this till you tell me it's cool. Okay?"

Juanita nodded and opened her eyes. The entire experience felt like a crazy, jumbled-up dream. A part of her was scared to death, horrified by what she'd seen. Another part of her felt like she was embarking upon the greatest adventure of her life . . . and the man who had saved her was the most handsome, sexy hunk she'd ever been this close to.

Tingles claimed her belly as she hunted through the medicine cabinet looking for mouthwash and spied small Dixie cups. There was baby lotion and Jergens lotion. She tried to forestall getting undressed as long as possible. But she knew in her soul that this barrio prince who stood like a soldier, back erect, gorgeous eyes alert to the darkness, would not turn around or fail her by breaking his honor.

Little by little, she eased her jeans down and then quickly turned on the water. "Don't listen. This is so embarrassing."

"I'll just sing," he said, laughing, and began humming a heavy rap tune. When she flushed, he laughed. "You're gonna have to holla and stomp your feet to drown me out when I go, girl. That wasn't nothing but a princess tinkle."

She laughed as she washed her hands. "You so crazy."

"Like none of what we're dealing with tonight is crazy?"

"It is crazy," she said, stripping off her clothing, by shy degrees. "But I'm not scared in here with you. And I'm sorta glad we met, anyway."

"You know, most guys meet a fine woman in a club, down on Venice Beach, walking down the street . . . but no. I have to meet the finest babe I've ever seen while on a motorcycle tear down a demon-filled street. That's the type of year I've been having. Truth be told, that's the kind of life I've been having. So, my bad if I wish I had met you under different circumstances . . . but I am glad we hooked up."

Juanita turned on the water and slipped under the spray without a word. He'd said she was the finest woman he'd ever met. Wow. A guy like him? He'd also said, in so many words, that he was unattached, since it was hard to meet people and he was having a bad year. Plus had said she princess-tinkled. She smiled as the warm water covered her and she doused her hair in it, finding a bar of Ivory soap on the rack. Her *papi* used to say that to her when she was a little girl . . . "go make a princess tinkle." She wanted to laugh and cry both at the same time.

"Your people are really nice, Jose. Thank you for sharing them with me for the night, and for taking me in . . . and for doubling back to pick me up on your bike. My family isn't as cool as yours."

"Yeah, well, you ain't never met my mom. She's a trip," he said, watching the window intently. The scent of Ivory soap was embedded in his nose, creating a memory template that he'd never forget. Wet woman splashing behind a thin curtain . . . naked. Trust was as thick between them as the growing steam and the heavy throb that had begun to cause a dull ache in his groin. Co-dependency—her dependent on him for safety, him dependent on her for hope, for balm to his wounded male pride . . . to make losing his mural, his last-ditch dream, worth it all, with both of them wrapped in the faith that they weren't crazy. They'd both seen it, had tribal elders confirm it.

"My mom is a trip, too . . . that's why I was out tonight," she said so quietly and in such a sad voice that he was tempted to turn around but didn't.

"Moms can be like that," he said, trying to sound nonchalant, but the response came out on a gentle rush of breath.

"You have any brothers and sisters?" She peered around the curtain and drew his attention away from his neutral post.

"No," he said slowly, unable to keep from looking at her squeaky-clean face and how the water ran down her wet hair, down her throat, and then slid away behind the semi-sheer curtain that barely concealed her wet cinnamon-brown skin. "Long story. But it's just me and her."

"Oh," she said, ducking back into the water behind the curtain.

Conflict tore at him. He wanted to keep staring at her and yet also needed to turn around to keep her from seeing the state she'd put him in.

"You and your mom had an argument?" He needed to talk, keep things moving in the bathroom. If it got too quiet, she might be able to hear him breathing through his mouth.

"I wanted to go out with friends," she said in a tight murmur, just above the spray. "But she slapped me and called me a whore—and I've never even *been* with a man. All I do is go to work, watch my little brother, clean up the house after him and Juan, my older brother, who she thinks walks on water, no matter what he does. Cook, clean, 'do this, Juanita,' 'do that, Juanita,' that's all I ever hear, ya know? I wanted to go to college one day but wound up working in a drugstore ringing a register, just to help Momma out. So, I just got fed up when she slapped me for wearing red and makeup, and I ran away. But I didn't ever think . . ."

"Hey, I hear you. Noticed you, like me, weren't in a hurry to make the call home. Maybe when we get outta here, huh?" he said, trying to mentally catalog everything this beauty had told him in one rush.

She, that fine babe, was a virgin—he'd heard that first. Then, his mind processed the rest: She didn't have a man. Had dreams that had been crushed by duty—he could relate— which meant that she had a good heart, a tender spirit, cared for people, and put family first. She didn't have a man? Shee-it. Problem solved.

"What were you doing out there?" she asked quietly, turning off the shower.

Jose let out a long breath. "I was almost dog meat," he replied, leaning against the wall with a thud as the grim reality finally hit him. "I was up on the scaffolding of the building that the city gave me a contract to paint a mural on. Up there, at night, by myself, studying the bricks and where to lay down the design—then cops pull up, hassle me, make me come down. In a weird way, they probably saved my life."

He heard the curtain yank back and steeled himself against the shudder of desire that ran down his spine.

"Ohmigod, you were out there by yourself, all alone, doing the mural, and could have been killed? You're an artist? Like a real artist, and went out there at night?"

The tone of her voice, the excited rush, and the awe that echoed in the bathroom made the muscle in his jaw pulse. No woman had ever listened to what he had to say with bated breath. No one had ever heard his tales of victory after near death like he was some street warrior returned from battle— he'd never had anything like the other *hombres* had to tell an adoring feminine crowd. But right now he had Juanita's full attention focused on him, her wet movements beneath a towel driving him to the brink of insanity; then the sweet smell of lotion and the sound of it being applied almost made him groan out loud.

"Yeah . . . I can draw," was all he said.

"But you were out there by *yourself,* Jose. Ohmigod!"

"Yeah. But it was cool."

"Whew," she whispered. "Okay, you can turn around now."

He shook his head no. "Uh . . . why don't you turn around so I can jump in there?"

"All right. I'm not looking."

She heard him drag in a deep breath and begin taking off his clothes. His sneakers fell to the floor in heavy thuds, and the vibrations made her belly quiver. This fine man was getting naked behind her back. This awesome guy had just stripped to the raw—this same man who had saved her life. He was an artist, single and unattached. The city thought enough of his work to give him a contract, at his age, so he had to be *ba-a-ad*. He was a man going places and a man unafraid. He made her feel safe and have hope and faith and something she dared not name. Just hearing him turn on the water and jump into the shower made her mouth go dry.

She peeped over her shoulder. "Want me to hold onto the gun?"

"It's a rifle," he said, chuckling, "but if it'll make you feel better, just keep the barrel pointed away from me, aw'ight?"

She laughed and didn't go near the weapon that rested on the floor. "That's okay," she said, stealing glances at his moving form behind the plastic curtain. Her body was responding against her will. The humid, foggy enclosure reminded her so much of the best parts of her crazy dreams . . . angry black smoke giving way to a thick rain forest–like mist . . . primordial steam, the sound of a waterfall. She was a water sign, Cancer, and the element was a part of her. That had to be it.

"So you hungry?" he asked over the din of the spray.

She towel-dried her hair harder, trying to wrest her thoughts back to appropriate topics. "Yeah, I guess."

"Cool. After I get out, we can go see if there's anything in the fridge."

By the time the water stopped, her heart was thudding in mild arrhythmia. When he leaned out of the curtain to grab a towel, rivulets of water running down his body, she didn't even bother to turn away. Toffee-hued bronze-tan skin cut through the steamy haze. Pure masculine scent mixed with the water and made her lean against the sink to stare. His chest was carved into two solid blocks of hard muscle, and as her gaze discreetly slid down his torso she had to bite her bottom lip to keep from going hang-jawed.

Perfectly sculpted abs in isolated free-standing muscles drew her gaze down to a silky thin line of water-slicked hair just under his navel. This wasn't the soft body of an artist; what Jose owned belonged to a warrior. Heaven help her, desire bathed her in a hot sheath of want. Her skin was on fire, her nipples were so hard they hurt, and the moisture that crept between her thighs made her face burn with sudden shame. He was the entire package—a decent human being, listening ear, soldier at the ready, generous of spirit to share his family, a man with integrity who had saved her life.

She turned her head like she'd been slapped when he swathed himself in a towel, but she noticed that he just stood in the tub, breathing in slow, paced sips.

He willed his legs to move, but they didn't cooperate. He begged his eyes to go back to an appropriate place, but they wouldn't listen. The finest woman he'd ever seen was leaning on his grandfather's sink in a white cotton nightgown that her wet hair had made cling to her. Nipples hard, dark brown hair making the gown sheer in all the right spots, curves unconcealed beneath the fabric. Just slap him. Adrenaline and the whole drama were clearly making him stupid. This woman trusted him and depended on him, but *por dios,* she was fine.

"You look much better after the water hit you," she said, trying to make a joke of their previously grimy condition.

"I'm a Pisces," he said, his laughter strained. "What can I say? Water is my thing."

For a moment she didn't answer, processing the comment a number of wicked ways. "I'm a Cancer," she said with a shy smile. "Water is my thing, too."

"Moonlight doesn't do too bad on you, either, moon child." He smiled and glanced at the window and then at her.

He stepped out of the tub and was standing two inches

from her. She tried not to glance down at his towel or the hard length it shielded and fixed her gaze on his eyes. He was standing so close that their bodies almost brushed.

"Any sweats or anything in there that I can throw on?"

"I think so," she whispered, and then pulled her gaze away from him with great effort.

"Give me a second; then I'll go find you something to eat."

Him for dinner was a viable option. She turned around quickly, wishing that the steam hadn't claimed the mirror so completely. She peeked but turned away and simply suffered at hearing him drag on the soft fabric.

"I'm decent," he said in a low murmur.

She turned to face him again, smiled, and stopped breathing as his body made a definitive tent in his gray sweats.

"You hungry?" he asked in a quiet, sensual tone that released a new flow of thick wetness between her thighs.

She nodded and swallowed hard.

"Me, too. Been a long time since I had anything good."

She stared up at him as he closed the distance between them and allowed his body to brush hers to get a towel to dry his hair. The sensation of his naked torso sweeping against her breasts almost made her gasp. Her stomach clenched, and his erection grazed her thighs, making her want to open them.

About to hyperventilate, she clasped the edges of the sink with both hands behind her. She'd never felt a man's body against hers, had never been touched so gently in an accidental rake of bare skin against cotton. Her nipples pouted with the urgent need for one more pass, one more feather-light contact. Even in the dense, steamy heat, gooseflesh had risen on her arms. But he simply stood inches from her, drying his hair, staring at her.

"Can I tell you something?" he finally asked, reaching past her again to slip the towel on the edge of the sink, his chest gently touching hers again when he did so.

She nodded quickly, his caress sending shards of lightning between her legs. "Yes," she breathed out. "What?"

"You are so beautiful that I really wanna kiss you, but I'm not trying to freak you out, after everything you just went through." He swallowed hard. "It's just that, I'm so glad you weren't hurt, so glad to be alive . . . and can't get the fact out of my head that we've been dreaming the same dream—and before tonight I didn't even know you."

She couldn't move or take her eyes off his as his finger softly traced her cheek and then found her ear to move her wet hair behind it.

"I don't want you to think I'm trying to take advantage of you, because I'm not . . . and it ain't like I'm trying to look for some payback for the ride. I don't roll like that."

It was the stone-cold truth. His actions were driven by none of those things. She was simply beautiful, a heaven-sent gift. A phantom beauty in the mist, sipping air, making his skin burn beneath too-tight sweatpants, making him remember how alone he was in the world—no touch, no mouth to hunger for his, no hands or body to make him know life was worth living.

He smiled a half smile. "Maybe I should have taken a cold shower instead. I'm sorry."

"I'm not," she whispered, her soft voice holding him for ransom. "Maybe we both should have."

The way she turned her head, bit her bottom lip, and gripped the edge of the sink tighter did something to him. He knew it was foolish, to go for it under the circumstances, but if he didn't touch her, he'd lose his mind.

Ever so slowly, he took her mouth, testing for acceptance as he closed his eyes and his tongue met hers. The warm, moist yielding of her soft lips drew his body nearer, yet he took care not to crush his to hers—he didn't want to offend her or scare her off. But the sensation of her satiny skin in patches against his made it necessary to swallow a groan. He deepened the kiss and allowed his palms to slowly slide up her rigid biceps, closing the small fraction of space between them until his pelvis welded with hers.

The sound of her voice trapped in their mouths made his tongue more aggressive, but he took great care not to move against her like he so desperately wanted to. She had sanctioned a kiss, had only said yes to that. She'd never been with a man and had almost lost her life. Her momma had put her out, or some variation on a theme. It wasn't about working on Juanita while she was in a vulnerable, messed-up mental state. Yes, he wanted her, but not like that in his grandfather's house . . . tears the next day, recriminations, no.

Yet his hands kept gliding up and down her arms and on each pass edging nearer to the side swell of her breasts. He couldn't help it. She tasted so good, smelled so sweet, his body ached for touch so badly, and she had turned him on so thoroughly. When her hips slightly lifted to press her mound against him harder, he allowed his thumbs to caress the sides of the breasts, gently tracing the heavy lobes that rose and fell with her shallow inhales.

She broke from the kiss, breathing hard, but didn't pull away. He loved how she stared up at him, a question in her beautiful brown eyes. His thumbs never stopped moving against the sides of her breasts. He never took his eyes away from hers. Compelled, his thumbs grazed her nipples, and she closed her eyes with a shiver. That was all he needed to witness. Permission granted to explore how far she wanted to go.

This time when he took her mouth, his lazy thumb roll back and forth became a quick flicker of attention that made her gasp. Her hands left the sink and found broad shoulders to hold. A man she'd just met on the back of a bike in a deserted street was between her legs, moving hard against her, making her cling to him, making her moan, making her ready to grab his back, making her lean her head to touch the medicine cabinet mirror.

Hot kisses along her neck stole her breath. Male hands both rough and gentle at her breasts made a whimper escape and fuse with the steam. It felt so good, so wonderfully, terribly good, as his body now created an insistent pulse, like he was trying to climb inside her, simply pull himself through the fabric, and God how she wanted him to do that.

Yet from some very remote place in her mind she'd been called out of her name, a vile word delivered by her mother that gave her pause. His family had offered them both trust and asylum, and an old Indian woman had kissed her cheek. Yet this man was coming out of his pants, the friction wearing loose the drawstring, wearing down her resolve, wearing a hole in her brain while wearing her out, hiking up her gown, making her bud ache with such agony that she almost cried and begged him to touch it.

"Your grandparents," she gasped in a rush as he suddenly bent, dipped low, and pushed her gown up to French-kiss her navel.

"They're cool; they're gone for the night," he said in a ragged whisper against her belly. "I'll be gentle."

He was on his knees on the bathroom floor, whispering promises with kisses against a place that only her fingers had ever touched. Her thighs parted without her rational consent. But she couldn't help it. He had spoken truth and torture against the swollen wet lips between her legs, finding spots that made her shoulders collide with mirror glass. If he didn't stop, she would lose her mind; if he stopped, she'd slap him. She covered her mouth to stifle the sound creeping past her larynx, but her hand fell away and her voice rent the room, echoing, bouncing off the tiles, a wail that she couldn't hold.

The scent of ready woman was all in his nose, had penetrated his sinuses, was in his mouth, and lit the back of his tongue to ignite his groin on autopilot. Damn . . . this was *the one*. Right here on the bathroom sink. Butter-soft thighs tensing and releasing, hot flow all over his face. Her tight, round ass lifting, hips jerking under his hold . . . sweet virgin essence washing his face, her voice a moaning plea for something more to quench her that only he had. Oh yeah . . . he'd be gentle but firm, would take her spilling tears of pleasure. Her hands had found his hair and had become fists—he knew exactly what she was trying to say.

He didn't need a bed; a bathroom floor would do. The wall, whatever, *oh, baby . . . yeah . . . just let it go like that when I'm inside you.*

It was impossible to catch his breath as he pulled her down to the floor with him. Her mouth fought his for more tongue, a deeper kiss, her hands seeming as though they couldn't touch enough of his skin fast enough. Her breasts begged to be suckled, and he obliged as he slid down his pants and nestled himself between her legs. Tears made her eyes shimmer in the lifting steam.

"I won't hurt you; I promise," he whispered, finding her slick entry point.

She looked up at him with eager, trusting eyes. "Just don't get me pregnant, okay?"

Her voice was so small and tight, just like he knew she'd be, that it split his conscience in two. "Okay," he said on a ragged whisper.

She closed her eyes; the rational side of his brain shut down with them. He entered her slowly, easing in just the head, and dropped down on his elbows to cradle her skull in a gentle grip.

"Take a deep breath," he said quietly, watching her expression. "Don't tense up, all right?" Agony clawed at his groin until it felt like his sac would be drawn up into his abdomen with each inhale.

She nodded quickly but kept her eyes closed.

"'Nita, look at me," he whispered, kissing the bridge of her nose and waiting until she did. "Trust me. It won't hurt in a minute. Don't take your eyes off mine," he said, allowing more of him to fill her.

She arched and he reached down with one hand to hold her hips steady, careful not to press his full weight down on her.

"It . . . oh God . . . it feels so good, but hurts a little, too."

He nodded, unable to speak for a moment, his eyes sliding shut as the sensation of a near convulsion swept through him. "I kn-n-n-ow," he stammered, then nestled even more of him within her. "Let me put it in slowly, then you get used to it, before I move."

A hard shudder claimed him as she stroked his chest, her graceful, soft fingers grazing over his nipples. When her hands slid over his ass, he was barely lucid. Every impulse within him hovered on the very shaky border of moving in hard-driving jabs, yet her tear-filled eyes held such trust that he had to open his, stare at hers, just to remain nearly sane.

In slow increments he entered her deeper, watching her writhe beneath him, the suffering of want becoming hot need as he lowered his weight on her fully and kissed her hard. Her thrashing, her touches, her soft moans that he swallowed, the tight, slick, contracting sheath she pumped against him in urgent mini-upthrusts, broke him. His hands found her wet hair once more, his tongue diving at hers the way he wanted to move inside her. Short, even strokes soon became longer thrusts bordering on desperation. He stopped when she cried out his name and spent hard, his burning forehead pressed against her shoulder.

"Why'd—"

"I *have* to stop. Now or never."

He clung to her, trembling, begging her with his mind not to move, lest he explode and accidentally fill her with his seed. But pulling out was going to be painful, worse than having dental work done without Novocain. He lied to himself, trying to make it seem rational that he'd pull out in a moment, as soon as that got easier to do. Never happen. It was gonna be a bitch no matter what.

He tilted his head, took a deep breath, and squeezed his eyes shut and withdrew with a hissing inhale. "Oh, shit. . . ."

Her caress found his face and her arms held him closer to her. "Papi, I'm so sorry I'm not on the pill."

"Shush," he whispered into her hair. "Don't call me sweet names while I'm in a way like this. Let me get myself together."

"But you let me over and over again." She hugged him tighter. "I never thought it could be like this."

Didn't she understand that she was making him crazy, making him rethink his position, lying between her spread thighs, his member pulsing, so close but so far?

"Baby—"

Her kiss stopped his words; the heat of her hand stole his breath.

"That's not fair," she whispered against his ear, her hand moving swiftly up and down his slick, engorged shaft.

In no position to argue, he grasped her around the waist tightly, convulsed with a low sonic-boom moan that bounced off the tiles, and collapsed, breathing hard.

Dawn crept through the windows, adding pink and orange paint to the white ceramic tiles around them. Only his deep pants chasing hers echoed within the tiny space.

"I think we need to take another shower before my grand-pops and *abuela* come home." He'd spoken without opening his eyes but could feel her nod and sweet acceptance with a kiss before she struggled to get up.

"Yeah, Jose, I'll *die* if your grandparents ever see me like this."

4

As he helped Juanita to her feet, after-the-fact guilt gnawed at him. Just seeing the slightest wince flit across her pretty face let him know he should have waited. A woman like this didn't deserve to have her first time be a heated rush on a bathroom floor. Damn, what had he been thinking?

Jose cupped her cheek. "I'm going to run into the kitchen for a second and will be right back, then——"

"No. You promised you wouldn't leave me," she said, holding him tightly, her eyes growing wide.

"How about this," he said softly. "You sit on the edge of the tub, hold the rifle, I'll leave the door open and will talk real loud—nonstop—so you can hear me. We'll keep talking during the thirty seconds it'll take. Then I'll wash you up in the shower." He held her face with trembling hands and kissed her gently. "You trust me?"

She begrudgingly nodded and loosened her grip on him. "Do I have to hold the rifle, though?"

"No, just stand by the door, then, and leave it open. Talk to me while I walk the short distance. It's only like twenty-five feet down the hall."

"What are you gonna do?"

"I'm gonna go get something that'll make you feel better."

He swept her mouth with another quick kiss, opened the door, and began talking loudly as he dashed through the house. "So, what are you in the mood for? Breakfast, a sandwich, maybe some soup?" he hollered as he yanked open the freezer, grabbed an ice tray, and ran back toward the bathroom.

"Wow, that was fast," she said, hiding her body behind a damp towel. She stared down at the tray of ice. "What's that for?"

He just smiled. "You'll see," he said, and turned on the shower water again, closing the bathroom door behind him. He motioned to the tub with a nod. "C'mon. Hop in."

She gave him a quizzical look but slipped into the spray like he'd asked. The sound of ice breaking filled the tiny room, and within moments he'd joined her in the water with ice in his fist.

"Turn around and face the water," he murmured against her neck.

She did what he'd asked but had questions. "What are you going to do?" She gazed at his fist, trying to keep her face out of the spray.

"Relax and lean back against me," he said in a gentle command, sliding one palm across her belly as he lowered his ice-filled fist near her mound. He kissed her shoulder. "Open your legs. . . . I know it's tender there, like a friction burn."

When she complied, he cupped his hand against her, allowing warm water to blend with the ice and pour a cool, soothing stream of relief over her bud, the swollen lips of her delicate flower, and where he was sure it hurt the most.

"Oh God . . . that feels wonderful," she whispered, melting against his chest the way the ice was melting in his hand.

"Bueno," he whispered against her ear. "All I ever want you to feel with me is good."

He applied a gentle caress to the fragile haven that had taken him in, and could soon feel a different slickness from just water spilling against his fingers as the ice disappeared. The sensation made him want to move against her again, but he'd already done enough.

"Hand me the soap," he ordered quietly. "Let me wash you off."

With her leaning against him, eyes closed, the spray pummeling her breasts, he lathered his hands and then gave her the bar of Ivory soap to hold. He took great care in sudsing her delicate throat, her collarbone, her arms and shoulders, and then allowed his hands to revel in the varying textures of her breasts, the soap a slickened glide over her soft skin. Her quiet whimper of pleasure made him focus on her nipples perhaps longer than he should have, but he couldn't help it. That part of her required special attention. A dull ache burning him again, he slid his hands away and simply kissed her neck to regain his focus.

As he repeatedly took the soap bar from her, he added more lather and worked his way down her torso and belly, stopping to spread wide, slow circles over her navel. She didn't say a word but just pressed her backside to him in a way that produced a shudder. The moment his palm slid against silky hair, he petted the tender area in silent apology. Next time would be the way she deserved.

He could feel her thighs parting but took great care to rinse soap away, lest it sting. He reached for the soap and then slid down to a squat behind her, kissing the firm rise of her behind while splaying his hands along her shapely legs to coat them, caress them, kissing the backs of her thighs until she fell forward with both hands pressed flat against the tile wall.

Looking up at her wet behind from that position was tearing him up. But rather than hurt her again in an impatient rush, he soaped the backs of her legs and slowly stood to make soapy swirls over the firm swell of her bottom. The dip in her spine called his name, made him kiss it deeply and then plant kisses up her spine, finding each vertebra to anoint with his mouth, followed by soap. By the time his hands slid over her shoulders, she'd released a low moan and had leaned against him again. Soap created a slick emulsion on her back and sweet ass, causing him to slide against the slippery surface and release a quiet moan.

They said nothing as they moved against each other, but he dared not enter her again. The first time had been Russian roulette. His shaft had filled so hard and so fast his greatest fear at the moment was that she was already pregnant. One drop was all that was necessary.

"I should probably make you something to eat," he murmured thickly against her hair. "If we keep this up . . ."

"I know," she whispered, "but . . ."

"I can't promise I can control it this time."

She nodded but didn't stop grinding her backside against his length. He understood more than she knew, and slid his hand down her belly until she moaned at the touch that found her bud.

"Is it still tender?" he whispered, gently massaging the outer folds that hid the pouting knob of flesh.

"It throbs," she whispered, shivering. "I've never felt anything like this in my life."

"The water's getting cold," he murmured into her ear, then swallowed hard.

"But it feels like it's on fire."

Her voice had come out in a quiet, strangled rush. Each time he moved against her, the muscles in her backside clenched, gripping him and driving him nuts. Cupping her breast with one hand, he kept the other palm moving in a slow, gentle graze against the tender region between her parted thighs. She needed to release again, and he could tell how close she was . . . just like him.

Water spilled down her chest and belly, and he caught it in a slight cup of his palm between her legs, allowing the water to add to his touch, sending it between the hot, sensitive lips in a pulse that matched his gentle thumb flick.

In total trust, she'd reached back with lathered hands, finding him, stroking him, almost making him forget that he couldn't put it in again. When she came hard, her grip made his eyes cross beneath his lids. His body found a demanding rhythm against the outside of her soap-slicked ass at the same time his arms found anchor around her waist. Close to madness, he forgot about the possible danger of a slip-and-fall injury; he had to let her worry about that. She braced her hands against the tiles; he braced for the swift convulsion that dredged his groin and sent jerking, twitching spasms into his limbs.

This didn't make sense. He lifted his head from her shoulder and they both turned around in the spray to rinse off again. He took her mouth hard this time and then held her face to look at her without playing.

"I have to put my pants on," he told her firmly, saying it out loud more for his benefit than hers. "We have to get out of the bathroom. One more go-round like this, and I'll lose it."

He stepped out of the shower and snatched his pants off the floor, wondering how in the world one could get out of a shower sweating. He didn't even bother to dry off, nor did he look back. The rifle went with him the moment his pants were drawn on, the fabric clinging. The soft padding of her bare feet was immediately behind him. The decision was clear—at full sunrise, he had to ride. At full sunrise, he had to find some gas. At full sunrise, he had to go into town. Full sunrise demanded action. Find a drugstore and some condoms.

Speechless, she slowly slid onto a kitchen chair, watching him quickly open and shut cabinets and the refrigerator and then reach down with plates and a bowl, slamming them on the counter hard. Eggs hit and splattered a black frying pan. Shells and egg whites got hurled at a trash can, leaving a long, clear ooze across the counter in the wake of his rush. All she could do was stare at it, remembering . . . the spilled whites a reminder to be more careful next time.

Bread got jammed into a toaster and the heating bar slapped hard to begin toasting it. Suddenly he'd slid two glasses on the counter and sloppily poured orange juice into them. Bacon went into a too-hot pan and sizzled. She tried to stand, but her legs felt like jelly. This man was so fine and so sexy, and the things he'd done to her body made her briefly close her eyes. But he seemed angry, like she'd really done something wrong. For a long while she stared at him, summoning the courage to find out what her offense had been so that she could swiftly correct it.

"Are you okay?" she asked softly.

"Yeah, I'm cool," he said, slapping eggs on a plate and flinging a piece of toast beside it.

She didn't say a word as bacon popped and sputtered, half-black on one side, half-raw on the other.

"Jose, what's wrong? If I didn't do something the way you liked back there—"

He stopped rushing about, let out a deep breath, and closed his eyes. "Hey, I'm sorry."

"If I didn't do it right, I'm—"

"No, it's not like that," he said, turning away. "Damn! Bacon's burnt. You okay with just eggs and toast?"

"I'm sorry if you're used to being with more experienced . . . I mean . . ."

He turned off the burners, leaned on the counter, and allowed his head to fall forward with his eyes closed. "'Nita, baby, I'm not angry at you; I'm angry at me."

"Why?"

He looked up at her and held her gaze. "I shouldn't have started all that in the bathroom. You deserved a better place, better circumstances, for your first time."

His urgent reply made her face hot.

"I wanted to as much as you did," she said quietly. "It was more than I'd ever dreamed of . . . the way you make me feel. But then you seemed angry and—"

"I'm not angry; I'm just so horny right now I can barely breathe." He turned away and began fixing their plates more calmly. "I've never been with nobody like you, 'Nita."

She watched his back expand and contract with deep inhales. It was as though she were witnessing his internal battle for composure displayed in every taut muscle that stretched beneath his skin. The sight of his raw arousal had reignited hers.

"There's a washer and dryer in the pantry," he said without turning to face her. "I'm gonna throw our clothes in, get dressed, and make a run into town. Cool?"

"Can I go with you?"

She watched him hesitate and his breathing become more labored.

"I'm gonna go pick up some supplies, and won't be gone long."

"Okay . . . but I just wanted to go to the drugstore."

He turned slightly and looked at her over his shoulder. "That's where I was headed."

"Why don't you sit down and have some breakfast?" she murmured. "The eggs are getting cold."

He nodded, pushed a plate toward her, and dug into his eggs with a fork where he stood, never taking his eyes off her. She stood.

"Tell me where the laundry is."

He indicated with a nod and sopped up egg yolk with his toast, shoving half a slice into his mouth. "I'll straighten up the bathroom," he mumbled over the food he was chewing. "I got the dishes."

"It'll be an hour to wash and dry everything."

He stopped chewing and looked at her, then at the kitchen clock, swallowing hard. "They don't have twenty-four-hour joints around here. We've gotta wait until nine, at least. Some stores don't open till ten."

"That's like four hours from now." She sat down with a heavy thud in the chair she'd abandoned.

He began to pace in front of the stove and raked his fingers through his hair. She picked at her eggs and sipped her juice, knowing exactly how he felt. There was nothing else to say as they finished eating. Jose washed dishes and straightened up the bathroom. She kept her focus on the task at hand, laundry.

As she was standing there in a white cotton shift, her feet bare, the old house had such a comfortable feel that it almost melted into her bones. No matter what happened, she'd never forget this. What had happened out there in the streets of LA defied explanation. Oddly, terror had been replaced by knowledge. Being terrified all alone was something wholly different from having a witness to share the horror.

There was finally someone else who had seen what she had. There was a family that understood her dreams, like no one else did. For the first time in her life, she knew she wasn't insane or possessed—demons did exist. Angels had sent her a warrior, and she didn't even receive a scratch. And this man's wonderful family of old Indian shamans had taken her in, would provide protection . . . she didn't have to go anywhere else in the world but here.

Juanita let her gaze slowly take in the small pantry. Everything within the wood-frame ranch house was neat and tidy and old-fashioned. Big rose cabbage floral prints in bright yellows and pinks were everywhere. The sofa and chairs were overstuffed, the electronics minimal and two decades old. Pictures of family hung on the walls. Sheer lace curtains blew at open windows, and ceiling fans and box window fans were the only defense against the desert heat.

She left the thudding dryer and peered out the back window. She loved the old porch in the front and the back that held wicker furniture. Chickens pecked at pebbles in the yard. A lonely, dilapidated toolshed stood leaning a hundred yards away across dried, brownish-yellow grass. An ancient pickup truck rested idly against a garage with no door. Jose's bike gleamed in the sunlight, marred by a dark green splatter she wished she could forget but never would.

Turning her attention to the positive, she spied tiny wild-flowers peeking out in spots along the edge of the shed and garage. Suddenly her prayer came back into the forefront of her mind. She had asked the Almighty for a quiet place . . . with flowers and trees and family and a loving pair of arms to hold her. "Thank you, God," she whispered, and hugged herself.

On a night when she was sure she would die, instead she'd become a woman. Warm arms had enfolded her, and the heart of a good man had beaten against hers. Heaven had sent a man so decent that he was openly losing his mind to be with her but had denied himself just to protect her from something neither of them was ready to deal with. That made her want him all the more, seeing his restraint. His gentle caresses in the tiny bathroom and knowing how close they'd both come to death had made her grasp life, cling to it, and experience it fully in his arms.

He'd cooked for her . . . saved her . . . breathed her name on a shudder. In this old, beat-up house filled with love, even in her bare feet and wearing a borrowed nightgown, she felt like a princess.

If he remembered correctly, the town had a run-down motel. Jose went into his old bedroom and stopped for a moment to take in the changes. Gone was his bunk bed. That had been re-placed by a queen-sized wood-frame one. His old pine dresser and drawing table and ladder-back chair were still there, though, and Pops and Nana had even framed his old sketches to hang in the new guest room. Jose's line of vision went to the blanket his grandfather had always tucked around him, and a sense of comfort began to thread through him. *This* was home, not East LA. This was the only place in the world where he felt unconditional love. What had he been thinking to ever leave? True, it didn't have the fast pace and excitement of the city, but there was something to be said for the stillness it offered.

He crossed the room and stared out the window, wondering if his grandparents would mind if he turned the old shed into a studio one day. His mural project was history, and with a woman, now, he needed to get his art thing going. He needed to figure out a way to support them both, as well as give back to his elders who had given him so much.

Jose pushed away from the windowsill, breathing in the new day. It was gonna be a hot one, up in the high nineties, could even top a hundred degrees—he could smell it in the air. When Pops came back, he wanted to sit down with the old man and ask a lot of questions.

The first one would be, how did the tribal council *know* what would attack them? The second would be, what was this strange gift he had to be a tracker? A nose. Jack Rider also had that same trait. He just wished he'd spent more time learning about that when there was a chance to. But he also wanted to ask his grandfather all about the demon world, how one fought them, how one protected oneself and one's family against them . . . were there more, or was there this whole other side of the universe that he had only just begun to see?

A small piece of notepaper on the wooden nightstand by the bed drew his attention. He went to it and carefully lifted it to read. His grandfather's scrawl was unmistakable. The note was cryptic, like everything the old man said:

> It will take three days and three nights to make the medicine. Learn your totem while we are away. Keep the house and your belief. There are more clothes in the drawer for both of you, as well as

something to help your stay. The days are short and
the nights are long. Make good use of your time.

"Cool," Jose said, crossing the room to pull open a drawer.

Three pairs of jeans and three T-shirts, along with a three-
pack of boxer shorts, greeted him as he peered inside the
dresser. But a small brown bag made him frown with curiosity. The moment he peeked inside the parcel, he froze. Pops
had left him *condoms*—oh, shit.

Jose quickly shut the drawer and then opened the next one
beneath it. Three pretty sundresses in yellow, blue, and pink
stared back at him. A plastic three-pack of girl's underwear
caught his eye, and there was another nightgown, this one pale
peach.

He pushed the drawer closed with a quiet thud. The old
folks *knew*? His gaze tore around the room as he further in-
spected for anything out of the ordinary. *They knew*. Had left
him and 'Nita in the house for three days and nights while
they went to go make spirit medicine? The realization made
Jose pace. He wasn't sure why all this was bothering him, but
it did. Plus, 'Nita might take it the wrong way. Then again, she
might be cool.

Some things were better separated from the knowledge of
the elders, especially like having a love jones and shower
sweats for a gorgeous woman. His face burned with humilia-
tion. If he used their quiet offering in the drawer, they'd *know*.
That would put 'Nita's business out there, when the woman
was trying to make a good impression. What had gone down
in the two-by-four bathroom was bad enough, but under
Pops's roof with Nana's and his knowledge?

It was still hours before the town stores opened and the
sleepy little commerce area woke up. Jose looked at the
drawer and then looked at the door. Aw, hell . . . he would just
have to get over it.

"Yo, 'Nita . . . wanna see some old sketches?"

5

The moment she heard Jose's voice calling out, it suddenly dawned upon her that she'd been all by herself in the pantry, standing near the washer and dryer, doing laundry for an entire fifteen minutes—*alone*. How had *that* happened? Wanting to be with him had her nerves so rattled that she'd temporarily forgotten about those *things* that had chased them? Was she insane!

Juanita ran to meet the voice that had become synonymous with safety. She couldn't sort out why Jose, this house, or daylight had chased away her terror or the images that by rights should have given her a nervous breakdown. All she was clear about was the fact that this man's presence made everything seem normal. His excited expression made her smile through the panic. He didn't even have the rifle with him. The only weapon he had, which instantly blew her away, was his brilliant smile.

She stood before him in the hallway, now nearly ready to laugh, as he shifted his weight from foot to foot like an excited kid with a secret.

"They redid my room, and made it into a guest room. But they didn't throw out all my old sketches. Wanna see 'em?"

How could she refuse an offer like that? Juanita's smile widened.

"You'd let me see your art?"

"Yeah. C'mon," he said, dragging her down the hall by her arm. "I forgot about half of this stuff. I used to have some wild-ass images in my head as a kid, and me and this older guy, Rider, used to hang out, practice sharpshooting cans . . . then I'd see stuff, could almost smell it." He turned to her as they entered the room. "I'm wondering, like, if we've been having the same dream, and hooked up like we've known each other for years, maybe some of the stuff I've drawn might be a trigger for you . . . like help you remember your dreams, too."

"Okay," she said, hedging, not sure if she had the special insight he was seeking. She would have been happy enough to see his work just on the basis of getting to know him better.

He took a deep breath and walked over to his old desk. "All right," he said, hesitating. "Granted, some of this stuff is rough." He ran his palm across his jaw, suddenly appearing shy. "I'm much better now, but, back then, I didn't know how to always get the shading right, or the depth perception to make things pop off the page in three-D, and—"

"Jose," she said, putting her hands on her hips and smiling wider. "Are you going to show me, or what?"

The fact that he'd grown shy about unveiling his work endeared him to her. The humility that had arrested him and had made him look away, along with all the qualifiers and disclaimers, made her want to hug him. She waited with great anticipation and much respect for him to share this intimate peek into his mind.

"Yeah . . . it's just that I only showed people the good stuff," he said quietly, motioning to a few framed pencil sketches on the walls. "I got all hyped when I thought about it, and may have spoken too soon. I never let anyone see my books, my pads—where I was just messing around." He turned away from the desk and leaned on the dresser. "It ain't nothing, I guess. Just some old kid nightmares . . . like you'd wanna see *that*. You'll probably look at them and go, 'This brother is touched—*loco*,' and then laugh, anyway."

She went to him and placed her palm gently in the center of his chest. "I would never laugh at something that came from inside you, Jose." She stared up at him. "A little while ago, you asked me to trust you—and I did. I've never let anyone get that close to me, or make me open up like that."

He covered her hand with his own, nodded, and drew a deep breath, then let it out through his nose. "Okay. But promise not to laugh or run screaming into the driveway to hitchhike a ride outta here."

She kissed his cheek. "Lemme see what's in there."

Slowly, he moved away from his perch against the dresser and she watched him go to the desk to extract several huge sketch pads. She sat on the edge of the bed and waited for him to sit down beside her.

"These were when I was in high school and used to visit here for the summer," he murmured, not looking at her as he opened the first book on her lap. "Wasn't much else to do out here; no clubs and I was too young for the one bar they had in town. So, I sorta amused myself and helped Pops. Nothing special."

She was rendered mute, her fingers tracing the edges of the exquisitely detailed drawings. A quiet gasp of appreciation was all she could initially offer him as she turned the pages. "Wow. . . ."

Every image was a finely crafted series of individual dots and hatch lines, if one looked closely enough. But upon her pulling back, the minute markings evolved into epic images of demons and angels in furious battles . . . smoke, fire, huge, sinewy protectors standing tall with outrageous weapons, holding the line with female warrior counterparts against evil. Juanita lowered her face to the pages to better see how he'd patiently, painstakingly laid down each black mark to expertly make an entire living dream come to life on a single page.

"Oh, my *God,* Jose," she whispered in reverence. "How long did it take you to do one of these, let alone all of these?" She hadn't even looked up at him. She couldn't look up. The question had simply spilled from her lips in honest awe. Each page was a living fresco, jogging her memory, making her mind flex and bulk with images of her own that matched what she saw.

"I don't know," he said with a shrug. "I lose track of time when I'm working. I get all caught up, and that would always get me in trouble at home . . . or at school," he said with a self-deprecating chuckle. "My mother thinks I'm a bum. Maybe she's right. You can't make money on stuff like this."

"Are you crazy?" Juanita whispered, turning pages, engrossed in his book.

"Yeah, totally," he said, laughing nervously and then standing to cross the room. "Told you."

She jerked her attention up to stare at him. "No. That's not what I meant." She held his gaze. "You're a freakin' *genius,* Jose. Why aren't you in art school, or in galleries somewhere? A bum? Are you nuts?"

His gaze left hers to seek the window. "Couldn't get my tuition together, and—"

"Did you ever apply for a scholarship, or send them your portfolio?" She was on her feet with a sketchbook extended. "With work like this, you could go *anywhere,* brother!"

"I never applied . . . didn't know they'd take me without cash on the barrelhead. Didn't wanna get my hopes up for nothin' that wouldn't work out anyway." He just looked at her.

"Did you ever show these to a guidance counselor at school?" Indignant, she put the book with the others on the bed and stared at him. "Didn't those damn people who are supposed to talk to kids about their future—because that's *their job*—ever tell you, 'Jose, man, you got skills. Lemme help you fill out an ap' to apply to a big-name university'?"

He didn't know how to answer her. No one had ever gotten angry at him for not using his art to better his life. No one ever had fire in her eyes because he might not have followed his dream or used his passion to earn opportunity. But this gorgeous woman nearly had tears in her eyes, hands on hips, and looked like she was ready to fight the whole world for his cause.

"Didn't they tell you that you could work as a cartoonist or that you could be the next great film animator—or even be the mastermind behind all those expensive video games, working for the big companies? Oh, my God, Jose!" she exclaimed, beginning to pace. "This is a travesty! A bum? Your momma called you a bum? Do you know that you could design video sets for the music industry, or, or . . . oh, help me, Blessed Mary!"

Juanita had placed her hands on top of her head and was now staring out of the window. Just seeing her so upset about no one understanding his hidden talent was blowing his mind.

"They all told me to stop dreaming . . . to get the three Rs of reading, writing, and arithmetic down. Said that my SAT scores were pitiful, like my grades. Said that I was wasting time doodling in notebooks, and—"

"They never saw your work?" Her hands slid off her head and hung loosely at her sides. "Never saw the quiet genius in you, a poor kid from the barrios." Her voice became a whisper of outrage. "Never thought you had dreams worthy of anyone's time. I know. Been there."

"The way you just broke down those industries and opportunities . . . you could be a businesswoman," he said, pushing off the dresser to go collect his books to hide them away again. This was too intense and had been a bad idea.

Her indignation made him nervous; he wasn't used to anyone caring so deeply about him. "You should be counseling kids, giving them hope and direction," he said, sudden depression weighing in on him. "Lotta parents just don't know what's out there, as far as different careers and stuff, and only want their kids to take the safe, guaranteed route . . . like a vo-tech school. I can't blame them." He shoved the books into the drawer and looked up at the few framed sketches on the walls. "You could be a talent agent, too," he said, laughing sadly as he thought about the mural contract that he'd lost. "'Nita, I was gonna paint the hell out of that wall . . . was gonna funk it out, trick that bitch out so lovely that there'd be accidents on the 405 from people staring." Jose let his breath out hard and turned around to look at her.

Tears stung her eyes and she swallowed hard. "How did you know?"

"Know what?" He hadn't meant to upset her by his outburst.

"That I wanted to be a businesswoman, not a cashier in a drugstore?"

"I thought that was a part-time thing, until you did your thing?" He closed the space between them. "With your mind . . . the way you just dissected my shit, pulled it apart, and came up with solutions that I couldn't figure out? C'mon, girl. Be serious."

"*You* be serious," she said, lifting her chin. "Vo-tech? You? I don't care who told you that; it's bogus."

"I just draw, but you seem like you were an As-and-Bs kinda student. Real book smart."

She turned away from him and went to stand by the window. "Yeah . . . I got straight As, but a lotta good that did me. When it came time to apply for college, they said that getting straight As at a low-expectations high school in the inner city wasn't as good as coming from a top-notch public high school, or private school. Plus, my momma needed help at home, and nobody was helping me find scholarships. I learned about all that career and scholarship stuff on the fly, when customers would come into the store to buy what they needed to go off to school. . . . I wanted to be them so bad, Jose, you just don't know—and I'd eavesdrop or make small talk to get them to tell me where they were going and how they got there, just dreaming. Then I'd sneak to the library and try to figure out what they meant. But I'd missed my chance by then."

"It ain't over till it's over," he said, coming to her and gently hugging her from behind. He placed a kiss on the top of her head. "You can still go if you want to; all you have to do is try."

She turned into his embrace and kissed the underside of his chin. "I'll take that advice, if you will. Deal?"

He nodded and shrugged. "I guess so—but *you* should go."

"So should *you*," she argued with a smile. Her fingers traced his mouth, her eyes following the invisible imprint of where her touch had landed. "Jose, you are so talented, have so much to offer the world with your inner vision. Promise me that, no matter what happens, you won't allow yourself to wind up in some dead-end job that will kill your spirit." She brushed his mouth with a kiss and then pulled back. "Do the wall, baby. That mural. Do it on paper, if you can't have the wall right now. Add that into your going-to-college-or-bust portfolio. Put your all into it, like you would have up on that scaffolding. Please, dear God, whatever you do, don't waste this gift."

The way her eyes searched his and her words coated his insides with heat lowered his mouth to hers in quiet surrender. Never in his life had anyone gone to bat for him like this, had ever pushed him so hard with such a tender shove. If he couldn't give himself over to his art completely, today, at least, he could give his all to her.

"Only on one condition," he whispered.

"Name it," she murmured, running her fingers through his hair.

"That you go to school with me and never stop looking at me like this when I show you my work."

"How could I stop looking at you like this, when you and your work makes me know there's still hope and love and beauty in the world?" She grazed his mouth with a kiss and then shook her head. "Jose, you also make me know that I'm not crazy to dream. . . . I've seen those same images before. They'd start behind my eyelids when I'd shut my eyes at night, like pinpoints of black dots fired by lights behind them . . . then the image would become clearer when my body would lift above it to see it all from an aerial view. And that's just how you drew the sketches—dot by dot."

"You serious?" he whispered, the words catching thickly in his throat.

"I swear it," she replied, staring at him without blinking. "The thing I can't understand is . . . how I know you?"

She pulled out of his embrace and wrapped her arms around herself. "I have to just say this, because my mind won't let it go."

He nodded and gave her space.

"I've never been so afraid in all my life." Her eyes sought his for confirmation and found it. "I didn't know you, had never seen you, had no reason to trust you." She looked away, shame glittering in her eyes made dazzling by the sunlight. "I don't just meet men in the street, jump on a motorcycle with them, and do the wild thing on a bathroom floor in their grandparents' house, of all places, for chrissakes." She covered her face with her hands and breathed in deeply. "I'm not like that, Jose. I have some pride and some decency, no matter what you might think. And yet I'm here in a borrowed night-gown, half-naked. I've just given my body to a man for the first time, and I don't even know his last name."

He went to her quickly and enfolded her in his arms. "Ciponte. My last name is Ciponte. And I know that you've never been with a guy like that, have to be freaked out, and have never *done it* before. That's why I was so angry at myself for going there with you; you aren't that type of . . . I mean—"

"I'm not," she said, huge tears spilling. "I have to get dressed and go home to my momma."

"I know, baby. We'll get dressed right now and I'll take you home. But I don't want you to think that all this was the norm for me, either. It's been a really long time since I had what you could call a girlfriend, or something. Years, and that's no bull." He raked his hair and kept his gaze on her, forcing her eyes to stay with his. "Guys get a bad rap for always being dawgs, but I swear on my father's grave, I've never had an experience like what we just shared. So, don't make it out to be dirty, in your mind. It was pure passion, from my point of view."

When she looked away, he returned her gaze to his with a gentle finger beneath her chin. "No, look at me—dead in the eyes so you can see the truth or a lie." He let out a long breath filled with emotion. "'Nita . . . No one has ever believed in me, treated me like I was their hero, given themselves to me without games. You think men don't have feelings? You don't think we ever dream of finding *the one*?"

He released his hold on her and went back to his desk, yanked out a drawer, and selected a pad. "Look at this one," he said, shoving the book toward her. "Every page owns my secret lover."

She cautiously accepted the book and he came closer.

"Look at her," he said, his voice becoming strident as he finally saw the eerie similarity between the woman standing in the room and the one gracing every page.

Growing more unnerved by the discovery, he led Juanita to the mirror that hung over the dresser and took the book from her to hold it up beside her face. "Same body, same hair. Every pose is you—same eyes, I just didn't have the rest of the face. The hero is standing in front of her, guns blazing, trying to keep demons at bay." Jose flipped another page and forced her to stare more deeply into the mirror. "Got her on his bike, rough-riding out of hellfire."

He flipped another page quickly, growing more urgent that she see into his heart. "Then he was so grateful to be alive that he made love to her in a tangle of passion in the mist—place to be determined, location unknown." He slammed the book shut and flung it on the dresser, bracing a hand against the furniture on either side of her body.

They both stared at each other's reflection in the mirror.

"Operative words—he *made love* to her, didn't screw her," Jose murmured, his eyes never leaving the mirror. "Would die for her, would take a bullet for her, would battle the darkness, just for her. Fell in love with her somewhere in the mist, I guess when he was losing his mind. I don't know when that happened, or how. I'm just the artist that draws them. All I know is, for years, he couldn't wait to go to sleep so she'd come to him in a dream. Years of wanting someone to see that he was a hero deep inside, and to have someone to call his own, someone who had his back, someone who could see what he saw and had vision. Artist by day, superhero by night . . . *Years,* 'Nita, that's how long he'd been waiting for her to step across the threshold of a dream and be made flesh, and be *real.*"

She nodded, tears now streaming down her face while she stared at his pain-filled expression. "Years of running through the darkness in dreams," she whispered. "Years of feeling different, and knowing she was . . . years of waiting for that voice she knew by heart in her head. Years of waiting for those right eyes that saw her as more than a booty call, some *chica* airhead to use and then throw away . . . hoping, believing, *knowing* there was only one man in the world who could chase the demons away. Only one who made her feel like a princess and special . . . who would make her body yield and then burn and give her all . . . and then feeling so foolish for having to bite her lip to keep from saying that she was falling in love with him the moment he took her in the steam on a bathroom floor."

His ardent kiss on the side of her neck caused a hard shiver at the same time his hands swiftly traced up her arms to produce a gasp.

"I can't explain this," he said in a hot whisper, aggressively nuzzling her neck. "I can't explain what we saw out there, or how I can be feeling this so strong with everything that just went down." He delivered mind-stunning kisses against her jawline and then shoulder. "I can't explain why I can't keep my hands off you, or can even think about something like that after what we just went through." He dragged his nose up the side of her neck and squeezed his eyes shut tightly, breathing her in. "I'll take you home, if that's where you wanna go. But don't ask me to stop feeling like this about you, okay?"

"I can't explain it, either," she said, her breaths coming out with the words in short, staccato pants. Her body moved against his and her voice became strangled as she tried to speak. "It doesn't make sense. After what we just saw we should both be so wigged out right now that . . . it doesn't make sense."

"Does it have to?" he said in a low rush, his hands covering her breasts. He dropped his forehead to her shoulder, gently kneading her flesh while capturing her nipples between his forefingers and thumbs. "All I know is you looked at my drawings like you were looking into my soul, 'Nita."

His voice fractured as he began to slowly pump against her backside through her nightgown. "All I know is that it's like I found you from somewhere in my mind, like some weird and wonderful out-of-body experience," he murmured, ending the statement on a deep, sensual moan. "And, baby, if you came to life from my sketches, I'm not ready for you to disappear yet . . . can't bear the thought of you being black-and-white, two-dimensional, anymore." He kissed the nape of her neck when her head dropped forward and her hands braced on the dresser. "Oh, *shit,* I need you in three-D right now."

Unable to withstand his impassioned outburst, common sense fled her as she reached back and yanked at the sides of his sweatpants, pulling them down over his hips. They both looked up into the mirror at the same time.

"Go 'head," she said on a hard exhale. "I've been waiting for you to step out of my dreams and become real, too."

For a second he didn't move; she didn't move. Then suddenly his hands raced up her sides, lifting her gown. He kept his eyes on her through their reflection and entered her tender, wet valley hard, sinking against her with an agonized groan. The new sensation lit her spine with fluid motion as her hands gripped the dresser's edge. She watched his eyes slide shut with an expression of pure torture.

"Oh, Jesus, if I don't reach into that top drawer right now . . . I'll get you pregnant today."

No words would form as he gathered her around the waist with one arm and yanked the drawer open by several inches. She didn't care what he did or that there was something hidden in there, as long as it would allow him to continue to be inside her.

Through half-closed eyes she watched him fumble with a brown bag, then a box, ripping and tearing away the cellophane covering like a madman, moving against her with insane thrusts that made her belly repeatedly collide with the furniture. Pleasure like she'd never known tore through her while she watched him struggle with the small foil wrapper, and she held on to the dresser, arms extended, head down, gasping.

The guttural sound he released deep within his throat fused with the sting of cold air against her back. Near weeping for his return, she arched into him, taking him in sheathed with latex. Instantly, strong arms gripped her waist, his hot cheek pressed against hers. She was blinded by the new sensation, and her legs threatened to go out from under her as he slammed pleasure into the tender place he'd so gently deflowered before.

Her hair swept the top of the bureau, swinging back and forth like a maddened feather duster. Tears blotted the surface, rolling down her cheeks to land in ecstasy-driven splotches. Her voice was not her own as it blended with his deep, grunting exhales, a unified chant till her nails raked wood severely enough to almost draw splinters. If this was what it was like, *don't stop*. If this was the next level, keep moving! If this was just the beginning, *por dios,* she would die and didn't care.

"Girl, I love you," Jose said on a hard shudder, then convulsed in waves of jerking thrusts.

Her body slammed against the dresser, the wind knocked out of her on a wail: "Jose!" Then wave after wave of womb-deep tremors consumed her, releasing bands of color behind her tightly shut lids.

The dresser held them both up, panting. She could feel his kisses pelt her shoulder blades. He was still rock hard inside her; a sob crested, and then she utterly broke down and wept in earnest. What was this sweet madness? No one had ever told her it could be like this. She'd practically been speaking in tongues, lost to reality. Strong arms were holding her; she could feel Jose extracting himself, breaking the connection to divine insanity. Reflex dug her nails into his hips.

"Don't move," she whispered between her teeth. "Not yet."

He nodded against her back, gulping air. "Tell me when. Did I hurt you?"

"No . . . it just feels so good. Don't take it out."

"Jesus," he said against her shoulders. "I've gotta put another one on."

Their eyes met in the mirror.

"What time will they come home?" Her glance went to the bed and then sought his again in the reflection.

"In three days," he said, swallowing hard and still gulping air.

"You sure?"

He nodded and stroked her hair. "Wanna go lie down in bed?"

She nodded but couldn't move.

◆ ◆ ◆

Every previous night of denied access took his mind, bent and snapped it, with her now under him in the flesh. Every touch she delivered against his skin made him insane . . . just like her voice, her scent, her seeking eyes as the sun began to wane. They had petted and fondled each other under the old Indian blanket until sweat stripped the linens and the arid desert air stripped their lungs. What was left on the bed was sticky and wet with spent love. His sweatpants were a ruined heap flung across the room to a vacant chair, just like her gown was a damp mess on the floor. The scent of pungent brand-new sex hung thickly in the room, growing denser with each encounter.

Time of day was lost. Thoughts of food went neglected. No matter how many times they had each other, their bodies still craved more. The need to make love seemed infinite, but the box had a finite count that brought sure panic.

"Just one more time," he whispered, his fingers lodged deep inside her. The scent of her in his sheets, in his hair, on his skin, was making him delirious as the sun went down. It felt like he was living his last twenty-four hours on earth before dying. But he couldn't care less as she straddled him, her lovely mound poised for his kisses as she went down on him and made him see stars.

No latex to dull the sensation of her tongue. No barrier to block the softness inside her mouth. No advance warning to prepare himself for the hard pull of her lips over the head. Nothing on this side of heaven to make him ready for the grip of her fist at his base. No way to keep from drowning in her sweet juices as he lapped them. Nothing rational left of his jellied mind as her sucking became more insistent. Impossible to stop the slow, hard implosion that sat him up in hard arches, made his hands grip the halves of her ass to open her wider for his tongue.

If there was something in the shadows coming for him,

then it had better kill him quick. If his people doubled back and came home early, so be it; he'd beg their pardon later. Because right now the only thing that registered was her tongue, followed by a lightning arc of current that ran down his spine, created epileptic seizures, made spasms dance through his limbs and stab his groin.

Near hysteria, he found himself sobbing against her wetness, breathing it in, almost choking on her sweet essence, and coming so hard he thought he'd go blind.

All he could do was collapse with her body a heap on his. Disoriented for several moments, he had to remember where he was, what time it was, feeling along her supple backside for confirmation that it had all been real.

"You want some water?" she whispered against his thigh.

He just gasped in air but didn't have the strength left to answer. His palm rubbed her hip as an immediate reply. "In a minute," he finally said, eyes still closed.

"We should get up and get a shower," she said, giggling. "The box is empty."

"This all started in the shower," he said, breaths ragged, and intermittently chuckling. "I'm scared of that room. Has powerful medicine in it."

"Our clothes are dry—the dryer stopped hours ago."

"You wanna ride into town before the drugstore closes, maybe stop at the diner to eat?" The thought of being in the house with her for two days and no way to make love to her brought instant clarity.

She kissed his thigh close to his sac. "I don't care if we stop at the diner, but we have *got* to go to the drugstore before it's full dark."

The feel of her hot breath against his inner thigh made him sit up and get focused.

6

The only rational thing to do, so they could get out of the house, was let the woman go into the bathroom alone.

"Open the window," he said as he walked down the hall with a rifle. "It's not dark yet, got a few hours, and I'm gonna go check on the bike—see how much gas is left to get us to town."

He didn't wait for her to argue. He was on a mission. He needed to score latex like a junkie needed to get crack.

Out the back door, down the steps, Jose went to his bike and groaned. Damn! His black beauty was running on fumes. Okay, new plan. The toolshed caught his eye. Maybe, just maybe, if there was mercy in heaven, his grandfather might have an old red gas can with a spit of fuel in it.

Jose jogged across the backyard, scattering angry hens. Resting the rifle against the outside wall of the dilapidated structure, he pulled the rusty door open with both hands. Allowing his eyes to adjust to the darkness, he squinted, searching for a light. But soon the low afternoon sun and opened door allowed his eyes to scan the interior. However, what he saw gave him pause.

It was a veritable artillery shed. Medicine wheels and amulets with eagle feathers covered the walls, along with silver stakes, crossbows, and bowie knives in varying degrees of blade length. He stepped inside, his curiosity dragging him over the threshold. In the center of the floor were strange circles and symbols, bones and stones, as though a hex or a ward against evil.

His gaze went to a litter of shells and dirt on the small wooden table by the wall. Jose approached it with care, peering down at the gleaming silver bullets and dark soil that had an incense fragrance. Jugs of water with war paint etchings from a time long gone sat beside the shells. He looked up at the crossbows and the long stakes plumed with eagle feathers.

They knew. Not just empathized or believed *but knew.*

Jose stared harder at the walls as dust motes danced and played in the murky stream of low sunlight. The interior had been whitewashed with war paint. The scent of white sagebrush hung heavily in the air, stinging his nose. A sense of calm, safety, spiritual fortress emanated from everything around him. Sagebrush and silver, chicken blood and burnt wood, all of it crawled over his skin in an odd sense of knowing. He was standing in the middle of a spiritual bomb shelter. If his people had built this, then what was coming?

Suddenly getting into town had less urgency. But finding gas to ride out a storm was still the thing to do. Jose walked through the shed with new reverence, only to be disappointed. He grabbed the rifle and jogged back to his bike, determined to rinse the demon gook off it before Juanita saw it again.

Hurrying with the task, he got the backyard hose and quickly blasted off the muck—this time more careful with the water that was scarce where his grandparents lived. Respect for them, what they knew, what they calmly accepted, what they'd built, entered him as he dropped the hose and ran up the back steps.

He passed Juanita in the hallway. "I'll be in and out in a few seconds." He knew he sounded panicked; he *was* panicked. But she didn't need to know why.

When he got out of the shower and raced to the bedroom, she had on her jeans and broken spike heels in her hands and was covering her breasts with her arm.

"Can I wear one of your T-shirts?" She gazed at him, chewing her lip for a moment. "My mother said the red halter made me look like a whore . . . and I don't want to look like that when I'm with you."

"You don't look like that to me, no matter what you wear." He pulled on his jeans and nodded toward the dresser. "You can have one of my T-shirts, and Nana left you some dresses in there, too."

"How did she know I was coming, Jose?"

They both stopped dressing and stared at each other.

"She's a seer," he said quietly. "Don't ask me how they do it; all I know is, that's what she is. *Abuela knows things.* So does Pops."

"I know things like that sometimes," Juanita said, going to the drawer to get a T-shirt. "That's why I know I don't want to wear this red halter right now."

He stared at her back for a moment and then found his sneakers and a T-shirt and she began to finger-comb her hair.

"When we go to the store, I'll get you a brush, too, and get us some toothbrushes—I need a razor," he said, rubbing his chin and trying to distract himself from the eerie feeling that had come over him. "But one thing's for sure; we've gotta get you some flip-flops, or something, until we can get you some sneakers."

Juanita bent without speaking and opened the bottom drawer. She slowly lowered herself to a squat, her hand stroking the doeskin dress. "There's moccasins in here with this dress."

Jose rushed to her side and stooped down to look, then snapped his glance to her quickly. "Full ceremonial outfit—how'd you know it was in there? 'Cause I damned sure didn't."

Juanita shrugged. "Can I wear the shoes, until I get some slides or flip-flops?"

He nodded and walked away, pacing in front of the bedroom door. "Let's make this a quick run. I think we should hang close to the house till my people get back."

Worry clung to him as Juanita kept a firm grasp around his waist. Dust stung his eyes and nose as they roared down the deserted strip of road, and he told her to keep her face pressed to his back to shield it from airborne debris.

Her wet hair whipped and slapped his neck, and the rose-orange hue of the setting sun made him push his bike to the limit. He had just enough in his wallet to put a couple of gallons in his tank, buy her some flip-flops, maybe a burger or two, a comb—but latex was king. If he'd known he was going on a serious road trip like this, he would have . . . done what? His ass was flat busted.

Jose almost cheered when he made it to the gas station and the old brave who ran it simply smiled and waved away his payment. He and Juanita shared a glance, and Jose walked over to the sun-blistered wicker rocker where the gas station owner sat calmly whittling down a stick. Even though he was nearly broke, Jose knew that the people in the town were poorer than that. He kept a respectful gaze on the gaunt, elderly silver-haired man who sat in the desert heat in a white sleeveless T-shirt and a pair of mechanic's uniform pants and worn leather slippers.

"Sir, it's cool," Jose said, extending a five-dollar bill.

"Your grandfather and I go way back. You're family." The elderly man glimpsed Juanita and kept whittling the stick into a sharp point. "We had a meeting, young Thunderbird. That which is within is about to come to the fore. You need everything you've got. The ancient spirits are dancing."

Jose folded up the bill and shoved it into his jeans. He hadn't a clue about what the old dude meant but also knew enough to know that once the elderly started talking in riddles, there was no arguing with them.

"Thanks," Jose said, quickly going to his bike and mounting it so Juanita could climb back on.

He was out.

Back on mission, he tried to wrest his memory back to the town layout. The streets were nearly deserted. Some stores already had their grates down. Full darkness wouldn't come until eight thirty, and judging by the height of the sun, it wasn't six yet. He stopped the bike at the corner of a strip of businesses. How did he know what time it was? He was freaking himself out and had to get a grip.

His gaze scanned the line of small stores, and when he spotted the old pharmacy he kicked the bike stand down in relief. "We can run in there, cool?"

Juanita got off the bike with a smile. "It's like the old West out here—like you see in the movies."

He laughed and slung his arm over her shoulder as they walked. "Baby, this place ain't changed since those times, believe me. That's why summer was enough."

Now, the challenge. It was simple enough to collect a pair of cheap rubber sandals, a plastic disposable razor, a comb, and a two-pack of toothbrushes, but this wasn't some impersonal, huge chain store where nobody knew your name. The real reason for the mission was up high on a shelf behind the counter, and the old lady who sat on a stool at the register fanning herself only spoke Navajo. How in the heck was he gonna ask Grandma for a double six-pack of Trojans!

Juanita edged away from the register. Aw, man, this was bad.

Jose dumped his stash of toiletries on the counter, and the old woman grinned a black, toothless grin and began ringing up his purchases. He spied Juanita glimpsing him from the corner of her eye. Okay. Cool. He lifted his chin. He was grown, was a man. So what if the old lady dimed him out to his grandmother? Pops had left a stash, anyhow.

"And, uh, two boxes," he said, pointing to the shelf behind the elderly matron. What was the word, what was the word— damn, he never learned the language cold like he should have!

She frowned and picked up two boxes of aspirin and began to add them to the items she was ringing up.

"No, uhm, not that."

She stopped and stared at him, then slowly put the items back, pointing at Pepto-Bismol.

The old woman was making him die a thousand quiet deaths, and he motioned with his thumbs higher to the next shelf.

She hesitated for a moment, then looked at Juanita, who had worked her way toward the door, and then looked back at him. Slowly, the old woman covered her mouth, giggled, nodded with a sigh, and jumped down off the stool to fetch a retail grabber stick. Jose sent his gaze down an adjacent aisle, too through. The boxes the storekeeper pulled down had so much dust on them he could write his name on the top. *Now* he had to check an expiration date, too, with Grandma staring at him?

Cringing, he pointed at the date without a word, trying to keep his dignity, act cool, nonchalant, like it was no big deal.

But when the old woman covered her mouth and burst out laughing, he was ready to forget it all. However, Juanita's shy smile bathed in setting sunlight made him endure while the elderly lady went to the back and brought out something with a fresher date.

She said something to him in Navajo that he didn't totally catch. Something about breathing new life. But he wasn't trying to hang around to hear all of that. He paid for his purchase, collected the bag, said a quick thank-you, and walked out the door ahead of Juanita.

She jumped on the bike behind him, laughing. "Oh, my God."

"Yeah," he said, finding it hard to laugh. "Like I said, this ain't LA."

He heard her stomach growl so loud that he thought the motor was already on. "You hungry?" he asked, stomping down on the pedal and realizing how starved he was.

"Can we grab a couple burgers and take them back to the house?"

"Yeah, but there's no such thing as fast food out here. We can get burgers at the diner and have them boxed to go."

"Then let's ride," she said, snuggling against him and laughing.

He loved the sound of her voice through his skin.

The smell of meats cooking, milk shakes, and coffee was making his stomach contract with need. They sat outside on the small metal bike rail to escape the inside fans that just re-circulated heat, waiting for their order, which was slow to come. Even though there were only a few truckers sipping coffee inside, the process of getting a couple of pops, two burgers, and some fries seemed like it took forever. But somehow, when he was with her, just laughing and talking, time didn't matter so much.

"If I hadn't dropped my purse back in LA, I would have been able to help out in the store," she said merrily, swinging her legs back and forth.

"It's cool," Jose said, enjoying her smile. "Like we're in this adventure together and I'd do it anyway, even if you did have your purse."

"Yeah, but you've gotta keep your ride straight," she said, nodding toward the bike. "It's beautiful."

"Ain't mine," Jose admitted, jumping down off the rail to go run his hand over the gleaming handlebar. "It's just a loaner."

"Who loaned you a bike like that? I mean . . ."

"Now you sound like my mom," he said, chuckling.

"Look, I wasn't trying to go there, but a bike like that, Jose . . . I don't want you to get yourself caught up in any—"

"It's cool, but I like that you're more worried about me than a fly hog."

"My brother . . . he deals, okay? And his friends, they do, too. I never rode in their cars and went with them because—just because. I don't believe in it."

He studied her sad face in the shards of sunlight that were left, loving every word she'd said. The rose-orange tinge made her complexion so beautiful. The way the breeze blew her wind-dried hair and she repeatedly removed it from her face and licked her lips, growing nervous. If she had any idea what her caution had just done to him . . .

"Remember that old guitar player I told you about?"

She nodded but wasn't looking at him when she did.

"My people did him a favor, a long, long time ago . . . maybe I was like five or so."

Juanita glanced up.

"He rode into town on this machine, lady on the back of it, near dead from a demon bite—legend has it." Jose stood taller and walked around the bike, touching it with gentle caresses, like he'd approached a shrine. "She was the love of his life, and he brought her to her grandmother, who later married my pops, became my *abuela* by marriage."

"What happened to her?" Juanita said, quietly rapt.

"Pops and *Nana* made good magic, but she crossed over and became a spirit."

Juanita covered her mouth. "Oh no, she died?"

Jose nodded. "Fucked my mentor around, you know. Rider sorta stood in every now and then for my dad, who died real young." He stared at her, smoothing his hand across the seat. "Dude left here, went to go lose himself in a bottle for a while to get over the loss, then little by little, once a year, he'd come back all sick for my nana to heal him. After a few days, he'd hang around and chill out with me . . . tell me stuff about me having a nose like him—a schnoz, he called it." Jose looked at her, hoping she'd understand. "Said I was a tracker, and needed to learn how to shoot dead-aim. Then he'd get all weird about legends and shit, talking about my destiny . . . would start sounding like Pops."

"He must have been in a lot of pain."

Jose nodded, his eyes locked on her sad gaze. "Until I met you, I couldn't really get with how deep it was for him." He shrugged and looked out into the distance. "One day he said he wasn't coming back for a while. The year I graduated high school . . . said to keep his lady clean, talking about this silver and black beauty that purrs in your crotch. Said where he was going he didn't need a chopper." The hard memory got caught in the lump in Jose's throat behind his Adam's apple, and he drew in a shuddering breath to dislodge it. "It's been years— ain't seen or heard from him. I keep the bike clean, polished, hoping he didn't do something crazy like put a bullet in his skull. He'd said he was gonna go join a band, some warriors or something." Jose let a hard breath out. "Who knows?"

Juanita slid down off the rail and came to his side, her graceful hand touching his forearm. "You keep the bike clean for him, okay? He'll come back."

"It's cool," Jose said, kicking a pebble away from a tire. "I'm just glad you believe me and didn't think I got it dealing drugs, like my mother. Have it her way and she'd take it to the scrap metal yard." Jose walked around the bike, his fingers grazing surfaces. "This is a custom-kitted Harley that the man designed and funked out himself."

"It's beautiful," she murmured, not sure what to say as she watched him go inside himself and bleed.

"It's a fucking fingerprint, a one-of-a-kind work of art. It's in every drawing I do. Respect," he said, his gaze catching hers in a sudden trap. "He told me a story about how he'd rid- den this halfway across the country with his woman bleeding on it after a demon attack. Until I saw what we saw, I didn't believe him. I thought it was the bottle and bullshit talking. But that night, last night, when you were on the back of this night rider, all I kept doing was praying to God—'ride me like the night wind, let me make it without one of those things slashing my woman,' that was my prayer. 'Don't let me drop the bike on a spinout.' "

"You didn't drop me, and nothing touched me, Jose," she said in a near whisper.

He glanced up at the waning sun and then stared at her. "If something like that ever were to happen to you, I'd be messed up—just like him. And he told me some crazy shit, that I've never told another living soul . . . said to bring me back his bike and he'd buy me my own, when I was ready to go demon-hunting with him." Jose raked his hair. "Said I'd be coming into some special powers, would learn how to track a scent like a bloodhound. Would join some underground group of warriors who had to protect this chick called a Neteru, or something, whatever that is. Then Pops keeps saying that I have Thunderbird in me, whatever that shit means. All I know is, since last night, my nose is . . . it's like I can tell the time of day without a watch, and can separate out scents like a damned hunting beagle. I don't know what I'm trying to say; all I know is the burgers and fries are done—and I shouldn't know that!"

"Let's go get our food and go home," she said as calmly as possible. She used her voice as a gentle prod, not fully understanding Jose's angst but feeling everything he'd said in her marrow.

He seemed so bewildered that she simply threaded her arm around his waist and leaned her head on his shoulder, walking him toward the diner. But as they stood at the register and waited for their food to be bagged, her gaze locked with her reflection in the shiny aluminum panels above the kitchen pass-through.

Much older eyes stared back at her, frozen in time. A pair

of sensuous male hands slid down her arms, but she couldn't see his face . . . couldn't see anything in the shiny surface but could feel it. Smooth enamel caressed the side of her neck, making her shiver with revulsion but also with desire. She suddenly felt drowsy—drugged. Yet a part of her was so wired that she almost screamed in the diner.

Juanita rubbed her neck with the palm of her hand to stave off the feeling of something touching her there. She sought Jose's eyes, but he was staring out the window, gaze locked on the nothingness in the parking lot. His profile was tense, his jaw muscle pulsing. Looking at him, his skin, she was drawn into his pores as his face suddenly became constructed by thousands of black dots. Darkness swallowed her whole as she stood in the diner by the register. She wanted to scream, tried to cry out, but something had paralyzed her vocal cords, her limbs; she could barely breathe from the crushing weight that pressed the air from her lungs.

In the faraway part of her mind she could see herself standing next to Jose in the diner, people moving about in slow motion while the waitress bagged their food. But she couldn't move as the interior of her waged war, struggling to break free of the black dots that were beginning to blot out the waning sunlight around her. Instinct told her to stay in the light, not to allow her soul to be covered over. Then her sight line became trapped in an inky splatter—that's when she saw them. *The feeding.*

A scream threatened to split her lungs, yet it couldn't break free as she watched the fanged creatures kneel over their limp, drained kill, heads thrown back, bulbous red eyes glowing, mouths washed red with gore. They had infested victims, mating with the dead, with one another, all of it a frenzied orgy of feeding and the carnal. Writhing bodies were everywhere. One of the creatures lifted an ashen woman's neck, then looked at her and turned the victim's face so that it could be seen.

Juanita's eyes locked with an older version of her own as the fanged, naked entity smiled, then viciously sliced into the victim's jugular with his huge incisors. Juanita stopped breathing, the scream still lodged in her chest. Perspiration coursed down her back. Her nails dug into her palms. She could hear her own heartbeat as the pain in her chest chased her pulse. Stroke, heart attack, one or both of the above, she was quickly losing consciousness but fought to remain awake. She knew in her soul that if she passed out, they'd have her.

"Darlin', you all right? You want some water?" the waitress said, nearing the register. "You younguns gotta be careful and pace yourself in this heat."

Juanita reeled and Jose's attention snapped toward her just in time for him to catch her before she fell.

"She don't look so good," the woman behind the register said, rushing over with a glass of water.

"My bet she's pregnant or high," the cook grumbled, and then went back to the fryer baskets.

Juanita clutched Jose's T-shirt as he helped her to sit on a counter stool and sip water. "We need to get out of here," she rasped, gulping water and wiping at the rivulets of sweat coursing down her temples.

"You gonna be all right to ride?" Jose asked, looking concerned and glancing out the window at the waning sun.

"When's the last time you ate, hon?" the waitress asked, setting the food bags on the counter.

"That's all it is," Jose said, grabbing the satchels and helping Juanita up. "She just needs to get something in her stomach."

The moment Jose and Juanita were outside alone they both began talking at once while they hustled toward the bike and he handed her the greasy bags.

"I know, I know, it was freaky in there," he said, nerves clearly shot.

"I couldn't move, Jose! I was just standing there one

minute, then I started seeing this horrible stuff, blackness was covering me, and I was choking on—"

"Sulfur," Jose said, finishing her sentence.

"You saw it, too?" She clutched his waist with the bags still held in her fists as they hopped on the bike.

"I didn't see it; I smelled it," he muttered, and then stomped down hard to start the motor.

7

Warm air slapped his face as he rode hard, but he tried to keep the speed to a level where Juanita could hold on to his waist with one arm. She held the bags; he held the handlebar. He talked, hollering over the roar of the bike, trying to rationalize the irrational. She listened, soaking it all in, holding out hope that he was right—that what had happened in the diner was just a freaky aftershock effect brought on by suppressing what had happened the night before. It was an unrehearsed dance of trust through the wind, down the dirt road, the family house a destination of sanctuary. The moment they crossed the threshold, he felt better.

It was near dark and his nose was picking up every scent in the house and beyond it, but burgers, fries, and two Cokes were calling his name. Why he was so hungry was a question he didn't have time to ponder. They both tore into the bags, swiping fries, stuffing their mouths, relief glittering in their eyes as they sat down heavily on kitchen chairs.

"I'm starved," she said through a mouthful of food. "I don't know why, but I am. After all this I should be ready to puke."

"I know. Ridiculous," he said, wolfing a burger and then closing his eyes. "I could eat a horse."

Slowly calm began to settle over them as they sloppily ate, licking their fingers and practically inhaling their food. He wondered what it would have been like to meet her under different circumstances and was glad that he'd shared so much with her while they recovered between lovemaking sessions in bed. It was odd, now, that they could just vibe, didn't need to say much, but could read each other even though only having known each other for such a short time. She was so easy to talk to. It was as though he could tell her all his dreams—even the crazy ones about joining a band—and she didn't laugh at him. He quietly wondered how things like that happened but was glad that they did. More important, he just hoped that he was right about her vision in the diner being set off by the past, not the future.

"Good thing you didn't join a band like you'd wanted; they'd put you out for eating up the concert door draw," she finally said, smiling and watching him devour his food in record time.

He glanced up from his Styrofoam and smiled, knowing that she was making small talk to stave off the earlier case of nerves. "Hey, they wouldn't put their lead drummer out," he said, banging on the table in a riff.

"You're pretty good at that, hmmm . . . maybe they'd keep you."

"Used to practice for hours, banging on anything around the house to keep my chops right," he said with a wide smile and striking the table to keep the conversation light— anything to keep fear at bay. "Would watch all the college bands on TV and could mimic whatever they did in a day; love the drums. Would work at it for hours till I got it down cold . . . sweatin' and thumpin' on the coffee table. You'd be surprised, but to play the drums, you've gotta be in serious shape. It ain't as easy as it looks."

"For hours," she said with a sly smirk. "Now I know why you've got a hard, soldier's body, not a soft, artist's gut." She laughed and shook her head. "I've experienced the upper-body strength that comes from hours of beating on furniture . . . sweatin' and thumpin', as you say."

They both laughed.

"I'ma have to practice some more tonight," he said, shoving another bite of burger into his mouth and giving her a sexy wink. "Bought two boxes." He lifted an eyebrow. "That oughta hold us till daylight."

"Man, stop talking trash and eat your food!"

Knees touching beneath the table, feeding each other fries, glances going between food and the other bag from the drugstore, they laughed like little children who had stolen fresh-baked cookies. Finally sated, they both leaned back in their chairs and groaned.

"We should have done this hours ago," he said, rubbing his stomach.

"I kept trying to make you get up, but you wouldn't listen." She giggled as she sipped her Coke loudly through a straw.

"And that's *exactly* why I couldn't get up," he said with another wink, standing to fold away the greasy containers.

"What?" she said, playing with the straw, complete mischief on her face.

He stood by the trash can with a smile, his mind working on a comeback, when a shadow flitted by his peripheral vision. His smile faded. She set down the cup gingerly, her smile fading, too.

"Jose, what is it?" she whispered.

He held up his hand, sniffed, and caught a whiff of sulfur. His gaze immediately tore around the room for the rifle, and he went to it and cocked back the hammer. "I saw something."

She stood, almost toppling her chair. "What was it?" she said in a fast, harsh whisper.

"I don't know, but it went past the side window." He stood

legs wide, braced toward the window, and then backed up to keep her behind him.

A thud on the porch made her cover her mouth in a silent scream. He held up his hand and shook his head, begging her with his mind not to shriek. Whatever it was had the same smell as the things that had chased them. The dank odor of rotting meat and sulfuric ash created a slurry of nausea in his gut. What had gone wrong? Pops and Nana had said the house was safe! Strong medicine was supposed to protect it. Panic-induced sweat made his T-shirt stick to him. But there was something else roiling in his system, something lethal and inspired by adrenaline.

"I'm going outside," he murmured, his voice a low growl.

Two small fists clung to the back of his shirt. "Oh no, the hell you aren't!"

"I'm damned sure not waiting for it to come in here and get us." Jose looked at her hard. "The sun just set; we've got twelve hours till daylight."

"Then we can just freaking wait in here for twelve hours with the lights on and live!" she whispered furiously through her teeth. "My momma said to pray the demons away!"

Another thud hit the porch, and then another sounded above them on the roof.

"You really think so?" he asked, shrugging out of her hold. "You stay here and pray while I blow the bastards off the porch."

Something insane had been embedded in his DNA, as he broke from Juanita's hold and stood by the door, opening it slowly, and then kicking it wide, gun barrel out first. She ducked down beneath the sofa and covered her head, and the moment he quickly peeked out, a hideous face with drool-slicked fangs leaned in. It was pure reflex. Dead-aim, center of the creature's head, and green gook splattered the porch with the shot. The smell of demon blood entered Jose's sinuses, connecting with a craziness encoded in his system like he'd never known.

Juanita's shriek blended in with hisses and snarls coming around the sides of the house. He ran to the steps and jumped down them into the front yard, spinning to catch an airborne predator in the center of its chest with a shell midflight. Two more creatures scampered over the flat rooftop and leaped, claws extended. Jose was down on one knee in seconds, pulled the trigger, and no shot rang out. But he held his position, gouging into the heart of the first beast as it attempted to land on him, then yanked hard to extract the rifle barrel and slammed the other one's skull with the gun butt.

Piles of smoking ash were all around him. He was pure motion. The thing that had fallen from the gun butt was only temporarily dazed. He needed more artillery!

Jose hit the front door and slammed it, hearing the thing behind him crash through the door. Kitchen knives in both hands, he flung them, sending blades into a yellow-green-skinned chest. Smoke and a sulfuric stench were everywhere. He could hear Juanita screaming, couldn't see her, but could smell her. He reached out, grabbed her arm, and hustled her through the house out the back door.

"Stop resisting; the house is about to be overrun!" he hollered.

"Not in the dark, not outside!" she shrieked.

He didn't have time to argue, just simply dragged her until she got with the program. She looked back and the windows were blackened by the unnatural infestation. Black ooze poured out of windows and cracks in the frame as Jose and Juanita ran across the open lot in a hundred-yard dash toward a rickety old shed. Once inside, Jose barred the door.

"*Now*, start praying," he said, yanking down a crossbow, loading it with silver stakes, and then opening the door wide.

He got the first creature that materialized in the chest, exploded it, and slammed the door shut again. Juanita stood cringing against the wall saying the Lord's Prayer between sobs.

"Say it like you mean it, sister!" Jose hollered. "Put authority in your tone, and back this shit up!" He whirled around, eyes wild. "Not on my land! Not in my grandfather's house! Not when I'm with my woman!"

A bowie knife went into his back jeans pocket, and he shoved a jug of water toward Juanita, frantic. "Get away from the walls; the boards are loose. Anything that comes near it can scratch you—splash the mutha, and get it away from the walls!"

She nodded, her face streaked with tears, and the moment a demon tried to get its claws between a loose board she screamed and flung a large splash against the wall. Horrible screeches and hisses became one with the smell of burning, rotted flesh.

"Keep praying—loud," Jose commanded, his gaze going to the ceiling, his nose instant radar.

Reloading the crossbow, he sniffed, took aim, and blew a hole through the roof, and a screeching, squealing demon dropped into the center circle on the shed floor, then caught flame. Spinning wildly, the thing on the floor reached to grab Jose's leg in a death cry, but a bowie knife ended the creature's suffering the instant Jose flung the knife down hard.

"Douse the bastard," he said to Juanita, who was clutching the water jug to her chest. "Do it now!"

She flung water at the thing from where she stood, hiccupcrying. Jose's attention went to the walls, sensing, smelling, and then a low, threatening voice laughed quietly outside the shed.

"You're one of us," it hissed. "Vampire. Distant cousin. A very young one, but the nose is a dead giveaway. You love the night, just like we do. It makes you stronger, just like the female in your lair made you fearless. We'll be back to finish this another time, half-breed. Maybe next time you'll get a nick or a scratch, perhaps a little bite, that will make you lose your human stink."

Drums and car horns crashed into the yard. Headlights lit the shed from the outside. Chants and voices, torches, were one.

What the demon had said made Jose's blood run cold. It had to be bullshit, because he could touch silver, stand in a prayer circle, endure the white sagebrush and sacred anointing water.

Jose opened the shed door, and a ring of pickup trucks filled with old men and women who had hands raised, pumping shakers, surrounded them. One-by-one they calmly climbed down from the vehicles dressed in full ceremonial garb, feathered headdresses bouncing as they stomped the dried grass under the moonlight and made a circle. Spitting and lighting fire to the ground, they walked with blind purpose, not even looking at Jose or Juanita. Women dropped bundles of sticks and sagebrush in the ring of dirt until it roared and sputtered with fury. Jose held Juanita close to him, a crossbow at his side at the ready.

His grandfather stopped and spoke first, addressing the spiritual war dancers in Creek, then Navajo, and then finally looked at Jose and Juanita.

"It is time to join the circle," the old man said as the drumming quieted and the chants subsided. "Under the silver of the full moon, learn your true destiny, young warriors. . . . Clan of the ancient Thunderbird, step forward."

Frozen where he stood, Jose gripped Juanita closer to his side.

"She is from the clan of the nighthawk and has seer eyes that understand the darkness. But you must step forward first."

Reluctant and glancing up at the shed roof to ensure no predators would harm her, Jose left Juanita to walk forward a few paces to stand before his grandfather.

A gentle, calloused hand petted Jose's face as a shaker hissed in his ear, and then his grandfather began a slow, stomping circle around him, dusting his body with a handful of eagle feathers, chanting in a deep tone he'd know in his sleep.

The drumming stopped when his grandfather stopped to face him. "Young warrior, they came for you early, because they sensed it was time when you left the house to go to town, son." Tears made his grandfather's eyes glisten in the moonlight. "The prophecy begins. . . . It will be hard, but we have made good medicine for you."

The circle shifted, and women shamans collected Juanita to make her stand by Jose before the roaring fire. Embers rose and carried on the wind like red-flecked fireflies. The silence created a natural harmony as fragrant sticks and twigs crackled and popped, and coyotes howled in the distance. Jose's grandfather waved two women forward; one was Jose's nana. The women came with bowls of oily water for Jose's grandfather to dip the feathers he clutched into, and he violently splashed the liquid across Jose's and Juanita's chests as though exorcising demons.

"Legend is truth; truth becomes legend. Without one the other cannot endure. We go back in time, many moons," he said as Native American flutes filled the quiet around them. "Eight generations ago, when the buffalo were plentiful, and the wolf could shift into man-skin and still run with packs at each full moon, it began on this land."

He paused and splashed Jose and Juanita with more of the strange liquid. Jose touched his chest with his fingertips as the substance started to make his skin tingle. He looked at Juanita and her lids were heavy. Instinct made him reach for her to hold her upright as she weaved a bit, appearing flushed and faint. The scent from the ministrations was strong, but he couldn't place it. He just prayed it wasn't some serious tribal hallucinogen, but everything was becoming hazy and his body felt too warm. Jose rubbed his eyes with his fists, seeing double. There was a ghostly layer of bluish-white aura around the old men and women in the circle, and his eyes went in and out of focus as it seemed like transparent forms of spirits wafted among the living, standing elders.

"A young warrior, our ancestor, was out chasing the shapeshifters . . . and he was attacked in battle by another beast." The old man paused and flung more oily water at Jose. "The beast with two fangs. The one that can only witness the shadows of the night. But the warrior was strong and did not die from his wounds."

The old man began chanting again and the drums accompanied his dance around the circle until he stopped and stared at the young couple once more.

"He sired many children, and only one lived to pass his seed to the next generation and then the next, all others dying young of blood diseases or sterile . . . then through the generations times eight you were born. Like your ancestor, part tracker, part the night itself. One day you will hunt what almost destroyed all generations to come. You will stand by one like yourself, a blood brother."

Jose's grip tightened on his crossbow. His mind was on fire like the inferno on the ground. Hot tears stung his eyes. What was his grandfather saying? He was a vampire, or part one, the undead! He didn't realize he was backing up and shaking his head until he almost bumped into another old brave. But Jose's grandfather's eyes held patience and such loving compassion that it made him swallow hard and stop.

"It is a gift," his grandfather whispered, his aged eyes holding Jose's gaze. "You can hold the sacred instruments of cleansing," he said, pointing to the silver stake in the crossbow. "You went into the place that is guarded by the Great Spirit," he added, motioning toward the shed with a wave of eagle feathers, "and the sunlight smiles in your hair. Do not fear. What you received from our ancestor is the best of the beast, making you a strong warrior—like the hunter who kills the bear but gains his strength. This is why you, alone, could defend a house from invasion. We had to see and know before we could complete the prophecy."

The old shaman moved the feathers about and used them to point to Juanita. "Your eyes will also guide him. You see through dreams and are his soul mate. You feed his hunger for the flesh and for the blood by living rhythm. . . . he needs you, like you need him. But you will also have the quest to find his blood brother with your night eyes, and bring them together as one."

"Rider's dead," Jose whispered. "He never came back for his bike. She'd never know where to find him."

"Rider is the brother of your soul, and lives," Jose's grandfather said quietly. "You will soon bring the bike to him. Your blood brother is younger than you, but older in spirit, and does not have the fangs yet, but soon will. . . . She is to wait with him until that happens."

Juanita shook her head and backed up to grab Jose's arm. "I'm not looking for vampires by *myself*!"

"You are to hold the place and hold the line for the coming female warrior, the Neteru, who will slay him the way you have slain the inner beast within my grandson," the old man said without blinking. "It is prophecy."

"He will come to you and trust only you for a while before the blood hunger hits . . ." Jose's grandmother said softly, touching Juanita's arm. "But Jose will come back for you, once the prophecy is complete. It is out of our hands; the ancestors have spoken. Your eyes will be blinded, but soon the second sight will reveal your purpose, child. Do not fear the wisdom of the ancient ones."

"We ain't breaking up; that's all there is to it. As soon as the sun comes up, we're out. I'm going to art school; she's going to college with me. I'm not living my life in this madness—you can forget that!"

Jose grabbed Juanita around the waist and raised a crossbow toward the patient souls who simply stared at them.

"When that which is within comes to the fore," his grand-father said in a quiet, serene tone, "you will be reunited. You were her first, and marked her soul with pure love. She was your first, the first to see you as a true warrior. That marked your soul with pure love. The darkness cannot eclipse a sun so bright."

"I don't care what you say; we're not breaking up so she can go hunting demons alone and I can go on some bullshit quest!" Jose shouted, staring at his grandfather and trying to stay on his feet.

"I'm not leaving him," Juanita whispered, holding Jose's waist tighter as she swooned. "I won't!"

"When the full moon calls the coyote and the demon is ash," his nana whispered, "then you will have each other again."

"When the sun draws your blood brother to dance with an-cient spirits . . . only when you step into the darkness without fear, and a light within burns brighter than that, will you taste your memory of this time." His grandfather began walking in a circle, touching the feathers to the ground. "It is done."

Shakers hissed; a slow drumbeat began. The flutes lilted a sad wail.

His grandfather's voice felt so far away, and Jose struggled to remain standing. He brushed the wet surface of his T-shirt and battled for consciousness.

"It is on your lips, the Thunderbird. Take back the night," a cacophony of faraway voices murmured. "Then it will fill your mouths and lungs to breathe new life again, and you will be home once more."

The last thing he remembered was having a very bad dream. His mother stood over him with her arms folded. Sunlight poured into the bedroom within their apartment. Bleary-eyed, Jose stared up at her frown and then blocked his eyes from the sun's glare. The taste of sulfur and a burger, dead meat, was stuck to the back of his tongue, nauseating him. The scent of white sagebush and campfire smoke clung to his clothes. Jose sat up quickly. The scent of a woman was a whispering memory from his pillow.

"Now that you're back home, don't you waste all day sleeping—you hear me, Jose?"

He stood, his eyes burning with tears. "Momma, how long was I gone?"

"Stop playing games with me, and clean up this place, at least, while I'm at work! I'm late and don't have time for your foolishness first thing in the morning." She strode to the door with her purse over her shoulder. Turning to him once, she glanced back. "Don't forget to put in an application to vo-tech school, all right?"

As his mother left, Jose just stood very, very still, watching the door. Drums were in his head; a sketch pad called out to him. There was an image stabbing into his brain. He finally had the rest of the face for the mystery woman in his dreams, but for the life of him wasn't sure why.

"Baby, this time I thought you were real," he whispered, and swallowed hard, his tongue tasting tears.

Juanita awoke from the sofa with a start at the sound of her baby brother's cries. She sat up slowly, scratching her head, and looked down at her red halter, remembering the party she never got to attend. Her mother's slap stung like a very old wound, and Juanita rubbed her face as the toddler wailed. She briefly closed her eyes, and for some unknown reason tears wet her lashes. The dream had been so vivid, so horrible, and yet so wondrous. He'd finally taken off his helmet, the fantasy lover in her dreams . . . and his eyes had been the most intense, gentle brown. He'd held her with sweet innocence and so much love.

She covered her mouth to keep from sobbing out loud and then ran up the steps to fetch the bleating child. She picked her little brother up from the crib as he stretched his arms out to her, and she hugged him, crying into his soft curly brown hair. "You be my hero, okay, *Papi*?" she whispered. "Mine only comes to me in my dreams."

EPILOGUE

Arizona, present day

Jose sat on the porch rail of his grandfather's house, his gaze on the horizon, his nose catching the fragrance of wildflowers on the early dawn wind. The smell of Jack Daniel's filtered into the layers of fragrances, and he didn't even have to look over his shoulder to know that Rider was moving through the house toward him.

So much time had passed, and yet there was subtle comfort in knowing that the entire Guardian team had been built body by body, each of the twenty-one members of the squad leaving something cherished behind to give of themselves to the world.

Warriors. Band to move about the country by day, demon killers by night. His art now was the weapons disguised as stage mounts. His dreams of personal freedom were long dead, like his mother and grandparents.

"Morning, partner," Rider said, bringing Jose a cup of coffee and handing it to him.

"Thanks, man." Jose took the coffee and let the aroma enter his sinuses.

"Least I can do for the shift change. You need a little

something extra in it this morning?" Rider asked, reaching into his back jeans pocket, extracting a silver flask, and pouring a healthy splash of Jack Daniel's into his own mug.

"Naw, I'm all right, man," Jose said, slurping his coffee but keeping his eyes on the horizon.

Rider leaned on a porch support beam and studied Jose with concern. "Dude, you've been up all night. It's daybreak. Shift change. You get to go to bed. That's how it works. Then, tomorrow night, some other poor SOB gets to sit up, walk point, and have his nerves screwed until dawn so a couple of us can get some rest and sleep with one eye open, watching the team newbies."

Jose gave Rider a sidelong glance. "I don't feel like going inside; is that all right with you?"

Rider held up a hand and his mug in front of his chest. "My apologies. My bad, as they say. Awful testy this cheerful sunny day, though, I might add."

"The house is overrun with warriors—it's like a damned army barracks in there," Jose said, slinging his legs over the rail and sloshing coffee on the porch as he stood. "That's not how it used to be. The bull is working my nerves."

"Let's me and you take a walk out of earshot, huh?"

"I'm cool, just need to get my head right this morning, is all."

Rider poured a long trickle of Jack Daniel's into Jose's mug and then capped his flask with a smirk. "That's why we should take a walk. Have your morning coffee and humor me."

"I ain't in the mood."

"Then keep me from accidentally dropping a lit cigarette as we walk and talk."

Jose sighed and obliged his longtime friend. What was the point in arguing with the insufferable Jack Rider anyway? The man couldn't be dissuaded by insults, and at nearly fifty, maybe older, Jack Rider was as rusty as an old barn nail. Jose began walking. He needed space. Rider hung back, lit a

Marlboro Red, and shoved the pack back into his jeans, catching up to Jose in long, lanky strides.

"So, she's back."

Jose stopped walking and just looked at Rider for a moment. "Yeah."

"Old bedroom is calling your name, but she's a brand-new Guardian on newbie lockdown—no fraternizing until all her powers of second sight come in full force, according to the house seer, the inimitable Marlene Stone. I take it that you're in such a foul mood, my friend, on account of the fact that Juanita needs to be judicious in her *experiences* until her third eye and special demon-hunting powers fully develop?"

Jose began walking again, taking a deep swig of his coffee.

Rider kept stride as his paces increased. "And the house now has a bunch of demon hunters in it, chasing the best memories of your life out the window."

Jose stopped walking. Rider's eyes held his without blinking.

"Been there," Rider said, then took a long drag on his cigarette and slurped his coffee. "Only my soul mate died. Went vamp, lives somewhere this side of hell, and I had to deal with it. Conversely, yours is in the house, alive, with her memory coming back by very fast degrees." He took another drag and studied the glowing ember, speaking to it in a philosophical tone. "Don't let the fact that she had to complete her mission to go bring your old line brother to us be a problem. Why stand on some old machismo ceremony? Bottom line is, *you* were her first; only a seer female could have smoked him out, blocked him from going after the Neteru before she was old enough to deal with a male with a lotta vamp in his veins."

Rider looked up from his cigarette and stared at Jose hard when he didn't respond. "The demon went to ash, *hombre*. You held his ashes. Dude crossed over and danced with the ancient spirits and went into the Light. Your skills came to the fore lovely, and you ain't scared of the dark, like you were when you were a kid. Embrace the opportunity. Embrace change."

Rider took in a deep inhale of fresh morning air when Jose looked away. "You're a nose like me—*smell it*. Change is in the air."

Jose glared at him from the corner of his eye. "That was seventeen years ago. A lot's changed. So? We ain't the same people we were."

"I might be several years your senior, but don't let this old Kentucky boy from a trailer park fool you. Smoke and booze ain't killed my schnoz." Rider gave him a sheepish smile. "What did the old man say? *Taste* your memory?" Rider chuckled and began walking back toward the house. "If you ask me, I'd damned sure let the Thunderbird be on my lips this morning, bro."

Screw the fate of the world; his was shattered. Jose stood in the driveway, his back to Rider, refusing to let his elder Guardian warrior brother see him slowly inhale the fragrance he knew in his sleep. His nostrils flared ever so slightly as Juanita's delicate scent wafted out from the house. Hurling the mug away, he refused to give into that delirium-producing connection. She'd awakened wanting him and was wet. He could separate that out from the thousands of other scents that barraged his senses, but none like hers could compete for his attention.

The night before had been an enigma . . . Juanita's memory had come back with a vengeance, and their reunion had been heated and grasping, urgent, frenetic, out in the depths of the night shadows while walking point. But now, standing in the driveway with the cold light of day facing him, what did that mean, really?

Her second sight hadn't fully come in; she was still in boot-camp early demon-hunting training. Another man had spent years with her, and how many lovers before that? The ancestors had robbed him of time and freedom, had stolen away what should have been. Yet in the quiet recesses of his soul he knew there was no other way. The demons would have relentlessly hunted him and Juanita down as an untrained pair and killed them if they'd run. It was their destiny to come into this group of night hunters—strength in numbers for those who shared this twisted but sacred path. The young female Neteru, the vampire huntress, had become his friend, his charge, almost his lover, and like all the other soldiers on the squad, his job was to be a defensive line so she could hunt.

The sweet fragrance from the house was beginning to make his hands tremble. Jose dug into his jeans pocket to find his Hummer keys. He was out. This morning he was off duty. But the strengthening scent made him look up to the porch. He couldn't move as Juanita stood in the door frame, a white cotton sundress slightly billowing around her shapely legs from the breeze. She said nothing as she opened the screen and walked toward him, spilling violet and baby powder and ready female fragrance in her wake.

"Hey," she murmured, tossing her long brunette hair over her shoulder. "You going into town?"

"Yeah. Just need to take a ride and get some air."

She descended the steps slowly, her flat sandals padding softly. "Mind if I tag along?"

Jose shrugged and opened the vehicle door. "Whatever."

She climbed into the vehicle next to him from the passenger's side and touched his arm. "Last night . . ."

"Was last night," he said, turning on the motor and shifting the gears into reverse.

"We need to talk," she finally said, resting her hand on his as he gripped the wheel.

They rode into town in silence. Good. What was there to say? At least she'd removed her hand from his, but his skin still burned where her caress had grazed him. The moment he pulled into the diner parking lot, he angrily put the vehicle into park and turned off the motor.

"All right, 'Nita," he practically shouted. "Talk. Get it over with."

"Last night was . . . the beginning."

He looked at her hard and then sent his gaze out of the driver's side window. "You're still in love with him. Too much time passed, the shaman medicine wore off too slowly, and I dealt with you not being in my life this long. I'm cool."

"Tell me last night didn't mean anything to you," she whispered.

The sound of her voice made him look at her. He could smell the salty, hot tears in her eyes before he'd even turned.

"Tell me what it meant," she said, swallowing hard. "All this time has passed and now—"

"Time passed," he said, fighting not to breathe her in. "You're a soldier; I'm a soldier. You met others and fell in love; so did I. We ain't kids no more."

"Then your memory didn't fully come back," she said, her voice low and urgent.

"My memory never fully left," he said, gazing at the way her figure had become even more voluptuous with age, her dark eyes more smoky and sultry. "Do you know how many years I chased the phantom memory of your scent? Your touch . . . your voice?" His gaze held hers in broken fury as his voice hitched when he spoke. "But you went to a master vampire, like it was nothing . . . didn't even—"

"Stop it!" she yelled. "It was nothing? He wasn't a vampire then and turned later, and it was part of my duty to keep him locatable. But what the hell do you think drew me to him!"

"The shaman—"

"No!" she cried, tears glittering but not falling. "He had your eyes! The voice, a vampire line brother's seductive whisper. I had been looking for you way down in my soul and found your near double!" She dragged her fingers through her hair and turned away, her voice going soft. "Just like you found my near double, time and time again, until you found me."

Shame stole the words from his mouth. He reached out to gently push the hair behind her ear, but she yanked it away.

"When I saw you in that cathedral," he murmured, "and you still didn't know me yet, I thought I would put my own nine to my skull."

She unfolded her arms and turned to him. "We'd just been chased into a corner on hallowed ground. . . . I didn't know it was you, at first."

He breathed in deeply and let the quiet shudder pass. "But you were so angry at me," he whispered. "You kept saying I'd left you, when that's not what happened, and then you pushed me away for months while we traveled back here . . . and for a while, even here, it was like I was some old, platonic friend."

She covered her mouth and inhaled sharply to hold back the sob. Slowly lowering her hand, she spoke toward the window. "It came back in snatches of memory. All I remembered was the pain of you leaving me, and I didn't know what I'd done wrong."

"Do you know how I felt when I first saw you again? That feeling that tore out my guts . . . felt like I'd been dropped from the twentieth floor in an elevator with no stops. My stomach was in my throat."

She turned and stared at him, wiping at her face.

"Your hair was all over your head. Your eyes panicked. It brought it all back, and here I was standing in a cathedral, armed, vampires on our asses, and all I wanted to do was hold you . . . but you didn't even know who I was."

Her hand reached out and cupped his cheek, and he turned his mouth into it to kiss it hard, covering her hand.

"And every day that I waited for you to remember, I lost a piece of my soul. Every day that I smelled your freshly washed hair, or saw it catch sunlight . . . or heard you laugh, watched you move around the house that we'd shared for one glorious day . . . I lost a piece of my soul. Every time I'd pass you in what's now become a safe-house barracks, and couldn't touch you to pull you into the bathroom or my old bedroom . . . each time that happened, something in me died, 'Nita." He caressed her face with one trembling finger. "Have you any idea what it does to me when I hear you take a shower? I have to literally leave the house."

"I remember," she whispered, moving closer and gently kissing his forehead. She brushed back his hair and then kissed the bridge of his nose.

"I was so angry at you," he whispered, and closed his eyes.

"I know," she murmured into his mouth.

"I don't want to *ever* feel that kind of pain again," he admitted quietly, ending the kiss but enfolding her in his arms. "Not when I love you like this."

"I swear to you, Jose, my memory is fully back. I love you so much. I'm not going anywhere ever again."

She immediately deepened the kiss, her hands tracing wide shoulders that had filled out with disciplined training routines, had been hardened by war and broadened by age and experience. Memory ignited within her touch, burning them both with bittersweet awareness of what they'd had and what they'd missed and everything in between that they'd been robbed of. His hands made fists in her hair, his tongue dueling with hers in a fire dance. Then he suddenly tore his mouth from hers as though a man drowning and dragged his jaw up her neck to whisper an urgent message in her ear.

"Just the scent of your bare skin drives me out of my mind; I can smell you in the house, tell when you're wet, know when you're moving around—I can't even train with you on the mats!" he said between his teeth. "You sweat, I inhale it, and then I have to be with you." He took her mouth again and punished it, breaking to gasp out his complaint. "Do you know how many nights I rode my bike around in circles all over Los Angeles, trying to track you on the night wind? Do you know! Then when I found you, you were with *him* and didn't know me?"

His intensifying passion sent her hands up his back. The need to have him recoup all the time that had slipped by made her pull him against her and roughly seek his mouth. She didn't care if all-night diner patrons walked by and raised an eyebrow. Didn't care that the windows had become fogged or that the air conditioner at full blast did little to cool the vehicle cabin. She had her first lover in her arms, her memory clear, the taste of him exquisite, and the Thunderbird was on his lips.

"I know you now, and won't ever forget," she said in a rushed, hot murmur against his neck.

"Don't leave me again," he whispered in gulps, crushing her against the seat. "Not even to die. Especially not that." He kissed her hard, sought her neck, his hands a coating of pleasure over the swell of her breasts till she gasped. "Don't ever forget how much I love you or how long I waited to find you again."

They were both crying, kisses cutting off sobs . . . thick, salty emulsion sheathing battling tongues, breaths hitched by emotion and intermittently halted by gasps.

"Take me somewhere quiet for the day, and I'll remind you of what I'd forgotten," she whispered, splaying her hands against his spine. "Let me show you there, in private, all day, what I had locked in my head . . . within nearly twenty years of deferred dreams." She nipped his neck until he groaned deep within his chest. "Let's make some brand-new memories."

He just nodded, swallowed hard, broke from the kiss, and started the engine, headed for the local motel with no name.

THE GIFT

by

Susan Squires

1

London, March 1820

"Rufford's done it! The bitch goddess is dead." Admiral Groton, in charge of the government's intelligence effort, waved a sheet of foolscap written in a masculine hand. He stood in front of huge windows that gave onto a rainy Whitehall Lane lined with the offices of the most powerful government in the world.

Relief washed over Major Vernon Davis Ware, Davie to his intimates. It was worth putting off his appointment with Miss Fairfield just to hear those welcome words. An image of Asharti rose to his mind, impossibly beautiful, her eyes gone red and deadly, her breasts brushing his bare chest. . . . He would not think of her. He had banished those dreadful weeks in El Golea when he was in her power from his memory. Now she was dead and all he wanted was a normal life. He was going to offer for Miss Emma Fairfield today and become a government servant in some boring diplomatic post with an intelligent and beautiful wife, if she would have him. And, God willing, he'd sire a family.

"I didn't think Rufford would prevail," Davie breathed. "He's well?"

"Who do you think penned the letter?" The only other occupant of the room was the Lord High Chancellor of England. The skin over the Chancellor's jowls was paper-thin and spotted with age. "Rufford has averted a world cataclysm."

The Admiral cleared his throat and frowned. His face, tanned from years at sea, had deep creases around his mouth. He was no stranger to worry. "The disaster is not yet averted."

"But the vampire woman is dead." It was unbecoming in a Lord High Chancellor to pout, but so it was.

The Admiral sighed. "Remember, Your Lordship, that these vampires have something in their blood . . . what did you say it was, Ware?"

Davie cleared his throat. "I'm not sure, sir. I only know its effect, and the fact that it can be passed through exchanging blood."

"Monsters," the Chancellor muttered under his breath. "They're monsters."

"Are plague victims all monsters?" Davie asked, in spite of the fact that he was questioning the Lord High Chancellor of England. "If the world is saved, Rufford will have saved it."

"The point is they can infect humans and make them vampire, too," the Admiral reminded his superior. "Asharti made an army of them. We're not out of the woods yet."

"But see here, Groton," the Chancellor protested. "You said Rufford and others . . . like him . . . they're on a campaign to wipe out her army. If he can kill Asharti, surely they can track down the ones who are newly made. You said they weren't as strong at first, didn't you, Ware?"

"Yes, I did, but they are still stronger than humans. And like a plague, they can spread." Davie managed a lopsided grin. "I wouldn't want to be in North Africa for a while."

The Admiral cleared his throat. "Yes, well. Rufford has requested the assistance of the British government. And he specifically asked for you."

It was Davie's turn to frown. His stomach churned. "What

do you mean?" He glanced from one to the other. The Chancellor wouldn't meet his eyes but paced to the window. Rain battered the panes in curtains. All his years sat upon the Chancellor's shoulders.

The Admiral had rather more courage. He fixed Davie with a steely stare. "We're to provide provisions and equipment. But their campaign requires someone who can move about in daylight to provide logistics. He wants someone who already knows what they are."

"No." Every fiber rebelled against returning to North Africa. "I'm going to make an offer of marriage today."

"Our future depends upon the outcome of this struggle, Ware." The Chancellor sounded almost remote. He clasped his hands behind his back as he stared at the street below. "He didn't ask for armies or navies. He didn't ask for Wellington. He asked only for you."

Damn Rufford! "What happens in North Africa does not concern us." He couldn't go back there for so many reasons, Miss Fairfield for one and memories of Asharti for another.

"Really?" The Admiral's acid tone cut through Davie's excuses. "And is that why you demanded our fastest cutter to take Rufford to Casablanca in the first place? Surely you thought the consequence was important to England, since we mustered every resource to send him on what we thought was a suicide mission. He went. He prevailed. And now he asks for our help, and yours."

Davie closed his eyes.

"You've got a box full of medals somewhere even if you don't choose to wear them in the drawing rooms of London." The Chancellor turned back to Davie. "After Waterloo you joined the diplomatic corps, so you've served your country several times. This is our most critical hour, not only as Englishmen, but as humans. Don't fail us now."

"We need to know what's going on down there, Ware!" The Admiral punched his fist into his other palm. "Of course we want battlefield dispatches, but we must keep an eye on Rufford and his kind as well. Do you think I sleep well at night knowing there are monsters living among us? Whatever you may say about them being victims, they're immortal, for Christ's sake, or nearly! They're unnaturally strong. They can disappear into thin air and they drink human blood. Perhaps worst of all, they can control minds. And for all his courage and his service to date, Ian Rufford is one of them. We need intelligence, Ware! What are their vulnerabilities? Who directs them?" He strode forward, his pale gray eyes boring into Davie. "So far, the only way to subdue one of them is with another one. Not something that gives me comfort, Ware."

So, they wanted to help Rufford but spy on him into the bargain. Well, Davie wanted none of it. "I won't go back there." He made his voice as flat as possible. "Rufford doesn't need my help. Good day, gentlemen." He turned on his heel as they exchanged glances.

"We'll be in touch," the Chancellor called after him.

Damn Rufford! Davie thought again as he pushed out into Whitehall Lane. He paused in the pillared portico of the Admiralty, only half-aware that the rain had stopped. He stared at the gaudy squadron of Horse Guards that trooped down the street.

It *was* that important that Asharti's minions be stopped. Only Rufford and his kind could do it. Did he know for certain Rufford *didn't* need his help to do the job? The man was true at the center, though Asharti had made him into a monster who drank human blood. If he trusted Davie enough to ask him for help . . . Davie sucked in the wet March air and slowly let it out. He remembered Rufford's own moment of decision, when he had known he would return to North Africa to face Asharti. . . . Davie had seen the despair in Rufford's eyes, the fear, and the certainty. Davie's dream of stability dissolved into memories of his time in El Golea . . .

El Golea, 1819

He shouldn't go to her. He knew that, somewhere deep inside himself. The jasmine that dripped from the pergola drenched the night in a flowery musk, but it could not obscure the scent of cinnamon and something else, exotic and sweet, that she exuded. He could barely see her in the darkness of the British compound courtyard. The thick-walled rooms that surrounded it were empty now. She had killed the legation, drained them of blood. They, at least, were at peace.

Only he was left. Why had she spared him? So he could serve her, night after night? He staggered out into the court-yard. No light shone from the surrounding windows, though her creatures were there, drinking and eating in the darkness. He heard their murmuring voices. He had nothing to fear from them. They dared not molest him. That was left to her. His gen-itals grew heavy with need. Revulsion washed over him. She commanded and his body obeyed.

The stars lit the night along with the sliver of a smirking moon. Ahead, her lithe form was a darker smear of black against the night. Though her back was turned, she knew he was there. Her hair, heavy and dark, cascaded down her back over the diaphanous fabric that barely concealed her form. Her garment might look gray in the darkness, but he would wager it was red.

He touched her shoulder. Her flesh was hot with energy. She turned. Her beauty struck him like a blow, as always. Her dark eyes, lined with kohl, glowed red. All thought of escape vanished. He knelt, knees wide, as she required. He was erect and ready. She bent over him and cupped his jaw.

"I have a task for you, my pretty," she whispered. "Well, two tasks."

He lifted his lips to her nipple and suckled through the sheer fabric.

Davie blinked against the spatter of raindrops as a last shower flapped against the paving stones of the Admiralty court. The shame of that time stayed with him even as the memories drained away. From the distance of London, and three months' time, he knew why he'd been left alive to serve and suffer. He alone had known where Rufford was. Rufford was the only one with a drop of the ancient blood, the only one who had a chance to best her. Davie had betrayed Rufford to her. He swallowed and Whitehall blurred before his eyes. It must be the rain. She could compel . . . anything—information, sexual service, *anything.*

Davie's jaw worked. She had sent him with a letter all the way to England, threatening all Rufford loved, knowing that would bring the man back to the North African desert, and into her clutches once again. Davie's ability to act as messenger was all that saved him from Asharti.

What did he not owe Rufford for that betrayal?

And he *had* sworn service to his country. What greater need could there ever be? No matter that he would be plunging into the middle of a war between what the world called monsters. His need for normalcy after his time with Asharti did not signify.

His shoulders sagged as he knew what he would do. Fear trembled down his spine. He'd thought he'd left behind the cursed sand of the North African desert forever. He was wrong.

And now he must disappoint the woman he loved and blight all chance for happiness.

Emma Fairfield sat in the breakfast room that looked out over the tiny back garden at Fairfield House in Grosvenor Square. The room was cheerful, its pale yellow walls and light Chippendale furniture a contrast with the bleak March rain that beat against the arched windows. Emma was arranging roses in a crystal vase. She managed to grow roses most of the year in the fourth-floor solarium, oranges, too, and peonies brought back from China by her great-uncle. He had been a true adventurer, the black sheep of the family. He was a rebel. Was that why she always liked him best? This bouquet was multicolored, some blossoms well opened, some mere buds. Creamy peach and white mixed with bloodred and pale pink in chaotic abundance.

"I thought we were going to receive a visit from that young man of yours," her brother said as he snapped the *London Mail* into new folds. They liked to sit here of an afternoon, rather than in the larger, formal rooms at the front of the house. Her brother was some ten years older than she was. He had never married. He never would.

"You might call him by name, Richard," she said calmly, clipping a stem with a small garden shears. "We've known Davie Ware since we were children. And he isn't mine. One doesn't own young men. He isn't even that young."

"Neither are you, Emma." Richard drew his handsome brows together and peered at her over the paper. "You'll be on the shelf if you ain't careful, girl."

"Three seasons isn't the end of the world, Brother."

"Not the point," he muttered. "You're too picky."

"Am I looking old-cattish, my dear?" she asked with a smile.

He put his paper down on his lap. He wore a red and black Oriental dressing gown and pasha slippers just now disposed comfortably on an upholstered ottoman. "You know you are well looking, Emma," he said severely. "That gold hair shines down anything in London. Your eyes are listed as cornflower blue at White's every time they're betting whether you'll accept the latest lovelorn sot. Which you have not. I've made a pony on you these last five times."

"You bet a hundred pounds I would refuse offers?" That took her aback.

"Well, normally I ain't a betting man, but . . . well, dash it, Emma, you refused a damned duke, didn't you? I can't see how you'd take that last puppy who spouted poetry all the time. Might as well wager if it's a sure thing."

"Richard," she reproved. But she had to suppress the smile

that threatened the corners of her mouth. She hoped he wouldn't notice. Then she cleared her throat. "And how are the bets running just now?"

"Fifty-fifty," he grunted. "They were three to one against until you danced four times with Ware at Almack's."

"And where is your money?"

"I haven't laid down yet," he said speculatively, "though I may. You toy with them. You're always so still and quiet, you fool people. But I know. You like to play."

"The whole thing is so boring!" She sighed. "I admit it was mischievous of me to act interested in them. But they enjoyed the dance."

"These are men's *hearts* you're playing with, Emma." Richard brought his blond brows together. He had the family's straight nose. His eyes were a grayer version of hers and he had the same full lips, though just now they were pressed together in a disapproving line.

"Their hearts were not engaged, Brother, except with the prospect of my income."

He grunted again. "Thank God for your fortune or you might have no offers at all. You've a blunt way about you, Emma; there are no two ways about it. Some say an acid tongue." He snapped his paper shut. "I like Ware. Maybe I should warn him off. Besides, I'm tired of watching them struggle to find the words when they ask my permission. And it all comes to nothing in any case."

"I wonder they ask you before they are sure of me."

"They *are* sure of you. And whose fault is that?" He shrugged, opened a fresh page of his paper, and hunched behind it. "I'll put down a pony this week."

"I wouldn't bet against this one, Brother." She placed a rose in the cut-glass vase.

His brows appeared over the top of his paper, then his eyes. He tossed it to the side and rose from his chair. "You mean . . . ?"

This time, she could not suppress the smile. Indeed, it was almost a grin. "He's going to offer, Richard. Lord knows I can feel it coming at this point. And I'm going to accept. So please be nicer to him than you were to the poet."

"Emma, Emma!" He descended on her and took her by her shoulders, holding her at arm's length. A crease appeared between his brows. "Don't let my badgering make you take him if you don't love him, Emma."

She raised her brows, her eyes unaccountably filling. She widened her smile to compensate. "But I do, Richard. That's the surprise. I didn't mean for it to happen. He picked me up from a fall off my pony and chased me out of his lily pond when I was a child. But when he returned from North Africa . . . Well, somewhere over the years he'd become a man and an interesting one at that. He's been everywhere. He has ideas." She shrugged. "He's only a soldier, but he has prospects in the diplomatic corps—"

"Tosh, you've enough money for him and a dozen others. Don't bother about that."

"Only if you won't. Don't make him feel paltry," she warned.

"Wares have been in Warwickshire since the Conquest. I have no complaints about his birth. I could wish he was not a second son. But Rockhampton says he'll try to get Ware onto his staff. He's got a bright future." He frowned. "Sounds like a dashed lot of work to me, but Ware seems to like all this rushing about in the diplomatic line."

"You've been doing research?" How dear of him.

"Well," he harrumphed. "You *are* m'sister." He tried to look severe. "He's like to haul his wife off to barbaric places. I won't dress it up for you. I know you fancy yourself a rebel, Emma, but are you ready for barbarians who don't even eat at a civilized hour?"

"I'll think of it as an adventure, Richard; truly I will." She kept her mouth prim.

"So you've decided." He nodded. "I thought so—saw how you looked at him."

"And that's the real reason you haven't bet against the match at White's," she laughed.

"Well, I can't say I like throwing money away."

"Provoking man! You teased me to get inside information out of me."

He drew her to him and hugged her. "You're more important to me than any bet at White's, no matter what I put about. I'll welcome your Davie, Emma."

She hugged him back. He was a most excellent brother. "I only hope we care for each other as much as you and Damien."

He put her from him and smiled affectionately. "That would be a lot to ask." Her brother's "friend" of many years was far more than that. "It will fall to you to get the heir. I'm sorry for that burden, Emma."

She sat again and picked up a rose. It was perfect, its petals bloodred velvet, half-opened, a promise of full-blown glory. It should go at the center of the arrangement. "You two are a marvelous example of constancy. The least I can do is provide the heir."

"More tea, miss?" She jerked around to see their old butler, Jenkins, peering through the door. The rose escaped her grasp. She grabbed at it. Its thorns pricked deep.

"Ouch!" she exclaimed. The rose fell to the floor. She grabbed her fingers and squeezed until blood welled. She sucked at the drops. It tasted of copper.

Her brother drew his handkerchief from his pocket. "Take this. You'll spoil your dress."

"I'll spoil your handkerchief." But she took it and wound it around her fingers. Blood stained it in a bright flower. Jenkins looked apologetic. "Jenkins, tea would be nice. And Major Ware said he would be late. Show him back immediately when he arrives."

• • •

"Ware," Richard said, pumping Major Ware's hand. "Good to see you."

Emma rose. The smile that burbled up from her heart at the sight of him faltered. He was pale, and a sheen of sweat had broken out on his forehead. He was a handsome specimen, a fact she had not recognized until she saw him again two months ago. How had she never noticed how clear and intelligent his blue eyes were? Sandy blond hair waved back from a broad forehead. His nose was straight and a little long, but that just spoke of character, which was a good thing, because his chin did not exactly shout it. What a dear cleft chin he had! She had never noticed how strong the column of his neck was or the set of his broad shoulders until he returned. *Certainly* she had never noticed how his thighs bunched with muscle under his trousers. His clothes were conservative but well cut. The military men all went to Weston for their coats. No padded shoulders or intricate neck cloths so high they pushed at Davie's ears. She'd wager he was beforehand with the world. Not a wastrel, her Davie.

But now he was clearly in distress. He nodded to her brother. "Fairfield." And he bowed over her hand. His was clammy as he held her fingers to his lips. Still, the shock of his touch did what it always did to her. She felt more alive, throbbing with awareness of him. "Miss Fairfield." She smiled inside to think that he was that nervous about offering for her.

"Well, well, I must go to . . . my steward. Not expecting you. Apologies and all. . . ." Richard snapped the door shut behind him.

Her brother's blatant behavior seemed to make Major Ware even more nervous. And . . . was that regret in his eyes? How . . . odd. "Won't you sit down?" She gestured to a chair upholstered in cheerful green stripes that defied the gray day.

Far from sitting, he paced the room like a caged beast, saying nothing, only occasionally clearing his throat. Was he so unsure of her answer? She sat calmly and waited for her still-ness to reel in his nervous energy.

He turned and came to stand over her. "Miss Fairfield . . ." he began after a moment.

She looked up and smiled. "Surely we have known each other long enough that you can call me Emma."

"Yes, well . . ." He ran a finger around the inside of his cra-vat. Then he seemed to sag. "Emma." Her name sounded like defeat when he said it like that. Was that right for one about to propose marriage? He eschewed the comfortable seat and sat on a Chippendale chair that looked too fragile for his bulk. "I know there are certain . . . expectations surrounding our rela-tionship. . . ." He cleared his throat, apparently uncertain how to go on.

"You mean the betting at White's?"

"They're not betting at White's!" He looked stricken.

She nodded in mock sincerity. "Richard says they are."

He pressed his lips together grimly. "I should like to be free to satisfy their expectations," he murmured, almost too low for her to hear. "But . . . I will be going away tomorrow."

Emma felt as though she had been slapped. "Where?" she blurted.

His eyes were pained. "I expect I'll start in Casablanca. Af-ter that, I don't know."

"How . . . long will you be gone?" she managed after a moment.

"I don't know that, either." He looked at his hands. He took a breath as though he had to fight for it. "It isn't my choice. . . ." He trailed off.

"Well, I'll be anxious for your return," she said carefully, trying to sense the truth of his feelings about this turn of events. Was he relieved that he was escaping the "expecta-tions"? He didn't look relieved.

He shook his head convulsively. "Everything will be

changed by then. A woman like you gets offers of marriage every week."

"I've managed to resist temptation so far." She couldn't believe she was telling him so clearly how she felt about him, not knowing if he returned the sentiment.

"It could be years . . ." he choked, turning.

Years? He *was* trying to put her off! Did he long to get away from her? Had she mistaken echoes of warmth for a childhood friend for something more? She had to know. "Surely a wife could accompany you, help you in your mission."

He turned a gaze on her filled with such longing and such . . . loss it almost staggered her. He swallowed. Then his countenance closed. "Too dangerous in Africa. And if . . . the worst . . . happened . . . a widow without being properly a bride . . . worse, alone in a strange land . . ."

He thought he would die there? *My God!*

"An unfair proposition all the way around," he croaked. "No, there are no obligations between us. You must look to your own happiness." He took a tentative step in her direction and another, until he loomed over her with all of his six-plus feet. Slowly he bent to her hand and lifted it gently with his own. The feel of his flesh against hers sent a thrill coursing through her. His hand was strong, the nails clean half-moons. He smelled like soap and lavender water. She was most aware of the muscle in his shoulders. She could hardly concentrate with the sensation of skin to skin assaulting her. "I shall always treasure our moments together."

That sounded so final! "I await your return, then. . . ." She tried to make her voice sound both stubborn and cheerful.

"No." He pressed his lips to her fingers. The touch made her feel faint with impending loss. "Move on with your life, Emma. I can promise you nothing."

That was it then. . . .

He snapped upright and let go her hand. All color drained

from his face. His eyes shone. "Your servant, Miss Fairfield." He nodded curtly, then spun on his heel and shut the breakfast room door behind him.

Emma was left staring at the closed door. Emotions careened and collided in her breast. Surely . . . surely his expression, if not his words, said he cared for her, that it was only duty that called him away. . . . Was she wrong about that?

The door creaked open and her brother let himself into the room. "Emma? I ran smack into Ware. He looked like he'd seen a relative executed. You didn't refuse him, did you, girl?"

"I didn't get a chance," she said, trying to make her voice light.

"He didn't offer?" Her brother was incredulous.

"It seems he's off to Africa tomorrow." She took up a piece of needlework at random. Her hands were shaking. "The expectations at White's will go unsatisfied." Her voice cracked on the last sentence. She despised herself for her lack of control.

"Oh, Emma!" Richard put a hand on her shoulder. "What a time to be mistaken in a suitor, just when you finally found one you liked." He sighed. "There will be others."

"Putting up with who I am because of my fortune, no doubt," she said bitterly. "I thought Davie . . . well, that he liked me as I was. If I can't have that, I'd rather be a spinster. Not a fate worse than death." But spinsterhood rankled. Marriage, too, with anyone but Davie, would gall her. What kind of diplomatic mission brought a certainty of death? Or had he just made that up to put her off? She watched her fingers pull small, even stitches through her needlework as though they belonged to someone else. Everything had changed.

Somewhere inside she felt a storm building, one that might sweep away her sanity.

2

The sun sank behind the Kasbah tents in Casablanca. Davie watched the light die from the third-story window of the room he had taken. Fear thumped in his chest. The night belonged to them. How would he find Rufford in this teeming city?

He lit a small oil lamp against the coming twilight. The Admiral had given Davie his fastest cutter. Supplies were diverted from a shipment to Gibraltar and sent to Casablanca. Whitehall was pulling out all the stops to give Rufford anything he needed for the war he was waging against the forces of darkness.

Darkness to darkness, monster over monster. Did it matter who won? Davie asked that question and answered himself a dozen times a day.

Yes. The world probably depended on Rufford's brand of darkness prevailing.

Davie had a hard time caring for the world just now. It was eleven days, ummmm, four hours, and twenty minutes since he had seen Emma Fairfield's face, incredulous, then hurt. That look had stayed with him through choppy seas and the smell of tar and salt water. She'd done everything but beg him to take her with him. A woman like Emma Fairfield did not beg. The need to be with her was a physical pain in his belly.

He went to the room's lone window, just an opening in the thick mud brick walls. He looked out across the city. Lights began to flicker as the Kasbah turned into a night market. The braying of donkeys and camels, the smell of spice and fruit and overripe meat, wafted up from streets that teemed with sellers and shoppers and no doubt something far more deadly. He could not have brought her into this chaos and danger.

"You came."

Davie whirled to see Ian Rufford standing in the shadows of the bare room, containing only a narrow bed and a dresser. He sucked in a breath. He thought he saw the gleam of red in Rufford's eyes. But then the man—if that was what you could call him these days—stepped out of the shadows and his eyes were as blue as Davie remembered them. Rufford had powerful shoulders and curling light brown hair worn too long and tied back in a black ribbon. The air was electric with the energy emanating from him. Davie recognized the telltale scent of cinnamon and something else, sweeter, underneath. They all had a variant of that scent and put out some version of that vibrating energy. The brute was handsome. So handsome he had enticed Elizabeth Rochewell into marrying him, even though she knew what he was. Davie and Emma Fairfield had stood up at their wedding. Davie still couldn't believe that Rufford had brought his new wife into the danger of North Africa. "How did you get in?"

Rufford shrugged. "Thank you for coming."

It was Davie's turn to shrug. "Rally round and all that." But he had been thinking about Rufford's wife. "I wonder that you didn't get your wife to see to your supply lines. She was a hand at organizing expeditions as I recall."

"My wife is doing just that for Khalenberg and Beatrix Lisse in Tripoli," he said. "The . . . extermination effort proceeds on several fronts. Urbano has Algiers."

Beatrix Lisse! Of course! The famous courtesan always wore perfume smelling vaguely like cinnamon. He should have guessed it wasn't perfume at all. "Why not send me to Tripoli and keep your wife by your side?" he couldn't help asking. Too late he realized that Rufford's wife might have left him, and the man just didn't want to admit that.

Rufford smiled grimly. "She can handle Khalenberg. You could not."

Davie was stung into a retort. "A slip of a girl?"

"She's our kind now," Rufford said. "And her blood is strong."

That stopped Davie. Elizabeth Rufford had been made vampire? A fate worse than death. Rufford once thought so, too. His saving grace was that he hadn't wanted to become a monster, had fought against it, hated it. Davie examined Rufford's face. The old pain and sorrow he had once seen there were gone. Rufford looked tired but . . . comfortable with himself, confident. Had he stopped hating that he was a monster? So much so that he made his wife into a monster, too?

"She was dying." It was as though he read Davie's thoughts. "My blood could save her. What would you have me do?"

Death is better than becoming a monster. That was what came of letting a woman come with you into dangerous climes. Thank God he had not been weak enough to ask Emma to marry him. Davie's heart clenched. He would probably never hold Emma Fairfield in his arms, now.

But he was not here to judge Rufford, or to mourn for what might have been with Emma. He was here to do his duty and help eradicate the remnants of Asharti's army, else humans would be kept as cattle and raised for their blood. He pushed the image of Emma's smile from his mind. "How goes the battle?"

Rufford didn't answer. His mouth set itself into a line and his jaw worked. "We need a safe house to heal during the daylight hours. We'll have to change the location frequently. Food, fresh clothing—African mostly, since we must pry them out of the local population."

Davie nodded. "Weapons? I brought an arsenal of guns."

Rufford shook his head. "Useless. Perhaps some sabers or cutlasses."

"Done. Bandages?"

Rufford raised his intense blue eyes. "No." He hesitated. "But we're going to need—"

Davie didn't want to hear the word. "I've been thinking about that," he interrupted. "Would it raise suspicions if I solicited donations? I could pay handsomely."

Rufford shook his head. "The city is frightened enough as it is. Bring five or six healthy specimens to the safe house each evening before we go out. We'll do the rest, and leave them with pleasant memories of a night of wine or love and money in their pocket they'll think they won at dice. We'll take a bit from each so no one is the worse for wear."

So. He was to be a procurer of blood. His face must have shown his revulsion.

"Look, Ware," Rufford said, his voice rough. "I'm not sure what you know of us, based on your time with her. Asharti," he almost choked on the name even still, "is not a good example of our kind. But you need to know our Rules."

Davie sucked in a breath and nodded. Rufford had suffered at her hands as well.

Rufford held himself still. The light of the lamp was the only flickering defense against the darkness that had grown in the room. Rufford stood outside its circle of illumination. His face was dimly visible in the shadows. "We have a parasite in our blood. We call it the Companion. It gives us strength. We can compel weaker minds as well as suggest memories. We can translocate—draw the power of our Companion until we pop out of space and time and reappear at a place of our choice within a range of a few miles. We are stronger than humans. The Companion rebuilds its host rather than relocating, so we heal wounds and life is extended . . . indefinitely." He made his tone matter-of-fact.

Immortal? The concept was too big to comprehend. Yet Davie knew from his terrible time with Asharti how true some of those impossible facts were. He had firsthand experience with compulsion. A woman of eight stone had brute strength that far surpassed his own. And he had seen Rufford heal a broken neck after trying to kill himself.

"We aren't harmed by garlic or wolfsbane or symbols of any religion. We don't sleep in the earth of our homeland. We have never been dead and we don't turn into wolves or bats. Those are superstitious myths."

"How can you prevail against your . . . kind if they are essentially immortal?"

"Decapitation. The head must be separated entirely from the body or it will heal."

Ugly. But at least there was some way to kill them. That's why Rufford wanted swords.

"You'll leave that to us, of course," Rufford continued. "Fedeyah and I—"

"Fedeyah! Asharti's second in command?"

Rufford nodded. "We are responsible for clearing the land west of the Atlas Mountains."

Davie's jaw dropped in horror and surprise. "*Two* of you? For all that territory? And one her servant? I would never trust him!"

"I do," Rufford said quietly. "With my life. Every night." He brushed aside Davie's outrage and glanced to the window. Outside it had grown full dark. "I must get to it. They are converging on Casablanca, which means this place will get more dangerous before it gets safer. That brings us to you." He turned back to Davie. "Don't go out at night. Stay at the safe house, no matter what you hear, no matter how badly you want to leave. Never touch us when we are wounded. Examine yourself for wounds and bandage them carefully before you get anywhere near us. A drop of our blood in the tiniest scratch or accidentally swallowed will infect you. You either die a horrible death or get immunity to the parasite from ingesting large quantities of vampire blood and become a vampire yourself. Not what you want, I'm sure."

The very concept made Davie's mouth dry.

"Think of your job as setting up a field hospital in a dangerous area." Rufford stepped back into the shadows. A more intense blackness seemed to whirl around him. "Begin tomorrow with finding a safe house. Leave the location here. Cover your tracks. They're everywhere."

And he was gone. Davie wondered where he and Fedeyah would find shelter tomorrow during the daylight. And he wondered just what he had gotten himself into. He had never felt so weak, so mortal. He turned to the window. Somewhere in the darkness Rufford and Fedeyah would do battle tonight with the remnants of Asharti's army converging on the city. He couldn't see them. But they were there. He stepped away from the window. Maybe they could see him.

Emma Fairfield stood next to the champagne fountain at Bedford House. She was very still. Couples danced in the precise dips and graceful patterns of a country dance. Ladies sipped punch and examined their dance cards. Dowagers in turbans and feathers rapped the knuckles of their equally ancient cicisbei. She could see tables of whist and pique through the card room door. It seemed unreal, it was so pointless. Richard danced courtly attendance on a woman he cared nothing for. He hated this evening as much as Emma did but had nothing better to do since Damien was gone up to Northumberland. Richard would have gone with him at any other time. They could be much freer there. In fact, Richard stayed in London only to give her countenance and allow her to have season after season where she refused all offers of marriage. She could not be so selfish as to let that go on forever. He glanced over to her. She made no sign. It seemed too much effort. Richard leaned in and spoke to a man on his left. The man—young Thurston, wasn't it?—glanced in her direction and then started across the room.

Emma breathed in and out carefully. It was only at her brother's instigation that she was here tonight. Actually, "instigation" wasn't the word. "Prodding." "Nagging." In the end it was easier to come. She need only stand and watch after all. But Richard obviously had other ideas.

"Miss Fairfield." Thurston bowed crisply before her. He wore the uniform of the Seventh Hussars. It matched his blue eyes. Too much gold braid for her taste. "May I have this dance?"

She looked at him. She should say something. What did one say? "No, thank you."

His expression was startled. "Uh. . . . Perhaps some punch?"

She shook her head. "No," she whispered.

"Oh." His dismay would once have been comical. But she didn't respond to absurdity anymore. She hadn't smiled for ten days. He glanced back to her brother, who made threatening expressions with his eyebrows. Thurston turned back and chewed his lip.

She looked at him calmly, not letting him see the knot of wormy despair that lurked inside her. No one must see that.

"Well then, I'll just be . . ." He took two steps back, turned, and retreated in disarray. She saw Richard sigh. She didn't move, just stood there, her hands folded quietly in front of her. The music seemed a desecration to her mood. She should never have given in to Richard.

Several young women hurried across to her as the dance finished, abandoning their partners with unseemly haste. "There you are Miss Fairfax," Chlorinda Belchersand called. Emma had known Chlorinda almost as long as she had known Davie.

That thought stabbed through her calm and made her gasp against the pain. Davie! Oh dear! She thought she had cried all the tears she had when she discovered he had wound up all his affairs and written out a will. That was when she was sure he wasn't coming back to her, ever. But tears closed her throat now against the thump of her heart. She fumbled at her reticule for a handkerchief as Chlorinda and Jane Campton arrived in a flutter.

"Where have you been hiding for ten whole days?" Miss Campton asked, breathless. "Did you have the influenza? You look very pale."

Emma dabbed her handkerchief to her eyes. It was easier to say nothing than to lie.

"Isn't influenza just horrible?" Miss Belchersand agreed, apparently willing to forgo Emma's actual participation in the conversation. "It makes your eyes water for days."

"I heard the posies were piled up in the foyer and you wouldn't see any of the young men who brought them." This from Miss Campton in a confidential whisper.

"*I* heard that you would have had several proposals of marriage if you were in any condition to receive them," Chlorinda revealed, not to be outdone.

"Well, she can receive them now that she's out and about again."

Emma couldn't think of anything more likely to send her to a madhouse than a proposal of marriage, or at least any proposal of marriage but one. She stared around the room as sets formed for the next dance. She wouldn't listen to their chatter.

"No one knows who to bet on next now that Ware is gone off," Chlorinda confided.

"Miss Fairfield would never have taken a second son without a fortune," Miss Campton sniffed, "and one tied to the diplomatic corps into the bargain. All those postings to vile places!"

"Well, she needn't have gone with him. An absent husband is a great convenience, and one dependent upon your money is even better. One would always have the whip hand, wouldn't one?" Chlorinda Belchersand's tone was arch.

Emma turned her eyes slowly toward the two women now talking to each other as though she weren't there. How had she never noticed how small and spiteful their eyes were?

"Well, who do you think it will be?" Miss Campton asked Miss Belchersand.

"I'm not going to accept an offer from any of these silly creatures," Emma interrupted. It was more than she had said at one time in ten days.

"You were always such a rebel, Emma." Chlorinda tittered. "What will you do? You can't live with that brother of yours forever."

"I *may* just set up on my own." She raised her chin.

"That isn't done! Everyone will talk about you!" Miss Campton said, horrified.

"Everyone seems to be talking about me now," Emma pointed out. "Men bet on the outcome of the affairs of *my* heart at White's. So why wouldn't I rebel?"

"Because society punishes rebels," Chlorinda said, now sounding truly worried. "You've refused all offers until you're nearly on the shelf. That's bad enough. But there *are* limits. If you set up for yourself, you won't be received. If you retreat to the country, you'll end up walking on the moors or whatever and dressing unfashionably and dying alone with only an aged housekeeper to note your passing."

"*You* have been reading too many novels," Emma said in a damping tone.

"You'll never know the touch of a man," Jane Campton said thoughtfully. How unexpected! A physical sense of yearning swept through Emma. That was a hard truth to bear.

Suddenly she wanted to shriek at these silly girls, at Thurston, at the dowagers and the cicisbei and the whist players. She wanted to shriek that they had no meaning in their lives, no love, and that pretending it didn't matter didn't fool anyone. Instead, she pushed past the two young women and bore down upon Richard. He turned in surprise.

"I have the headache and I'm calling for the carriage, and you may take me home or not as you please," she said, through clenched jaws. If she clenched her jaws she might not scream.

Richard raised his brows. "I'll call the carriage." He turned to the Countess Lieven, with whom he had been conversing. "Your servant, my lady. Duty calls."

Emma turned and stalked out of the hall without looking back. Inside she was seething. Davie had done this to her. She was certain he loved her. It had been written in his expression of loss that afternoon at Fairfield House. He *had* been going to offer for her, until he felt some wretched sense of duty and protectiveness that sent him off to Casablanca without her.

The whole town had become intolerable and she didn't know whether to cry or shout defiance at the unfairness of it all. Where was all her vaunted calm? Lost. And she didn't know how to get it back.

3

It was almost dawn. Davie waited in the darkness of the tiny whitewashed house. The windows were covered over with black cloth. Rufford and Fedeyah would be here soon.

He should leave. The weapons cache must be moved and the food supply replenished. Then he would bring several young men and women for Rufford and Fedeyah when they woke. They drained a little blood from each, as the donors drowsed and smiled, and stored it in two leather sacks. They needed it most when they arrived, wounded, just after dawn. Davie had never seen them return from a night of fighting. But he had seen the results of the battle. The city was buzzing with fear. Twelve decapitated bodies had been found in an alley to-day. Twelve! The number of Asharti's followers in the city had been growing. And they were not as discreet as Rufford and Fedeyah. Human bodies drained of blood were being noticed, even in a city where the poor died on the streets every day. Citizens were leaving if they had the means to do so. Davie dreaded a panic that would send the population of the African metropolis streaming into the desert and certain death by exposure or setting sail for Gibraltar in unsafe craft that would leave them at the mercy of the weather and the sea.

With the turn of days, he had been lingering longer as dawn approached, tempted to stay. *Curiosity killed the cat.* Possibly quite literally in this case. Who knew what feral monsters Rufford and Fedeyah became after a night of killing? They never let him into the room where they slept. By the time he returned in the late afternoon, they were sitting in the chosen house, with the remains of the food he had brought scattered over a table, making plans for the night. This campaign was taking a terrible toll on Rufford. The man's grim determination had been slowly turning into a heartsickness that was palpable. And Fedeyah? Davie had never trusted the Arab and couldn't read his face. Fedeyah followed Rufford's orders, just as Davie did, though the Englishman was something like a thousand years younger than the Arab.

Davie felt he was doing too little, that he was protected from whatever put such a charge on their souls. At the very least he could witness that cost. So he sat, quiet, as the gap around the cloth that covered the window lightened. He laid a sharp cutlass across his knees, lit a fresh candle, and waited.

The two whirlpools of blackness did not surprise him. He had seen vampires translocating many times. But he was shocked at the figures that materialized out of the darkness onto the terra-cotta tiled floor. They were covered in wounds that showed bone and guts and shouted death. He jumped to his feet. Rufford took a single step forward. His soft leather boots gushed with blood. He was naked except for a cloth around his loins and those boots. His burnoose had apparently been ripped from his body. Davie had been in the Peninsular War. He had seen wounds and death aplenty, but nothing quite so vicious as Rufford's. It looked like an animal had raked him with six-inch claws. Shoulder gaped over ligament; chest showed bone; belly revealed intestine; thigh showed layers of muscle.

Rufford toppled to the floor.

Davie rushed forward. "Rufford!" Fedeyah sank to his knees. He, too, was wounded, but not like Rufford.

"Get from us," Fedeyah gasped in his heavily accented English. "The blood!"

Davie stopped, swallowing hard. Fedeyah's wounds were already beginning to close. Rufford didn't seem to be making the same progress. The scoring Davie could see on his back still bled. The dirt floor was dark with blood. "Can he die?" Davie croaked.

"No," Fedeyah panted. "But drinking blood can give him strength and spare him pain."

"Right, right." Davie scanned the room. "Blood." There it was, on the crude wooden table. He lunged for the leather water sacks. When he turned back, Fedeyah lay on the floor in semiconsciousness. His wounds were visibly healing now.

Davie took a breath. Very well. It was up to him. He held up his hands to the light of the candle, front and back, checking for cuts or scrapes. Nothing. He could do this. He knelt beside Rufford. The man's pale English flesh was an anomaly in this land of sun and sand. Davie sucked in a breath and turned Rufford over by the shoulders. Davie's hands were slick with blood. He heaved the nearly naked man into his lap, not looking at his belly or the wounds in his neck and chest. Holding up his head, Davie got the nipple of the water sack between Rufford's lips and squeezed. Thick, half-coagulated blood oozed from the corners of Rufford's mouth before he gasped and choked and swallowed. But then, barely conscious as he was, he sucked greedily.

God in heaven, what am I doing? Davie might burn in hell, but he wouldn't let a man suffer. When Rufford had taken what there was, Davie laid him down and took the other sack to Fedeyah. Davie roused the Arab, who raised himself on one elbow and took the water sack. Fedeyah upended it over his mouth and squeezed. Blood arced into his mouth. His wild black hair was caked with dirt and dried blood. As Davie watched, a scalp wound closed and sealed itself. Fedeyah leaned against a wooden chest, breathing hard.

Davie turned to Rufford. The belly wound was healed enough so that no intestines were visible now. The gleam of bone had gone from his chest. As Davie watched, Rufford opened his eyes. They radiated pain. His gaze darted about the room until it fell on Davie. "You shouldn't be here," Rufford croaked.

Davie leaned down and hoisted him up by one arm, though Rufford protested weakly. He got his shoulder under Rufford's arm and pulled him onto one of the beds, a simple wooden frame with rope netting supporting a straw mattress. Fedeyah crawled onto the other one. "You were in no shape to get to the blood," Davie panted.

"Doesn't matter," Rufford muttered. A cut on his temple sealed itself and faded into a pink line of new skin. "I'd heal sooner or later."

"If it weakens you for tonight, it matters. Looks like last night was a near thing."

"More all the time." Rufford's voice was bleak. "They make their own reinforcements."

Davie glanced to Fedeyah, who seemed to be dropping off to sleep. "You took the brunt of it," he said to Rufford.

"I have an Old One's blood. I am the stronger. It's up to me to protect him."

"Seems they know that. They're going for you."

Rufford nodded. "Word is out. We no longer have to look for them. They find us."

This whole campaign seemed hopeless to Davie. "Can just two of you turn the tide?"

"Beatrix sent word to all the cities and even to Mirso Monastery itself. They will come. Some to Tripoli, Algiers, and here. We must hold out until they get here."

"Then I hope they arrive soon."

"I'm more worried about Tripoli."

Ahhh. He was worried about his wife. Davie couldn't imagine having the woman you loved in a situation like this. He looked away, remembering Emma. He saw her in the breakfast room in the Grosvenor Square house. The room was light with gentle English sun. Her skin was clean and pink. He would never see her again.

"Miss Fairfield?"

Davie stared at him. The man *could* read minds!

"No," Rufford said, a small smile touching one corner of his mouth. "But your thoughts aren't hard to guess. I'm sorry I made you leave someone you love behind."

"How did you know it was Miss Fairfield?"

"It was written all over you two the day I married Beth. Did you tell her?"

Davie shook his head. "I was on my way to propose when Whitehall called."

"You didn't go through with it?"

Davie shook his head. "Couldn't make her feel . . . obligated, under the circumstances."

"Probably wise. Spunky, that girl. Stood up for Beth when no one else would."

Davie smiled. No one could help liking Emma. He looked away, lest Rufford see his weakness. "She was my best hope for a . . . normal life. After . . . you know. After . . . her."

"I like Englishmen," she said. They were in the chambers of the former ambassador in the English compound in El Golea. She lay across the huge bed of English walnut carved and inlaid with rococo magnificence, her body draped with strips of almost transparent cloth. A spill of heavy black hair splayed out over the rich cut-velvet spread. Her nails and lips were painted gold. Her nipples were dusted with it. Kohl lined her eyes. She wore a wide necklace of interlaced gold links to which had been attached hundreds of tiny gold disks, each set

with a tinier jewel. Her wrist had a bracelet of the same. They tinkled when she moved.

She was the most beautiful woman he'd ever seen, and he had never been more frightened of anyone. He knelt on the cool tile beside the bed, head bowed. He was naked, as always, knees wide, his most private parts vulnerable to her. She did not allow him even a scrap of cloth to cover his loins. He was full, if not fully erect. Two round marks punctured his flesh over the big arteries that ran down into each thigh from his groin. That was one of her favorite places to feed. She had him shaved and bathed daily and whipped almost as often with wide leather straps. She liked fresh welts but didn't want them bloody. If he was too injured, he would lose the strength to service her. He had become dulled to the horror of compulsion. Revulsion at her habits was a luxury not allowed a slave. The time when he had been Major Vernon Davis Ware, attaché to Lord Wembertin, was a distant dream.

"Come, Englishman," she whispered, beckoning with one long golden nail. Her eyes went red. He felt the familiar tightening in his balls, the throbbing in his cock that signaled a full erection. She could keep him hard all night, and she would. He crawled up onto the bed and lay beside her, his cock stiff now. He thumbed her nipple because that was what she wanted. She commanded, though she didn't speak. He obeyed. He kissed the top of her breast. She ran those long-nailed hands through his hair, over the welts on his back and buttocks. Then she lifted his chin with one finger even as she grasped his cock with the other. His throat was bared to her. He saw the glint of her canines in the darkness, felt the sharp pain. She sucked only lightly, a prelude to excite her as she writhed against him and pulled at his cock. The sensation cycled up to excruciating, but he wouldn't come. She hardly ever let him ejaculate. She liked to keep him raw and needing. With a jerk she pulled her teeth from his neck and lay back on the pillows. She wanted him to lick her.

She spread her legs and he knelt between them. She tilted

her hips up. He parted her fur with his tongue and tasted her musk as he slid his tongue up and down to her point of pleasure, teasing her toward her release. As her excitement grew, she held his head to her pelvis and ground against him, moaning. Then her hips began to jerk and he sucked on her small nub, harder and harder, drawing out the sensation for her. When at last she could stand no more, she cried out and fell back. Her eyes faded from red to jet-black.

"I like you, Englishman," she said. She could speak many languages and did, seeming to choose them at random. He understood her when she spoke French or Arabic, Latin or Greek, but lost her when she started speaking the guttural one that sounded a little like German or Russian but wasn't. "But I find you have been keeping secrets from me."

Fear cycled up through Davie. What secrets could an attaché to an incompetent ambassador in a godforsaken place like El Golea have that she could want? He crawled to her side again. Should he beg forgiveness? Should he speak at all?

She arched. He had been well trained. He bent to suckle her nipple. The gold dust tasted bitter and metallic in his mouth. "I am told, slave, that an Englishman crawled in off the desert here some months ago. He had the marks on his body." She fingered the twin wounds at the inside of Davie's elbow. "Do you remember this man, slave?"

"Yes, Goddess," he said, around her nipple, which had tightened. She would be ready for his cock soon. She meant Rufford. He knew now how Rufford got those wounds. He understood the pain that drenched the man's eyes, why he said he had turned into his own worst nightmare.

"Where is he now, slave?" she whispered. Poor sod. Hadn't Rufford suffered enough?

"He's gone." There. He could give her that. That couldn't hurt Rufford.

Compulsion slammed into him. His cock grew painfully hard. "I know that!" she barked. "Where?"

Davie let out a moan. His balls were swollen almost to bursting. A molten core of fire was trying to get out through his cock and couldn't. "England." She couldn't reach Rufford there. How he longed to be in England with Rufford! He bent to kiss her. That was what she wanted. Her lips were soft, but he knew they covered fangs that would bite and suck yet tonight. She thrust her tongue into his mouth and lifted her hips again. He tore himself away and lay between her thighs, his cock aching as it trembled at her entry.

"Where in England?" she hissed.

He held up her hips and thrust inside her, hard, ramming his cock home. It was excruciating for him. She wanted it harder yet. She wasn't pleased. He slid in and out. Where? She wanted to know where. He couldn't tell her. He'd pretend he didn't know, even to himself, and then he wouldn't tell her. His cock screamed for release.

"Where?" Her eyes were full red now.

Stanbridge. *Rufford said he was going home to Stanbridge. He couldn't help the thought. No! He should never have remembered it. He pumped inside her. She bucked in counterpoint. He bit his lip until it bled, trying not to say the word. He leaned down into her. She licked the blood from his lip. That brought out her canines. They pierced his carotid on the other side. She clung to him and sucked as he rammed his cock home. He felt her womb contract around him with her orgasm. His own cock was beyond pleasure and well into pain.*

At last she lay back on the bed, panting, and allowed him to withdraw. His cock was raw, still throbbing with sensation.

"I was distracted," she said conversationally. "Now, where were we?"

Her eyes went from burgundy into carmine.

He panted against the word that thundered in his brain, pressing to be uttered. He twisted away, but she grabbed him by the nape of the neck and with incredible strength brought him round to face her. "I know you know," she whispered, almost inside his brain.

"Stanbridge!" he cried, and collapsed beside her. Betrayer! His eyes filled.

"That's better," Asharti soothed, stroking his head. "I'm surprised you had so much resistance left in you. You'll leave tomorrow for England, with a letter."

He raised his head. Leave? He shut down the hope that might just show in his eyes. Leave her? His betrayal had earned him freedom. Guilt washed over him.

"But first, tonight, you must be punished for your resistance."

Davie blinked as the tiny house and the smell of blood flickered back into his consciousness. He pulled his mind away from El Golea before he could relive that punishment. But Asharti could never be banished for long. He was doomed to relive that time again and again, maybe for the rest of his life.

Rufford gripped Davie's arm. "She's dead. I saw her die."

Davie closed his eyes once. "Is she? She seems fairly alive to me."

Rufford took a breath and sat up. His body was covered with scars that were disappearing fast. Davie saw the older scars, though, that he had first seen when Rufford dragged himself in off the desert in El Golea, twin circles at throat and groin and the insides of his elbows, jagged tears in his pectorals and his thighs, scars of a whip across his shoulders. They were made before he gained his power of healing. They said he knew what serving Asharti meant. "There is life and . . . love after Asharti. Take it from me, Ware." His eyes were blue pools of pain and determination.

Davie chuffed a bitter laugh. "Are you sure? We're barely hanging on against her leavings, and I'm not sure you can last much longer."

"I'll hold out. I have to."

◆ ◆ ◆

I'll go to Northumberland, Emma thought. *Surely things will be better at Birchwood.*

She tossed her gloves on the dressing table. She was still agitated from leaving Bedford House in a huff. Flora, her maid, unpinned her bodice and untied her skirts. She let the skirt pool at her ankles. Flora helped her shrug off the bodice and unlaced her corset, saying nothing. "You may go, Flora." Emma drew the chemise over her head and slipped on the nightdress Flora had left.

Things wouldn't be any better in the country.

Love didn't come along every day. But against all odds, Emma *had* found love. She loved Davie. Probably had loved him for years. That was why she never mistook girlish crushes on a man in a uniform or with a handsome face for real love, and why she could refuse dukes and poets in the face of betting at White's. And since she'd found love, she wasn't content to be a spinster. She wanted more of the feeling she got when Davie took her shoulders or brushed his lips across her hands. Much more. She wanted Davie in her bed making love to her, and at her side at the breakfast table planning their day. She wanted to share his life, and give pleasure and comfort to him in all the ways a woman could. She wanted to grow old with him and wise.

She crawled into the great bed in the room reserved for the lady of Fairfield House. A fire crackled in the grate, its warmth proof against the capricious March winds.

The worst of it was that Chlorinda and Miss Campton thought her a rebel because she was willing to be a spinster if she couldn't have love. No, the *worst* was that she thought herself a rebel. What had she done but refuse a few offers of marriage that were distasteful to her and occasionally speak too bluntly to be conventional? What kind of rebellion was that? It hadn't cost her anything. And what if she set up housekeeping

on her own so Richard could retire to Northumberland with
Damien? Would that be rebellious? Hardly.

No, rebellion would be chucking it all to go after the man
she loved.

She sat up. The room seemed to expand and contract
around her as everything changed. Her mind darted in a thousand different directions.

Why not? What did she care for danger, or hardship?

But what if he didn't love her? She thought back to that day
in the breakfast room and their painful conversation. He loved
her. She was sure of it. Duty was in the way. What of that? She
could help him execute his duty. That was what people who
loved each other did.

The whole problem with being a woman was that you had
to wait for a man to give you what you wanted. You couldn't
make a push for it yourself.

But why? Davie didn't think he could ask her to sacrifice
her comfortable ways. But that was exactly what she wanted
to do. She wanted to make her rebellion real.

There would be a cost. She'd be leaving behind everything
she had known, including Richard. She'd never be received in
polite society, ever. There was danger, according to Davie.
Davie might be angry. Probably would be angry. She might
die with him.

And what of the cost if she didn't even try? A dry descent
into a half-life of regret. That was all she had to look forward to if she retreated from this moment without taking any
action.

Plans formed and re-formed in her mind. Could she do it?
How did a gently bred young woman just up and leave for
Casablanca? Money, of course. A companion, no, two. Where
to get them? She mustn't tell Richard until after she had gone.
He wouldn't understand. But Damien would help her. He al-
ways had a soft spot for her, and he had an interest in getting

her off Richard's hands. Besides, Damien was a believer in
true love. He'd brave Richard's wrath. Passage on a packet.
Could she even find Davie in Casablanca? Surely the embassy
would know where he was. Unless the worst had already happened. But she wouldn't think about that. She'd write to
Damien first thing in the morning.

4

Davie strode through the dusty streets of Casablanca wearing leather boots, a vest over his bare chest, and the loose pants identified with Berbers. Not that anyone would mistake him for one. His pale skin had tanned and his light hair was concealed by a head cloth, but his light eyes betrayed him. The saber hanging from his belt clanked against his thigh. The city would be unbearably hot if not for a hint of the sea in the air. The sun beat down remorselessly even in April. Behind him two bearers he had hired only this morning carried a large wooden box of sabers and a huge pack filled with food, leather pouches of blood, and clean clothing. They had no idea what they carried, and he was careful never to use the same ones twice. He chose only those sitting full in the sun to be sure they weren't vampire, just in case the scent of cinnamon was masked by the aroma of spices or the smell of camel dung.

How long had he been doing this? Forever. It must seem longer to Rufford and Fedeyah. Now Davie stayed each dawn until they arrived to be sure they could get the blood they needed to heal. The toll their campaign took on them was horrible to behold. There was no question of retreat, though. If humans were raised for their blood and vampires multiplied indiscriminately, both races would die out entirely.

He fingered the message from Admiral Groton demanding a full report on the status of Casablanca and Rufford's plans for coordinating the effort against Asharti's army. Davie didn't think he wanted Whitehall interfering with Rufford, now or in the future. Rufford was a moral man. Davie smiled to himself. He had never thought to say that about a monster. But it was more than he could say of Whitehall on occasion. He trusted the future of the human race more to Rufford than the Admiral and the Lord High Chancellor.

Davie directed the bearers into a side alley and up the stairs into a small apartment that would be their shelter tomorrow. He would sleep here tonight to ensure that no one but him was waiting for Rufford and Fedeyah.

Cinnamon! Davie jerked around, scanning the tiny winding street lined with bright fabrics drying in the sun and filled with children laughing as they darted over the cobblestones. He could see no one suspicious. Lord! He was getting jumpy. He dismissed the bearers, unpacked his supplies, then ventured out to scour the city for tomorrow's safe retreat. Finally, his work done, he returned to the house he had left at dawn to check on the vampire warriors as they slept the day away and tried to regain their strength.

He slipped into the darkened house. Lately they were so exhausted they had been sleeping like the dead. He grimaced at the image. They weren't dead, though. Vampires were very much alive. He moved quietly through the front room, the table still strewn with the remains of their repast, and into the dim sleeping quarters.

There was no reason he should sense trouble. The cinnamon scent could have belonged to Rufford and Fedeyah. The presence he felt could have been theirs. But it wasn't.

There! The wind flapped the dark fabric at the window and let in enough light to gleam against metal. Davie didn't stop to think. His sword slithered from its scabbard. The shadow, a deeper black in the dark, whirled to face him. His two charges stirred from their sleep. He raised his sword, not quite sure of his target. Metal bit into his side. He grunted with the shock of pain. Rufford rose. The sword in Davie's side was pulled out. The shadow was moving left, toward Rufford, sword up. Rufford's neck! Davie lunged forward, swinging the saber with both hands. It struck and stuck. He felt a warm splash across his face and chest. He pulled his sword away and tried to find an opening to strike again. Rufford struggled with the intruder. He couldn't risk wounding Rufford. Something thumped onto the floor. The vampire's sword clattered away. Fedeyah crouched, fighting another attacker. Davie turned to Fedeyah's foe, but Rufford, moving too swiftly for Davie's senses, was there before him. Did Rufford grab the intruder's head with both hands and simply wrench? Davie must have been mistaken. He was feeling dizzy now. It was dark. He sank to his knees.

Rufford turned from the shadowy figures lying on the packed-earth floor, and dragged Davie into the front room. Fedeyah lit a candle. Davie looked down and saw that his flowing pants were soaked with blood that was oozing from a wound in his side. Blood was splattered across his chest and leather vest, too.

"Got you good," Rufford muttered, sitting him forcibly in a chair. Davie craned to see into the room beyond, now dimly lit by the glow of the candle beside them. A body was clearly visible. It didn't have a head that he could see. "You almost got his head off." Rufford knelt beside Davie to examine the wound. "Saved my neck."

"It's hard to decapitate with a sword," Fedeyah observed as he ripped a clean burnoose into strips. "You have strength."

"Rufford had to finish the job," Davie said through teeth clenched against pain.

Fedeyah examined the wound. "Thrust clean through. Nothing vital touched."

Rufford touched the blood sprayed across Davie's torso. He looked up, shock in his eyes. "Some of this blood isn't yours." He pulled Davie's vest away. Davie looked down. The splatter of blood crossed his chest diagonally and splashed across the wound gaping in his side.

"Must be his. . . ." Davie stared up at Rufford as the implications washed over him. Vampire blood. In his wound. "My God. . . ." He looked around wildly. "Water! Flush it out."

Rufford straightened and put a hand on his shoulder to hold him in the chair. "Too late."

Davie slumped. He was a dead man.

In that moment all he could think about was Emma. He realized that somewhere inside he had held out hope he would survive this nightmare and return to Emma. Now, she would never know why he had left or how very much he loved her. He remembered her sweet face, anxious with concern for him, trying to tell him in every way allowed how much she wanted him. A vision of her as a tomboy, holding up her skirts to wade through his lily pond after frogs, slipped through him. At seventeen to her nine years, he had seemed so much older and wiser than she was. He felt a smile tremble on his lips. He had known nothing about her then, and now that he knew, he would never get to tell her just how wonderful she was.

"Guess we'll have to find you another procurer," he managed.

Rufford stared at him, brows knit. Suddenly Rufford jerked away and began to pace furiously, hands clasped behind his back. His knuckles were white. A burning started in Davie's side. He blinked several times, trying to master it, but it seemed to creep into his veins. Fedeyah stood over him, sympathy in his eyes. "How . . . how long?" Davie asked.

"Several days. A week. Not a pleasant death," Fedeyah remarked. He glanced to Rufford.

"You'd . . . you'd better leave me, then." Davie was having

trouble getting his breath. "I'll draw a map . . . to your next . . . safe house."

Rufford ran his hands through his hair. That loosened the ribbon that bound it, and it cascaded over the shoulders of his burnoose. "Damn it, Fedeyah, we can't serve him thus!"

Fedeyah nodded, thoughtful. "I remember thinking the same of you once."

Rufford came to stand over Davie. His face was grim. "I have the blood of an Old One in my veins. My blood can give you immunity to the Companion and it will do its work quickly."

Davie cast about for meaning. "Make me . . . vampire?"

Rufford nodded. A muscle jumped in his jaw where he clenched his teeth.

"I thought the point . . . was to eradicate . . . made vampires." Davie wondered if the smile he managed was wry.

"You've got it wrong." Rufford's eyes were hard. "Fedeyah and I are both made vampires. The point is to stop those who would upset the balance of the world."

"I don't want . . . to be a monster." What had happened to his brave words to the Lord High Chancellor about vampires being victims, not monsters? They seemed naive. No, with reality staring him in the face, he realized he'd rather be dead than one who drank human blood.

Rufford nodded. "I know. I felt the same. But it doesn't have to be like that. You don't know the . . . joy of being one with your Companion. It can be . . . good. In all senses of the word."

"Doesn't look . . . very good . . . from here." The burning was consuming his vision. He felt light-headed, whether from loss of blood or the infection he didn't know. "Think I'll decline."

"I could force you," Rufford's voice grated out.

"You won't." He counted on Rufford's moral compass.

Rufford frowned and Davie knew he was right about him.

"You could use the Companion to do good in the world. If I made you, you'd be strong. We could use the help."

Ahhh. Playing on his sense of duty. Smart man, Rufford. Did Davie owe the world even becoming a monster? And what if they won through, unlikely as it seemed at the moment? He was left with eternal life and drinking human blood.

And yet . . . would he leave Rufford and Fedeyah to pay the price while he escaped with a few days of pain into death? His thoughts were getting muddled. Suddenly he seemed like the defector, betraying Rufford yet again. "I . . . don't know." Rufford seemed to be looking down at him from the end of a long tunnel. Could he abandon them just when things were darkest? "Give me your word you'll kill me if we prevail."

"If you still want it, I'll kill you. I give you my word."

He blinked. Was Rufford sincere? When had he not been? "Do it." He was about to become a monster.

Then the tunnel closed, and he saw nothing.

He was tied, spread-eagled, to the ambassador's bed. Asharti hung like a nightmare above him, her eyes glowing red. He was naked. Juice from the melon she was eating dribbled on his heaving chest as she sat beside him. The pain in his loins was almost unbearable. He writhed in his bonds, but there was no escape. She had been at him all night, bringing him up to a need that was painful, using him for her own pleasure without letting him release the molten fire inside him, opening wounds and licking them. How much more could he stand?

Not that he did not deserve it. She was punishing him for withholding information from her. He deserved the punishment for betraying Rufford. His cock throbbed against his belly. He groaned, much as he hated to give her the satisfaction.

"And have you learned your lesson?" she whispered, leaning down to his ear.

"Yes," he gasped. "Yes."

"I'm not sure." She pouted, tossing the melon rind to the floor. "And I must be very sure before I send you into the world. You must know what is in store for you if you disobey me."

The throbbing in his cock ramped up another notch. "I . . . I do!" he cried. "I understand."

She put a hand on his cock. He tried to wrench himself away, but he was bound too tightly. The scrape of her palm against his flesh was excruciating. She began to stroke him.

"God have mercy!" he panted.

Her throaty laugh shook her breasts. "No, my pet. You must ask me for mercy. I am your Goddess, not your paltry Christian God." She increased the pace of her hand moving up and down his cock. All the while her eyes glowed red. "Beg me for mercy."

Davie could hardly breathe. Fire seemed to be eating at him from inside. Still he hesitated. She could make him beg. But she didn't. She wanted him to abase himself on his own, damn her! But what use was pride when he might burst into flame at any moment?

"Goddess . . ." He gulped for air. "Have mercy on me."

She leaned in and brushed his lips with her own. "No," she said softly, and pierced his throat with her canines.

He was burning up. He rolled his head from side to side, trying to escape the flames. He heard moaning. And voices.

"Rufford, he needs you."

"I'm nearly healed."

"He can't wait."

That was Fedeyah. Davie opened his eyes. He lay on a bed in a darkened room, naked, just like his dream, only he wasn't tied down. And it wasn't the ambassador's great Tudor bedstead but a simple straw mattress on a wooden frame. Sweat-soaked sheets were bunched around him. Davie looked around, expecting to see Asharti waiting in the corner to torture him, but he saw only Rufford outlined in the doorway. The vampire was stripped to the waist. His torso was covered with half-healed wounds.

"Water," Davie croaked.

Rufford sat on the edge of the bed. "Water isn't what you need." He grabbed a great long knife from the bedside table and calmly sliced his wrist. Blood welled. Davie could smell it. Something inside him rose up and shouted in joy. What was that, that felt so . . . alive?

Rufford swiveled around and lifted Davie's head, holding his bleeding wrist to Davie's lips. "Quickly, suck before I heal."

Revulsion filled him. But another part hissed, *Yes!* He bent and sucked. The blood tasted like copper life flowing down his throat. He drew at the wound greedily. A sense of well-being flooded him. The burning itch along his veins receded. Too soon, the wound closed. He only just managed to restrain the urge to ask Rufford to open himself again.

Rufford seemed to read his thoughts. "In another hour or so, when I have rested." In truth, Rufford looked awful. There were dark circles under his eyes. His wounds were healing slowly. Had he drained his strength so that Davie could make peace with his infection? Davie lifted a hand to his sweaty brow and pushed back damp strands of hair. The lingering fear from his nightmare still vibrated inside him.

"Thank you," he said hoarsely. "Not sure thanks is enough for what you've done."

Rufford shrugged. "I'm making reinforcements. Strategic use of my blood. You should thank Fedeyah. He's been taking care of you."

Fedeyah came up behind Rufford with a fresh linen cloth and laid it over Davie. "Thank you, Fedeyah," Davie whispered.

Fedeyah grunted in acknowledgment. "Food?"

Yes. He could eat now. He nodded.

"I think you've turned the corner," Rufford observed, standing.

"How long has it been?" This was the first time Davie had even a mild interest. It felt like he had been dreaming of Asharti and burning inside forever.

"Two days. Would have been faster, but nights have been taking their toll on me."

"How bad is it?"

"People are leaving the city. Some panic and hoarding of supplies. More of the enemy coming in. Most are newly made, but they act together. Difficult."

"What he means is that blood is running in the streets." Fedeyah presented a bowl. Davie could smell the dates and goat cheese, along with the scent of the soap used to wash the linen, his own sweat and the mustiness of the earthen floor, the faint whiff of rancid oil in the bottom of a disused amphora in the corner. He heard the skitter of rats and the call of an imam far away. His senses poured information over him.

Rufford shrugged, trying to look confident. "Reinforcements will be here soon."

"When can I help?" Davie asked. Suddenly he realized how strong he felt, how . . . whole. Was this the joy Rufford talked about? Lord, there was some part of him that *liked* being a monster. He shoved it down. No, he didn't. He sacrificed himself to the cause of mankind. He would suffer being the stuff of nightmares in order to fight the greater nightmare. It was a fate worse than death. His opinion hadn't changed about that. But it was a price he would pay, at least for a while. Either he would be killed in battle or, if they won through, Rufford would kill him.

"Soon. I'll give you blood as often as I can. And there are things you must learn."

Translocating, Davie thought. *Feeding*. He shuddered and

wasn't sure whether it was horror or ecstasy that trembled down his spine.

"One other thing I should tell you. The Companion with its will toward life gives us . . . more intense sensations of all kinds." Rufford got a secret smile. He raised his brows and shrugged. "It makes relations between a man and woman . . . well, the phrase 'joys of the flesh' takes on a new meaning." Rufford sighed. Was he missing his wife? "Don't be surprised by the frequency and power of your erections, especially at first. Later you'll get more control."

This all sounded like Asharti. Her ghost seemed to hover in the room, laughing that throaty contralto laugh. She had needed constant satiation, regardless of the cost to others. A horror of premonition shot through Davie. "Tell me I don't have to be like her."

Rufford chuffed a laugh. "You don't. You won't be. And how I wish there had been someone to tell me that when she first made me."

Everything had changed, except one thing. He had lost Emma. Now he was separated from her not just by distance but by his very nature. "I only hope Emma never knows what I've become. I could not bear her revulsion."

Rufford looked at him for a moment. "She didn't strike me as a fragile flower. Beth liked her. And Beth doesn't like the kind of woman who goes into hysterics."

"I'm not talking about having the vapors over some social slight. The stakes are a little greater than that, Rufford."

"Well, you know her better than I."

"I'm just glad she's safe at home. I wonder you can bear to have your wife in danger."

"It wasn't my choice," Rufford said softly. "Women have minds of their own, especially Beth. And in a partnership you must treat their desires as equal to yours or you will lose them."

Advice on women from a vampire? And one who made his beloved into a vampire, too.

"Rest," Rufford commanded. "I'll be ready to give you more blood in an hour."

Emma Fairfield came down the gangplank to the quay from the xebec that had brought her on the last leg from Gibraltar. The solid land beneath her feet felt strange. It had been three weeks since she had left Portsmouth. Not as fast a trip as she would like. But the captain of the packet she had booked passage on for her and her three companions had gotten wind of evil doings and political upheaval in Casablanca and set its passengers down in Gibraltar. It had taken several days to find a Turkish trader willing both to try to get its cargo into Morocco and to take her up. In Gibraltar she'd sent the two women home in the propriety of each other's company under the protection of Mr. Stubbs. She had only required their company in order to book passage in the first place, since no respectable English ship's captain would entertain taking a single lady aboard. Thank goodness the Turkish captain had no such nice compunctions.

During the journey she had managed not to let the doubts about what she was doing creep in. There was too much to do to pacify her wrangling companions during the first leg of the journey and too much fresh and strange to be interested in at Gibraltar. Then with the necessity of bribing the Turkish captain and hiring bodyguards for the second leg of the journey, she'd hardly had time for second thoughts.

Now she was here, where Davie might be.

She was surprised that there were only three ships in the harbor and very few people on the quay. Her experience with harbors said that they were usually teeming with workers and passengers and sailors. Those in evidence here seemed to be hurrying about in a sort of random panic. The city spread out above her, the whitewashed adobe buildings with their red tile roofs marching up the hill. Palm trees drooped in the hot April sun. The bougainvillea might be colorful beneath the fine coating of dust, but one couldn't really tell.

She swallowed. Second thoughts came down in buckets now. It suddenly seemed very much harder than she imagined to find Davie. He had said he'd start in Casablanca, but that didn't mean he was still here after more than six weeks.

Well, no use crying before the milk was even surely spilled. The first thing was to acquire a roof over her head. She stalked up to a single cart, finished dumping its cargo unceremoniously by the dockside. The driver shook his head and made a woeful sound when she asked after the Prince Hotel. He dropped her and her trunk in front of a modern building in the Georgian style without ceremony. A stream of obviously English people flooded into the street.

"You there, with the cart!" an older man accosted her driver. "To the harbor. I hear a ship has come in."

"That's my cart," a hefty woman with several ostrich plumes in her brocade turban protested in a screeching voice. Several others joined in the melee. Emma looked about for a doorman. Not seeing one, she hoisted her trunk by one handle and dragged it through the doors.

Inside, chaos reigned. The uniformed attendant behind the desk was arguing with several people. Luggage was stacked everywhere and guests, predominantly men, were rushing about with neck cloths askew and without apparent purpose, contributing to the pandemonium. "Excuse me," she shouted to the man behind the desk, as several of those accosting him threw up their hands and rushed away, creating a gap. "May I check in?"

"Check in?" The man frowned. "Everyone's checking out!"

"Why?" she asked. Several people turned to her in astonishment.

"The embassy evacuated," the deskman explained.

"Blood in the streets," a portly woman wailed.

"The end of the world as we know it." This from a gentleman with long white mustachios.

"The place isn't safe for civilized people."

"Murders every night."

"People drained of blood."

The crowd parted as several more people just dropped their bags and ran for the door under the onslaught of this litany.

Emma felt the blood drain from her face. Davie had said it would be dangerous, but the reality of a city in panic shook her. He must be here. But if the embassy had been evacuated, how would she find him? She took hold of herself and gave herself a mental shake. Let them panic. She had a purpose. She had to find Davie.

The man behind the desk looked around wildly at the crowd rushing for the door and simply deserted his post. *Good,* Emma thought. She grabbed a key labeled "106." That might be on the first floor. She dragged her trunk upstairs. She didn't stay long in the room, though. She pushed out through a lobby now nearly empty and into the heart of the city.

What few people were left all seemed to be hurrying this way and that with bundles on their backs or chickens under their arms or carts full of rugs or furniture or pots, whatever they had. Panic crept into Emma's soul. She tried to stop several people to ask them if they had seen a tall, blond Englishman, but they shook her off and hurried on.

Tears of frustration welled up into her eyes. Had she come all this way only to be denied by a city in panic? She found herself at the open-air market surrounded by stone arches of Romanesque design. Most stalls had already been deserted and their goods abandoned. Some were being looted openly. Others had their wares scattered and broken. Shouts echoed around her. As she turned, she saw in the harbor below a ship weighing anchor, its sails flapping into place. Only one ship remained. Retreat was being cut off even as she failed in her purpose. A man with very bad teeth leered at her and said something unintelligible. He grabbed her arm. She twisted away and ran farther into the market, ducking under cloth hung over ropes for display.

Her breast heaving, she crouched under the fabric. Her breath slowed. She looked up. They were burnooses. That would cover her blonde hair. She pulled one that looked smaller off the line and over her head, twitching up the hood. There, that was better. Now what to do? She peeked over into the next stall. Canvasses stretched across wooden frames were stacked neatly against the tables. She spotted charcoal. The stall belonged to an artist. . . .

Emma had an idea. She slipped into the stall. A charcoal . . . canvasses, and a knife.

Very well. If she could find some nails and a hammer, she had the beginnings of a plan.

They swung through the empty streets, silent, senses pushing out into the night, searching for the ones who would be waiting. Davie saw clearly in the dark now. He no longer wondered why Fedeyah and Rufford never needed candles. He had been hunting with them for nearly a week. Rufford insisted he act only as backup since he was still so newly made. But that did not make the battles any less horrific. Or his horror at his new condition less intense. He wondered that Rufford and Fedeyah were still sane.

Everything had changed in the last week. Davie could call his Companion and use its power to draw the darkness for translocation or to compel a weaker mind. His strength amazed and appalled him, as did the painful burns sunlight caused on skin and eyes. These were signs that he had left his humanity behind. And the sexual need was so intense it had been a torment during the last days. He clung to Rufford's assertion that he didn't have to be like Asharti, but privately he had his doubts. Who knew to what he would stoop when the need for blood or sexual fulfillment raged through his body?

Whenever Asharti seemed near enough to invade his thoughts, he would conjure up an image of Emma and let the love he had seen in Emma's eyes the last time they met banish his memory of Asharti's whips and fangs. Images of Emma did not banish the erections, though. Quite the contrary. And thinking of how repulsed she would be by his new nature created bleakness in his belly but didn't counteract the power of her image on his body.

Perhaps worst of all was the strange exhilaration that threatened to overwhelm him sometimes. How dared he feel so alive, so whole, when he was a creature of night and nightmares? Would he burn in hell for what he had taken from Rufford?

"We'll have trouble feeding with all the humans leaving town," Rufford muttered as they strode down a winding alley toward a broad avenue lined with jacaranda trees.

Davie still chose to take his blood from a cup filled by Rufford or Fedeyah from the wrist of a donor. He couldn't bear to think of drawing his power to elongate his canines and plunge them into a living throat.

They'd been having trouble feeding at all since Davie couldn't procure for them in daylight hours. They holed up wherever they could, easier in the last few days with so many houses vacant. They'd tried feeding before the nightly conflict began, but often the battle came to them before they were ready, with so many of Asharti's minions about. After the battle, they were in no condition to find what they needed. They'd gone without last night. With no blood, how would they keep their strength up?

Rufford backed against a wall at the corner of the boulevard and peered around. Suddenly he straightened. "Well, Ware, do you happen to have a relative named Davie?"

Davie gave a start. "It's Vernon Davis Ware," he said in a low voice. "My family and oldest friends called me Davie." Why had Rufford grown curious now?

Rufford simply pointed. Davie peered into the night. A canvas was tacked to a building across the alleyway at the other corner of the intersection. On it was written, clearly, in charcoal or some such, "Davie Ware. I'm at the Prince Hotel."

Davie was drawn across the alley, enthralled. Who knew him as Davie that might be here in Casablanca? And what was that stuck over the nail that held the canvas?

God! It was a lock of yellow hair, bound by a strip of ribbon.

He turned on Rufford. "Miss Fairfield!"

The scent of cinnamon wafted down the boulevard. "They come," Fedeyah said. Davie drew his sword. Damn!

"Get to the Prince Hotel," Rufford said through gritted teeth.

"I won't leave you two to face them." Shadows drifted out onto the boulevard.

"Think, man! You can't leave her alone in Casablanca now."

Davie counted. Eight? His gut twisted. Rufford was right, but his duty was here. "Why did she come?" he muttered.

"You have to ask?" Rufford's grin was wicked. He motioned with his head. "Lucky dog. Get out of here."

"Four to one," Davie warned.

"We've had worse." When Davie still hesitated, Rufford lifted his brows. "I've got Old blood in my veins, man."

Davie took a breath of night air, redolent with jasmine and ominous with cinnamon. "I'll be back as soon as I can."

"You'll never find us. We'll use the hotel as our safe house." Rufford drew his sword as he scanned the street. "Protect her. We'll see you at dawn."

Davie took off at a run for the waterfront.

5

Emma sat, quiet for the first time in days, and looked out on the night from her small balcony. It wasn't that she wasn't frightened. She was. But there was nothing more to be done. She had posted her signs all over the city this afternoon even as the teeming hordes left town. The harbor was empty. The last ship had sailed on the evening tide. From where she sat she could see several fires burning in the town, but the looting now seemed sporadic. She had gathered lamps from several other rooms to be sure she had enough oil, and locked her door. She was going to sit here day and night with a light burning like a beacon until Davie came for her. She wouldn't let herself think of how angry he would be that she was here or that he might not even be in the city to see her signs. Every piece of common sense said this would work out badly. So she resolved not to listen to her common sense.

The hotel was quiet behind her. The shouting in the streets had grown distant. So she clearly heard the pounding of boot heels taking the stairs up from the lobby two at a time. Her heart leaped into her throat. She would be raped and killed in the next minutes, or . . .

She looked to the door. He burst through it as though it were made of paper, lock and all. "Davie!" She ran to him without thinking, relief flooding her. The door twisted into the room on broken hinges. He took her in an embrace that was like to break her ribs. She didn't care.

"Emma!" he said into her hair. "Emma, what are you doing here? This is no place for a woman." But the chastising nature of the words was lost in his lips moving through her hair, his breath warm. He was wearing only a shirt open at the collar and trousers and boots. He hadn't shaved in several days, but that didn't make him seem unkempt, only rugged and more male than she remembered. She had never seen him without a coat and waistcoat. The hardness of his body beneath his shirt and the exotic scent of cinnamon he wore combined to assault her senses.

But he'd asked a question. What was she doing here? And she'd never really thought what she would tell him. He held her away from his body and looked at her with hungry eyes. His gaze roved over her and stopped at her hair. "Oh," she said apologetically, shaking her head, now full of unruly blonde curls. "I cut off all my hair to make the signs."

Davie gave a lopsided smile. "I like it." Then his grin collapsed. "Oh, Emma, it's too dangerous here. You shouldn't have come!"

She couldn't avoid this. "I . . . I couldn't sit at home and let you face . . . whatever it was you were facing. And don't you dare tell me I'm only a woman and I couldn't help." She felt a strange anger rising in her breast. What was she angry at? That he put himself in danger? That he hadn't offered for her? That he hadn't had the courage of his convictions. . . .

She gathered herself. "If you don't love me, Major Vernon Davis Ware, tell me straight out and I'll go home. But if you do . . . then we belong together, no matter the circumstance. I'll not be a burden on you. And I'll stay out of the way. But I can help you; I know I can."

He looked at her with such intensity in his eyes it made her feel faint. He seemed so . . . alive. He was magnetic, hypnotic even. Had he been this attractive when she'd last seen him? It must be the air of danger that made him seem to vibrate with energy. "This isn't a diplomatic mission, Emma. It's a war."

"Plenty of women follow the drum." She swallowed. "I'll work in the hospital with your wounded. I've volunteered in the hospital in London, you know. Or I'll cook, or I'll wash for your men. I'm not proud, Davie, and I'm not delicate."

He was running his hands up and down her arms from shoulders to elbows, apparently unaware that he did so. His gaze roamed the room. "Emma, Emma, you don't understand."

She grew surer of herself. "You must tell me you don't love me if you want me to leave."

"You know I love you," he almost snapped. "Or you wouldn't have come here. . . ." He seemed to recollect himself. "Your reputation . . . did you have a companion? Your brother?"

"I hired two females and a retired officer as escort." He looked relieved. Well, he'd better know the worst. "I dismissed them in Gibraltar. How could I bring them here with all the rumors of blood in the streets?" Now distress furrowed his brow. "I don't care a jot for my reputation, Davie. I love you. I'll bind your wounds, and barter my jewels for chickens for your stew. I can't stay at home going to parties where the worst thing anyone can imagine is that Lady Jersey is with someone else's child again. And don't think I'll ever love anybody but you. You were talking nonsense that day in Grosvenor Square. If you won't have me, I'll go to Paris or Vienna and set up on my own and I'll die without knowing the joys of marriage. I won't settle for some loveless union with a duke or a poet."

He smiled ruefully and sighed. Then he touched her cheek with the back of his index finger and stroked gently. "My brave, rebellious Emma. You always did have more courage than any ten girls put together."

She wished he would take her in his arms again. As a matter of fact, she wished he would do more. She wanted to cross some line from which she couldn't retreat. In spite of her brave words, she needed to put England and home and small social concerns beyond her reach, to remove any risk that she might just run home with her tail between her legs if the going got rough. Today in Casablanca she had realized that the going might get very rough. She wanted to leave who she was behind entirely. She slid her hand up behind his neck and pulled him down to her. He looked . . . well, frightened. She brushed her lips across his, not quite believing she could be this bold. She really was a rebel!

"Emma," he breathed into her mouth. "You don't know . . . what I might . . . do."

"Yes, I do, Davie," she said with more confidence than she felt inside. "At least I know what I'm hoping you'll do." To punctuate her statement, she slid her hand underneath the open collar of his shirt. The skin at the nape of his neck was damp in the heat of Casablanca. "We love each other. You're going to show me how to love you." She was going to give up her virgin state in order to cross her line. All she had to do was convince him.

"You must save that for your marriage bed." He was breathing hard. She sidled into him and felt the shocking hardness under his trousers roll against her hip. He wanted her!

"That can be my marriage bed," she breathed, pointing to the bed in the other room of the suite. "When we can find someone to perform a ceremony, we will make it official." She saw the conflict churning behind his eyes. How dear that he was so concerned for her he would try to suppress his physical desires. But she wasn't going to let him do that. "If you want me, take me," she challenged. "But know I don't give myself lightly. It will be our troth."

• • •

A thousand thoughts careened and collided in Davie's head. The thing in his blood shouted down his veins, throbbing with life and a sexual intensity that muddied his thoughts. He shook his head as though to clear it. He couldn't make love to Emma. Who knew what he might do when in the throes of passion? And he couldn't marry her either. She didn't know he was a monster. He couldn't let her stay in Casablanca where horror stalked the streets. He'd be dead soon, or, if he lived through this terrible campaign, he'd live forever. Neither would be good for Emma.

And yet . . . she needed the protection of marriage, at least in name. He could not let her go to some foreign city alone, to fall victim to the first rogue she met. If she bore his name, he could write to Charles. Davie's family would look out for her. Then she could return home to the comfort of England and her own family at least. He'd make up some tale as to why she had abandoned her chaperones. He'd think of something.

Very well. He'd find someone to marry them, if he lived through the night. He swallowed and tried to breathe, and took her in his arms. "I am yours," he whispered. "For as long as I live. My name will be your protection, and all that I have."

"For better or worse, 'til death do us part," she recited.

He swallowed, then nodded.

"Then love me."

The thing in his blood sang out in agreement with her, but that was too dangerous. He couldn't give in to passion. He thrust himself away from her and stumbled to the doors open to the balcony. He leaned against the wall. "I dare not consummate our marriage vows," he choked.

She looked stunned and hurt for moment. Then he saw her muster herself. "You won't get off so easily," she chided, her tone deliberately much lighter than his. "You've practically promised me a night of lovemaking, and I shall hold you to it."

He jerked back to her. "I'm not safe," he said through clenched jaws.

"You'd never hurt me," she said, trying to smile.

"I'd never want to." His eyes were wild now. "But people like me, they . . . they hurt people like you. I know. I used to be like you. Someone . . . hurt me."

Her brows contracted. "Hurt physically?"

He nodded, a jerky motion, cleared his throat. "You wouldn't think it possible, I know—a woman hurting a man. But it is." He almost choked on those words.

"A woman hurt you when she made love to you?" She sounded incredulous.

He swallowed and looked away. "Yes."

There was a moment as she digested that. Finally she said, "Whatever has happened to you in this godforsaken place, you are still you. You're a good man, Davie. And you love me. I trust you." She went up behind him and put a hand on the muscles bunched in his shoulder. The water was rising against the dam inside him. She sucked in a breath and put her other hand on his hip. The feel of her hand on his flesh beneath the fabric sent an electric charge straight to his loins. "And whatever happened before, you need a woman who loves you and wants to give herself to you." He turned, tentatively. She smiled. "I think I fill the bill."

Sweet, giving Emma. Her generous nature, her courage touched him deeply. He couldn't let her think he didn't want to make love to her. "Oh, God, Emma! I want you, like . . . like I've never wanted anything or anyone before."

"Then take me, because I want you just that much in return." Her voice was calm, though he could see her heart pounding in her throat. The dam inside him burst. He couldn't resist her. But he could resist the thing in his blood. He'd make sweet love to Emma and give her something of a wedding night, in case he was dead tomorrow, and she a grieving widow.

◆ ◆ ◆

He swept Emma up as though she weighed nothing and carried her into the bedroom. The feel of his hard chest against her breasts made her shudder. At last! Whatever had happened to him in the past, she knew she could heal with time.

"I'll keep control, Emma; I promise," he said as he laid her across the bed and began to strip off his shirt. It was dim in this small room. Only the light from the lamps in the sitting room cast a glow through the doorway. His pale, muscled torso and shoulders made her suck in breath. His chest was covered with curling light hair. His nipples looked soft. She licked her lips and thought what it would be like to kiss them. He sat beside her, pulled off his boots, and began unbuttoning his trousers. Then he stopped, swallowed once, and ducked his head. "I'm sorry. This shouldn't be a rushed affair."

"Then you'll help me undress?" His trousers, partially unbuttoned, gaped over his belly, only just concealing what she wanted most to see. She swallowed.

He did help her undress. He took the pins from her dress one by one as though it was a precious ritual and untied the skirt, unlaced her light corset, pulled off the sleeves until she was standing in her chemise. Her nipples, turned suddenly sensitive, pressed against the fine linen fabric. She felt so vulnerable, unlaced in front of him. She sat and unrolled her stockings herself, as she glanced under her lashes to see him taking off his trousers and smalls with far less ceremony. He turned from her, but not before she had seen his erect member rising out of a nest of hair a shade darker than the blond on his head. It was so much larger than the statues she had seen. Well, *that* was rather . . . intriguing. Could all that fit inside her? She wanted to touch it, examine it. And that thought, in turn, made the throbbing between her legs turn . . . wet.

She let her gaze rove over his tight buttocks, strong thighs, the muscles moving in his back as he folded his trousers. His shoulders were wide—wait, what were those marks? She peered at him in the dim light. Scars. Deep furrows where wounds had healed without benefit of stitches.

All his talk of being hurt became real. Someone had hurt him terribly, purposefully, once. Could he mean a woman did these things to him? All Emma could think about was that she wanted to take that hurt away. She wasn't experienced in love-making, had never even seen a man in the state he was in now. But she was a rebel, wasn't she? She would cast aside maidenly shrinking from the act and try to give him pleasure, show him that love could be generous and sweet. . . .

Davie turned away, ashamed at the throbbing erection that must shock her. Lord knows he'd had erections so frequently in the last week he should be used to it. But the thought of making love to Emma had induced a need that was almost painful in its intensity. He'd had those kinds of erections only with . . . her, but never of his own volition. He wouldn't think of that.

He was having trouble thinking at all. He shouldn't make love to Emma. It was his duty to restrain himself. She shouldn't give up her virginity. He couldn't marry her when he would be dead in a matter of days one way or another. He should send her home. How? The ships had left the harbor. But she must be married, mustn't she? She couldn't return home after traveling unescorted without the protection of his name, even if he himself was dead. Alone in Vienna or Paris? Unthinkable. What to do? Could he keep control? She must never know he was a vampire. He must never hurt her. His breathing grew ragged. How had he let her talk him into this moment, when he was naked and needing and not thinking clearly at all and she was there sitting on the bed behind him wearing only a chemise, her nipples clearly visible, and that halo of hair glowing in the dark . . . ? He could smell her musk of desire, feel the throbbing of blood in her veins. He closed his eyes, knowing he was lost.

He was going to make love to her, and in spite of the fact that he hadn't had blood in two nights, he would muster control of his urges and give her only tenderness and slow enjoyment in her first sexual encounter. He would find the strength. He had no choice.

He did not lay down his folded trousers but clasped them at his loins before he turned back to her, his unruly cock pressing insistently against the fabric. He gasped. She had shrugged out of her chemise and now sat, naked, on the edge of the bed, with a shy smile. She was the most beautiful thing he had ever seen. Her breasts were as full as he'd imagined them, her legs long and shapely, and there, at the vee of her thighs, was the delicate curling blonde thatch that called so to him.

She held out a hand. He could not help but go to her. As he stood before her, she gently took his trousers from him and dropped them. "Would you keep me from enjoying all of you?" she whispered. Even in the dark, he could see her blush. But then, mustering her courage, she reached to stroke his cock, gently, caressing the underside, thumbing the tip. He thought he might pass out. "It's so silky soft," she marveled, "and yet so hard."

"I'm . . . glad it . . . pleases you." What did one say to a beautiful woman admiring her very first cock? Especially when one was busy wondering how one would avoid throwing her back on the bed and plunging said cock into that little vee of curling hair? Her hand cupped his balls and lifted them gently. They were so damned swollen and heavy they filled her hand.

"I've heard that these are very tender. Does this give you discomfort?"

He took two breaths before he could manage, "No."

"I can feel the stones inside."

"So can I." That was enough. He couldn't bear any more of her gentle explorations, so different from . . . No. He

wouldn't think about her. It was time Emma had some pleasure. And he knew what pleasured women. He had been
taught. He had . . . her to thank for that. He picked Emma up
and placed her on the center of the bed and lay down beside
her. He must introduce her slowly. She might be frightened if
he asked to lick her or, worse, asked her to lick him. And then
there was the fact that she was a virgin. She might be in so
much pain after he broke her barrier, pleasure might not be
possible. That meant he had to hold himself in check even
longer. She must be pleasured first.

He brushed his lips across her forehead. His cock lay, hard
and needing, against her soft white thigh. He willed it not to
throb against her, without success. He could feel the blood
pulse in the arteries just under her jaw. He put down all
thought of blood ruthlessly and moved his lips down to hers.
Her mouth opened to him easily. She had been kissed before.
Someday he would want to know by whom. He licked the inside of her lips and then caressed her tongue with his. She returned the caress, making a little sound as she pressed her
breasts against his chest. Her nipples, now tight buds, seemed
to burn his flesh. He ran one hand down her back to cup her
buttocks, squeezing gently. She took her lead from him and
did the same. Her fingers trailed fire over his body. He had
never felt the sensations of lovemaking so intensely. The
aroma of her was so layered with complexity! He could distinguish the smell of the charcoal she had used to write the signs,
the spices from the market she had been in, the musk of her
desire, and underneath, her own sweet signature of scent. And
she was alive with blood. But he couldn't think about that.

Now to bring her slowly and inexorably to her pleasure. He
laid her back and sucked at first one nipple and then the other.
She gave a little moan of pleasure and arched up to his kisses.
What a sensual creature she was! As he sucked, his hands
explored her body, smooth hip, tight belly, and then the thatch
of hair. She spread her legs so that he could have easier access

to her. That sweet act of giving touched him. He slid a finger inside her folds and felt the viscous fluid of desire there. Her bud of pleasure was already swollen. She gasped at his touch.

"Oh, Davie!" But she didn't pull away.

He slid down between her folds and put his middle finger into her tight passage. Her blood throbbed against his hand. He pushed deep, felt the barrier of the hymen. But . . . yes, it was partially torn already. Thank goodness for all her tomboy ways, climbing trees and riding ponies. She had probably been torn a little long ago. It would make tonight easier for her.

He turned his attention back to her lips and kissed her long and hard as he fingered her rising nub with his thumb. She brushed her nipples across his own instinctively searching for more sensation. God, but if he were given enough time he would show her everything. A woman like her should have the full experience of lovemaking and do it often. With him. She was gasping now, into his mouth. He lowered his lips again to her breasts and pulled gently against her nipple as he rubbed her slick membrane. He thought she was near. He mustn't keep her this close to her release for too long, or she might not plunge over the edge. He stopped all movement, all sucking, for a long moment; then just as she began to move her hips, seeking the return of sensation, he redoubled his efforts. She arched against him almost instantly, crying out over and over as he sucked and rubbed. He kept her going until her body jerked away of its own accord and she lay there in his arms, gasping, the pulse in her throat throbbing at him, aching to be opened. His Companion prodded him. He clenched his jaw and refused.

It was exciting to see her orgasm. She came to it so naturally. He lay there, cradling her in his arms, as her breathing returned to normal. He was nearly sure he could give her another one, if he waited for a moment to enter her. She opened her eyes. They were hot with desire. "That was marvelous. Is this what married women get to do?"

"As often as they want it."

"I will want it often." Then she looked conscious. "I had thought . . . that it happened with . . . with your . . ."

"My cock?" He smiled. "It does. And other ways as well."

"Well, then, I think I want your . . . cock."

The word on her lips, breathed into his ear as she touched the organ in question, drove down to his loins with exquisite torture. She rubbed the head again, only this time the clear liquid of his restraint was slicked over his burning flesh. "God, Emma," he choked. He raised himself and parted her knees, then knelt between them. A rising film of red desire seemed to coat his body. He wanted her, wanted . . . *wanted*. Lord help him go easy in spite of the flames that threatened to consume all control. He held himself above her and positioned himself at the entrance to her tight shaft.

"This might be uncomfortable," he said.

"Davie, I want your cock." Her tone was urgent. She wanted restraint no more than he.

He pressed inside her. She was so tight around him. A little farther . . . there was what remained of the barrier. He pushed home. She sucked in a breath as he filled her. That was all. Then he pulled almost back to the entrance, plunged again. This time she arched her hips and he lost all restraint. He slid in and out. He pulled her against him, showing her the dance in counterpoint that gave them both most pleasure. God, could he wait for her to reach her climax? His blood roared at him. His shaft throbbed inside her tight sheath. Emma, this was for Emma, not for him. She gasped, her panting growing quicker.

He pulled her up and held her against him while he knelt on the bed, moving her easily up and down on his shaft with his newfound strength. She arched her neck just in front of him, making small sounds with each stroke. No, he wouldn't answer the blood he felt throbbing in her throat. He wouldn't do what had been done to him. . . .

And then she shuddered and made small yipping sounds as her muscles contracted around him, milking his cock. He exploded. The world went red. He spurted his soul out in a stream of molten lava, even as blackness threatened to overwhelm his vision.

He blinked as the room wavered back into view. What kind of an orgasm was that? He had felt as though he was . . . what? Transformed? Reborn? But he had managed not to take her blood. A new world opened up in front of him. He could resist the need. It had been sexual intercourse, extraordinary, but ordinary after all.

Emma was looking at him with a soft expression in her eyes.

"Did I hurt you?" he asked.

"I felt a twinge only. Nothing compared to what came after. You know," she mused, "the first time was very good, but the last time with you inside me felt more fulfilling. You said there are other ways?"

He smiled and nodded. "Lots of other ways."

"I want to know them. How many times can we do it?"

"I don't know," he said, barking a laugh. "A lot of times."

"Good," she said, snuggling into him.

"Maybe not an infinite number just in a row," he amended. "After a few we will have to rest. But there is always tomorrow. . . ."

Rufford! Rufford and Fedeyah would be coming at dawn. If they survived the night. They had been doing their duty and suffering for it while he had been dallying here with Emma. He raised himself on one elbow. And when they came, they would be wounded and bloody, and they would heal too quickly. He had to keep Emma away from that and from knowing that her only protection from monsters was another monster. She must never know what he was.

But first, he'd let her show him how many times she'd like to be loved tonight.

"We're going to get some visitors at dawn," he said, looking at her tenderly. He was supremely sorry this night had to end.

They had made love to exhaustion. She was just stretching awake from having slept for a few hours. He drew her into his chest. There was no stopping time, though. "They need a place to recuperate from their battles. It . . . it has been my job to attend to them, and I must go when they come. And tomorrow night, I'll be with them, fighting."

She, too, raised herself on one elbow. Her lips were swollen from kissing, her cheeks and breasts still flushed. "Of course. I can help. I can take care of your compatriots, and you, God forbid, if comes to that."

"They have their own ways. There's nothing you can do." He hated rejecting her offer.

She looked at him strangely. Then she sat up. "Vernon Davis Ware, if you think I came all the way to Casablanca, married you—which I just did, minus the minister—just to have you keep me at arm's length, you'll have to think again. Whatever trials you have ahead are my trials. Do you understand?"

He did. But of course she had no idea what she'd gotten herself into. When it got close to dawn, he'd lock her in the room next door to protect her from the knowledge of just what she had married, for however brief a time. At that thought, winter seemed to blow into his soul, bleak and sere. And even more concerning, a little fire in that frozen landscape would not go out and hissed into the blowing snow, *The blood is the life!*

6

How dare he?! Emma thought as she rattled the doorknob. *He's locked me in!*

She whirled and put her back against the door. She'd moved into the adjacent room at his insistence, because of the broken lock. Here she was, dressed in serviceable clothes and sensible half-boots, ready to go down and help him and his friends, and now he was trying to protect her from the ugliness of his life. She wouldn't have it.

She pushed off the door and went out onto the balcony. The sun was rising behind the city, for it created an answering glow out over the harbor, now empty of ships. *We'll just see about that.* She climbed up on the wooden chair and from there to the sidewall of the balcony. *Don't look down. The gap isn't more than four feet. Hardly more than a step.*

She held her breath and jumped, teetering on the wall of the balcony to her original room until she could grasp the striped awning and lower herself down. She dashed out through the broken door. Now to find her quarry. Where in the hotel would she be if she had just come in from battle? There were probably forty rooms here. No, not in a room. She'd be in the kitchens.

She went cautiously down the great staircase, then wended her way to the back from the lobby. She heard them before she saw them.

"Lord, Rufford, if reinforcements don't come soon . . ." Davie, sounding shocked.

"They'll come. . . ." A weary baritone she recognized. She had stood up at his wedding to Beth Rochewell. Ian Rufford was here with Davie?

"Fedeyah, sit down. Drink this." Davie in his most commanding Major's voice.

"Enough! There is so little." An Arab accent. "Save some for Rufford and yourself."

She slid quietly toward an open doorway from which the voices came.

"I'll find more." This from Davie, but he wasn't sure. She could hear it in his voice.

"You can't go out in daylight." Mr. Rufford gasped for breath. "You'll fry."

"The city is deserted, except for them," the Arab muttered. "Unless Allah provides, we must do without."

Emma peered around the door frame. At first she couldn't quite take in what she was seeing. Davie stood over Mr. Rufford, who was laid out on one of the long wooden tables in the center of the kitchen. He cradled Mr. Rufford's head in one arm and was helping him to drink from a cup. Mr. Rufford's mouth was stained red, along with everything else. Blood was everywhere. Terrible wounds were revealed by the shredded clothing still clinging to Mr. Rufford. On the hearth of the great fireplace filled with spits and pots sat an Arab man with sad eyes, also wounded. The whole place smelled of blood. Shock and revulsion cascaded over her.

"I should never have left you to face them," Davie said, his voice soaked in guilt.

Mr. Rufford put up a hand and looked around. How was he still breathing? "Come in, my dear Miss Fairfield," he said hoarsely.

Davie swung round. The Arab looked up. She sighed and stepped out into the doorway.

"Miss Fairfield! Get back to your room!" Davie cried, laying Rufford back onto the table. He strode across to her and took her shoulders.

"Miss Fairfield"? "Get back to your room"? "As you recall, *Major Ware,* as soon as you can find a minister, it will be Emma Ware. And I told you when I accepted your proposal to share your life last night that I share it all, whether you like it or not." She looked to the other men. She was about to ask how she could help when a cut across Mr. Rufford's forehead sealed itself before her very eyes. She gasped. *What is going on here?* Davie tried to turn her about and hustle her from the room, but she pulled out of his grasp. She glanced across to the Arab. The pink weal of a scar slowly disappeared from his cheek.

"What are you?" she whispered to Mr. Rufford, ignoring Davie's sputtering protests.

"Don't tell her," Davie warned.

"We are not like you, Miss Fairfield," Mr. Rufford said, getting up to one elbow. "Not anymore." A sword wound on his chest began to close.

She swallowed and tried to breathe. "I see that." She turned to Davie. "You might as well tell me." He looked away, ashamed.

"Perhaps it would be easier if I tell you, Miss Fairfield. I'll be stronger in a bit." Mr. Rufford lay back, obviously exhausted.

She wanted to know now. Davie was leaning against the window frame as though defeated. She turned to the Arab. "You tell me."

The Arab glanced to Davie. "We have a thing in our blood, miss. It changes us."

"How?" She crossed the room to him, slowly. "How does it change you?"

"We are strong. We heal and live long. Sunlight is painful. We can move unseen."

Davie turned from the window, his expression fierce. "I don't think you're doing it justice, Fedeyah. It's a disease, Emma. We're vampire. We're immortal unless we're decapitated, and we drink human blood. No way around that. And Fedeyah forgot to mention the fact that we can compel weaker minds. We can make people do things they don't want to do."

They were vampire? The word echoed in her mind with horrible reverberations.

"God in heaven," Davie continued, rolling his head, "we can't even commit suicide! Rufford knows; he tried often enough. We're monsters, Emma, once we're infected. Monsters." This last was said on a note of such despair, her heart went out to him.

She stood, blinking stupidly, wondering what to do, what to think. Vampire, human blood, immortality. And Davie, her Davie, was condemned to this? She glanced to Rufford, who seemed only half-sensible, his wounds slowly resolving themselves. The red trickling from the corner of his mouth was human blood. How could she think that so calmly?

"Who did you kill tonight?" It was as though someone else asked the question.

"Others of our kind, made by an evil woman. Not pretty." Davie's mouth was grim.

Decapitation. She would wager it wasn't pretty.

"They want to rule the world," the Arab said. His voice grew incredibly sad. "They make more vampires. It would destroy the balance. We make jihad against them."

"Balance? What balance?"

"We do not kill humans for our blood," Fedeyah explained. "We don't make others of our kind. There are Rules. Rules they do not obey."

"And these Rules wouldn't condone marriage to a woman who isn't like you, would they?" She turned to Davie. Anger boiled up out of her belly uncontrolled. Davie drank human blood and was going to live forever unless he was killed in some horrible way fighting a war against monsters like him. "You knew that last night. And you let me think we could be happy together." Tears sprang from nowhere.

"Go back to your room, Miss Fairfield," Davie said. His voice was distant. He turned back to the window.

She whirled and ran down the corridor and up to her room. The damned door was locked, so she went into her original room and pushed the door back into its frame, no matter how silly that was. She couldn't lock out the creatures downstairs. With their strength they would just push through an unlocked door or a locked one. She remembered how Davie had burst into the room. She threw herself on the bed, sobbing, because all her innocence was lost and all her future, and the world held monsters and one of them was Davie.

She came out of a sleep feeling drugged and groggy. It was twilight. The sky outside the window was purple, edging into indigo. Someone was knocking at the door.

"Miss Fairfield?"

One of the monsters, she thought dully. *Mr Rufford.* "Come in." What did it matter?

He pushed the door in gingerly. He was clean, shaved, no blood in sight. He wore a shirt open at the neck, black trousers, and riding boots to the knee. His brown, curling hair was tied back in a ribbon, just as it had been in St. James's Church when he had married Miss Rochewell. *Hmmm.* Emma thought about that.

He made a small bow. "Are you well? I thought you might be hungry." She got up on one elbow. He carried a plate: cold roast beef, horseradish, some radishes and small tomatoes, a chunk of bread. She was famished. How could her body betray her emotions so? Without waiting for an answer, he set the plate down on the table beside the bed. She sat up and touched her hair. "You look fine." He hesitated, looking as though he thought he should go but wanted to stay.

She didn't want him to go, she decided. In the shock of the moment in the kitchen, she hadn't realized what to ask. Now she did. "Won't you sit down?" she asked, gesturing to a chair.

He hesitated, then sat.

Emma's mind churned. She thought back to the wedding. "Miss Rochewell, I mean Mrs. Rufford . . ." She frowned. "Where is she now?"

"She serves the cause in Tripoli." The grimace around his mouth said he didn't like it. That was interesting, though. Beth Rufford was allowed to help the cause.

"Did she know?"

His blue eyes looked up sharply. "When she married me? Yes. A tribute to her courage."

Miss Rochewell had accepted that Mr. Rufford was vampire? How could she? Still . . . Emma sorted through what she knew. Drinking human blood—bad, but as long as they didn't kill . . . How could she be thinking that? Strong—that was fine. Compelling people against their will—bad again, but a good man could refrain, couldn't he? It occurred to her that compulsion might be one way a woman could hurt a man during sex. She wondered how Davie had been "infected" and whether it had anything to do with the evil woman who made vampires. And yet the most important thing Emma wanted to know might only be answered by this vampire sitting across from her who had married a mortal woman. "How . . . how does she bear the fact that she is mortal and you are not?" In some ways it came down to that.

Mr. Rufford took a breath. "She doesn't have to. She isn't mortal anymore."

Emma felt her eyes get big.

"As I said, she has courage." He looked fond and . . .

proud. He shot her another sharp glance. "Beth and I accept who we are. More than accept. I can't explain. Major Ware may accept someday. I hope so. I promised to kill him if he demanded it. I hope I won't have to keep that promise." Mr. Rufford rose. "Eat. Keep up your strength. We must go soon. The jihad calls."

"Wait! How . . . how is one infected? How was Davie infected?"

"The blood from one of us must be ingested, or introduced through a cut. Major Ware came to serve our cause here in Casablanca as a human. It was an incredible thing to ask of him, but we needed someone who could go about in daylight. He was infected while he defended Fedeyah and me."

"How . . . did he get the scars I saw on his body?" She felt herself flush.

"Asharti." Mr. Rufford set his mouth. "She made the army we fight. We have all suffered at her hands." He nodded curtly, his confidences at an end. "Stay in tonight. The streets will not be safe." He slid out quietly.

Emma took up the plate and absently crunched a radish. Davie thought he was a monster. But Rufford didn't. He loved his wife. They had accepted . . . more than accepted that they were vampire. What did that mean?

Emma rolled up a slice of beef and dipped it in horseradish. Where else could one get beef and horseradish but in an English hotel, even on the other side of the world? English people always took who they were along with them. A fault perhaps. But therein lay a truth. Didn't one always take oneself along no matter how strange the destination? Were she and Davie any different at heart than they were yesterday? Mrs. Rufford joined her husband even when she knew the truth about him. Mr. Rufford must have made her vampire in spite of these Rules or whatever they were, and he loved her, and . . .

And what?

And that changed everything.

Emma stared at the whitewashed walls of the room, painted crimson with the last of the dying sun. She was strangely aware of her lungs pushing air in and out of her chest, her heart thudding. The decision that rattled in her brain demanding to be made frightened her.

She had thought she was a rebel because she refused to marry someone she didn't love. True rebellion was deeper than that. She thought she was bold chasing after Davie to Casablanca. She didn't know then what "bold" meant. Now she would find out what she was made of. She was at the extreme edge of experience, and yet there was one more step to take. She had wanted to cross some line that would cut off all retreat to her humdrum life in England by giving up her virginity. Now she knew that wasn't a bold enough line.

The sky was lightening out the window of the hotel kitchen. Emma was ready for the return of the warriors. Could she face the kind of wounds she had seen yesterday morning? Could she bear to see Davie hurt? No time for those thoughts now. She had hot food prepared, a hearty lamb stew. She had ripped up some hotel sheets for bandages, though she wasn't certain they would be useful. One thing she knew they'd need she didn't have. Blood.

Or maybe she did.

Crashing sounded from the front lobby. Looters? The hotel had been deserted all day. Or maybe it was Davie coming back. She picked up a butcher's knife and ran to the front.

A ragged man knelt before two others, sobbing, pleading in Arabic. She might not understand the words, but she understood his horrified expression. He knew his life hung in the balance. The scent of cinnamon filled the air. He had obviously tried to take refuge in the hotel. Unsuccessfully. At her appearance his two persecutors swung around. A wicked grin stole over the face of the taller one. He saluted her. Both intruders had an avaricious gleam in their eyes. The stouter one turned back to the sobbing man. The one before her stalked forward two steps. His eyes turned red. There was no other word for it. And the grin on his face now included canines elongating into fangs. Panic soaked her. She had to run!

But she didn't. She walked forward though she knew she shouldn't, even though she was afraid. She struggled against the impulse, but still she took step after step, her chest heaving with useless resistance until she could feel his reeking breath, hot on her face. Behind her nemesis she heard a very human shriek, then a horrible burbling sound. She thought she might be going to pass out, because there was a whirling blackness just at the edge of her vision. The creature held her close. Red eyes filled her vision. She prayed to faint. The creature wrenched away from her and she fell to the floor. Above her, Davie shouted like a berserker as he slashed at her attacker.

Still dazed, she saw that Davie was already wounded in a dozen places. And there was Mr. Rufford. How was he still standing? But they were, fighting the two attackers. On the floor near the door was the ragged man, his throat ripped out. The scene taking place around her seemed unreal, it was so horrific. Emma heard Davie's grunt as a blade found him, a shriek of anguish as Rufford felled one. She felt the splatter of warm liquid and blinked when a head rolled past her.

It was over. The lobby seemed strewn with body parts. Davie sank to his knees in the gore. Mr. Rufford wavered on his feet but went to help him. A whirling darkness dissipated in the corner and Fedeyah stepped out of it. She was beyond surprise.

Fedeyah came to help her up. "We have rats in the house," he observed. "That makes forty." She saw that she was still gripping the silly butcher's knife. She let it clatter to the floor.

This? This was what they had been facing every night?

Mr. Rufford pulled Davie's arm over his shoulder. "To the kitchens."

Emma trailed in their wake, still blinking. They staggered into a kitchen, filled with the smell of spiced lamb stew and her neat rows of rolled bandages. Fedeyah sank on the raised hearth. Mr. Rufford heaved Davie up on the huge wooden table and then simply sank to the floor, his back against a table leg. Davie didn't move.

"What, what can I do for you?" she asked faintly. Her rolled bandages seemed ludicrous.

"Blood," Mr. Rufford breathed.

She felt her own blood rush from her face.

"No, no." Rufford shook his head wearily. "Not from you. From the dead man by the door. It must be from the human."

She swallowed. Very well. She grabbed an intricately painted terra-cotta bowl and turned to face the lobby. She kept her mind tight, small. *Step. Step. Step. Survey the room. Find the ragged man. Did the ragged tear in his throat still bleed? Yes. Step. Step. Kneel. Hold the bowl. Keep your mind a blank. Don't look at his opaque eyes. Keep your stomach clenched.* The flow slowed to a drip. *Look at the bowl. Not full. Survey the room. Blood everywhere. But not human. This is all the human blood. Is it enough? Stand. Wait for the room to steady. Step. Step. Step. Careful with the bowl.*

She fell to her knees in the hallway and vomited onto the tiles. But she didn't spill the precious bowl. Then she staggered up. *Push into the kitchen. Kneel in front of Mr. Rufford.* "Is it enough?"

She saw the answer in his look. "Give it to Fedeyah and Ware. I'll do."

Now was the moment. "I'll take care of Major Ware," she whispered, and offered the bowl to Mr. Rufford.

He peered at her through exhausted eyes. A small smile curved his lips. He nodded, took the bowl, and gulped his half. The gray in his complexion faded. "I told him he was a lucky dog."

She chewed her lips and glanced to Davie. "This doesn't seem lucky."

"It will, if we can prevail against the tide."

"I hope you're right." She took the bowl to Fedeyah, who drank the balance. Both he and Mr. Rufford were healing faster. Only Davie remained still and bleeding. She glanced to Rufford. "How . . . how do I do this? Must I cut myself?" She hoped she had the courage.

To her surprise, Rufford pushed himself up and looked around. Then he pulled Davie from the table, hefted his limp form across his shoulders, and staggered to a little storeroom off the main kitchen. There he laid Davie down across some sacks of flour. "Gently," Mr. Rufford said. "Lie by his side. He will know what to do." He stumbled from the room.

Emma looked around and saw a flint and candle. She lit the candle and shut the door. The smell of flour and dried beans was overwhelmed by the cinnamon scent of Davie and the smell of blood. She swallowed. *No time to lose the courage of your convictions.* Davie needed her. And if what he needed wasn't just in the ordinary line of mending handkerchiefs and hosting his dinner parties, well, that was just what she had escaped London to avoid.

She tried not to look at his wounds as she lay down. She was dimly aware that he had cuts and gouges over much of his body. His clothes were in tatters. *He'll heal,* she told herself. *Just like Rufford and Fedeyah.* She pressed herself to his side and felt the warmth there. She brushed the hair back from his forehead. There was a gash on his cheek that didn't seem to be healing at all and one on his shoulder, peeking through his torn shirt. "Davie," she whispered. His eyelids fluttered. "Davie, wake up and take what you need."

The blue eyes opened, struggled to focus. Then he turned to her. "You shouldn't be here, Emma," he whispered. "You shouldn't have seen—"

"This is exactly where I should be," she corrected. She tried to keep fear from knocking against her ribs as she saw his eyes flicker red.

"No," he gasped in a strangled sob. His eyes faded to blue. He wrenched his head to the side. "I'm a beast, Emma."

She reached to his jaw and gently turned him back to face her. "You're my Davie. I'm your Emma. Nothing has changed. I want you, Vernon Davis Ware. And I'm not going to give you up just because you're immortal and strong. Or over the blood. Miss Rochewell didn't give up Rufford."

"You don't know—"

"But I do. Surely nothing can be worse than tonight."

"One mortal, one not . . ." He shook his head ever so slightly.

She left that for later, just put up her chin and bared her throat to him.

His eyes began to glow faintly red. "I can't take from you. . . ." This was a desperate sob.

"You're not taking, my love. I'm giving. It's different." She stroked his jawline as his eyes went fully red. Would he growl as those in the lobby had? Would he rip her throat?

Instead he kissed her, gently. His lips brushed her chin, her jaw. "I don't deserve you," he murmured. Then he kissed her throat. She forced her shoulders to relax. She stretched her head back, waiting. But he continued to kiss her so softly, so tenderly, that she began to feel the wet between her legs. She remembered yesterday, making love through the sunlight hours, sweet pleasure rolling through her again and again at Davie's touch. And when the twin points of pain finally came, they were all mixed up for her in lovemaking. Davie filled all her senses, even pain. She moaned as he clasped her to his body and sucked rhythmically.

"Ahhh, Davie, Davie," she murmured, and held his head against her throat. The pain was over. All that remained was the sensation of being one with him, possessed. The throb of her heart was meant to push her blood into his mouth. The great artery in her throat was meant to be opened by him. Her hips began to move of their own accord as they rocked together. And then there came a feeling of . . . distance, as if she were floating away on the tide of their passionate exchange. She relaxed into his arms.

The moment she went limp, he wrenched away with a cry. "Emma, Emma, did I take too much? God, what have I done?"

She looked up at him, sleepy. "No. That was . . . exciting." She noticed that the wound on his cheek was closed. That brought her up sharply. She shook off her lethargy and examined him, as he hung over her. If she didn't bestir herself it would be too late. But no, the wound on his shoulder was still open and seeping. She raised herself on one elbow and pushed him firmly onto his back. He looked surprised. Then she bent her head, pulled back his tattered shirt, and, taking only one breath for courage, licked his wound.

The taste of his blood was copper, thick. Not unpleasant. She licked again, just to make sure she got enough. The wound closed under her lips.

He gripped her shoulders, his glare fierce. "What have you done?" he cried.

She looked at him calmly, more calmly than her thumping heart might indicate. "I have fulfilled a vow. For better or for worse."

"You don't know!" He sat up. With the strength lent by her blood, his wounds were disappearing quickly. "You'll die without the immunity of a vampire's blood. . . ."

"How lucky that I know a vampire. You won't let the Rules stand in the way of my immunity, will you, Davie?"

"Emma." His eyes filled. "I will likely die tonight, Emma. We can't hold them. Forty we killed tonight and still they come and come. You'll be left alone to die horribly."

"We both could die tonight, Davie. Or any other night. One just can't know the future."

"You don't know what you're in for. You can't."

"Probably neither of us do." She smiled ruefully. "But we'll face it together."

He grabbed her, shook her until she thought her teeth would rattle, and then took her in a fierce embrace. She could hear him trying to suppress the sobs in his chest. There. That was better. "I wanted to protect you."

"Do your best, Davie. I permit you to protect me from anything but you."

"I never wanted this for you."

"And what I want, does that not count? We are a partnership." It was her turn to disengage herself and hold him away from her. "An equal partnership."

"Woman!" he half-laughed, though his cheeks were wet.

"See?" She smiled. "You didn't know what you were getting into with me, either." She sobered as a flaming sensation coursed along her veins. "Mr. Rufford may not be happy over what I've done. And you must wait to give me immunity. You can't be weakened with the odds so great." Suddenly things she hadn't anticipated came rushing in. She felt her eyes go big. Now was not the time for her to become ill and be a burden on him.

He rose and handed her up off the flour sacks, his mouth a grim line. "Just let Rufford try to hinder us. Let us see how he and Fedeyah go on. They didn't have blood tonight."

She followed him, dousing the candle. "They did have blood. I collected a bowlful from that man in the lobby, the one who wasn't vampire. Or what was left of him."

He turned a shocked countenance on her. "You . . . ?"

"I managed." She didn't tell him she had vomited.

He chuffed a laugh and took her hand. Rufford was sitting at the table in front of the hearth, tucking into a bowl of the stew. Fedeyah was pouring wine. He handed Davie a glass. Their wounds were hardly more than scars.

"Miss Fairfield?" Fedeyah asked, waving a full glass of wine. "You look pale."

"Thank you." She nodded.

"She needs blood, Rufford," Davie said, without preamble. His voice had iron in it.

"I thought she might," Rufford remarked. "Excellent stew, Miss Fairfield. We are not used to such expertise in the kitchen. Or should I call you Mrs. Ware?"

"That can wait until we find a Christian minister," she said, suddenly shy. The room was doing funny things around the edges.

Mr. Rufford peered at her. "Take her upstairs where she can be comfortable, Ware."

"I mean to give her what she needs." Davie said it as a threat, a promise. Emma smiled. He had decided.

"My blood will do the job faster. I'll send up a cup later. Between us we can muster enough to make her way easier than yours was."

"My blood is hers," Fedeyah said from somewhere far away.

Emma felt her knees grow wobbly as the fire in her veins raced up toward her heart. She wanted to thank them, to apologize for being so much trouble . . . but she couldn't seem to make her mouth work. Then Davie swept her up in his arms. She felt his heart beating against her breast. . . .

Night. Blessed darkness! Moonlight shone in through shutters thrown wide to the night air. She was alive! She touched the wool of a fine red robe she had been wrapped in. She could feel each individual thread in it. The scent of jasmine drifted in through the window. How had she never noticed how wonderful jasmine smelled? Joyful life flowed through her veins . . . she felt . . . *more* than she had ever been. Where was Davie? She must tell him how wonderful she felt.

She heard noise in the street below. She threw off the covers. How long had she lain here? She remembered Davie sitting with her, Davie making her drink the thick, sweet copper-flavored blood drained from his wrist or sent up from Rufford and Fedeyah. The pain had been dreadful, but always Davie was there to soothe her. . . .

She leaned out of the window. In the street below, Davie, Rufford, and Fedeyah stood, backs together, sabers drawn, and in a semicircle around them stood what? Fifty? A hundred? Eyes glowed red on both sides. She stifled a cry.

"Strategic retreat, Ware?" Rufford whispered. She heard him clearly, though.

"What use?" Davie answered, iron resolve in his voice.

"Very well. The last stand against chaos starts here." Rufford straightened.

Lord, God, if such as I am now may pray to you, then help them! she thought.

But dash it all, she dared not leave it only to God. Strength rushed through her. She would not again stand by stunned while they fought for their lives as she had in the lobby that first night. She whirled from the window and hurried down the stairs. The lobby had been cleared of corpses. Her bare feet slapped against the cool tile. Over the fireplace in the lobby hung a display of crossed swords. No paltry butcher's knife for her tonight. She climbed on the hearth and stood on tiptoe. If Davie was going to die tonight in some gesture of sacrifice and duty, no matter how futile, then so would she.

She had a moment of doubt as she reached for the heavy weapon. She was only a woman. But she hefted the sword easily. She was that strong! She didn't stop to wonder. The red robe she wore was a native burnoose, richly embroidered at the edges, much better than her English dress for moving about in. She raised her sword and ran for the street. She had no skill with such a weapon. But that was not the point, was it?

The three men standing in a semicircle against the hordes glanced back. Rufford smiled. Fedeyah touched his forehead once. And Davie, about to protest, closed his mouth firmly over whatever he would have said. She took her place beside him.

He looked down at her with such love in his eyes that the thing inside her welled up and shouted gladness. Life seemed to hum in her veins. But there was no time to tell him. Movement made her glance out at their enemies. The wall of red eyes ahead advanced. Who were these men? Why were they here? Only what they wanted was plain. They wanted the four before them dead. Fedeyah and Rufford spread out to give themselves room to swing their swords.

"Decapitation is the only way," Davie whispered, his eyes hard. "It's difficult. Aim for the neck. I'll finish them."

Emma swallowed. Killing people? Had she thought this through? Even such creatures as these? But what choice was there?

At that moment, a heavy man in the center let out a piercing ululation, and the line broke into a melee of bodies as they charged forward. This was it, the doomed last stand against chaos.

Emma hefted the sword with both hands. Davie stepped in front of her, slashing. A body launched itself into the air from the side. Emma held her sword out, frightened. The body was impaled upon it, wrenching it from her grip. She shrieked in horror. But then the creature stood. He slashed at her. A cut opened on her shoulder. She gripped the hilt of her sword where it protruded from the creature's breast and pulled. Davie slashed at the vampire's neck. She didn't think anything happened, but the creature fell back. She pulled her sword back with both hands and slashed at the neck of an oncoming boy, even as horror shrieked inside her. The blade thunked against something. A horrible cut opened up, but the boy raised his sword. Davie cut at three others now descending. Shadows cascaded behind them. There were too many. Rufford fought like a slashing demon. Too many!

In the center of the melee, whirling darkness spread, obscuring even the closest of figures. Emma just pushed the young boy vampire with the glowing eyes and blood spurting from the cut she'd made back into the crowd. The darkness was everywhere, in among them. Had she not seen that strange kind of darkness before? A cutlass found Davie, and another vampire was twisting Davie's head. Emma slashed at those arms furiously. The attacker fell away, howling. A hand grasped her shoulder. She turned. Another young man hardly out of his teens hissed at her, brandishing a knife. She pulled away.

Time slowed as combatants on both sides took in a new reality. The darkness was seeping into the earth, it seemed. And taking its place, standing among the attackers, still like statues, were perhaps twenty men and women, some dressed as monks, some in rich garb from many nations. The stillness lasted but a moment. They began to move almost faster than the eye could comprehend, rending, slashing at the hordes. And their eyes glowed red.

"How did you hold out?" a tall man with luxuriant mustachios asked. Emma sat in a corner just behind Ian Rufford, hoping not to be noticed. The power careening around the room was intimidating. Energy vibrated in different notes and tones. Davie had taken several of the newcomers upstairs to bathe and dress, but perhaps fifteen of the victorious were arrayed around the grand dining room in various states of dishevelment. Wounds were healed and now a cold collation and the hotel cellar's finest vintages were being consumed with relish by monks and noblemen alike. "Must have been the blood of the Old One that runs in your veins."

"We would not have held through tonight if you had not come." Rufford frowned into the dregs at the bottom of his glass.

Emma recognized the stunning woman with hair like banked coals who poured Rufford another glass of wine. Beatrix Lisse, Countess of Lente and toast of London's male society. It was disconcerting, no, stunning to discover that she had been vampire all along.

"Why so anxious, Rufford?" the Countess asked. "Asharti's army is broken."

"Here," he growled. "But there is still Tripoli."

"Ahhh," she said in recognition. "John sent word. Tripoli is secured. Your Beth is fine."

Rufford relaxed.

"We expected two of you. Yet we find four," the Countess observed, glancing at Emma.

Davie's new kind might not be welcoming to newly made vampires, since they had just spent some effort to eradicate an army of them. Emma tried to think what to do about that, but she was having trouble concentrating on the talk around her. Thoughts of Davie kept creeping into her mind and down lower to the point between her legs. The flood of life that coursed through her veins seemed to conjure thoughts of Davie, naked and needing. She wished he would return. But maybe that would only make it worse.

"Ironic, isn't it, Beatrix?" Rufford asked, twirling his glass. "Four made vampires, two actually by Asharti, were the only thing standing between Asharti's army and success." He said to Emma confidentially, "The Countess was my instructor in the ways of being vampire." Then he turned back to Beatrix Lisse. "You didn't mind using made vampires when it was the only chance you had to kill Asharti, did you?"

"Point taken," she conceded.

"And I called for Ware. He came, knowing exactly what he was up against. He kept us provisioned and provided logistics for nearly two months."

"Courageous fellow." There was still a tone of reserve in her voice. Emma could see that several of the others were listening.

"He got infected saving my life, Beatrix," Rufford said, his voice hard. "I couldn't let him die, any more than Fedeyah could let me die."

"And you?" the Countess asked Emma, with sweetness that Emma knew masked dangerous power. "What brought you all the way from England to a place like Casablanca?"

Emma lifted her chin. "I came to help Major Ware."

"She and I were betrothed." Davie came down the main staircase, himself washed and dressed. The coat didn't fit him exactly. It was probably "borrowed" from one of the departed hotel guests. But to her he had never looked better, more English, more hers. Now she recognized the vibrating intensity the Companion gave. The fact that Davie had just lied to save her face was dear. "She sacrificed as much as anyone for this cause. I made her vampire. Blame me."

Emma stood. She couldn't let Davie take responsibility for this. This was on her head. "No, he didn't, Countess. I couldn't gather enough human blood for all three of them. So I gave him my blood." Davie came to put his arm around her. She smiled at him, getting courage from his straight back. He was proud of her. She turned to the Countess. "And then I licked his wounds. I couldn't let his condition stand between us. In short, I did it for love. And you won't understand that, but it's the truth."

The Countess glanced to Rufford, uncertain.

"True," he remarked. "Of course *you've* never made anyone for love. John Staunton, Earl of Langley, for instance. Why, I'll wager he's always been vampire—"

Beatrix Lisse threw up her hands. "Ahhh! I can't police true love. The Elders must grow used to it." She poured wine into her own glass, frowning. "These outposts never have champagne . . . ."

Davie sat next to Emma. The others began planning to spread across the city to be certain the stragglers from Asharti's army were no more. Davie took Emma's hand. It sent what must be the same electric shocks through her body as it had in the breakfast room of Fairfield House, but now they seemed magnified a thousand times.

"You are under no obligation, Emma," Davie murmured. He glanced down at their joined hands, unable to meet her eyes. "I know the Companion in your blood must seem a . . . a violation. If you want to cry off. . . ."

"A violation?" She drew her brows together. Did that mean he was the one who wanted to cry off now that together might mean forever? Should she free him from his vow and let him have time to decide?

No, dash it all! What good was being a rebel if you couldn't tell the truth and demand truth in return and damn the consequences? She'd know how he felt for certain if she could look into his eyes. Diplomat or no, he wouldn't be able to hide how he felt about her. That was why he wouldn't look at her, because he knew his eyes left him vulnerable. She lifted his chin.

What she saw in his eyes was so complex she needed a moment to interpret it. He had put up a wall. He thought he was making his eyes calm and flat. But underneath was such longing that no wall could hide it.

She smiled. "Can you call the life we feel, this sensation of wholeness, a violation? I call it a gift."

"The gift comes with a few drawbacks," he managed, swallowing.

She smiled and gave a tiny shrug. "So does life."

He cleared his throat. "Does . . . does that mean . . . ?"

"It means I have no intention of releasing you from your promise, Davie Ware. It means I want to know what all this sensation flooding me will feel like in bed naked with you, with your lips on my body and your cock between my thighs. I have been unable to think of almost anything else for the last hour. Am I making myself clear enough here?"

He flushed and laughed, whether in embarrassment at her

language or in sympathy with her wishes she'd wager even he wasn't sure. They noticed the silence around them at the same time. They turned their heads.

The others in the room were staring at them, some with frank amusement in their eyes. Emma felt her rebellion dissolve into a fiery blush.

Davie stood, squeezing her hand for reassurance. "I . . . I crave a boon," he announced to everyone and no one.

"We *are* leaving you alive," the gaunt vampire with the mustachios noted.

"Once I would not have counted that a boon," Davie said. He looked down at Emma and his eyes were soft. Then he glanced to Rufford. "I release you from your vow, you know."

"Thought you would," Rufford said wryly. "I'm glad my services will not be needed."

"Yes . . . well," Davie continued, surveying the room. "I was wondering if any of you monks from Mirso Monastery are . . . are priests or . . . or capable of performing marriage rites. Miss Fairfield and I have recited the vows . . . unofficially, but we'd like to consecrate them."

A small man in a simple black woolen robe stood. "You could call us experts in Vows. I'll perform your rites."

"Brother Flavio, would the Elders approve? The Rules dictate that we live one to a city. That doesn't allow for marriage." The mustachioed vampire frowned.

Brother Flavio cocked his head. "I wonder if that Rule is the reason no children are born, Delanus. These two are new enough that they might get precious children." He looked from Rufford to the Countess and back to Emma and Davie. "We have several pairings represented here. I don't think they mean to live one to a city." He approached Davie and Emma. He had to look up into Davie's face. He searched it for what seemed a long time and then turned his attention to Emma. She couldn't help but flush, but she held her head high and looked him straight in the eye.

"Kneel," he said.

Davie grabbed a cushion from one of the chairs for her knees and knelt beside her. He fairly glowed. And she knew that before she had crossed her line she had only been half-alive. Her spirit was strong now and she wanted Davie in a spiritual way that was much larger than she could have imagined before and in a profane way as well.

Brother Flavio motioned to Rufford and the Countess, who came to range themselves on either side. "You two shall witness, who have gone before."

"Your blood calls, one to the other, life to life," Brother Flavio intoned. "Will you answer her blood, Major Ware?"

"I will," Davie said firmly in that baritone rumble she loved so.

"His blood calls to your blood, Miss Fairfield. Will you answer?"

"I will," she said, thinking how far the drawing rooms of England were behind her now.

"Then for all the years there are, the Companion will sing inside you, one to the other."

It *was* like a singing, a humming vibration of energy deep in her veins that sang to her.

"You are now joined."

Applause broke out around the circle that had gathered. Whistles sounded. "Here, here!" and, "A toast!" "Ware, you dog, kiss her!"

Davie leaned down. His eyes glowed, not red but blue. "Forever," he murmured, and just brushed her lips.

"Forever," she whispered, and pulled his head down to kiss him thoroughly. Sensations flooded her that could not be described but hinted that a lifetime of trying might be worthwhile.

"Whoa, boy!" Rufford chortled, patting Davie on the back. "Get thee upstairs for that sort of thing. My virgin eyes are seared with such displays of passion."

Davie got up and pulled Emma up beside him. He tucked her into his side. She fit well there, and the warmth of his body made her blood rise. "As you will." He nodded crisply and pulled Emma toward the stairs. At the bottom, he paused. "Consider my duty discharged, Rufford. This is no place for my wife. You'll have to clean up the remains here yourself."

Davie had given over duty for her sake. It was the final gift that he could give her. Emma saw Rufford grin. "I recommend the New World," he said. "Plenty of room there."

The sun was rising outside. She knew it even though the draperies of their room were pulled shut and the shutters latched against it. The world already seemed new. They had the whole day ahead of them for loving.

A forever of days.

THE
FORGOTTEN
ONE

by

Ronda Thompson

With love to Joanie, Teresa and Cheryl. We've had some great laughs together, girlfriends! Oh, and what the heck, to Gerry, too, who brought us all together.

1

Blackthorn Manor, England, 1821

Lady Anne Baldwin had a reputation. And not a good one, or rather, too good of one. She was said to be kind and sweet, well mannered, and docile as a lamb for the most part. She'd tried hard her whole life to be a pleasing child to an aunt and uncle who found themselves suddenly burdened with an orphaned child when they planned to have none of their own.

But sometimes Anne did not feel like being good. Tonight was one of those times. She'd stolen from the manor house in the middle of the night to ride her horse across the moors. Something strictly forbidden to her since childhood.

A midnight ride in itself wasn't so daring, not since Blackthorn Manor in Yorkshire was quite isolated and she doubted that she would encounter anyone . . . but perhaps she might encounter some *thing*.

It was rumored that wolves still roamed the sparse woods surrounding Blackthorn Manor. The night was dangerous. And it was the prospect of facing it head-on that made Anne's heart pound faster, her blood sing through her veins. A wild hair had put her upon the path to rebellion. Anne had become bored with herself, and so she imagined others must find her every bit as boring.

No one had come to call on her since she took up residence at the country home. In three months' time she would turn twenty-one and not an offer for her hand on the table. It was because she was boring, Anne conceded. But she vowed she would change that . . . at least for one night.

The stable was dark and deserted. Anne hadn't thought to bring a candle or a lantern. Being bad was new to her, or she supposed she wouldn't have taken time to dress in a modest riding habit, stockings, and sensible boots or put her hair up. She should have crept from the house with her hair down, clad only in her nightgown. The fact that she hadn't disappointed her.

Storm, her mare, startled Anne when she nickered a greeting.

"Quiet," Anne whispered. "You mustn't wake the stable help. We are having an adventure."

A bridle hung on a peg next to the stall. Even in the dark Anne had no trouble finding it, then slipping it over Storm's head. A saddle would be more difficult. She'd have to go to the tack room and probably bang about until she woke someone. Did she dare ride bareback? Doing so would also call for her riding astride.

Once, when Anne was twelve, she'd told her old groom, Barton, that she wished to ride astride like a man. Barton had nearly fallen from his own mount in shock. He'd said a young lady must never embrace a horse between her legs. He'd said it wasn't proper. But it was a night for brave deeds and Anne decided she would ride bareback. She further decided that she would do so with her hair down, clad only in her underwear.

Reaching up, she unpinned her hair, allowing the thick mass to tumble down around her shoulders. With more trepidation, she considered the buttons down the front of her modest riding habit. She debated whether undressing might be carrying the rebellion a bit too far, then realized it was a sensible thought and she was to have none of those tonight.

After Anne rid herself of the gown, she shivered in the night air. Groping in the darkness, she found a bench, hiked up her petticoat, and balanced her foot on the bench. She removed her boots and rolled a delicate stocking down her leg.

She was in the process of removing the other one when she felt the first strange sensation. That of someone watching her. Gooseflesh rose on her arms. She glanced around the dark, deserted stable. Storm snorted and stomped in her stall, as if the horse also caught wind of something amiss.

"Is someone there?" Anne whispered.

No answer.

"Easy, girl," she soothed the horse. Anne suspected the animal had sensed her own sudden unease and was simply reacting to it. She glanced around once more but saw nothing . . . but wait, she did see something. Along the front stalls she saw a pair of glowing eyes.

Her heart lurched. What was it? A wild animal? But it couldn't be unless it was perched upon something, for the eyes were not close to the ground but higher up. A flint struck. The small flame moved to the end of a cigarillo and for a moment too brief to identify features, revealed that the presence with her was at least a human one.

"Are you a horse thief?"

The breath Anne held escaped in a relieved sigh. "You frightened me," she said. Whoever the man was, she didn't recognize his voice. "Who are you?"

He didn't answer; instead she felt as if his eyes were moving over her. Anne knew that was impossible. He surely couldn't see her any better than she could him.

"I'm the new stable master," he finally answered.

She'd heard her uncle mention securing a new man to run his rather impressive stable. Although sheep were the best they could do in the terrain, Uncle Theodore had a weakness for horses and prided himself on having the best. Should she introduce herself to the new stable master? Manners dictated that she should, but would he tell on her? Anne knew that her guardians, the Earl and Countess, would consider her behavior tonight inexcusable. They might go so far as to ban her from the stable and riding altogether. What difference would it make if she lied? He couldn't see her.

"I am Lady Anne, ah, her maid," she said. "I thought I'd go for a midnight ride."

"In nothing but skin and silk?"

Heat flooded her cheeks. How could he possibly know she wore only her unmentionables? He must have heard her moving about and somehow deduced she was undressing. "I borrowed the lady's riding gown, but then thought better of wearing it."

"You don't talk like a servant."

Drat, she was as unskilled at deceit as she was at being bad. Anne should have thought to mimic the cockney accent of most of the servants. He spoke with a different accent, as well. His words carried a soft burr. Scottish?

"My lady insists that my manners be highborn, even if I am not," she explained.

"And where are you off to? To meet a lover? Did you undress to save time?"

Again, the fact that he knew she wore only her undergarments unsettled Anne. Her plans must be abandoned now, all things considered. "I've changed my mind about a midnight ride," she said. "I'll just gather my things and go."

The glowing tip of the cigarillo fell to the ground. It disappeared a second later, Anne assumed beneath his boot.

"No need to go . . . without."

What did he mean by that? Anne groped in the darkness for her discarded clothing. When she straightened, she felt him at her back. His heat penetrated her chilled skin. He pulled her hair over one shoulder.

"Your lover will be sorely disappointed."

His familiarity with her stunned her, or Anne assumed that was the reason she stood rooted to the spot. "It makes no matter to me," she managed to say, her voice breathless.

Ever so soft, his lips brushed the side of her neck. "Then it makes no matter to me, either, lass."

A shiver raced up her spine. Her face flamed. "What do you think you're doing?" she demanded, her voice stronger.

"I don't think I'm doing anything," he answered. "I know what I'm doing."

He pulled her against him. Shocked, Anne dropped the clothing she had gathered. His body was hard . . . everywhere. He was taller than her; she could judge that much. Taller. Bigger. Stronger.

"I insist that you release me this instant," she warned. "I am not the sort who—" Anne abruptly cut her sentence short. She'd told him she was a maid, had not corrected him when he'd assumed she was off to meet her lover. She'd lied to him. What should she do now?

"Do you know how sweet you smell?"

The deepness of his voice raised the fine hairs on her arms. Anne had never heard a voice quite like his. Deep yet soft, lilting. It was hypnotic.

"I'm wondering if you feel just as good."

Slowly, his hands slid up her rib cage. Anne swallowed loudly, but again, she did not struggle. She wasn't certain if she was hypnotized or frozen with fear. His hands stopped just below the lower fullness of her breasts. A second later he cupped her firmly. Anne gasped. No man had dared touch her intimately before. She turned her head to protest, but he captured her mouth before she could utter a word. While his mouth boldly claimed hers, his scent found her, almost as physical as his touch.

It was an earthy scent, musky, male, mesmerizing. The scent filled her head with visions of naked bodies entwined upon rumpled sheets—of sweat-slick skin and quiet whispers. She moaned softly against his lips, and never breaking contact, he turned her to face him. His mouth pressed against hers until she opened to him. Then his tongue slipped inside.

Anne had never had a man's tongue inside of her mouth, and if anyone had told her men were wont to do such things, she would have thought it repulsive. But it wasn't repulsive. His slow invasion made her breathless. He tasted of mint and a hint of tobacco. His scent fogged her mind as his mouth worked against hers and stirred feelings she had never felt before. What was happening to her? Why couldn't she push him away? Bite him, do whatever she must to be free of him? Why didn't she want to?

"Please," she whispered.

"Please what? Do this?" He stopped kissing her long enough to press his warm mouth to her ear and nibble her earlobe. His thumbs brushed across her nipples and sent a jolt all the way down to her woman's core. Her knees shook beneath her petticoat. She ached in places she should not ache. None of this should be happening.

Sin had come to live in her stable and Anne was allowing it to have its way with her. She had wanted to do something daring tonight, but never had she imagined this. She shook her head, trying to clear her mind. It was if he'd cast a spell over her and she couldn't break free. But she must.

"You take liberties," she managed to say, and thank God her voice sounded stronger.

"I take what I can get," he countered. "I take what you will give me, and I'll give you all that you desire in return."

It took almost more strength than she had for Anne to step away from him. His hands dropped away from her breasts, and still they tingled from his touch. "And what do you have to give me?" she asked, her voice too snooty to be that of a maid. It was, in fact, a tone Anne never used. She wasn't the type to lord it over the servants.

The man reached forward and pulled her back into his arms. "Enough to satisfy a little thief out for a midnight tryst with her lover. Enough to bet you'll be back for more of the same tomorrow night."

His hips pressed against her, and innocent or not, Anne thought she understood what he offered her. She also understood that what he offered her was quite a lot. A maid for one night and she had been set upon and kissed for the first time in her life, touched in places no other man would dare touch her, and promised something she had no idea if any woman should or would want. At least Anne *thought* she knew what he had offered her.

"What is it you think to give me again?" she asked, staring up at him, although she couldn't make out a single feature upon his face.

He bent close. "Pleasure beyond your wildest imagination. You wanted a midnight ride. I'll give you one you won't forget."

When she swallowed, Anne was embarrassed to hear the gulping noise she made in the silence. No other man had dared to speak to her in such a manner. "You are arrogant," she said.

"Just confident," he argued. "There's a nice straw mattress in the loft overhead." His mouth brushed her neck and she shivered. "Come with me."

Anne had carried being bad too far. But she had trouble thinking when he stood so near, when he put off that intoxicating scent, when he whispered foul things in her ear. She realized she wanted to go to the loft with him. Whatever he was doing to her, she wanted more of it. But Anne was not a serving maid in truth, she was a proper young woman, and she was on the verge of making a mistake that could ruin the rest of her life. She found the sense to push him away and take a step back.

"I must return to the house. Maybe another maid will happen along shortly and you can try your luck with her."

He pulled her back into his arms. "I don't want another. She couldn't be as beautiful as you are to me. Or smell as sweet, or taste as good, or fire my hunger as no woman has fired it before."

Anne had been complimented by men, but never so boldly. This man was obviously trying to seduce her. And it was working. She was so very close to surrendering. Her will, usually too strong for her own good, seemed to melt away in his arms. This was ridiculous and she had carried the game too far.

"If you do not step away and allow me to leave, I will scream," she said.

The man withdrew so suddenly she shivered with the absence of his heat. Her eyes had adjusted just enough to the darkness to make out the white of his shirt. He seemed now to be leaning against a stall.

"No need to scream, lass. I never meant to keep you against your will. I thought you were looking for sport. I only meant to provide it."

Something in his lazy manner, his calmness when her nerves were rubbed raw, her senses more heightened than they had ever been in her life, greatly annoyed Anne. "You are very accommodating," she snapped, and felt an irrational flare of jealousy. Jealousy of herself? She was confused and needed to escape the devil and his intoxicating scent.

Quickly Anne bent and retrieved her things. "You'll see to the horse," she instructed automatically, then realized her tone was that of a person used to issuing orders and having them followed. "I mean, please," she added. "I've bridled her."

His teeth flashed white in the darkness. "I'll see to her," he said. "And I'm thinking on another night, I'll see to you, as well."

She wanted to argue the matter with him, but Anne had already said too much in his presence. He might not recognize her face in the light of day, but if she continued to converse with him, he would recognize her voice.

As much as she wanted to flounce away, her head held high as if his last statement had not affected her, Anne had no choice but to move slowly through the dark stable. She felt his eyes watching her. Even that was almost like a caress. Good God, who was this man who could so easily turn a female's mind to mush with nothing more than the sound of his voice, the touch of his lips, his strange scent? She pitied the poor maids sure to run across his path in the days ahead . . . or was "pity" the right word?

Anne made it to the door without falling flat on her face and hurried outside. She needed fresh air to clear her head. The back of her neck prickled and she knew he watched her even now. The temptation to turn and look at him in the moonlight nearly got the best of her. If she saw his features, then he'd be able to see hers.

Come tomorrow, Anne must pretend that she had never met the man who'd nearly seduced her tonight. Pretend she had never felt his mouth moving against hers, the brush of his fingers upon her skin, never heard the sound of his husky voice. Tonight she'd told her first lie. Anne supposed tomorrow she would try her hand at acting.

2

It was early the next morning when Anne met him. Her eyes felt swollen from lack of sleep. She'd lain awake much too long thinking of him once she'd reached the safety of her bed. Her lips were swollen, as well, and she knew what that was from. Lost in thought, she sat quietly dining upon breakfast with her aunt and uncle when a stranger entered the room. Anne had never seen the man, but she knew him instantly.

Her nostrils flared, her heart skipped a beat, and the hairs on the back of her neck bristled. The man didn't look her way but strode past her straight to her uncle.

"You sent for me, my lord?"

Her uncle dabbed his mouth with a napkin. "Yes. I thought you should meet my niece. She frequents the stable much more than the Countess and I find agreeable, but because she does, I will provide an introduction. You should know who she is and how she is to be treated when she visits the stable to ride."

The new stable master inclined his head. It was a dark head. His hair was as black as a moonless night. It hung to his shoulders, was thick and curled around his collar. His lashes were just as dark, just as thick, shielding his eyes from her until he glanced up and in her direction. Anne forgot to breathe. He pinned her with ice blue eyes and she couldn't seem to form a simple thought. He stared, and she stared helplessly back.

Slowly, the rest of his features came into focus. High cheekbones, chiseled jawline, indentations along the sides of his mouth . . . a mouth shaped with a gentle hand when nothing else about him hinted at any tenderness. He was big, and broad, and beautiful. And for a moment, she thought she had seen him somewhere before, but she knew she could not have.

"My niece, Lady Anne Baldwin," her uncle's voice managed to penetrate the fog in her head. "Lady Anne, this is our new stable master, Merrick."

"Lady," the stable master said softly.

Anne knew she had to respond. She couldn't say his name. It was too intimate. "Mister . . . ?" She let her voice trail.

His eyes never left her. "Just Merrick. I've no last name. Born on the wrong side of the blanket. You may call me by my given name."

She simply nodded but refused to do so.

"I'll tell you what I tell the rest of those who work for me," her uncle interrupted. "You are to treat my niece with the utmost respect. She spends far too much time riding her horse and lurking about the stable when she knows her aunt and I do not necessarily approve of her fondness for such things. We indulge her here in the country where it makes little difference. But being in charge, I expect for you to watch out for her, and of course with as much distance as possible between the two of you while you do."

"Uncle!" Anne was embarrassed by his instructions and by his bluntness in her company.

He held up a hand. "A man must know his place, Anne. Sometimes a man must be told his place so that he doesn't forget."

"Really, my dear," Aunt Claire fussed. "Must you embarrass the girl so early in the morning? I'm certain our new man knows good and well his place, don't you, Merrick?"

As if reluctantly, the stable master's intense gaze swung from Anne toward her aunt. "I've been put in it enough times to know it, my lady," he said.

"Interesting." Aunt Claire's gaze slowly swept over him. "That you have an English name and a Scottish accent."

"My mother was Scottish," he explained. "Grew up listening to her, so naturally I would speak as she spoke. Whoever my father was, he asked her to give me an English name. Not his name, mind you, whatever it was, but an English Christian name."

"That will be all, Merrick," Anne's uncle piped up, dismissing the man. "My niece rides every morning at ten o'clock sharp. Her horse is the bay mare in stall five. Be sure that the horse is ready for Lady Anne."

Anne couldn't ride this morning. It was out of the question. She needed time to gather herself. "I will not ride today," she blurted. "I-I don't feel well," she explained to her aunt and uncle, who both looked surprised by her statement.

"I would have a word with your maid."

Anne's eyes snapped toward the new stable master. "What?"

"Your maid," he repeated. "I would like a word with her."

"Old Bertha?" Aunt Claire's brow furrowed. "Why on earth would you need to speak to her? Not that she could probably hear half of what you say. She's going quite deaf in her old age."

The new stable master didn't look surprised. He knew. Anne suspected he'd known all along. But how could he? He couldn't have seen her last night. She couldn't see him in the darkness.

"Never mind then," he said. "I assumed the lady might take her maid to ride along with her and I meant to question the woman regarding which horse she would use, but if the woman is old . . ."

"You will ride with my niece," her uncle instructed. "At least until I can decide upon a suitable groom. Her old groom is no longer with us. Ride with Lady Anne, but a proper distance behind her, of course."

"Of course," he said, and Anne detected a hint of sarcasm behind his cool expression. He was of the serving class. But he did not like it. Not one bit.

"Is that all, my lord?" he asked her uncle.

"You are dismissed," Uncle Theodore answered, returning to his breakfast. "Don't forget my instructions regarding the gray filly."

The stable master turned to leave. Anne was curious about all that went on in the stable. The gray filly was a particular favorite of hers, although the horse belonged to her uncle. "What about the gray filly?"

Merrick, as he would have her call him, hesitated, glancing toward her uncle. " 'Tis none of her affair," he said to the man. "Go on now about your business, or rather my business," her uncle added with a chuckle.

Uncle Theodore's good humor failed to make Merrick smile, and Anne found herself wondering what he might look like if he did. Would it soften the hard lines of his face? Merrick left the room and she stared after him until she felt her aunt's regard. Anne blushed and quickly turned her attention back to breakfast.

"He's very handsome, your new stable master, dear," Aunt Claire commented. "I am not certain he was a wise choice when we still have a young, beautiful woman beneath our roof. Rather like putting a fox in charge of the henhouse."

It bothered Anne somewhat that her aunt had referred to Blackthorn Manor as belonging to Anne's guardians. The house had belonged to Anne's mother and Blackthorn Manor, along with a large inheritance from her mother's lineage, would become Anne's when she turned twenty-one. Still, she said nothing. Anne felt certain it was an oversight.

Uncle Theodore had inherited Anne's father's title, but her father had been a "naked" earl, in that he had no property that went with his earldom. It had been Anne's mother who had married beneath her. A love match. Because she had no brothers or male relatives left living on her mother's side, Anne's son, if she had one, would someday become a Marquess.

Uncle Theodore waved a hand. "As long as the hens mind themselves, so will the fox." He glanced up, sharing a peculiar look with his wife that Anne had trouble reading. A warning?

Uncomfortable silence settled over the table. Anne was still curious about the filly and thought her uncle might be more talkative now that the stable master had left. "What are your plans for the filly?" she ventured again.

"Unsuitable conversation for a young lady," he said, frowning at her. "It is not your concern, Niece."

"Yes, Uncle," Anne replied dutifully, although his refusal to discuss the matter only made her more curious. Maybe she'd been too hasty in her decision to stay indoors this morning. The stable master knew what plans her uncle had for the gray filly. If she asked, he'd have to tell her, wouldn't he?

"May I be excused?" she asked. "Perhaps a short rest this morning will see me feeling more myself."

"Yes, by all means go and lie down for a while," her aunt said, patting Anne's hand absently, a required response rather than a heartfelt one. She tried not to be resentful. Her aunt and uncle had become her guardians when her parents had contacted a fever abroad and both died, leaving her orphaned at the age of ten. But she'd never felt truly loved again, not as her parents had loved her. Her aunt and uncle had been staying with her at Blackthorn Manor when the news of Anne's parents' deaths reached them. They had simply never left.

Her father and uncle were brothers. There was no one else to take Anne in, and perhaps had there been, she would at least have the knowledge that her aunt and uncle chose to raise her because they wanted to, not because they had to. Anne excused herself, rose from the table, and went upstairs.

Old Bertha had nodded off in a chair and snored softly. Anne's riding habit had been laid out. She couldn't avoid the new stable master forever. Besides, she wanted to ask him about the filly and her uncle's plans for the horse.

Merrick smelled Lady Anne's sweet scent before he saw her. He had a gift for scent and for sight. He always had, but he obviously couldn't read a lady's mind, because her sudden appearance surprised him. He stood before the gray filly's stall, thinking his new employer was an ignorant man who didn't deserve the fine horses he owned. He turned and saw Lady Anne at the stable entrance. She was dressed for riding.

"Change your mind?"

It was a question that might hold two meanings, and by her slight blush he knew she was quick-witted.

"Yes, I have decided I shall *ride* this morning," she stated, stepping into the stable's dim interior. "Will you saddle my horse?"

"That's what I'm here for." He moved away from the gray's stall. "To see to your needs."

Her blush deepened. "There is no call for this to become awkward. You made a mistake last night and we shall both forget it today and move forward."

Merrick paused before the bay's stall. He lifted a brow. "I made a mistake? I wouldn't have had you had you not lied to me."

But that in itself was a lie. Had Merrick known she was the niece of his employer last night, it still wouldn't have stopped him. She was the most beautiful woman he'd ever seen. Merrick had never reacted so strongly to a female before, be she a serving maid or a highborn lady. He found Lady Anne Baldwin irresistible.

Her hair was the color of rich maple syrup and when down, as she'd worn it last night, cascaded in waves to her slim waist. Her eyes were a warm shade of brown. Her lashes were dark and thick, and her skin was as pale as cream. Some might consider her mouth too generous, but Merrick liked her full, lush lips. Her figure was every man's dream. The lady wasn't for the likes of him, but that didn't stop Merrick from wanting her.

"It was wrong of me to lie," she admitted, biting her fuller lower lip. "I feared you'd tell my aunt and uncle what I was doing and I knew they would not be pleased. I thought they might ban me from the stable and riding."

Judging by what he knew of her aunt and uncle, Merrick imagined they would not be pleased to know of her actions last night, certainly not his. "Then it can remain our little secret." He bridled the mare, opened the stall, and led the bay out. He glanced at Lady Anne, noting that her chin rose a notch.

"I would think that would be more to your advantage than to mine."

Merrick quelled the desire to roll his eyes and stopped before her. "I'm not so ignorant that I don't know that. There's no need to threaten me, lass."

Anne hadn't meant to. She'd always prided herself on being kind to others, even to those of a lower station—even to those considered outcasts among society. Why now was she putting this man in his place? Why did she feel threatened by him? Her gaze roamed him and she knew the answer. He was dangerous. Being bad wasn't so difficult, after all. One just needed the right incentive. The right incentive stood before her now, tall and handsome as sin, staring down at her with his rebellious blue eyes.

"I'm not like them," she insisted. "I am not a snob."

His gaze ran the length of her and back again. "Yes, you are," he said. "You just don't know it yet."

She watched him lead Storm to the tack room and tether her. Anne was trying to think of something to say when he moved past her, walked to the end of the stable, and led a leggy black stallion from his stall. She'd never seen the horse before, and in an instant she forgot her crossness with the new stable master.

"He's beautiful," she breathed. Anne loved horses and considered herself a fine judge of horseflesh. The stallion was built for speed. His head was small, his neck thick, and his long flowing mane and tail were well tended.

"He is a fine horse," Merrick agreed, stopping before her so that Anne could reach out and stroke the horse's silky coat. "But he has no pedigree. Caught him as a wild colt and brought him up myself. Don't know his lines, just as I don't know my own. We're both bastards, I guess."

Anne lifted a brow. "Does he resent it as much as you do?"

His blue eyes widened in surprise for a moment, as if he hadn't expected her to be intuitive. Then he shrugged. "No," he answered. "But he's too dumb to know the difference. I guess he's blessed that way."

Realizing Merrick's parentage was obviously a sore subject, Anne didn't comment further. Instead she watched as he went about the business of saddling Storm and the black. Merrick moved with a grace few men, even those of the gentry, possessed. Black trousers hugged his slim hips and muscled legs to the point of near vulgarity. He wore a white shirt, coarse but clean, open at the neck, so open in fact that she saw a portion of his tan chest and a glimpse of dark chest hair. For some reason, that struck Anne as indecent, as well. Or perhaps it was simply her reaction to him that was improper.

The lack of shine on his knee-high boots reminded her that

he was of the working class and had no valet to see to them nightly. His hair had hung loose when he'd intruded upon breakfast in the house, but now he'd secured it with a black ribbon. Doing so only accented the chiseled lines of his face and made his stark blue eyes stand out. She had to admit in that moment she'd never seen a man as handsome as he was.

Just looking at him filled her stomach with butterflies. Her blood raced through her veins and catching a normal breath was difficult. Oh yes, he was dangerous. Anne would have to watch herself around him, which was something she had never had to do before.

"I'll give you a hand up," Merrick said, and she realized she was still staring and the horses were saddled and ready.

Fighting down a blush, she walked around Storm where he waited. The sidesaddle perched upon the mare's back made Anne frown. It was a reminder that her adventure last night had not included her dream of riding astride like a man. Her thoughts scattered with Merrick's hands encircling her waist. They felt warm even through her lightweight riding habit. He lifted her into the saddle as if she weighed nothing. He stared up at her for a moment and their eyes locked. It took a great deal of willpower for Anne to glance away.

Flustered, she steered her horse around the big stallion and out into a rather dreary day. Anne was thankful for the cooler air to revive her. She wished Merrick had not been given the task of escorting her on her rides. She feared no good could come of the two of them spending time together.

3

Trying to concentrate on the ride and forget her escort, Anne took a familiar path through the fields along the north side of the manor house. The smell of rich dirt and clean air always made her feel better. Anne was a country girl at heart, if she could get on well enough in the city.

"What are my uncle's plans for the filly?" she called over her shoulder, expecting Merrick to be following at a discreet distance as he'd been told to do.

"I recall hearing your uncle say it wasn't your business."

She turned to find Merrick beside her. It didn't surprise her that he hadn't followed her uncle's instructions. Anne suspected Merrick seldom followed anyone's rules but his own.

"As my uncle said, I have a fondness for horses and the stable. The gray filly has excellent lines. He isn't going to sell her, is he?"

Merrick's lips suddenly curled slightly at the corners. "No," he answered. "She's in season. He wants to breed her."

Anne realized why her uncle had refused to discuss the issue with her. Such things were not discussed in the presence of ladies. She was always told to stay away from the stable when the breeding took place. The new stable master seemed to take delight in saying something so shocking in her company. She wouldn't give him the satisfaction of making her blush again.

"To which stallion?" she asked. "I hope not Ascot, the large sorrel. He's too big boned. A colt produced by him would likely be too large for the filly to deliver. I'd personally choose Shadow, the charcoal stallion. He's smaller, and the coloring would suit, I'd think."

When Merrick didn't respond, she glanced toward him. His lips were still curled in that disturbing way that drew her gaze to them, but in his eyes shone a glimmer of respect.

"My thoughts exactly," he said. "Your uncle doesn't strike me as the type of man to appreciate my advice, however, so I'll not be giving it."

"It is your right, isn't it?" Anne asked. "To advise him on such matters? I thought that was the reason he hired you to run his stable."

He laughed and she saw the flash of his white teeth again. "He hired me to say he got the best. He likes the best, your uncle. Your aunt, too, I'm thinking."

Now he had overstepped his boundaries. Anne bristled. Her aunt and uncle did always require the best of everything, but that was beside the point.

"That is not a subject you are familiar with and you should refrain from pretending that you are," she scolded. "And aren't you supposed to be riding a proper distance behind me?"

The smile faded from his lips. "When I become familiar with the path, then I will ride discreetly behind you, my lady. If that is your wish," he added, as if the matter might be in question.

"Why wouldn't it be?" Anne asked defensively.

"I never said it was," he countered.

"You hinted at as much," she huffed. "You mustn't assume to know me or what I would or would not prefer simply because you made a mistake last night."

He lifted a dark brow. "Are you saying you didn't make one? Maybe you didn't mind giving me the wrong idea so much."

His easy ability to fluster her had Anne feeling a temper that was usually nonexistent in her. Instead of arguing with him, she turned her attention to the path, kicked her heels into Storm's sides, and took off. Anne let Storm have her head, both of them familiar with the path. Merrick pulled up next to her a moment later.

Storm was fast, but Anne doubted that she could outrun the black. The stallion was bigger and stronger. Anne, however, sat lighter in the saddle. She was feeling a rebellious streak again and urged Storm into a faster gait. Ahead the path narrowed, leaving the open fields and winding through wooded ground.

Anne supposed it wasn't a considerate thing to do, forcing the man to follow her in a dead run across a path he was not familiar with, but she suspected she could leave him behind easily enough. He should be put in his place . . . although she was never one to really think of "places" and "putting people in them" before.

Maybe she only wanted to show off. Anne seldom had an opportunity to display her riding skills. The paths in London, Rotten Row and the like, were tame for her talents. A log had fallen across the path ahead and she and the mare took the jump easily. Deeper Anne wound her way along the path into the woods, always aware that the stable master and the stallion were nearly on Storm's rump.

When the path widened, Merrick was suddenly beside her. Ahead, the path narrowed again and she couldn't let him get out in front of her. Then it would be a case of him leading and her following. Anne urged Storm on.

Merrick swore, then loosened the reins to give the stallion more freedom. The animal lunged ahead so swiftly that Anne felt a sinking sensation. Her mare couldn't match the stallion's speed. Just as Anne had wanted to avoid, Merrick pulled ahead when the path narrowed and she was forced to follow instead of lead.

The path widened again and they were in a meadow. He slowed his horse, and when she pulled up beside him Merrick reached across and snatched Anne from the saddle. She was so startled by the move she immediately struggled and almost toppled to the ground. A strong arm settled around her waist and he easily brought the headstrong stallion to a halt. Merrick let Anne slide to the ground and quickly dismounted.

"What do you think you are doing?" she demanded, for the second time in the space of a few hours after being in his company.

He dropped the reins to the stallion's bridle and pulled her a short distance from the excited animal. "I'm doing my job," Merrick shot back. "Making sure you don't break your pretty neck while trying to show me up and put me in my place."

"I am a very accomplished rider," Anne defended. "I thought you would have noticed that."

Merrick stared down at her. For just a moment, his blue eyes softened upon her. "I did notice," he said. "But I won't have you getting hurt my first day on the job because you wanted to impress me."

Since she'd just more or less admitted she was trying to impress him, Anne saw no reason to deny it. "Did I impress you?" she asked instead.

A smile tugged at the corner of his sensuous mouth. "You're a skilled rider," he admitted. "You have lovely form. You might have given me more of a race if not for the sidesaddle. It weighs more."

Anne glanced at her horse, the mare having come to a halt as soon as her rider was no longer at the reins to guide her. "I hate the saddle," Anne admitted, then bravely announced, "I'd like to ride astride, like a man."

She expected her declaration to shock him. Even old

Barton had been shocked when she'd announced the same thing at the age of twelve. Merrick simply shrugged. "Then why don't you?"

Of course he wouldn't understand. Anne would enlighten him upon the subject. "It isn't considered proper for a lady to . . . to ride that way," she informed him. "My aunt and uncle would never allow it."

Merrick glanced about the clearing. "I don't see your aunt and uncle."

Anne came dangerously close to smiling. How simple his life must be compared to hers. She envied him in that moment. Anne had spent the good portion of her life heeding all the rules of society in order to please her aunt and uncle. In order to win their love.

"My old groom, Barton, nearly died of shock when I suggested it at the age of twelve." Recalling Barton brought tears to her eyes. Anne had been very fond of him. "He passed on just last month. I miss him."

Merrick placed his finger beneath her chin and forced her to look up at him. In his eyes was an expression so soft it melted her heart. It took her off guard—reminded her of the power he'd held over her the night before. Anne pulled away and blinked back her tears.

"You must think I'm silly," she said, walking toward Storm to gather the mare's drooping reins.

"I don't know what I think," she heard him say to her back. "And I usually know right away."

Anne decided then and there she must squash her unruly feelings for a man she hardly knew. It would be much better if they were simply friends. She took a deep breath and turned to face Merrick.

"Can we start over?" she asked. "I feel as if we've gotten off on the wrong foot with one another."

For some reason, her suggestion made him smile. Not a genuine one but more of a smirk. "Do you think you can geld me with an offer of friendship? Do you think that will make me forget what you feel like, and smell like, and taste like?"

Heat exploded in her cheeks and shot through her body. Anne had never met a man she couldn't tame with a show of good manners and an offer of friendship. But she sensed that this was a man unlike any she had met before. "I believe you have the wrong impression of me."

He sauntered toward her. "Now that's where you're wrong, lass. I think I might know you better than you know yourself."

When Anne looked up at him, she tried to appear as calm as he usually did in her presence. "What does that mean?"

The softness returned to his eyes and Anne thought that expression alone might be more dangerous than the scent he'd put off last night in the stable.

"You long to be something that you're not. I understand that well enough. You want things you cannot have. I understand that, too. You want to ride your horse astride like a man, at midnight, in nothing but your undergarments. What are you running from, Lady Anne? Or are you running in hopes you'll find whatever is missing in your life?"

The man had no right to ask her such personal questions. He had no right to assume so much about her. And damn him, he had no right to know her better than she knew herself, just as he claimed. This intimacy between them had to stop.

"I wish to return now," she said stiffly. Anne turned to mount her horse. Merrick was at her back in an instant. His hands closed around her waist.

"Not yet," he said. "Not until at least one of us gets something we want."

4

Anne wheeled to face him, nearly colliding with him, he stood so close. Her eyes made it past the dark hair teasing her from the open collar of his shirt, up across his broad shoulders, the dark whiskers on his chin and cheeks, to his icy eyes, but no, they were not cold. The heat was back in them. His gaze lowered to her lips and they parted as if he'd commanded them to do so. Would he kiss her again? Was that the something he wanted? And did it matter what she wanted? Or did she want the same thing?

He lifted a hand, almost touched her hair, then quickly withdrew it. "You wanted to ride astride like a man, and today you will."

Merrick turned from her and walked to the stallion. He unsaddled the horse in short order while she stood reeling from the onslaught of his nearness, her lips tingling in anticipation of a kiss that had not come.

"You are going to do it this time, aren't you?" he asked while carrying the saddle to her mount and laying it on the ground. "I'd hate to go through this trouble only to see you bolt and run away like you did last night."

A teasing light had entered his eyes, but Anne did not find him amusing. Staying last night had been out of the question. No telling what might have happened had she not regained her senses and fled to the safety of the house. And no telling how often she would wonder exactly what would have transpired between them if she hadn't escaped when she did.

"I will ride astride," she assured him.

He didn't comment but unsaddled Storm, then saddled the mare with the lightweight English saddle he'd used on the stallion. Merrick adjusted the stirrups, then turned to her.

"Up you go."

Anne glanced down at her skirt. "I wish I owned a pair of men's trousers. And tall boots like you are wearing."

He placed a hand against his heart. "I might not survive such a sight. You have lovely legs, lass."

She fought down another blush. Had Merrick seen her legs? And how had he seen anything at all when she hadn't been able to make out so much as his silhouette in the darkness? He couldn't have, she assured herself.

"I'm not sure how to proceed," Anne tried to change the subject. Only she had to bring it back around when she glanced meaningfully at the skirt of her riding habit.

Merrick motioned her closer with a jerk of his head. "Come on, I'll help you up, then you'll have to figure out the rest."

"And you won't say anything to my aunt or uncle about this?" She wanted reassurance.

"You have my word."

For some reason, Anne believed him—felt certain she could count on his word. Why, she had no idea. Maybe the man really had cast a spell over her. She allowed him to give her a leg up. In order to sit the saddle astride, she had to bunch her skirt up around her knees. It left her stocking-clad calves bare to his eyes, but she hoped he wouldn't look. He did.

"Very nice," he said. "Just like I remember."

Ignoring him, Anne urged Storm forward, awkward at first with her position astride the horse. It took Anne only a few paces to become braver and urge the bay into a trot. The sensation was strange, to say the least. Anne decided a gallop might prove less disturbing and soon she was on the path, racing along astride and realizing how cruel it was to make women ride sidesaddle.

She laughed out loud with the sheer freedom she felt, glanced behind her, and saw Merrick riding bareback behind her. He looked like a barbarian and her heart made a funny lurch inside of her chest.

"So what do you think?" Merrick called, quickly catching up to her.

"It's wonderful," she called back. "It's the way a horse was meant to be ridden. I shall never want to ride sidesaddle again."

"And what about riding in your underwear, bareback, at midnight across the moors? Are you still brave enough to do that?"

Anne slowed her mount. Was Merrick teasing her? "Not with an escort," she assured him.

He smiled in answer. Just at breakfast Anne had wondered what it would be like to see him smile. She decided she was better off not knowing. He had a smile that could melt winter.

"Would you do it if you had a pair of men's trousers and boots?"

She cocked a brow. "And where would I get those?"

He shrugged. "I could get them for you. The lad who sweeps out the stalls, Brennan, he's not much bigger than you."

What Merrick said was true. The stable boy was only ten but tall for his age. And Anne supposed his feet were still small. Did she dare? She had wanted to dare last night. But last night had proven a mistake, and she had a feeling meeting the new stable master in the dead of night for a midnight ride again would be another one.

"May I go alone?"

He shook his dark head. "I cannot allow that. You can go if you let me go with you, to watch after you."

His suggestion annoyed her. If her aunt and uncle were not particularly affectionate people toward her, they had made certain Anne had been well chaperoned all of her life. She wanted the freedom of riding alone.

"I don't need looking after," she said. "I'm a grown woman and, as you said yourself, a skilled rider."

Merrick leaned forward in the saddle and scratched his chin. "Have you ridden bareback before, then?"

Anne frowned. "Well, no, but—"

"When I feel you know what you are doing, then you can go alone and I'll keep your secrets."

Anne wasn't a mistrustful person by nature. But she wasn't as innocent as she'd been just the day before. "Why would you do that?" she asked.

He glanced at her and winked. "To see you in the trousers of course."

She had no idea if he was teasing her. Considering what had happened between them the night before, she thought she should ask, "You won't try anything like you did last night, will you?"

Merrick shrugged. "Probably. It's in my nature to ravish any young woman who stumbles across my path in the night." His expression was perfectly serious.

"Then I must decline."

The serious expression he wore disappeared and he surprised her by laughing out loud. Anne didn't care to be laughed at.

"What is so funny?" she asked stiffly.

He pulled up and stopped his horse. Anne did likewise. "Last night I didn't know who you were. Today I do. That changes everything, lass."

Anne ignored the slight sting she felt to her ego. "You said you would not forget," she reminded him.

Heat flared to life in his eyes as he stared at her. "Oh, to be sure, I won't. But a maid looking for sport with her lover, and a lady only wanting a midnight ride on her horse are two different things. You're safe with me . . . I think."

It was his afterthought that made Anne nervous. But that trepidation was easily outweighed by a chance to do something she'd wanted to do for a long time. It was a chance that might never come her way again.

"All right," she said. "Meet me at midnight in the stable. Have the clothes with you."

Merrick had to wonder if he'd taken leave of his senses. Making offers, keeping secrets, getting too close to a woman he had no right to get close to. Lady Anne was a proper lady. He was a bastard, a stable master who made a good enough wage to support a common lass, but not a grand lady like his employer's niece. Not that Merrick was thinking of wedding the tempting Lady Anne, but he was damn sure thinking of bedding her.

He had the clothes, paid for with a coin to the lad and a promise from the boy that he'd not ask why the new stable master needed them. He had the horses saddled and ready. He had everything but a brain in his head. He almost hoped she wouldn't come. It would be better for the both of them if she regained her senses and decided he wasn't a man to trust with either her secrets or her virtue. She'd probably be right in thinking that, although he'd always tried to be a man of his word before.

There was little in life Merrick had besides his word and his skill with horses. He recalled giving his word to another woman. His mother on her deathbed. She'd told him not to go looking for his past. She'd told him to be content with what he'd been given in life. Not to dream of things beyond his reach. And Merrick had promised.

Now he was sniffing around a woman's skirts he should not

be sniffing around. Merrick and Lady Anne were as different as night and day. Merrick was, in fact, different from any man he knew. He had strange abilities that his mother hadn't even known about. He had his secrets even if he chose not to acknowledge his differences most of the time. He did not understand his "gifts" or why they had been given to him. He wasn't sure they were gifts. Perhaps they were instead a curse.

Although his mind told him it would be better if Lady Anne did not appear tonight in the stable, Merrick watched the door for her. He willed her to him, and by doing so he went back on his word to his mother. He wanted all he promised her he would not want. Deep inside, he resented that his blood was somewhat blue but still ran red like that of the common man he was.

His mother, God rest her soul, had taken his father's name to the grave with her. Whoever the man had been, Merrick resented the hell out of him. How could a man treat a child like a dirty secret? Like a mistake, easily ignored and then forgotten? While the man was alive, he'd made certain that Merrick and his mother were provided for, but after his death, it was as if he'd wanted to bury his secrets along with him. Merrick, only a young man at the time, and his mother were suddenly forced to work at whatever jobs they could find in order to support themselves. He supposed that made them no different from most, but he had wondered if while he and his mother scraped and starved, somewhere the man's legitimate children were living in the lap of luxury.

The horses had always come naturally to Merrick. He knew a good bloodline when he saw one. He knew what mare to breed to which stallion in order to produce a better horse. He knew how to care for the animals, how to clean up after them, how to ride them. He'd made a name for himself in his profession, if it wasn't the grandest profession a man might strive for, and if his name was only his first name. Still, he'd learned to be content . . . until last night.

He caught Lady Anne's scent before she reached the stable. Why did she have to smell like that, like a gumdrop, all soft and sugary and melting on the tongue? Why did she have to feel like fine silk beneath his calloused hands? Why did she have to taste like heady wine, warm and wet and intoxicating? Why did she have to trust his word when already his body stirred to life with want for her and he was thinking of going back on it?

"Merrick," she whispered in the darkness, and even the sound of his name on her lips nearly caused him to groan.

"Here," he said, then had to clear the huskiness from his throat.

"Do you have the clothes?"

"In the tack room," he answered. "I've draped them across your sidesaddle. The boots are there on the ground next to them."

"You will stay out here while I change?"

She was still wary of him. Which proved she was smart as well as pretty. "Unless you need my assistance," he answered.

"I won't," she assured him.

"Hurry up, then. We don't have all night."

His abnormal hearing tortured him with sounds of her undressing a moment later. The brush of cloth against skin. The pictures forming in his head. He wanted to see her in the moonlight. See her beautiful face light up with laughter as it did when she rode astride earlier. Why had such a woman not already been claimed? Were the men of her station all daft? She was everything he would want in a woman and nothing he could have.

"I'm ready."

Lost in his thoughts, Merrick hadn't been listening for her approach. He saw her outline in the darkness. If he wanted to, if he looked long and hard enough, he could make out her features clearly, but they needed to get away from the stable.

"I'll give you a hand up. We'll unsaddle the mare once

we're away from the house, and I'll teach you to ride bare-back."

She brought her sweet scent and her soft woman's curves around the horses to stand next to him. When his hands encircled her small waist, he wanted to teach her far more than just to ride bareback. Her lips were innocent last night. Lush and ripe and he thought she might have never been kissed before. At least not properly.

He lifted her easily and she scrambled into the saddle. Merrick walked around her and mounted the black. Like thieves, they rode quietly from the stable, only daring to pick up their pace once they'd gone a distance from the house.

Finding the meadow again, Merrick drew the black to a halt, dismounted, and went around to assist Lady Anne. She came into his arms perhaps more easily than was wise, then stood before him, staring up. The moonlight bathed her lovely features in soft white light. Her eyes sparkled and her hair hung down her back almost to her hips. He ached inside just looking at her. Ached as he had never ached before. Wanted as he had never wanted before.

"You're so beautiful," he said, staring down at her. "You turn a man's mind to mush and make him forget his promises."

The smile hovering about her lush lips faded. She met his stare and he thought he saw the same hunger he felt staring back at him from her warm brown eyes. Then she shook her head as if to clear it. "You gave me your word. Was I a fool to trust you?"

So it would seem. Merrick had never been subtle about his wants and desires. "I want to kiss you again."

Even in the darkness, he saw color creep into her cheeks. "Then I should demand that you take me back to the stable and end this fool's errand."

He agreed, but his desire to know her more intimately kept him from saying so or doing what he knew would be best.

"Why do you think doing something you dream of is foolish, Anne?"

Anne had expected him to either try to kiss her or take her back to the stable. She was surprised that instead of doing either, he'd asked her a question and seemed genuinely interested in her answer. She wasn't used to anyone really caring about her feelings. She wasn't used to anyone really caring about her. Oh, she liked to fool herself into believing her aunt and uncle simply had trouble displaying affection, but she knew that was not the case. And she somehow blamed herself for being unlovable.

"What difference does it make if I learn to ride bareback, or if I ride astride?" she said with a shrug. "Neither are subjects I can discuss with anyone. Neither are skills I can show to anyone. And neither are certainly accomplishments my aunt and uncle would be proud of."

His warm hands closed around her shoulders. "Have you never done anything just for yourself? Just because it pleases you, and to hell with everyone else?"

Nothing except her riding, and ladies were certainly known to enjoy a good jaunt, if few might admit they had an interest in all that Anne was interested in. Breeding, racing, all things related to horses. There were men who loved such things, as well, but so far, she hadn't met one who she thought would understand her own love of them.

"It would be different if I were a man," she explained. "Because I am a woman, I must be pleasing. I must be kind and considerate to others. I must want what all young women of my station want. To dream of doing or being something other than what is expected is foolish."

He pulled her closer. "It is never foolish to have dreams of your own. For some of us, that's all we can have. And why do you seem resentful of your life when it seems to me that you have everything?"

"Not everything," she argued, then realized she was revealing too much about herself to him. How pathetic she would sound if she told him she did not have the one thing she wanted most in life. To be loved. Just for herself. "But I sound shallow and unappreciative," she added, lowering her gaze. "You must understand that all that is really expected of me is to make a good match. To be pleasing so that a man will want to marry me. It's a woman's place to make her husband's life comfortable. To bear his children and run his home. At least it is that way for women of my station." Oddly enough, Anne's guardians had not pushed her to marry, had not seemed concerned over her lack of suitors even though Anne was nearly twenty-one.

Merrick suddenly released her and turned his back. "I see what you're saying. I suppose women of my class can only aspire to bear a man of your class's bastards and hope he doesn't die and leave them and the children to scavenge for themselves."

Anne realized she had been insensitive. She must sound like a total ninny to him, whining about her privileged life. "I'm sorry," she whispered. "Is that what happened to your mother?"

He turned back to her. "We didn't come here to talk about me. I thought we came so you could dare to do what you've been wanting to do. If you don't have the spine for it, let's go on back. Some of us cannot sleep the day away when we've stayed out too late the night before."

She had wounded him. She had stirred resentment in him. Anne hadn't meant to do either. But he was right. She'd been given this one opportunity to do something just for herself. Merrick had given her the opportunity, and however wrong it was, she couldn't help but come close to loving him for it.

"All right," she said. "Enough talk about matters neither of us can control. Tell me what to do."

Merrick stared at her a moment longer and Anne was

afraid he'd changed his mind. Then he sighed and moved past her to unsaddle Storm. Once he'd laid the saddle and blanket upon the ground, he swung up easily onto the mare's back.

"Watch me first," he said. "You have to hold on with your legs. Press them good and tight against the horse's sides. Like so."

Anne watched as he took the horse around in a circle. He walked the mare first, then nudged her into a trot, and then a gallop. Watching him made Anne feel odd again. All achy and feverish, as if she'd come down with an illness. Regardless of his bloodline, Merrick, with no last name, was quite something to look at. Again, Anne couldn't help but feel as if she had seen him somewhere before. Perhaps in her dreams.

Storm was known to be headstrong at times, but Merrick commanded her far better than Anne ever had, and the horse seemed to sense he was a man who would brook no nonsense from her. Anne wondered if he handled all females the same way.

"Are you ready to try now?"

"Yes," Anne answered. "But I believe you make it look much simpler than it is."

He drew the mare to a halt beside Anne, threw one leg over, and easily slid to the ground. "You'll do fine," he assured her. "You'll do fine because it's something you want to do. Maybe something you have to do."

Suppression and being a female born in a man's world went hand in hand together. Anne was used to suppressing her wants, her desires, her dreams, even her thoughts. She'd never met a man who encouraged a woman to be daring. It was a refreshing change for her.

"I'll help you up, since you have no stirrups," he said, and bent, folding his hands into a makeshift step.

Anne placed her hand upon his shoulder, feeling the sinewy muscles beneath his shirt. She put a booted foot in his hands and he hefted her easily up onto the horse's bare back.

"Remember to grip her with your legs," he instructed, and Anne tried not to blush in the moonlight.

Legs and gripping anything with them would be considered vulgar for a man to discuss in the presence of a lady. Recalling she wore men's clothing, Anne decided tonight that neither was she a lady nor was Merrick a gentleman. She nodded and took the reins draped across Storm's neck.

Anne started out slowly, getting used to the feel of the horse beneath her without a saddle. She walked Storm in a circle a few times before she felt confident enough to nudge her into a trot. The uneven gait nearly unseated Anne and she urged the mare into a smoother gallop.

"You're a fast learner," Merrick called. "You're doing fine."

Concentrating on keeping her seat, Anne called, "Can we go to the moors? Ride across them bareback in the moonlight as I dreamed I would do?" She glanced at him.

He shook his head. "Not tonight, lass. You need more practice before you dare that."

Who knew if Anne would have the courage to sneak from the house again and slip away with the new stable master? She could come to her senses at any time. Revert to her old ways of being good and chaste and totally boring. Her aunt could suddenly decide the country was too uneventful for her and demand they all pack up and leave for London. Tonight might be the only chance Anne had to realize her dream.

"I'm going," she decided. "Stay behind if you want. In fact, go back to the stable, so if I'm discovered or something happens to me, you won't be held accountable."

Having issued her orders, Anne turned Storm toward the path that would eventually lead her to the moors.

"Come back here, Anne," Merrick ordered. "I said you weren't ready yet."

Anne nearly obeyed simply out of habit. The need to rebel had taken root inside of her now and she wasn't sure she wanted to staunch it. Who was he to command her anyway? Merrick wouldn't tell on her, since he'd been a party to helping her tonight. Not unless he wanted to lose his position.

Already knowing him a good deal better than she should, Anne wouldn't put it past him to come after her and drag her from the horse's back. Anne kneed the animal into a gallop. Behind her, she heard Merrick swear rather loudly.

The path was easy to follow due to the bright moonlight shining down from above . . . at least until Anne was deep in the woods. She heard the pounding of hooves behind her and knew Merrick followed. Anne also knew that he would easily catch her if she stayed to the path. In a split-second decision, she reined Storm off the path.

Because Anne had a good sense of direction, she thought she could make her way easily to the moors. What she didn't anticipate was the difficulty of maneuvering a horse through the thicker forage or the log in her path she saw too late. Jumping on horseback was a good deal more difficult when the horse wore no saddle. Anne lost her balance and fell.

The fall jarred her to the teeth. The breath had been knocked from her and once she could breathe again, she sat up, trying to determine whether she'd been hurt. She moved her legs back and forth, her arms; nothing was broken. As Storm had been taught, the mare had come to a halt with no one guiding her by the reins. Anne slowly rose from the ground, her bottom still stinging as she moved toward the mare.

Suddenly Storm's head came up. The mare snorted, then her eyes rolled back in her head, and she shied, taking off through the woods as though the hounds of hell chased her. Anne wanted to cry. She should have listened to Merrick. He had been right. She wasn't ready to attempt what she had. Now she was afoot, lost in the woods, and alone. Or was she?

The hairs on the back of her neck prickled. She had a feeling she was being watched. What had frightened Storm? The horse didn't usually shy easily. Glancing around, Anne noticed how much darker it was at night when the trees overhead blocked out the moonlight. She had trouble distinguishing shapes. She also had trouble telling direction. Where was the path? If she moved in that direction, surely she'd come across Merrick in search of her.

She took a step, but movement from the corner of her eye had her wheeling to the right. Anne squinted into the shadows. Another shape joined the first. And then another. Wolves. Her blood turned to ice. So, the legend was true. There still were wolves roaming parts of England.

Anne dared not take her eyes off the still shadows, wondering how much longer they would remain still. She needed a weapon. Glancing down, she tried to make out the shape of a branch, a rock, anything she might use in her defense. A shadow had moved closer when she glanced back up. Anne swallowed hard.

"Don't move."

The instruction was no more than a whisper; then she felt Merrick's heat at her back. Her knees nearly buckled with relief. A shadow crept closer. Eyes glittered in the darkness. Her heart rose in her throat. Merrick stepped in front of her, blocking out the danger, protecting her from her own foolishness, perhaps with his life.

The shadows continued to move in until they were surrounded. Frightened, Anne slid her arms around Merrick's waist and pressed her face against his back. His heart thudded beneath her ear, strong, steady, but not racing wildly the way hers did at the moment. Silence echoed around her; then very soft, very low, she heard a growl. It resounded not from the beasts of the night but from the man who stood before her against them.

Gooseflesh rose on her arms. Anne didn't know whether to release her grip around Merrick's waist and run or hold tighter to him. She closed her eyes and prayed. How long she stood clinging to him, she did not know. It seemed like an eternity.

"It's all right now, lass. They've gone."

Anne opened her eyes, although the darkness that surrounded them was much like having them closed had been. She didn't see anything in the shadows, but that didn't mean there was nothing there.

"Are you certain?" she whispered. "How do you know?"

"Because I know," he answered, turning to face her. "They've gone and taken their scents with them. They were only curious to begin with. Curious to know what kind of fool walks alone in the woods at night."

A touch of embarrassment mingled with her fear. He was right; she was a fool. Anne might have considered herself boring the day before, but she hadn't considered herself foolish until tonight.

"I'm sorry. You were right," she admitted. "I shouldn't have gone off on my own. It was foolish and dangerous."

He didn't respond, and when she glanced up at him, Anne gasped. His shadow stood tall and dark against the night, but his eyes glittered like those of the beasts of the forest.

"Your eyes," she whispered. "They glow in the dark like the eyes of an animal."

He glanced away from her, as if to shield her from the sight. Anne recalled the low growl he'd issued while she had clung to him in fear. And his scent, the one she smelled on him now. The one that overpowered fear and confusion and attracted her to him even when common sense said she should run away. There was something very strange about Merrick. But perhaps it was only hysteria that made her think so.

"Merrick?" she whispered. "Who are you? I mean, really?"

5

It was a question Merrick had asked himself many times in the past. Who or what? He knew he was different from other men. He did not understand why. He'd been able to read the wolves' thoughts or, rather, sense what they were feeling. He had warned them off and they had gone, no doubt as frightened of the strange human as humans would be if they knew the whole truth about him.

"I'm just a man like any other," he lied. "I simply have some rather odd abilities."

One of those abilities allowed him to see her expression in the darkness. For a moment she had been frightened of him; now her brow wrinkled and natural curiosity took over.

"What sort of abilities?"

The path Merrick walked was a dangerous one. He shouldn't have told her as much as he had. And yet he wanted to tell her. Why would he? It was bad enough that so much already stood between them. Their stations in life. Why would he want to broaden the gap? Maybe to put distance between them. Maybe to simply see her reaction.

"I can see in the dark," he answered. "I see your face. Last night in the stable, I saw you as clearly as if it were daylight, standing in your underwear, rolling your stockings down your shapely legs. Your chemise had a red silk rose sewed to the front of it."

Her eyes widened. She took an unconscious step back from him, and Merrick tried to ignore how much that affected him. "How could you know that?" she asked. "How could you see that clearly in the darkness? It is impossible."

He wished it were impossible. Merrick felt her withdrawing from him. Even if her mind told her it was impossible, her conscience had begun to fear him. It was what he'd wanted, to put distance between them. But it didn't feel like what he wanted at all. No, if he was honest with himself, he'd admit he wanted her back in his arms. He wanted to kiss her. He wanted to do more than kiss her.

Perhaps it was an unconscious act on his part, but he knew by the slight flare of her nostrils, the way her eyes suddenly became heavy lidded, that he put off the scent. The one that attracted women to him. Merrick knew that wasn't right. He knew, but whatever instinct inside of him wanted to seduce Lady Anne Baldwin took over. He wanted her to desire him as much as he desired her. He wanted to forget about his strange gifts and the gap that separated him and Anne. He wanted her to forget, too.

Slowly, he leaned down and captured her parted lips. They were as sweet as he remembered and more responsive than they'd been in the stable. He was no longer a stranger to her, which seemed to be working to his advantage. She moaned softly when he traced her full lower lip with his tongue. She opened wider to him and he slanted his mouth against hers, exploring her, tasting her, seducing her.

Anne pressed against him and he pulled her closer, molding her soft curves against him. He cupped her breast, his blood heating in his veins when she did not pull away. She gasped softly when he brushed her nipple with his thumb through the fabric of her shirt. He wanted her naked. He wanted to touch her skin.

Merrick backed her against the trunk of a thick tree. He kissed her neck, worked the laces at the front of her shirt loose until the material gaped open and he could slide his hand inside. Conscience whispered that this wasn't the same as the night in the stable. He knew who she was now. He knew she was innocent. Still, he could not stop himself.

Anne knew she should stop him. Her mind was fogged with passion. Passion she had never felt before. What was it about this man that she could not resist? Maybe a combination of everything about him. His mouth moving against hers, his hand against her breast, excited her beyond common sense. She could even ignore the rough bark of the tree pressed against her back if only he kept kissing her . . . touching her.

His mouth moved to her neck, biting her skin gently before he moved lower, pushing her shirt aside. The feel of his moist mouth against her nipple, even through her chemise, sent a jolt through her. Anne twisted her fingers in his long hair and tried to remember to breathe.

"Do you know how beautiful you are?" he whispered against her skin. "How perfect in every way?"

Anne had never felt beautiful before. Certainly men had told her she was, but none had made her *feel* beautiful. On a deep level Anne knew that she craved Merrick's touch so much because she had been denied affection growing up. He gave her what she had been denied, and in turn, she wanted to deny him nothing. But as right as it felt, Anne knew that what was happening between them was wrong.

Resisting him became more difficult when he took her nipple into his mouth and sucked gently. Her nails dug into his scalp. Her knees nearly buckled. The place between her legs grew moist. She ached there, ached as if her body needed something her mind could not comprehend.

Anne sank deeper into the fog of her desire. His warm mouth traveled up her neck again; then he was kissing her. When he thrust his tongue into her mouth, Anne responded likewise. That's when she felt his teeth. They were longer than she knew them to be . . . almost like fangs.

She opened her eyes and thought he looked different. His facial features were somewhat blurred. She tried to struggle, but he pinned her securely against the tree. With his body pressed against hers, she felt his arousal for her. Then she couldn't swear to it, but she thought he growled.

"Merrick," she whispered. "You're frightening me."

His mouth was on her neck again. She felt the sharp sting of his teeth before he suddenly wrenched himself away from her. He turned his back; then he disappeared into the forest. Anne blinked into the darkness. Her heart pounded inside of her chest. He'd left her alone.

A wolf howled in the distance and Anne sucked in a breath. She fumbled with the gaping edges of her shirt and pulled the garment closed around her neck. Slowly, she slid to the ground. Where was Merrick? And why had he left her alone in the darkness?

When a twig snapped, she jumped. A tall shape broke from the shadows. Merrick was now standing before her, staring down. "Come, Anne," he said. "Let me lead you to Sin."

"Sin?" she whispered.

"The stallion. I'll take you home."

For the briefest moment she thought she couldn't trust him. Her eyes had adjusted enough to the darkness to see that he held his hand extended toward her. What had happened a moment ago? Had she imagined that he had looked and seemed different? She had been frightened earlier. Perhaps her fear had only carried over.

"Anne, take my hand," Merrick coaxed softly.

She slid her hand into his larger one. They were the hands of a workingman, but they had felt like silk against her skin a moment earlier. He pulled her to her feet. Anne swayed slightly. She felt dazed, out of sorts.

"What is happening to me?" she asked. "Why do I respond to you as I do, and what do you want from me, Merrick?"

He didn't say anything for a moment. Perhaps he didn't know the answer. Then he said, "For right now, I want to take you home. I want you to be safe."

Safe from the wolves or safe from him? Anne wondered. She should go home. She should go home and slip back into the safe, boring life she had known before she had kissed him in her stable. A stranger. A man who worked for her uncle. But a man who made her feel as she had never felt before. A man who was not afraid to show her affection. A man who said she was beautiful.

Merrick pulled her along behind him through the woods. The path was actually not that far and they stumbled upon it, startling the black stallion that had stood waiting for their return. Merrick spoke softly to the animal and he gentled. Merrick climbed up into the saddle and pulled Anne up in front of him.

"What about Storm?" Anne roused herself from her dazed state to ask. "And the saddle and blanket we left behind?"

"I imagine Storm has headed back to the stable. If she's not there when we return, I'll go back out and find her. I'll fetch the saddle, too."

He would cover for Anne. Erase her mistakes tonight. He had possibly saved her life earlier. Merrick with his odd abilities and his scent that still affected her. He could have taken advantage of her in the woods. Anne was fairly certain she would have allowed him to seduce her fully. Why hadn't he? And had she only imagined that his features had blurred for a moment, had seemed misshapen, his teeth like fangs?

Of course she had. The wolves had given her a fright and she had been still reacting to that. The feel of his hard chest pressed against her back affected her now. His strong thighs molded on either side of her. Anne needed a distraction. He walked the horse, she assumed for her benefit, but the slow pace only prolonged the torture of being pressed against him.

"Why do you call your horse Sin?" she asked.

"Because he's as dark as sin."

The silence between them stretched again. Merrick's heat penetrated the back of her riding gown and she wondered what it would feel like to have his bare flesh pressed against hers.

"He seems fast, your horse," she blurted.

"Yes," he responded, and his breath brushed her ear, causing her to shiver. "Fast as any I've seen."

"Do you race him? I would, if he were mine, that is, and of course if I were a man."

"I race him," he responded. "Mostly at small country fairs, and only if the purse is fat. The horse loves to run. He likes the competition."

The horse didn't seem in the least bit anxious to hurry them back to the stable at the moment. Anne wasn't even certain they were headed in the right direction now that she thought about it.

"Merrick, do you know where you're going?" she asked. "I don't think this is the path back to the house."

"I know where I'm going," he assured her.

A few moments later they left the shelter of the trees behind them. Merrick pulled the stallion up and Anne gasped. Ahead of them, the ground bladeless and cracked, lay the moors. Moonlight shone down and the ground stretching before them looked strangely beautiful.

"Are you ready, Anne?" Merrick asked close to her ear.

She knew now why he had brought her here. Her heart soared that he would, that he knew how important it was to her—to live this one dream.

"I'm ready," she whispered.

"Hold tight."

He kneed the stallion and they shot forward into the moon-light.

It wasn't exactly Anne's dream of being in her underwear, alone, and riding bareback, but it was better. Better because she had Merrick to share the moment with. He laughed along with her, and she knew that he shared her joy. He understood her as no man had ever understood her before. And he was right. Everyone should have a dream, even a small one like this.

6

Anne laughed out loud from the sheer joy of racing across the moors in the moonlight, the wind in her hair, Merrick at her back, his arms around her holding her securely in front of him. He was right. She'd never been on a horse as fast as the stallion. Sin's hooves thundered along the cracked ground, throwing clots up in their wake.

"Want to go faster?" he leaned in close to ask.

"Oh yes," she breathed; then they both leaned in together and the stallion shot ahead.

Her blood sang in her veins. Anne closed her eyes and simply lived in the moment—felt the horse powerful and sure-footed beneath her, felt the wind dance across her face and a man's strong heartbeat against her back. She never wanted it to end, but of course it had to.

Merrick slowed the stallion. Sin's breath fogged on the air as he snorted a protest. Merrick knew the horse well. The stallion loved to run.

"There's a fair in the shire not far from Blackthorn Manor next week," she told Merrick. "You should race Sin there."

"And will you come to watch us run?"

Anne loved country fairs, if her aunt and uncle found them boring at best. "If my aunt and uncle will bring me," she answered. "They don't usually care for such things. My aunt would rather attend a grand ball in London."

"And what about you, Anne? What do you prefer?"

He'd brought the stallion to a halt. The moonlight bathed the land around them in soft light, again making her marvel that such a harsh landscape could be beautiful.

"I prefer the fair," she answered honestly. "Although my aunt would count it as time spent wastefully. There are no fine gentlemen at the fair for me to attract. There is no agenda there that she would approve of. No marriage mart."

Merrick pulled Anne's now tangled hair over one shoulder. The brush of his fingers against her neck made her shiver. "Why are you not wed already, Anne? Are the gentlemen in London all blind or daft?"

She could only be honest with him. "I am boring."

When he laughed, his warm breath caressed her ear. "You, boring? A woman who sneaks out of the house in the night and strips down to her underthings so she can ride her horse across the moors? A woman who ventures into the woods alone to confront wolves? A woman—"

"I don't usually do those things," Anne interrupted, turning so that she could see him. "I'm having a rebellion. I'm quite certain it will pass."

"Will it?"

His mouth was suddenly only a whisper from hers. Had he brought her out here to finish the seduction? Something wicked inside of her said if so, that might not be a bad thing. The ride had fired her blood. The ride and Merrick wrapped around her. Tonight might be all they had together. Anne knew her rebellion couldn't last. At some point she must regain her senses and return to her boring and predictable life . . . but perhaps not just yet.

• • •

The lady wanted him to kiss her. Merrick was tempted. Tempted nearly beyond his control. But something odder than normal had happened to him tonight. In the woods, while he'd been kissing Anne, touching her, wanting her like he had never wanted a woman before, something had stirred beneath his skin. He'd felt it rising up in him. It had come very close to consuming him . . . whatever the hell it was.

His lust for her had turned animalistic. His thoughts had become disjointed, as if they were slipping away from him. As if he were transforming into something else. For a moment, he'd actually been afraid that he might hurt Anne. That fear was the one thing that had penetrated his lust for her and caused him to break away, to disappear long enough to pull himself back from the brink of whatever was happening to him.

Now she tempted him to lose control again. In the past, women of Anne's station had come to him, sneaking to the stable where he worked in the dead of night. They had wanted sport with him, and Merrick had used them, he supposed, for whatever revenge against their class he harbored in his heart. But Anne, she was not like those other women. What he felt for her was not the same. And what she made him feel was like nothing he had felt before.

He took pleasure in her joy. Her innocence was like a balm to his jaded soul. What he wanted from her was not a few stolen moments in the night. He very much feared what he did want. It was all he had promised his mother he would forsake.

"If I were a gentleman, I would take you to the fair," he told her, brushing a tangled lock of hair from her beautiful face. "I would drive you in a smart buggy and show you off. I would wear your favor upon my arm as I raced Sin."

She smiled at him in the moonlight and his heart twisted inside of his chest. "But I am not a gentleman, Anne. You must not forget that."

Her sweet smile faded. In the moonlight, he saw the blush

bloom in her cheeks. "You are more of one than you know,"
she said softly. "Or you would not be warning me not to lose
my head. You would not be reminding me of my place, and of
yours."

It was defiantly out of his character. Merrick had never
minded taking what was offered, secretly resenting that he
was at times treated like a fine stud in the stable and not a
man. He had thought Anne was different, but was she? Perhaps she thought of him the same. A diversion from her ordered life. Just a part of her rebellion. Then should he feel any
guilt about seducing her? Having his sport with her as she
would have hers with him?

Her eyes were large and innocent as she stared into his.
Soft as the eyes of a doe. No, he was not wrong about her,
even if he wanted to tell himself he was at the moment. "You
want more than I can give you, Anne. More than a man like
me will ever be able to give you. I'll take you home now."

For a moment, her gaze upon him sparkled, as if her eyes
had filled with tears. "Is it so much to want?" she whispered.
"To be loved?"

Was that what she wanted from him? Merrick had trouble
believing that. More than likely, she was simply confused about
what love was. Not that he really knew himself. He had never
been in love with a woman before. He certainly knew what it
was like to be rejected. He would spare himself that with her.

"I'm sure you are loved, Anne. Your aunt and uncle—"

"Have trouble showing affection toward me," she interrupted. Anne blinked back her tears. "I've done everything I
know to do to win their hearts, but I feel as if I have failed. I
wonder if the fault lies within me. If there is something about
me that is unworthy of love?"

Was that what she thought? How could anyone not love
Anne? She was good and sweet and beautiful, and he'd known
that about her instinctively. He'd known she was the opposite
of him. Maybe that was why he found her irresistible. She was

everything he was not. She had everything he did not. But then, perhaps they were more alike than he knew. They both wanted what they could not seemingly have.

"You are not unworthy, Anne," he told her. "Maybe they are unworthy of you." And so was he.

Merrick turned the stallion toward Blackthorn Manor. Anne settled back into the saddle before Merrick. They rode in silence. He savored the feel of her against him. Her sweet scent in his nostrils. A moment in time when nothing separated them, even if tomorrow everything would return to the way it should be. Anne in her grand house. He in the stable. She a lady waiting for all that she deserved in life, all he felt would be hers in time. And he . . . Well, Merrick wasn't even certain what he was. A man Lady Anne Baldwin should stay far away from. He did know that much.

The fair in Devonshire was a grand sight; Stalls of merchants, horse trading, sheep trading, and even a traveling show performed. Anne weaved her way through the crowd, her pace leisurely so that her beloved Bertha could keep up. Her aunt and uncle strolled ahead, dressed as if they visited a grand ball rather than a country fair. Anne had decided upon a simple day frock, modest bonnet, and one of her oldest shawls. She didn't want to stand out in the crowd.

She had too much pent-up energy to play the part of a grand lady today. Since she and Merrick had snuck away into the darkness she'd stayed away from the stable. She was frightened, Anne admitted. Frightened of her feelings for Merrick. No good could come of them, but knowing that didn't seem to stop her from wanting to be with him.

Merrick was here today. He'd left at daybreak, advising her uncle to bet money on him and his stallion in the race. If it weren't for the prospect of making money on a wager, she doubted her aunt and uncle would have wanted to attend the fair at all.

A woman telling fortunes called to Anne as she strolled past. "Come let me tell your fortune, good lady."

Bemused, Anne paused at the brightly colored tent. The fortune-teller's eyes were heavily made up. She wore a scarf tied around her head and a ring on every finger. Anne reached into her reticule and removed a coin. "This is all I have," she said, which was not entirely the truth, but all she had for such silliness as having her fortune told.

The woman snatched the coin and grabbed her hand. She studied Anne's palm. "You have a long lifeline," she said. "But I see trouble ahead in your future."

Anne supposed most people should expect trouble of some sort or another in their future. She merely smiled at the woman.

"There is a man," the woman said, looking up at Anne from beneath her lashes. The woman glanced down again, then suddenly released her hand. Her eyes widened. Her dark complexion paled. "Beware of the wolf in your stable," she whispered. "Stay away from him or bring his curse down upon you both."

Anne blinked down at the woman. "Beg your pardon?"

"Go now," the woman commanded. "I can do no more than warn you."

Anne felt cheated, to put it mildly. There was no wolf in her stable and she'd expected to be told she would meet a special man and have a bright future. It was the sort of thing a woman wanted to hear. Suddenly Anne wondered if the wolf the woman referred to might in fact be a man whom she should avoid.

"Is this wolf in my stable a man or a beast?" she asked the woman.

The fortune-teller shuddered. "He is both," she answered, then rose and disappeared into the crowd.

Gooseflesh rose on Anne's arms. She pulled her shawl closer around her.

"There you are, Lady Anne," Bertha huffed beside her.

"I had lost you in the crowd for a moment and was sorely worried."

Still unnerved, Anne reached out and squeezed her maid's arm. "I'm fine. I stopped to have my fortune told."

Bertha snorted. "That was a waste of coin. Suppose she told you you'll soon meet a nice young man and have a happy future together. Those types always tell a body what they want to hear."

Bertha's words only further unsettled Anne. So she had thought, as well. A disturbance farther down the stretch of vendors and performers drew her attention. Horses churned up dirt in the air. The horse races were about to begin.

"Come, Lady Anne," Bertha instructed. "Your aunt and uncle will wonder what's become of us. We're to join them to watch the races and have a nice lunch."

Anne's maid never missed a meal, which was obvious by her rounded frame. Bertha hurried Anne down the lane toward the meadow where the horse racing would take place. Anne couldn't help but glance over her shoulder toward where she'd last seen the fortune-teller. The woman stood staring after her. Quickly Anne turned away.

She spied her aunt and uncle resting on a blanket spread on the ground. Millicent, her aunt's personal maid, had come along, hefting things from the buggy for her mistress's comfort. The woman knelt upon the blanket unpacking lunch.

"There you are," Aunt Claire called upon seeing Anne. "Come and sit, Anne. We are famished."

Dutiful as always, Anne hurried toward the blanket and seated herself. "I can't thank you enough again for bringing me today, Uncle Theodore and Aunt Claire. I know you both find these fairs boring, but I am having a wonderful time."

Absently her aunt reached forward and patted Anne's hand. "Wish a social engagement would put the sparkle in your eyes and the blush in your cheeks like this crude affair. Perhaps you were never meant to live the life of a social wife. 'Tis no wonder a suitable gentleman has not offered for you, Anne. You have odd likes for a well-bred girl. You must have gotten that from your mother's side."

Anne stared down at her clasped hands. "I'm sorry to be such a disappointment to you, dear aunt," she said. "I will try harder to gain the attention of a suitable bachelor when next we visit London."

"Leave the girl alone," her uncle fussed. "We want her to be happy in her match, don't we, lady wife?"

Her aunt patted Anne again. "Of course we do. Take your time, Anne. There is no hurry."

Aunt Claire's attitude was strange indeed. Most mothers were so desperate to find suitable matches for their daughters that nothing else was thought of or discussed from the time the girl became old enough to marry. Since her aunt and uncle displayed little actual affection for her, Anne suspected they'd be all too happy to rid themselves of her. Perhaps it was because she'd been so obedient trying to win their love she was not considered much of a burden.

"I should try harder," she admitted. "I'll be twenty-one soon, practically considered on the shelf."

"We thought we would stay in the country until after your birthday," her uncle piped up. "We thought you would enjoy it more if you could ride your horse and wander about outside like you love doing."

Anne was surprised. Her birthday was a good three months off. She couldn't see her aunt spending that length of time away from her London parties and social friends. Anne had in fact thought her guardians might throw her a birthday ball. It would be an opportunity to attract male suitors for her.

"How kind of you," she said in earnest. "I do prefer the country over the bustle of London, but I know that both of you prefer our time in the city."

"It is your birthday," her aunt said, forgoing the hand patting this time. "We want you to spend it as enjoyably as possible."

A bout of tenderness for her aunt and uncle overcame Anne. She supposed she sometimes judged them unfairly. Simply because they were not free with their affections didn't mean they didn't care about her.

"It would make me very happy to spend my birthday in the country."

"Then it is settled," her aunt said, eyeing the food her maid had set out for them. "Let's dine before the horses stir up even more dust and ruin our meal."

They set about having lunch. Anne found her appetite lacking. She was nervous. Maybe for Merrick and the black. Maybe because of her encounter with the fortune-teller. No one seemed to notice how sparsely Anne ate. Her aunt and uncle were too busy talking about the latest London gossip.

"Two of them married now," Aunt Claire said. "Some say they are being allowed into society because of their affiliation with the dowager. I say it's shameful. I'm happy Anne didn't go all soft in the head over Jackson Wulf like every other woman he flashes those dimples at."

Anne's attention snapped toward her aunt. She spoke of the Wulf brothers. The wild Wulfs of London, as some called them. Suddenly a realization struck Anne as forcefully as a blow. "Wulf," she whispered.

"What, dear?" her aunt questioned.

Grappling with the sudden dawning of who Merrick reminded her of, Anne merely shook her head and didn't answer. Merrick was the spitting image of Jackson Wulf, only he had dark hair instead of light and light eyes instead of dark. No wonder she felt as if she'd seen him before the first morning she met him in the dining room.

How uncanny that they should resemble each other so much, at least in facial features and stature. Her gaze automatically strayed toward the meadow where the horses were being lined up. She couldn't see over the crowd and rose, shading her eyes against the sun.

A few tall men blocked Anne's view. "I can't see," she said to her aunt and uncle. "I'm just going a bit toward the front."

"Bertha, go with her," her aunt instructed. "She'll be gawking and unaware if someone is picking her pocket."

The maid, still involved with her lunch, grumbled, placed her plate aside, and lumbered to her feet. "Getting too old to chase after her," she complained.

Anne didn't wait for Bertha. She hurried into the crowd, now driven to see Merrick. She paid no mind to the people she shoved her way through. Standing now at the front of the crowd, she searched the riders preparing their horses for the race. Merrick was already seated upon his great black stallion. The two of them made a formidable sight. Both dark. Both magnificent.

Her breath caught in her throat as Merrick pranced the stallion around the other riders, obviously with the intention of intimidating them. Merrick's hair was tied back, calling attention to his striking good looks. He wore a white shirt, open at the neck, ruffled and seemingly out of place among the country's simpler folk. He wore tight black breeches and his boots were now polished to a high shine. She'd never seen a more handsome man. Besides the rest of the Wulf brothers.

All were handsome indeed. Jackson was a close friend of hers. They had met abroad just last year. He had since married. A woman some claimed was a witch, but Anne had liked Lady Lucinda the moment she had met her. By God, Merrick did look like Jackson. He looked like him enough to be his brother.

She must tell Merrick about his uncanny resemblance to Jackson Wulf. It might answer some of the questions Merrick had concerning his parentage. But then again, it might simply make trouble for the Wulf brothers, and Lord knew, they had enough of that dogging their heels as it was.

Anne was at an impasse over her sudden suspicions. She valued her friendships with Jackson, had found him funny and charming and none of the things that were often rumored about him. But Merrick might find comfort in at least knowing where he came from, if in fact her suspicions were correct. And how could they not be? Merrick had to be a Wulf; that was all there was to it.

"*Beware of the wolf in your stable.*" The fortune-teller's warning suddenly came back to Anne. Not the wolf but the Wulf. Merrick was admittedly illegitimate, but he was a Wulf nonetheless. She was fairly bursting to tell him she had solved the mystery of who his father had been.

The riders lined up before her. Their horses stomped and pranced in readiness for the race. Behind her, she heard men making wagers. Merrick was a favorite, most betting on the Earl's new man.

She also heard murmurs among the women present. Hushed whispers regarding the stable master's handsome looks and fine form—talk that made her back stiffen.

"I imagine Lady Baldwin spends more time than usual around her husband's horses these days," one woman joked. "Hear she likes her lovers young and virile."

"She'll not be disappointed with that one, then." Another woman laughed. "Suppose the man is used to servicing his employer's women, like any good stud."

The women tittered and Anne moved away from the talk and the ill feeling it brought to her stomach. She'd noticed the way her aunt eyed Merrick that first morning in the dining room. Saw the way her gaze swept over him in an assessing manner. Anne hadn't thought much of it, other than that he was the type of man who drew a woman's notice, young or otherwise. Surely her aunt had not approached him in the stable and dangled herself before him, suggesting she was ripe for adventure herself.

Sudden jealousy ripped through Anne. She had no right to feel the emotion. She had no right to suspect her aunt was anything but taken with his looks, without acting upon her interest. Then Anne recalled her uncle's warning to them about the hens behaving themselves. Had his statement been aimed at his wife, rather than Anne?

"Nonsense," she scolded herself. She had never felt jealousy over a man and didn't like the emotion. It made one think irrationally. Wanting to soothe her sudden worries, she glanced around in search of her aunt and uncle. They had joined the crowd of onlookers for the race. They stood a few feet away, her aunt staring at Merrick as he took the stallion through his paces, while her uncle clearly made wagers on the outcome of the race.

Merrick, as if feeling Aunt Claire's regard, glanced toward the woman, held her brave stare for a moment, then looked away, she supposed in search of younger, prettier sport. His eyes landed upon Anne. She tried to look away, but she couldn't. Funny, she had never felt the flutter in her stomach and the leap of her pulses when Jackson Wulf looked at her. So much alike and yet so different.

A trumpet sounded and Merrick glanced away, his interest now trained upon the race. Anne flushed that he'd managed to hold her gaze and glanced around uneasily. She saw her aunt staring at her, her disapproval obvious by the scowl on her face. Anne refused to feel ashamed, having heard what she just had about her aunt and her taste for younger men. It was obviously all right for her to behave badly but not for Anne. She lifted her chin in a show of defiance, rewarded by her aunt's sudden look of surprise.

A shot was fired and Anne returned her attention to the race. The horses and riders bounded forward and cheers went up from the crowd. How she longed to be part of the race. To be riding at breakneck speed across the meadow, her hair flying behind her, astride and in control of the horse. She became caught up in the activity and shouted along with the crowd when Merrick pulled ahead of the other riders.

It was over almost before it began. Merrick was easily the

winner, and most of the crowd pushed forward to offer con gratulations. Anne could do no such thing. It wouldn't be proper, but for a moment she longed to be among those gathered around Merrick. She longed to throw herself in his arms and kiss him.

Guilt over her brave thoughts made an appearance. She glanced back at her aunt and uncle, hoping they had not witnessed her enthusiasm for the race. They weren't paying any attention to her but seemed to be involved in a heated argument. She'd wager it had something to do with Merrick. Glancing back at the stable master, she noted that he also seemed focused on her aunt and uncle.

It was absurd, but if Anne didn't know better, Merrick appeared to be listening to their conversation. He couldn't possibly hear whatever they discussed at the distance between them, not to mention the shouts and claps on the back from those gathered around him, but when he glanced at Anne, she read a certain amount of alarm in his usually cocky expression.

A moment later he was distracted by the presenting of the purse for winning the race. Her aunt and uncle were suddenly beside Anne.

"Let's go home now, Anne," her aunt instructed. "I think you've had enough excitement for one day."

The disapproving scowl still shaped her aunt's thin lips. Usually, Anne would have been devastated to bring either her aunt or her uncle the slightest reason to be disappointed with her. Today, it seemed less important. Nevertheless, she fell dutifully in step with them and returned to their carriage.

Merrick would come home, too, although she doubted he'd ride along with them. He seemed to like being on his own. A lone wolf. A Wulf in truth, she remembered. Would she tell him of her suspicions? Would it solve anything or just create more trouble?

7

It was none of his business, Merrick tried to assure himself for the hundredth time since he'd returned to the manor house. He was a servant, nothing more. It wasn't his place to interfere in Anne's life. Still, the conversation he'd overheard between Lord and Lady Baldwin bothered him. Should he tell Anne what he'd overheard, and would she believe him if he did?

Merrick paced the dark confines of the stable, plagued by indecision. He'd never gotten involved in such matters before. But then, he already was involved, whether he wanted to be or not. Damn his abnormal hearing and everything odd about him. It was a curse at times.

But Anne needed to be warned. He cared about her too much to see her cuckolded. She'd stayed away from the stable now for a week. It was just as well, since he'd been breeding the gray filly and knew Anne's uncle would not have wished her to be a witness to the breeding. Still, it had eaten at Merrick not to see her. It had also made him realize just how enamored of her he was. Which did him little good.

Even though it was late in the evening, Merrick thought it

best to speak to Anne immediately. He knew which room upstairs belonged to her. He'd seen her standing at the window gazing out a time or two during the past week. Merrick would throw a rock to get her attention. He nearly ran into her on his way out of the stable.

"Good Lord," she gasped. "You scared me half to death. What are you doing slinking around this time of night?"

She'd given him a start, as well. "What are you doing slinking around this time of night?" he shot back.

"I need to talk to you," she answered. "Privately, so I thought it best to wait until everyone had gone to bed."

Although he was curious as to why Anne had sought him out, his concerns over what he'd heard earlier were uppermost on Merrick's mind. "I need to talk to you, too. I heard something today I thought you should know about."

"Heard something?" Her brow furrowed. "That concerns me?"

They stood at the entrance to the stable, in plain sight if anyone cared to look or was up at this late hour. Merrick took her arm and pulled her inside.

"I overheard your aunt and uncle arguing at the fair."

Anne eyed him oddly. "How could you have heard them? From what I saw, you were never within speaking or hearing distance of my aunt and uncle this afternoon."

He wouldn't go into detail about his abnormal hearing abilities. He'd already told her too much about his strange gifts. "I heard them," he insisted. "And they were arguing about you."

Although she was clearly confused as to how he could have heard a conversation take place between her aunt and uncle, a light of interest flickered within her lovely eyes. "Arguing about me?"

"Yes," he answered. "Your aunt was worried about the two of us. About the way we looked at one another. She said they'd done their best to make certain you didn't find a man to marry who was acceptable and she wouldn't let you make a mistake with one who wasn't."

"What?" Anne shook her head. "That makes no sense. It isn't as if they don't want me to marry, simply that no one suitable has offered for me."

"Anne." Merrick took her shoulders between his hands. "I imagine more have asked than you are aware of. You're lovely. And sweet. They don't want you to marry because if you aren't by the time you turn twenty-one, your inheritance is to fall under their control. They want your fortune, Anne."

She took a step back from him as if he'd delivered a blow. "That is not true. I am to gain my inheritance when I turn twenty-one. It's been understood for some time."

Merrick had to make her understand. "Only if you are married, Anne. I heard them say so. Otherwise, they are to take control of your inheritance until you turn twenty-five, at which time I imagine it will become yours whether you are married or not. I'm betting they'll have it spent by then, or tied up so you can't get it."

She looked stunned. "But it's my inheritance," she insisted. "I never knew there was a stipulation of marriage involved."

Anne didn't want to believe him, Merrick realized. She still clung to the hope that her aunt and uncle cared more for her than their actions showed. "They didn't want you to know. They are heavily indebted. I heard your aunt say so when she argued with your uncle about it, though they kept their voices low. Even the roof over their heads will someday pass to your husband. They stand to lose everything if you marry, Anne."

Doubt still clouded her eyes. It was hard for her to trust a stranger's word over what she wanted to believe about her aunt and uncle. "I have no wish to hurt you, Anne," he said. "If you don't want to believe me, then don't. At least I told you what I heard and my conscience is clear."

His duty done, he thought he'd turn from her and go back

to the loft where he slept before he gave into temptation and pulled her into his arms. Merrick remembered she'd come to tell him something. "What was it you wanted to tell me?"

Still wearing a dazed expression, she chewed her full lower lip. "I . . . it was nothing. It was none of my business, just as this is none of yours. Never mind."

He'd hurt her whether he wanted to or not. Even if Anne had long suspected her aunt and uncle did not love her, hearing they only thought of her as a means to an end, fulfilling their own selfish desires, had hurt her deeply.

Merrick understood the pain of not being wanted. Still, maybe she needed to sleep on what he'd told her before it could penetrate—before she accepted that he had no reason to lie to her. He started to turn away from her again when his sharp ears caught the slight snap of a twig underfoot. The scuffle of slippers against the pebbles that made a path to the stable from the house.

"Someone's coming," he said. "Better hide until we see who it is and what they want."

Anne seemed to mentally shake herself. She glanced around. "I don't hear anything."

"Quiet," Merrick warned again. He took her arm and led her toward an empty stall. "Go in there and don't come out until whoever it is has left."

"But," she started to protest. Merrick didn't allow her. He gently pushed her inside the stall and hoped she'd stay put. He didn't need to be found with her alone this time of night.

A figure appeared at the stable entrance a moment later. Merrick wasn't surprised by her visit. It was Anne's aunt. The woman had been ogling him since the morning he was introduced to her. He was used to such visits from his previous employers' wives. Merrick was usually amused by their interest, but not tonight, and not this particular woman.

"Can I be of assistance to you, Lady?" he asked.

She sashayed toward him. "I hope so. I noticed something that distressed me today and thought we should clear the matter up. I didn't see call to involve my husband."

"I don't imagine so," Merrick said drily.

"It concerns Lady Anne," the woman forged ahead. "I fear she may be smitten with you. And that you might take advantage of her innocence."

"Do you now?"

The woman stepped closer. Anne's aunt wasn't an unattractive woman, but she was nearly old enough to be Merrick's mother and the scowl she usually wore had deepened the lines in her forehead and around her mouth. "I've seen the way you look at her . . . and the way she looks at you. Anne is a beautiful young woman and I don't doubt you find her to your liking, but I won't have you making sport of her."

Merrick leaned casually back against the stall where Anne hid. "It's honorable that you want to protect her."

She shrugged. "I suppose even a sensible girl like Anne's head can be turned by a handsome face. And I am sure that you are well used to women throwing themselves at you, Merrick. There is no need, however, to go sniffing around her skirts when another option is open to you."

Although he knew what her answer would be, Merrick asked, "What option is that?"

Her hand shot out and her fingers traced a lazy path up the front of his chest. "Me, of course," she answered. "Despoiling an innocent is one thing. Having a dalliance with an experienced woman is another. My husband bores me and has since a week into our marriage."

Merrick didn't want the woman touching him, but Anne needed to be convinced that her aunt and uncle did not have her best interests at heart, no matter if she wanted to believe otherwise. "Are you worried that I'll ruin Lady Anne before you can marry her off?"

"Don't be silly," the woman snapped. "To be honest, I was

simply feeling a bit like she'd intruded upon my territory. I consider everything on this property mine . . . you included." The woman cocked her head to one side. "Now that you mention that, however, it is not a bad idea. You see, I would prefer that Anne not marry. It would be to my benefit if she does not."

Merrick knew every word from the woman's mouth shattered Anne, but maybe Anne was too innocent for her own good. "So now you're asking me to ruin her so she won't be a fit wife for a gentleman of her own station?"

"It is a possibility," the woman answered. "But first, I want my fill of you. Do we have an understanding?" ·

He stopped the woman's hand from traveling farther up his chest. "No. We do not. I am not yours to command. You don't own me like I am a horse in your husband's stable. I have no wish to bed you, Lady."

Her face, maybe once pretty but now only bitter, suffused with color. "Are you refusing me?"

"I don't have many rights, but I imagine deciding who I pleasure and who I don't is one of them," he assured her. "Go back to the house and get what you need from your husband."

The woman's mouth fell open. "It's Anne, isn't it? You only want her."

Merrick thought about his answer. "I care for Anne. I would not demean her in the manner you want me to, and certainly not for your own gain."

"How do you know it would be to my gain?" The woman's eyes narrowed upon him. "And why would you care as long as you got what you want . . . unless." She suddenly laughed. "Oh dear, you're in love with her."

Was he? Merrick had never been in love before. He only knew he wanted to protect Anne. He wanted her to be happy. "You should go," he said to the woman. Anne had heard all she needed to hear.

"Poor fool." The woman clucked. "Even Anne knows her

place in life, and yours. Don't think you're the first to be smitten. We've had to beat the suitors back with a stick, although Anne is not aware of that. I'd prefer she stay in the dark. Let her think she is not interesting enough to capture a man's attention. At least for a while longer."

"I can tell her what you've said to me," Merrick said.

The lady lifted a brow. "You wouldn't dare. And she wouldn't believe you anyway. Anne sees the best in us and always has. She is cursed that way, I suppose. Poor thing, so hungry for love."

Anger for Anne churned his gut. "How can you not love her?" He hadn't meant to speak the thought out loud.

Lady Baldwin drew herself up straighter. "I have done my duty by Anne. I didn't want children. I don't even like them, but my husband convinced me there would be rewards by taking Anne in and raising her. I will not see my just rewards stripped from me. And I think your time here has come to an end. You won't cooperate and I will therefore see you dismissed. I'll simply tell my husband you are not only trying to get Anne into your loft, but you have propositioned me, as well. Pack your things; you'll be gone come morning."

With that warning, Lady Baldwin turned and stormed from the stable. Merrick waited a moment to make certain she had gone. He opened the stall behind him and went inside. He found Anne huddled on the straw-covered floor. Her hands covered her face and her shoulders shook. His heart broke for her. He bent beside her and gently touched her.

Anne glanced up, tears streaming down her face. "I didn't want to believe you. I'm so blinded by my own hopes at times. I feel like a fool. Does that make you happy?"

At one time, Merrick supposed it would have brought him some sense of pleasure to expose her aunt's deception, to tear a family apart, one of the upper classes anyway. Merrick felt no pleasure in seeing Anne's tears. They tugged at his heart. "I'm sorry," was all he could think to say.

In her pain, he expected her to lash out at him, and he would understand, but instead she only covered her face with her hands and leaned into his body. "What am I going to do?"

Merrick took her shoulders and forced her to sit. "Look at me, Anne. You need to get married. And the sooner the better."

She blinked up at him. "Married? To whom?"

"To whomever," Merrick insisted. "The two of you can slip away to Gretna Green. You can marry before your aunt and uncle can stop you."

Anne ran a shaky hand through her hair. "It's impossible. First I'd have to go to London to find someone, then talk him into marrying me. My aunt and uncle would never let me go without them. I can't go alone. Not all that way without some type of protection. There are thieves on the roads. It wouldn't be safe."

Merrick would be dismissed tomorrow anyway. "I can take you to London, Anne. Now, tonight. I can protect you."

Her large doelike eyes lifted to him. She reached out and gently touched his cheek. "Why would you? Why do you care, Merrick?"

Why indeed? He'd never stuck his nose in matters that weren't his business before. But Anne felt like his business. "I know what it's like to feel as if you mean nothing to someone. But you aren't nothing, Anne. I won't have them making you feel that way."

Even though her heart was broken, Anne felt it flutter to life in that moment. No one had cared about her like Merrick seemed to care. He encouraged her hopes and dreams. He had protected her when she needed protection, and he had exposed her aunt and uncle's deceit to her, when she'd been too innocent to see it for herself. Anne couldn't think of one gentleman in London she would wish to marry. But she did know one man who made her feel like no other man made her feel, or no other man ever would.

"Marry me, Merrick," she whispered.

His eyes widened for a moment. "No, Anne," he said softly. "You can't marry me. You know that."

"I can," she argued. "We can run away together tonight, just like you said. We can go to Gretna Green."

Merrick shook his dark head. "You don't know what you're saying, Anne. You're upset, not thinking clearly."

Anne knew exactly what she wanted, maybe for the first time in her life. She loved Merrick. How or when or why didn't seem to matter at the moment. She knew he cared about her, if of course he didn't love her. But she was used to that. She had to make him want to marry her for reasons that would best benefit him. She sadly understood that now, too.

"You are bitter because of the life denied to you," she said to him. "What better revenge than to marry into it? All I have will become yours. You won't have to sleep in a stable anymore, Merrick."

He shook his head again, but Anne saw that he was thinking about what she'd just said. Considering her offer. "If all you have is going to a man anyway, why not just let your uncle have it?" he reasoned.

Anne wouldn't lie to him about that. "I am angry," she admitted. "And hurt. I've spent my life dancing to their tune in hopes of winning their approval, their love. I will have stipulations if you marry me."

He lifted a brow. "Such as?"

"My independence," she answered. "I expect to do as I please."

"And what would you expect of me?"

Staring into his eyes, she wanted to say that she expected him to love her, but Anne had learned her lesson about love. She knew now that it wasn't something one person could wrest from another. It had to be given willingly, freely. "I expect you to do as you please, as well," she answered. "As long as it doesn't interfere with what pleases me."

He made a snorting noise. "You want me under your thumb."

That was not what Anne truly wanted, but she couldn't tell him what she really desired. It would show him that she had learned nothing. "I am not as blind as I was yesterday, or even the day before. I understand now that my vision of the world has not been a true one. People are not good and kind simply for the sake of being so. They always want something."

Her answer broke his heart. Merrick had shattered her view of the world. He had already stolen her innocence. But she was right. What better revenge against a class who had wronged him and his mother than to marry into it? To have all that had been denied him? To have everything . . . but Anne. Still, he wasn't a fool. And Anne needed his help.

"All right," he said. "I'll marry you, Anne."

Anne ran her sleeve across her nose. "I haven't any money of my own."

Not a problem at the moment. Merrick supposed not a problem in his future, either. "I have the purse I won today. It will get us where we need to go and back."

They stared at each other in the darkness. Merrick felt her sudden indecision, was glad for it, to be truthful. He'd be a fool to refuse her offer. But if she decided to come to her senses, he couldn't say he wouldn't be relieved. She drew in a deep breath a moment later.

"Saddle the horses," she said.

8

Merrick and Anne were camped not a day's ride from Gretna Green. Anne had changed into the stable boy's trousers and boots before they stole from the stable. Merrick had proven unsurprisingly useful on the journey. He knew when to take to the woods and when to use the road. Where to find fresh game. He knew too many things for a mere mortal man. Tonight he'd said they could have a fire.

They sat before it now, eating a roasted rabbit he'd caught and skinned earlier. Merrick sat across from her. His eyes glittered in the darkness. Anne tried to tell herself it was due to the flickering firelight . . . but she'd seen them gleam before when there was no fire.

She hadn't told him about her suspicions regarding his father. Their flight from Blackthorn Manor hadn't given her time to think about anything but getting away. But now she had to tell Merrick. He deserved to know.

"I've been meaning to tell you something," she said.

"What's that?"

For a moment Anne was mesmerized by the sight of

Merrick licking grease from his long, slender fingers. The meat was somewhat messy and it wasn't as if they were afforded the luxuries of home.

"Anne?" he asked.

She tried to regain her thoughts. "I believe I know who your father was."

His strange eyes pinned her in the darkness. "How could you possibly know that? I don't even know."

Anne used the coarse britches she wore to wipe her own greasy hands. "When I first saw you, I mean in the light of day, I had the strangest notion I had met you before. The day of the race, I realized it was because you are the spitting image of Lord Jackson Wulf. The reason it didn't immediately dawn upon me is because you have dark hair and light eyes and with him it is the opposite."

Merrick's brow furrowed. "Wulf? I've heard of them. Any man who knows anything about horses has heard of them. Never seen them. They don't spend a good deal of time in London to my knowledge."

"No," she agreed. "They prefer the country estate for the most part. They . . . well, there is talk about them."

His eyes met hers again. "Cursed," he said softly. "It is said they are cursed by insanity."

Anne waved a hand in dismissal. "I don't believe they are cursed. Lord Jackson is really quite nice if one takes the time to get to know him and as sane as the next man. I am not familiar with the other brothers but assume they are also as well mannered when the mood suits them. Lord Jackson and I are friends."

Merrick lifted a brow. "Friends?"

She might be fooling herself again, but Anne thought she caught a note of possessiveness in his voice. "He's married," she blurted. "I mean, he wasn't when I first met him abroad, but he is now."

Merrick continued to study her, as if trying to decide if her friendship with Lord Jackson might have been more than innocent. Finally, he asked, "And I look like him?"

She nodded. "More than a little. Too much for it be coincidence."

Lifting a water skin, Merrick took a drink. "The father is dead, if I recall."

"Yes," Anne responded. "A little more than ten years ago. He . . . he killed himself. They say he was mad when he did, and his wife insane, as well, when she went shortly after. It caused a scandal."

He was silent, as if mulling over what she'd told him. "What you say may be true, Anne, but I don't suppose it makes any difference now."

His response surprised her. Anne rose from the fallen log she sat upon. "No difference? To know you are a Wulf? To learn that you have half brothers? That makes no difference to you?"

Merrick shrugged. "It doesn't change anything for me, Anne." He stood as well. "I'm still a bastard. A secret my father wanted to keep hidden from the rest of the world. His dirty deed. I doubt the brothers would welcome me into the family with open arms, would be willing to share their lives and their wealth with me. I've still got nothing. No name, and now, no position."

Anne walked around the fire to join him. "Tomorrow, that will all change," she reminded him. "Tomorrow, you will have all that I have. More important, you will have your revenge."

His glittering gaze bored into hers. "And you will have yours. Right, Anne?"

She had to look away from him. For her, the marriage was not simply a matter of revenge. But Merrick need not know that. "Yes," she answered. "I will have my revenge."

The touch of his fingers upon her chin was gentle. He

forced her to look at him again. "You should want more than that, Anne. Me, I cut my teeth on a need for revenge. But you're not like me. You're different."

Tears burned her eyes. Anne blinked them back. He was wrong. She was bitter. "I've wasted my life trying to be the person I thought my aunt and uncle wanted me to be. I've wasted my life trying to make them love me. That's all I wanted, to be loved again."

His fingers brushed a stray tear from her cheek. His eyes were soft as he gazed down at her. "And you deserve to be . . . loved. I'm thinking I cannot do this, Anne. Marry you. Not even for revenge."

Would Merrick reject her, as well? This possibility had not occurred to Anne when she'd ridden off into the night with him. "You don't want me, either," she whispered.

His eyes closed for a moment, as if her accusation hurt him. "I wanted you from the first moment I saw you. There are things I don't even understand about myself, Anne. You are good and kind and innocent, and you deserve better than this. An arrangement."

She'd believed if she hardened her heart against the world, it might spare her from ever feeling pain again. But now Anne understood that she was all that she had aspired to become while growing up. Her heart was soft, and it was soft for this man. She reached up and touched his cheek in turn.

"You are a better man than you give yourself credit for being. No man has ever made me feel the things that you make me feel."

Merrick suddenly pulled away from her and turned his back. "I make all women feel things," he said, his tone harsh. "It is one of my 'gifts.'"

Anne wasn't certain what he meant. She supposed she could count the way he looked as being a gift. His voice, low and lilting, that flowed over her like sweet honey syrup she imagined could be counted as a gift, too. But Anne knew her attraction toward him went beyond his outer beauty. His scent, even though it attracted her, could not make her feel something she didn't honestly feel inside.

Whether he wanted to have them or not, Merrick had morals. She strongly suspected that he would not take her innocence tonight without wedding her on the morrow. Which left Anne no choice but to seduce him. She couldn't turn back now. She didn't want to turn back.

Anne closed the distance between them and touched his shoulder. He turned to look at her. Lifting herself on tiptoes, she pressed her mouth against his. Although inexperienced in the art of seduction, Anne sensed that she must rid herself of all inhibitions—simply act upon her emotions and let them carry her away, and him with her, she hoped.

Merrick's lips were warm, firm, and, unfortunately, unresponsive. She glanced up at him from beneath her lashes. His eyes were open. She ended the contact.

"Tell me you want me, Anne."

Surely he knew that she did. Surely he had the experience to know. "You know that I do."

Merrick shook his dark head. "No, I don't know. Is it the scent on me that makes you want me? Does the reason have anything to do with me at all? Tell me you want *me,* Anne. Only me."

He reached out and pulled her closer. His scent was in the air now and Anne had to admit it was a strong aphrodisiac. But it was the man she wanted. The man who had taught her to ride a horse bareback, who had taken her racing across the moors in the moonlight. The man who had saved her from wolves. The man who cared enough about her to warn her of her aunt and uncle's deception. The man who would turn his back on a fortune because he thought she deserved more than a bargain for the sake of revenge.

All of her life, Anne had been waiting to be loved again.

Longing to be loved again. In that moment, she realized that Merrick did love her. Perhaps he did not even know it, but she knew it, and for the moment, that was all that mattered.

"It's the man I want, Merrick," she answered. "It's the man I love."

His eyes flared in the darkness. "Do you love me? A bastard? A man with strange gifts he cannot understand and a heart bitter against a world that has no proper place for him?"

Her arms went around his neck. "Your place is with me. Destiny brought us together. I need your strength and you need my softness."

Slowly, he lowered his head. His lips brushed softly across hers. "You have strength enough on your own, Anne," he said.

"Make love to me," she whispered. "Share all that you are with me. And I will share all that I am, or have, with you."

Merrick made a low sound in his throat, nearly a growl. His eyes flashed blue fire in the night. "Don't tempt me, Anne. You know I want you."

She lifted her chin. "Then take me, Merrick."

He smiled at her daring. "You would trap me into taking your innocence so that I am honor bound to say the vows tomorrow. Very clever, Anne."

Although what he said was true, he needn't make it sound as if that were Anne's only reason for wanting him. Who better than him? A man who understood her love of horses and riding? A man who would let her have her independence and who wouldn't mind so much if she wanted to be bad on occasion, perhaps as long as it was only with him? There was no wrong in tricking him into making love to her. Anne loved him. He might not say the words, but he loved her, as well. Or she thought he did. Was she fooling herself again?

"Do you love me, Merrick?"

He brushed a stray lock of hair from her face. "You're a hard woman not to love."

It wasn't an answer. Not really. "Do *you* love me?" she repeated.

He looked away from her. She thought he wouldn't answer; then he glanced back into her eyes. "You know I do."

Her heart pounded in her chest. Joy rose inside of her, because she knew he wasn't lying to her. He wasn't trying to deceive her. At long last, she had what she wanted. Bravely, Anne reached down and pulled her shirt and chemise over her head. She stood before him bare to the waist.

"Show me you love me," she said.

The fire in his eyes flared. His gaze roamed her naked flesh. Everywhere he looked, her skin heated. Her nipples puckered in the cool night air.

"Jesus, lass," he whispered, his voice low and raw sounding. "You're beautiful. Your skin is like fine porcelain—so pale and smooth I wonder if you'll break if I touch you."

"I will not break," she assured him, her own voice breathless. "Touch me and see."

Merrick's eyes locked with hers. He reached out and touched her cheek, caressing her gently before lowering his hand to her breast. She fit into his hand as if she were fashioned for him alone.

She gasped softly when his thumb brushed across her sensitive nipple. He bent forward, kissed her neck, then moved lower until his tongue performed the same tantalizing dance that his thumb had a moment earlier. Anne twisted her fingers in his thick hair. Her knees nearly buckled when he took the straining peak into his warm mouth and sucked. He straightened, gazed into her eyes, then picked her up in his arms as if she weighed nothing.

Their blankets were spread for the night and he took her to his, lowered her gently, and knelt beside her. "What do you know of matters between men and women, Anne?"

"Nothing much," she answered. "My aunt didn't speak to

me of such things. My maid told me there would be pain my first time with a man."

Merrick ran a finger down her arm. "I don't know about being with a woman her first time. But I know there can be pleasure between us. Are you willing to go through the pain first?"

He offered her one last time to regain her senses. Anne didn't want to regain them. She did trust him. She had to trust him. There could not be love without trust.

"Yes," she answered. "I trust you, Merrick."

Slowly, he pulled his shirt over his head. Anne hadn't seen him without a shirt, and she quickly surmised it was something she wanted to do often in the future. His skin gleamed in the moonlight.

A smattering of dark hair covered his chest, tapering down into a thin line that traced a path down his corded stomach to disappear into the top of his trousers. She wanted to touch him. Wanted it badly enough to reach out and run her fingers down his chest. He was warm to the touch, as she knew he would be. She didn't know that a man could look soft and feel hard. There was no excess to be found on him. Only steely muscle and glorious tawny-colored skin.

"You are beautiful," she whispered.

"Come into my arms," he commanded. "Feel my skin against yours. Feel the differences between us."

She went willingly. The touch of her skin against his was like nothing she had experienced before. He tangled his hands in her hair and pulled her head back. Then he lowered his mouth to hers and kissed her.

They sank into a kiss where mouths were fused, tongues clashed, and gentleness slipped away on the night breeze. The soft down on his chest teased her nipples and sent heat coursing to the place between her legs. He lowered her to the blanket, mouths still joined, skin against skin. Only when her head touched the ground, cradled by his hand, did he end the kiss. Merrick stared down at her, hypnotizing her with his strange night eyes; then he bent to kiss her neck.

Lower he traveled, finding her nipple and drawing it so deep into his mouth that her nails dug into his shoulders. Her hips arched upward as if by some uncontrollable force. Between her legs, she began to throb. Slowly his hand traveled down her body. He came to the tie on her trousers and loosened it, then pulled the trousers down her hips and legs.

Anne was a modest person by nature. It wasn't so easy to leave the past behind in one night. But when Merrick kissed her again, she began to relax. While he distracted her with the skill of his mouth, he introduced her to the skill of his fingers.

The first touch made her jump, to have his hand there, where no man had been before. He did not soothe her with soft words but continued to kiss her, doing nothing more than stroking the curls that shielded her mound. It wasn't so awkward, Anne decided, more distracted by his tongue delving into her mouth than what purpose his hand might hold.

When she didn't resist, he became bolder. Gently, he slid his finger into her cleft and rubbed a place where all her sensation must surely lie. Anne gasped and tried to close her legs.

"Don't," he said softly. "Don't shut me out. Let me bring you pleasure before I bring you pain."

Her face flamed with embarrassment. "I—I'm wet there for some reason."

He smiled and gave her a soft, quick kiss. "If you weren't, I wouldn't be doing my job. You're wet there so our bodies can join. It's to welcome me in, so don't shut me out."

Anne willed her body to relax. She'd never imagined what all intimacy with a man entailed, but she rather thought it would be a quick affair, both only exposing the necessary parts to complete the act, then quickly righting their clothing and going to sleep. *Necessary parts* stuck in her head.

"Am I allowed to touch you, as well?" she asked. "I mean, wherever I wish?"

He lifted a brow. "Curious?"

"Yes," she answered.

He bent and kissed her again. "My body is yours tonight." He suddenly stood, slipped off his boots, then reached for the ties of his Cossacks. Ann turned on her side, placed a hand under her head, and watched him. She thought he took an abnormally long time to untie the fastening of his trousers. She might have even thought he was stalling, that he might be more modest than he pretended to be, but then she realized she was holding her breath, her eyes glued to the ties as his fingers leisurely undid them, and what he did he did for her pleasure.

Finally the ties were loosened and he slid his trousers down his hips, past his legs, and stepped from them. He straightened and stood before her naked. She supposed her eyes widened— resembled two twin moons. Whispered words from the ladies at the fair like "stallion" came to mind, and with good reason.

"Do you like what you see, Anne?"

She glanced up at his face. Shadows hid his features, but his eyes still glowed blue. Slowly, her gaze ran the length of him again. Past his broad shoulders, his muscled chest and flat abdomen, to the member jutting proudly, and rather impressively, away from his body. His hips were slim, his flanks smooth; his muscled legs were long and dusted by dark hair.

"Yes," she whispered. "Whatever your bloodline, you are a fine specimen of a man."

He came to her, bent beside her. Even though his eyes were on fire, his touch was gentle. He kissed her softly—teased her lips until her arms slid up around his neck and her fingers twisted in his hair. He lay beside her and pulled her into his arms and the contact of flesh against flesh, male against female, warmed her body and crashed through any defenses still standing. Slowly, he traced a finger down her body from neck to navel, and then lower.

"I want to touch you, and taste you, and make you mine . . . forever."

She wanted that, too. To be claimed by him, to claim him in turn. Bravely, she reached out and touched him, let her fingers slide down his broad chest, his flat stomach, to wrap around his sex. He jerked slightly and Anne quickly snatched her hand away.

"Did I hurt you?" she whispered.

"No," he assured her. "Just took me a bit by surprise."

Again she reached out and touched him. "Is it always so . . . so . . . ?"

"No," he assured her again. "Although around you, yes, most of the time."

She wanted to ask him more, but he bent toward her and kissed her again. Anne was innocent, but not so innocent that she didn't understand that he was finished talking. He moved lower and kissed her neck, then lower. While he teased her nipples with his teeth and tongue, his hand slid down again to her woman's mound, and she did not shut him out. He stroked her there as he had done before, stroked her until she bit her lip and moved with and against the pressure of his fingers. A force built inside of her—a desperate need—a hunger she had never felt before.

Her breath now came in ragged gasps. Her nails dug into his back, and beneath him she bucked as if she had no control over her body. He increased the pressure, and when he slipped one finger inside of her she nearly came up off the blanket.

"Easy," he said against her lips, and Anne thought it was the same tone he used to calm skittish horses. The pressure stopped and she wanted to whimper—to beg—but for what she still wasn't certain. Gently, he spread her legs with his knees, then settled between them. Instinctively, Anne tensed beneath him, but he kissed her, distracting her sudden trepidation, and when he made no further move, she began to relax, to savor the feel of his mouth moving over hers, his tongue delving into her mouth in a rhythm her hips wanted to match for some odd reason.

His hand slid between them again and he took up the torture. He'd told her she was supposed to be wet there, and Anne was glad of it or she would have been terribly embarrassed. He used that wetness, rubbing her sensitive nub until she thought something inside of her would burst. Then she felt him poised at the entrance to her woman's passage.

He was big there, just like the rest of him was big, and she felt him stretching her with the tip of his member. He moved a little ways inside of her and she gasped with the pressure. He gasped, too, but it was a different sort of distress, she thought.

"Damn," he whispered. "You shouldn't feel this good. I'm trying to go slow with you, Anne. It's damn hard to do when you feel like this."

And having said as much, he thrust in deeper. The pain was sharp and stabbing and caught her by surprise. She didn't scream, although the gasp that emerged from her lips was more forceful than the last. Tears stung her eyes, and for a moment she wondered how he'd managed to seduce her into this position. He moved in deeper and she steeled herself for more pain. It didn't come. Not that she wasn't very aware of him, his size filling her, stretching her, but there wasn't pain, only pressure.

"Now that the pain is over, I can please you," he said. "Are you all right?"

She nodded. He kissed her deeply, while below he slowly but steadily invaded her body. He moved, and he moved in such a way that stimulated her, just as he had done with his fingers earlier. It wasn't unpleasant.

Her hips arched against him. He sucked in his breath and plunged deeper. She sucked in her breath, too, and then her body took over, her instincts, her passion for him, and gentle wooing slipped away. His scent filled her senses and something primitive rose up inside of her. Her nails dug into his back, her teeth nipped at his neck, and he thrust deeper, harder, forcing a moan of pleasure from her. She began to tingle, then to throb where they were joined. Desperation made her move wildly beneath him. He pulled back, twisted his hand in her hair, and stared down at her, his eyes aglow with passion.

That's when she shattered, when the pressure had built to the point it would no longer be contained. Warmth spread over her, and her body continued to buck and convulse against him, and still he moved, still he thrust, only extending the pleasure until she thought she would die from it. Only when she thought she could stand no more did he thrust deep inside of her, groan her name, and hold himself there, still, as if he were poised on the brink of death. Then she felt him shudder. She clung to him, their hearts pounding wildly against each other, bodies coated in sweat, breathing fast and erratic.

She thought it had ended, the storm that raged between them, battered them, spat them out upon the shore to do nothing but lie exhausted, but then Merrick groaned and rolled away from her. He doubled up, clutching his stomach.

Anne struggled to turn on her side. Her limbs felt as if they had no bones. "What is it, Merrick?"

He didn't answer, but his body jerked. Anne wasn't familiar with lovemaking, but she didn't suspect this was part of it. "Merrick," she tried again. "Look at me. Tell me what is wrong!"

He tilted his head back. His eyes glowed blue, which was not something she hadn't seen before, but as he gasped with the pain, the moonlight gleamed off of his teeth, and they did not look like they had a moment earlier. His eyeteeth had lengthened and strongly resembled fangs. She touched his face and he grabbed her wrist. Anne nearly screamed. His fingers were bent, his nails jutting from his fingertips like claws.

Staring down at his hand, as she did, Merrick quickly released her. "What am I?" he whispered, and his voice came out garbled. "What am I?" he shouted, his voice in agony as his body began to convulse and contort.

Anne scrambled away from him. She grabbed her blanket from the ground and wrapped it around her. Trembling, she watched, both helpless and terrified. What she saw taking place before her could not be real. Such things only happened in nightmares. Merrick still lay on the ground, naked, contorting, but as she watched, hair began to cover his body. His limbs shrank, his features changed, and where once a man lay on the blanket it was a beast that rose on all fours and stood staring at her in the darkness.

"Merrick?" she whispered.

The beast did not respond. Instead, it glanced skyward at the full moon. The wolf howled, and in that sound Anne heard all the sorrow and anger of a man betrayed.

The animal lowered its head and stared at Anne. It peeled back its lips, displaying impressive fangs. *Loved by him as a man, killed by him as a beast.* That thought floated through Anne's mind before the darkness crept deeper into her vision, surrounded her from all sides, swallowed her whole.

9

The sun peeking through the trees woke Anne. She was curled in a ball, her blanket clutched around her. For a moment she couldn't remember where she was or why. She tried to move and her muscles protested. The ache between her legs brought the night before flooding back. She sat abruptly and glanced around the campsite.

Merrick sat on a log staring at her. He'd donned his trousers and sat with a blanket wrapped around his shoulders, shivering. He looked human again . . . almost. His eyes were haunted.

"What happened to me, Anne?"

She didn't want to think about that. She wanted desperately to pretend last night had never happened . . . at least up to a certain point. "You turned into a wolf."

He blinked. "What do you mean? I acted like a beast?"

Anne had trouble grasping what had happened last night, much less explaining it, and to the person it happened to. She could only be straightforward. "No, Merrick. A wolf. An animal. You turned into one before my very eyes."

He ran a shaky hand through his hair; then he held his

hand in front of him and stared at it. "What you're saying is impossible."

"It is possible," she countered, tugging her blanket tighter around her in the chilly morning air. "I would have never thought so . . . until last night."

He rose and shrugged from his blanket. "We must have dreamed it," he said, and the look in his eyes begged her to agree with him.

Could Anne pretend? Her whole life had been a pretense up until now. She must be honest with him and with herself. "Your gifts," she said. "Could this be another one of them?"

"Gifts?" he growled. "If what you say happened to me did, it's no gift, Anne. It's a curse."

"What do you recall of last night?" she asked.

His angry features softened for a moment. Merrick joined Anne, bending beside her. "Us," he answered. "Together. As one. Then the pain. The horrible pain. After that, nothing until I woke naked and shivering in the woods this morning."

Anne glanced down at her hands clasped around the blanket. "I thought I was going to die," she confessed, glancing back up at him. "When you stood before me as a wolf, I thought you would kill me."

His eyes misted and he glanced away from her. "I would never hurt you, Anne. I'd take my own life before I'd let myself, in any form, take yours." He glanced back at her. "I've got to go from here."

Today was to be her wedding day. And no, it would not have been a grand affair with flowers and a church and all of society turned out, but whatever it was, it was meant to be hers. Last night, Anne had found all she was looking for in this man. She couldn't let the dream go.

"Maybe it won't happen again." Perhaps it was wishful thinking, but Anne wasn't certain she wasn't right. Perhaps last night they were both drugged, drugged on each other, when she thought he'd turned into a wolf.

"What if it does, Anne?"

"What if it doesn't?" she countered.

He stared into her eyes for a long time before he said, "All right. I'll give it one more night. I hope it's not a mistake, Anne."

Merrick went hunting in the afternoon. His senses, always stronger, he suspected, than those of a normal man, were now heightened tenfold. He heard as he had never heard before. Saw movement in the brush and the distance no mortal man could see. At times, when he spotted an animal, he did not see the animal at all but only the blood pumping red through its veins.

Could what Anne said happened last night have really happened? Flashes had gone through his mind all day. Flashes of them together, making love, then the pain, the sight of his hand, covered in hair, claws jutting from his fingernails. He felt almost sick now with the memory of it . . . sick, and yet as he watched Anne move around the camp he felt something else. Something primal. The instinct to mate with her again.

Merrick shook his head and tried to dislodge the thought. He'd spilled his seed in Anne last night, certain that he would marry her today. If he really was this beast now, this man by day and an animal by night, he could not marry her. And yet he might have planted his bastard. He above all men should know better than to do that to any child.

"Anne, come here," he called.

She glanced up from throwing another handful of branches on the fire, where a spit roasted their supper. He hoped she would show wariness of him, but she did not hesitate to come to him.

"What is it, Merrick?"

She stood before him, so beautiful, her eyes etched with worry . . . worry for him, he realized. "Sit." He nodded toward the place next to him.

"But our supper—" she began.

"Can wait," he finished.

Anne sat beside him. He took her pale, delicate hand in his. "Tonight, once the moon is up, if it happens again, I want you to make me a promise."

"That tree," Anne said, nodding in the direction where their bedrolls were spread. "I can climb it easily if—"

"No," he interrupted, staring deep into her eyes. "I don't want you to run from me, Anne." Merrick took the pistol from his waistband and handed it to her. "I want you to kill me."

Her lovely eyes widened. She refused to take the weapon he tried to press into her hand. "No, Merrick," she breathed. "Don't ask me to do that. I love you."

His heart twisted inside of his chest. He took her hand and forced the pistol into it. "If you love me, you'll do this for me, Anne. I'll have no life. A man by day, a beast by night. I'd be better off dead."

Tears filled her eyes. She shook her head. "You can have a life, Merrick. One with me. Like we planned. I've been thinking. We could go to the Wulf brothers—"

"No," he interrupted her. "I'll not crawl begging to them. I have my pride, Anne. If they are my blood kin, our father wanted them to have nothing to do with me or he'd have seen that I was raised alongside of them. He'd have seen they knew about me before he died."

"But maybe they know what is happening to you," Anne persisted. "It is said they are cursed. Perhaps the curse is not one of insanity as all believe. Maybe they suffer what you now suffer. Maybe they know a way—"

"Anne," he said more gently. "Don't you see? It's because our father must have known something was wrong with me that he kept me a secret, hidden away, ashamed and embarrassed about me. No, I'll not go to them."

She threw the pistol down and rose, staring down at him. "You'd rather die?" she asked. "Is that it, Merrick? Your pride is worth more than your life, than our life together?"

He rose to meet her glare for glare. "We have no life together," he drew out as if she were a slow-witted child. "Not if it happens again tonight. Now, promise me."

Anne shook her head. "I will not promise you. I don't think you would harm me, Merrick. You could have last night. I was unconscious. You might not remember what happened, but I believe you are still somehow you, even when the beast has taken your physical form."

"You believed your aunt and uncle cared more for you than they did for your inheritance, too," he reminded her unkindly. When she took a step back from him, as if he'd struck her, he felt like a beast indeed. "Forgive me for that," he said softly. "It was a cruel thing to say."

Anne straightened her spine and lifted her chin. "The truth is often cruel. So while we are on the subject of honesty, maybe you should examine your own motives for refusing help of any kind from anyone. I think you like it, Merrick. Being a bastard. Being bitter. Wanting your revenge. If you have all that, then you don't need anything else, or anyone. You don't have to be responsible. You don't have to share your heart. You don't have to give. You don't have to succeed where you feel your father has failed. You don't have to one day look in the mirror and realize that you are just like him."

"I am not like him!" Merrick hadn't meant to shout— didn't mean to make her jump—but dammit, he was not like the sorry excuse for a man who must have spawned him. He'd never abandon a child of his . . . or would he? For all he knew, he was already doing that. Merrick was no longer hungry. He needed time to think. Time alone. He walked away.

He halfway expected Anne to stop him, but she did not. It was better that she didn't. His physical hunger had disappeared, but his hunger for her was another matter. He wanted her. But if he could not have her in love, he should not take her in lust. The man knew that . . . the beast that prowled inside of him did not.

10

Anne had dozed off when Merrick woke her. He crawled into her bedroll naked. She had begun to fear he wouldn't return. She'd checked the horses tethered in a nearby meadow often to make sure the stallion still grazed alongside her mare. Anne had eaten, cleaned their camp, done all she could think to do to bide her time; then she'd become sleepy without anything to distract her.

"Anne," he breathed, pulling her close to him. She went willingly, snuggling into his warmth. His hair was damp. He'd obviously found a stream to bathe in, and she longed to do the same. She'd cleaned up as best she could earlier with water from their flasks.

"Do you know your scent travels through the forest and finds me no matter how far away I go?" he asked, nipping gently at her throat. "Your scent will always call me back to you. I cannot resist it."

Her hands traveled over him as if she had no will over them. Could she and Merrick have been dreaming last night? Could two people, joined in body, in soul and heart, share the same nightmare?

More than anything, Anne wanted to believe they could, that they in fact had. Her hands, moving over his warm, muscled flesh, told her he was only a man. He pressed against her and she felt his readiness for her. Her pulses leaped. Anne closed her eyes and refused to think about what had happened last night. Behind closed lids, she wouldn't see if his own eyes were glowing blue in the darkness. "Kiss me," she whispered.

He did, very gently, which nearly broke her heart. His body shook with his need of her, and yet his lips were tender. She knew in that instant that she should never fear him. No matter if they had shared a nightmare or if the nightmare had been real, Merrick did not have it in his heart to hurt her. Whoever he was, whatever he was, she loved him.

Her hands crept into his hair and she slanted her mouth beneath his, opened wider, and invited him to invade. He did. Tenderness burned away beneath the rise of scorching passion. Suddenly he was pulling at her clothes, and she did all she could to aid him. Their breaths grew ragged between kisses. His hands moved over her, everywhere, on her breasts, down her stomach, between her legs.

She was already wet for him by the time his fingers stroked her. He moaned into her mouth and parted her legs with his knees. He'd been gentle upon his entrance last night. Tonight he forged ahead, thrusting deep in one smooth motion that made her gasp.

"Wrap your legs around me, Anne," he commanded.

Without hesitation, she obeyed him. He grasped her hips and thrust deep again, and again, over and over until she tingled, ached with both pleasure and pain, holding on to him as he took them over the edge of sanity. He became primal, biting at her neck, but never hard enough to draw blood, and she in turn used her nails on his back, urged him onward, became as primal as he. The tension coiled inside of her—grew until she exploded. She arched against him and screamed his name.

One deep plunge and she felt him pulsing inside of her, felt him spilling his seed.

She clung to him, both of them gasping for breath, their hearts beating wildly against each other . . . then the first spasm of pain took him. Merrick jerked away from her.

"The pistol, Anne," he ground out. "Get the pistol!"

She sat, clutching the blanket to her naked breasts, staring down at him. Their eyes met and locked. Slowly, she shook her head. "No, Merrick. I will not."

Pain made him spasm, made him curl into a ball, his knees up against his chest. His eyes glowed blue, but even in the darkness, she saw them fill with tears.

"Please, Anne," he managed. "I would die if I ever hurt you. I love you."

Reaching out, she touched his hair, smoothed it from his face. "I trust you, Merrick. Now you must find the strength to trust yourself."

"Damn you, Anne!" he shouted. "Your trusting heart will get you killed!"

Another spasm, one stronger, took him. Anne scooted away from him. She came up against the tree she had told him she would climb if she felt threatened, but she didn't ready herself to leap into action. The pistol was in a pack she'd placed at the base of the tree. With trembling hands, she reached inside the pack and drew the weapon out.

Before her, on the blanket where they had just made love again, Merrick danced the dance of the wolf. His body twisted and turned. The hair came, then the teeth, the claws, his body shrank, and then he was gone. The wolf came swiftly to its feet.

Despite what she'd told Merrick, her first instinct was to grasp the pistol securely, lift it, and take aim. The animal stared deep into her eyes. They were Merrick's eyes looking at her through the face of a wolf. Anne lowered the pistol.

"You want to kill me, then go ahead," she said softly. "But the man you share your skin with will be very angry."

The wolf cocked its head to one side. A moment later it turned and trotted off into the night. Anne released the breath she'd been holding. She laid the pistol within reach and tugged the blanket up around her. She would wait until morning to see if Merrick had told her the truth. If her scent would always bring him back to her.

Anne spent the whole night waiting, listening, hoping Merrick would return to her in the form of the man she loved. A twig snapped and she glanced up. Merrick stood naked in the bushes. He shivered in the morning air. Anne clutched her blanket tighter, rose, and went to him. They simply stared at each other for a moment before she stepped forward, opened her blanket, and enveloped him inside with her. His skin was freezing.

"Why didn't you do what I told you to do, Anne?" he asked against her hair. "We both know now it was no dream we shared."

"And we both know you didn't hurt me," she countered.

"Yet," he ground out.

She tilted her head to look up at him. "Why must you believe the worst of yourself, Merrick?"

He met her gaze with a hard one of his own. "And how can you stand here with me, sharing your warmth, when you know what I am now?"

She pulled the blanket tighter around them. "Because I love you," she answered. "That's what love is, Merrick. It is unconditional. Is your love for me not the same?"

He struggled out of the blanket and away from her. Merrick walked to where he'd discarded his clothing the night before and began to dress. "It's because I love you that I must do what is best for you, Anne. I'm taking you to London."

Her heart sank. "London?"

"You surely have friends there you can stay with. You'll find yourself a suitable man and be quick about it, just as you should have done from the start."

Anne frowned at him. "I am not leaving. We are one day's ride from Gretna Green and I intend to go there, and to marry you, just as we agreed."

Merrick tugged his shirt over his head. "I won't marry you, Anne. Not now."

They were back to this again. Anne felt frustration knot her stomach. "Then you will take me home," she said. "Not to London."

Merrick paused in his dressing to rub his forehead. "You cannot go back there and you know it. Not until—"

"I will not marry another," she interrupted. "I will go home and make the best of my life, wiser now where my aunt and uncle are concerned. Maybe in time you will come back. Maybe in time you will love me as I love you."

He cussed and stormed to her side. "It's not that I don't love you, Anne. You know I do. But—"

"But your pride will keep you from having all that should be yours," she interrupted again.

Merrick wondered what was wrong with the lass. Couldn't she see it was impossible for them to be together now? That he was cursed? That she would be cursed right along with him? Never mind she would have been regardless of what he was but because of who he was. It was foolish of him to agree to her proposal of marriage. What had he been thinking? That she could make him more than he was?

She had already made him more than he ever dreamed he'd be. Loved, by a woman like her. Thoughts of revenge against her class had faded beside the wonder of her love. He'd judged all by the actions of one man. Anne had shown him there was goodness still left in the world, kindness to be found from others, never mind if they lived in a grand house or a stable.

Through her, he had felt hope. Hope that he might rise above who he was and be a better man. Now he knew being a better man had nothing to do with what side of the blanket he was born on or where he called home. But he learned these lessons too late. Now he was not even a man. He was something else.

Merrick stared down at Anne, standing with her blanket draped around her, chin held high. Even without her fine clothes and her fancy manners, she was a lady through and through. His mother would have liked her. And Anne was right. It was his cursed pride that made him less than he could be. It had always been his pride.

"What would you have me do, Anne?"

Her eyes softened. "I want you to marry me, Merrick. I want you to go to your half brothers and speak to them about what has happened to you. If they invite you into their lives, then you must accept and claim them as your kin. Just as I will."

He took a deep breath. His pride was a hard thing to set aside, but for her he would. "If that is your wish, Anne. For you, I will surrender my pride. For you, I will do anything."

Her face seemed to light from within. Her smile nearly blinded him. She started to reach for him, but the pain suddenly came upon Merrick again. He doubled over. He placed his hands on his knees, trying to catch his breath. The next pain sent him to the ground.

"Merrick!"

Anne's voice came to him from a long way off. Sweat beaded his brow. This could not be happening. It was the light of day, not night, with a full moon hanging in the sky. Could this curse be something that grew stronger daily? Would he soon cease to be a man altogether?

"Merrick!"

He felt Anne's hand upon his shoulder and twisted away from her. "Don't, Anne," he warned. "Stay back. It's happening again." His eyes frantically searched the camp. "The pistol, Anne! Where is it?"

"I won't use it. I don't need it," she said, bending down beside him. "I trust you, Merrick. You still haven't learned to trust yourself."

She was vulnerable. She did not even have her clothing to protect her from his teeth, his claws, should he attack her. Trust was easy enough when he had control of himself, but when the animal took him . . .

"Where is the pistol?" he repeated, another sharp pain cutting into his stomach.

She didn't answer, but her eyes moved toward the pack at the base of the tree where she'd spread their bedrolls for the night. Merrick staggered to his feet and toward the pack. Anne was on his heels and they both grabbed for the pack at the same time.

"No, Merrick!" she sobbed.

He pushed her away and reached into the pack, removing the pistol. The pistol was cold in his hand and he shook so badly he wondered if he could cock and shoot it. Damn if he would live his life as an animal. He steadied the gun, stared down the long, smooth barrel; then his gaze lifted to Anne. Her beautiful eyes were awash with tears, pleading, loving. She held out a hand to him.

"Don't do this to me," she whispered. "If you take your life, you take mine."

He hesitated.

"Trust in yourself, Merrick," she said. "Trust in me."

Could he? He'd never trusted anyone besides his poor mother. She'd trusted a man once. A man who had pushed her aside quickly enough when he learned she carried his child. It was man's nature, Merrick had since learned, to take the easy road. It had been his . . . until now. Slowly, he lowered the weapon.

"For you, I promised I would do anything. I will trust as you trust, Anne."

Suddenly Merrick was thrown backward against the tree. It knocked the air from him, and as he opened his mouth to gasp, a blue light spilled forth. His vision blurred. His throat burned. Tears ran from his eyes and he could not close his mouth, could not breathe. The light took form, took shape, that of a wolf. Only when the shape was complete and stood between him and Anne could he suck air into his lungs. The animal stared at him as he struggled to regain his breath. Merrick stared back.

"Begone with you, wolf," he growled.

The shape slunk slowly off into the woods.

"Merrick!" Anne was beside him, her cool hands brushing his hair from his face. "What happened?"

He wasn't sure . . . but he felt different now. Different than he'd ever felt before. It was almost as if he were blind, deaf, but no, his abilities had only weakened to what he supposed normal people saw and heard. He glanced up at Anne's pale face.

"I think it's gone from me," he told her. "The gifts, the curse, whatever it was. It is gone."

"Gone?" she whispered. "Are you certain, Merrick?"

He was, and Merrick didn't know how he felt about that yet. The gifts had been part of him; the curse had only come recently. He was only a man now. But no, he was a man in love with a woman. One who would stand beside him, cursed or no.

"I'm certain," he answered.

Anne sat back on her heels, looking rather stunned by what had just happened. "What should we do?"

There was only one thing to do. Get on with the rest of their lives. He took Anne's chilled hand in his and kissed her fingers. "I'm thinking we should be off to Gretna Green. I plan to marry you today, Lady Anne."

Her lips trembled when she smiled, but she was made of sturdier stuff than she knew. Then she frowned. "It has just occurred to me that you have no last name to give me, Merrick."

He thought on that, but only for a moment. "My name is Wulf, Merrick Wulf, and I'm thinking after we get ourselves wed, it's time to pay my half brothers a visit. We may need their help in the coming days."

Tears glistened in her eyes. "You would do that for me?"

Merrick pulled her into his arms. "I told you, I will do anything for you, Anne."

"Anything?" she asked, glancing up from beneath her lashes.

She was naked beneath the blanket and Merrick was thinking it wouldn't take him long to recover from becoming a man and only a man. He thought he knew what his lady love wanted.

"We've got all day to get to Gretna Green," he said, bending to kiss her. "What would you ask of me, Anne?"

She placed a finger against his lips to stop him. "I want to ride your horse, bareback, in nothing at all."

Merrick blinked down at her. It wasn't the start he'd imagined to their new life together, but as he'd promised, he could deny her nothing.

"And you will," he assured her, bending to kiss her again. "But later."

Also available from *New York Times* bestselling author
Sherrilyn Kenyon

Dark Side of the Moon

The latest novel in the sexy, suspenseful
Dark-Hunter® series

Coming in December 2006
ISBN: 0-312-93434-3

The Dream-Hunter

The first novel in a breathtaking new series—first
time in print!

Coming in January 2007
ISBN: 0-312-93881-0

"Kenyon's writing is brisk, ironic, sexy, and
relentlessly imaginative."
—*The Boston Globe*

AVAILABLE FROM ST. MARTIN'S PAPERBACKS
sherrilynkenyon.com
Dark-Hunter.com
Dream-Hunter.com

Don't miss the next two books in the bestselling
Vampire Huntress series from L.A. BANKS

"A master of the genre." —*Zane*

THE DAMNED

"All hell breaks loose—literally—in the complex sixth
installment. . . . stunning."   —*Publishers Weekly*

Coming soon in January 2007
ISBN: 0-312-93443-2

AVAILABLE FROM ST. MARTIN'S PAPERBACKS

THE WICKED

*The legend continues with this new novel about the
deep, dangerous passions of the Undead*

Coming in February 2007
ISBN: 0-312-35236-0

AVAILABLE FROM ST. MARTIN'S GRIFFIN
www.vampire-huntress.com

Stay tuned for the new novel from
New York Times bestselling author

SUSAN SQUIRES

☾

ONE WITH THE NIGHT

*Far from the glittering lights and shallow bustle of 1822
London lies another world of shadows, secrets, and seduction...*

Coming in April 2007
ISBN: 0-312-94102-1

"Squires charts a new direction with [her] exotic,
extremely erotic, and darkly dangerous Regency-set
paranormal tales."
—*Romantic Times BOOKreviews*

☾ ☾ ☾

AVAILABLE FROM ST. MARTIN'S PAPERBACKS
www.susansquires.com

Look for the next new, wondrous novel from
New York Times bestselling author

RONDA THOMPSON

THE CURSED ONE

*The Regency werewolf series keeps getting better,
and hotter, with this latest romance about the Wild
Wulfs of London...*

Coming in December 2006
ISBN: 0-312-93575-7

"A deliciously dark world."
—*Romantic Times BOOKreviews*

AVAILABLE FROM ST. MARTIN'S PAPERBACKS
www.rondathompson.com